Laura Andersen has ~~one~~ B~~……~~ 805 4 ~~en, and a~~ college
degree in English that ~~……~~ by reading
~~……~~

The Boleyn King

A NOVEL

Laura Andersen

EBURY
PRESS

3 5 7 9 10 8 6 4 2

First published in the United States in 2013 by Ballantine Books,
an imprint of The Random House Publishing Group,
a division of Random House, Inc., New York.

Published in the UK in 2014 by Ebury Press, an imprint of Ebury Publishing
A Random House Group Company

The Random House Group Limited Reg. No. 954009

Addresses for companies within the Random House Group can be found at:
www.randomhouse.co.uk

A CIP catalogue record for this book is
available from the British Library

The Random House Group Limited supports The Forest Stewardship Council®
(FSC®), the leading international forest-certification organisation. Our books
carrying the FSC label are printed on FSC®-certified paper.
FSC is the only forest-certification scheme supported by the leading environ-
mental organisations, including Greenpeace.
Our paper procurement policy can be found at:
www.randomhouse.co.uk/environment

Printed and bound by Clays Ltd, St Ives plc

ISBN 9780091956486

To buy books by your favourite authors and register for offers visit:
www.randomhouse.co.uk

To Angie, Katie, Lori, Marianne

and the Loco Lizard:

Without your faith

and your dare

I would never have jumped

AUTHOR'S NOTE

O<small>N</small> J<small>ANUARY</small> 29, 1536, Anne Boleyn, Queen of England, miscarried a baby boy of approximately four months' gestation. It was the beginning of the end for Henry VIII's second queen, for Henry was forty-five years old and desperately needed a son. Although his passion for Anne had been both strong and enduring—sufficient to separate the English Church from the Pope's authority—the miscarriage was the final blow in an already wavering marriage.

Anne's fall was swift and brutal. On May 2 she was arrested on charges of adultery and treason. On May 17 five men were executed for having allegedly committed adultery with her—including her brother, George, Lord Rochford. On May 19 Anne was beheaded by a French swordsman on Tower Green. On May 30 Henry married Jane Seymour.

What if Anne Boleyn had not miscarried? What if she had brought the pregnancy to term and delivered a healthy boy in the summer of 1536? What if Henry only ever had two wives and Anne's son, not Jane Seymour's, became King of England?

And what if, in the end, Elizabeth Tudor still became queen?

The
Boleyn King

PRELUDE

28 June 1536

FOR ANNE BOLEYN, the world had narrowed in the last twenty hours to this: candle flame and darkness, stifling heat aggravated by leaded window glass and heavy draperies, bed linens that could not be kept clean, and the familiar pain of a child wanting out of her body.

And overriding it all, a terrible, clutching panic.

Anne was no stranger to childbirth; she had borne a whole and healthy daughter not quite three years ago. But she had not been afraid that time. She had been newly crowned, had finally taken her place openly at Henry's side, had seen her rival banished and her own family promoted. And she had been absolutely certain that the child she carried then was a boy.

The wrenching disappointment of Elizabeth's birth had faded slightly with the girl's obvious health and intelligence. No one could doubt the little girl was Henry Tudor's daughter—not only her red–gold hair but her entire presence shouted the assurance of her father's blood.

But Henry already had a daughter. He had not divorced the popular Catherine of Aragon, defied the Holy Roman Emperor, and wrested control of the Church from papal hands in order to have a second daughter. He needed a son. A son Anne had been meant to give him. She had already failed not once but twice: there had been a boy a year after Elizabeth . . . a boy who never even breathed.

Anne moaned with a mix of pain and fear—fear of the pale, blonde Jane Seymour, whom Henry had plucked out of Anne's own household to make his mistress. *There's the black humour of fate,* Anne thought. *Doing to me what we did to Catherine.*

And now Catherine was dead these five months, and as far as most of Europe was concerned, Henry was legally single. Anne's enemies scented blood. If this child was not a living boy . . .

"Your Majesty," the midwife said, "it's time to push. It shouldn't be long now."

"That's what you said at noon," Anne snapped back. At dawn, when her pains began, they had closed the single window she'd been allowed to open this last month and now she had no clear idea of just what hour it was. After sunset at the least.

She stifled a scream as the midwife pulled her legs apart and two of Anne's ladies held them back.

"Push, milady," the midwife instructed from the stool where she sat with skirts tucked between her legs, ready to guide the child out.

Anne focused all her power and managed to push twice before the pain eased and the midwife allowed her a brief respite.

Please let it be quick, she intoned silently to God, *and please let it be a son.*

She felt the rising wave of another contraction and braced herself, wishing passionately that Marie were with her. But her favorite lady-in-waiting had been caught unaware mere hours ago by her own childbirth pains. Anne spared a moment's thought for the Frenchwoman's too-early labor—she should ask after her; her own ladies were in and out of the room bearing news to the king, whispering to the midwife and each other in a way that made Anne want to scream. But then she was overwhelmed by her own body and forgot about Marie.

This time she let the sound of her effort leak out, half push and half sob. Then a swift burning and the midwife exclaimed, "Slowly, milady, the head is out."

But Anne could not go slowly. She gave one mighty push and felt a rush of relief as she could, for the first time in months, take a deep breath.

She lay back, exhausted and wanting only to sleep.

The midwife bundled up the screaming child—at least it was alive—after a quick check and handed it to a waiting maid. Then, without speaking, the midwife stood and walked over to the drapes. She pulled back on one and then opened the casement window to let the air in.

Anne squeezed her eyes shut. Had it been a boy, everyone would have been shouting the joy of it to the heavens. No, no, no! she wailed inwardly. Another girl. Behind closed eyes, she could see Henry and Jane and knew she was in the greatest trouble of her life.

"Your Majesty," the midwife said softly. "Open your eyes."

Anne made herself look. It wasn't the baby the midwife was indicating—it was the dark skies through the window.

"Not an hour ago, there was a rush of falling stars—one of the women told me. Do you know what that means?"

Anne didn't have the energy for any reply, let alone the furious one she wanted to make.

The midwife smiled brilliantly. "It is a sign, Your Majesty. A sign of God's good pleasure on you and all England. He has given us a prince. A Prince of Wales to follow in his great father's footsteps."

Anne's heart stuttered. "Truly?"

"Truly, milady. We will wash him and then take him to the king. His Majesty will be well pleased."

Anne shut her eyes again, so as not to weep openly. *Henry will be pleased,* she thought. *And I . . .*

I will remain queen.

CHAPTER ONE

I am seventeen today and have decided that, although I shall never be a scholar like Elizabeth, I can at least keep a diary. My history is quickly told—daughter of a French mother and an English gentleman, no siblings, and no parents since I was eight. My full name is Genevieve Antoinette Wyatt. It was Elizabeth who first called me Minuette. I was born more than a month before I was expected, and the first time she saw me, Elizabeth thought me too little for the name my French mother had given me. She attempted to call me Mignonette—meaning dainty and darling—but her three-year-old tongue did not pronounce it properly. I have been Minuette to my friends ever since.

The importance of this day goes beyond just my seventeenth birthday—today I return to Elizabeth's household after an absence of two years. Queen Anne has been my guardian since my mother's death nearly nine years ago, and I spent my childhood with Elizabeth. But when I turned fifteen, the queen took me into her own household in order to train me properly for Elizabeth's service. I have learnt to stand quietly when necessary, so that I am almost forgotten. I have learnt to remember names and faces, to know the habits of noblemen and the

*idiosyncrasies of ambassadors. And I have learnt to lock away secrets,
for a lady of the privy chamber must be able to keep her own counsel.*

*Elizabeth has come to Hampton Court not only to reclaim me but
also to join in the weeklong celebrations for William's birthday. There
will be feasting and dancing tonight, and I will pretend, as I always
have, that the celebrations are half for me. But today the only
celebration I truly care about is seeing my friends. Although Queen
Anne spends much of her time with her children, I have not seen either
of them for a year. Last summer the queen decided I was too dependent
on others, and so I was left behind every time she joined the court at
Whitehall or Greenwich or Richmond. I spent six months at Hever
and six months at Blickling Hall as her resident lady. A great privilege,
to be sure—but I would have given up any privilege to see my friends!*

*Dominic has come as well. A waiting woman told me that Master
Courtenay rode in after dark last night and is even now with the king.
I have not seen him for a full sixteen months, not since he was named
Lieutenant of the March along the Welsh border. I am sure he could
have managed to visit at least once in all that time, but his letters
always pleaded duty, a virtue to which he is too much wed. I wonder
what he has brought me for my birthday. I hope it is fabric—velvet or
satin or shot silk. But it is probably only a book. Dominic has always
thought it his calling to teach me to be wise.*

Minuette closed the diary, pristine vellum pages bound by
soft calfskin, and marked her place with a bit of burgundy velvet
ribbon.

The sharp, familiar voice of Alyce de Clare came from the
open doorway behind her. "Are you still here? I was looking
forward to having the chamber to myself for once."

Minuette swiveled on her stool and smiled. "You know you
will miss me as much as I'm going to miss you."

Alyce was nearly three years older, and she, like Minuette,

came from a relatively unimportant family. Alyce had come to Queen Anne because her father had been a secretary in Lord Rochford's household. The queen's brother could be as difficult to please as Anne herself, but both of them were quick to reward loyalty. Alyce's father had served Rochford long and well (and discreetly), and his daughter had been rewarded with a place at court where she might be expected to make a good marriage. She and Minuette had been steady chambermates for the last two years.

Alyce attempted a smile, but it didn't touch more than the corners of her mouth. "You will be too busy being important in Princess Elizabeth's household to remember to miss me."

"Of course I'll remember." Minuette stood, which meant the shorter Alyce had to look up a little. "I just wish . . ."

"Wish what?"

Minuette hesitated, but she knew that this might be her last chance to speak her worries. "Alyce, I'm worried about you. I think . . . I think you are in trouble. I would help you if I could."

Alyce's brown eyes blanked—a skill most women picked up rapidly in the queen's household. On Alyce, it had the effect of sharpening her generous mouth and rounded cheeks, so she looked more like a statue of a woman rather than her usual vivacious, warm self. With distant courtesy, she said, "I can't imagine what you mean."

"You should speak to the queen," Minuette said firmly, letting her eyes linger on Alyce's waist. Though still tightly cinched beneath a yellow-and-black-patterned stomacher, it had been growing thicker over the last eight weeks. "Someone will tell her soon enough, and you know how she hates gossip."

For a heartbeat Alyce seemed to teeter on complete denial, then with a rush of emotion she said, "And you know very well that the queen will be angry no matter who tells her."

Minuette did know. But she put a hand on the stiffly embroidered sleeve of Alyce's yellow dress and said gently, "You will have to act very soon. If I can help in any way—perhaps I could speak to Elizabeth—"

"No!" Alyce jerked away, her waist-length brown hair swirling. "Don't tell anyone. Certainly not the princess. She is the very last person who would help me."

"Elizabeth is my dearest friend, she would—"

"Princess Elizabeth is her mother's daughter." Alyce smiled fully this time, a bitter and twisted smile that broke Minuette's heart. "The rising star and the setting sun . . . but both of them can burn."

"Who is the father?" Minuette asked quietly. It was a question she had pondered often the last few weeks. One would think that, in the close quarters of the court, she would know whom Alyce had been dallying with. But her friend also knew how to keep secrets.

Alyce shook her head. "You are not meant for these sorts of games, Minuette. You are too trusting and too generous. Those qualities will hurt you one day—but not through any action of mine. Forget what you have guessed. I can take care of myself."

She turned away with the grace of a sylph and vanished as suddenly as she'd come. Minuette sighed, knowing she would hold her tongue, as Alyce had asked. For now.

Dominic Courtenay fingered the necklace he had bought at the abbey fair in Shrewsbury: cabochon-cut sapphires and pearls to circle the neck, with a filigree star pendant. Neither exotic nor terribly expensive, but Minuette had little jewelry of her own and she delighted in impractical gifts.

He had just finished tying up the pendant in a square of fabric when William opened the door without knocking and shut it in the faces of those who followed him everywhere. He was dressed for sport, in a linen shirt and leather jerkin.

"Why is it," William said accusingly, "that you are the only man in England who keeps me waiting?"

Dominic gave him a wry smile. "Because I'm the only man in England who still thinks of you as Will rather than as the king."

William snorted and crossed the room. Picking up a sheet of heavy paper from the desk, he read a few words aloud. "'Once there were four stars' . . . you wrote down the star story for Minuette?"

Dominic pulled the letter away and said, "It's not easy to share your birthday with a king, especially not one whose birth was attended by such signs as stars falling from the sky."

"It's a fair enough gift."

"What did you get her?" Even as he asked, he wondered why it sounded like a challenge.

"It's a surprise. And speaking of gifts . . ." William's voice trailed off meaningfully.

Dominic shook his head. "I thought you were anxious for sparring practice."

"Only to prove that my reach is longer than it was when you left—you might find it harder to disarm me."

Dominic cast a measuring eye over the boy he had known since birth. It was true that he had gone some way to matching his father's height. Still, Dominic was five years older and a natural swordsman. He didn't think William was his equal yet; they would find out soon enough in a fair sparring bout.

Only once had Dominic made the mistake of going easy. When William was ten and had been king just six months, he and Dominic had spent the morning fighting with wooden practice swords. But William grew impatient with the clumsy replicas and demanded real swords. The swordmaster hesitated, but a nod from Lord Rochford, who was watching their practice, sent him scurrying off.

William caught the implied permission from the Lord Protector. He said nothing, but Dominic saw the set of his still-childish jaw as they were laced into the bulky, padded jerkins that would be some measure of protection against blunted steel.

For the first time ever, Dominic allowed himself to make mistakes as they sparred—nothing obvious, or so he thought. Just a misstep here and a delayed feint there, enough to give the younger boy the edge.

But he had miscalculated. Without warning, William threw his sword straight at Dominic's head. Only a quick duck saved him from being hit squarely by the hilt. Too surprised to move further, Dominic stood silent as William marched up to him, the command in his voice making up for the fact that he was six inches shorter. "Don't you ever do that again."

"Do what?" Dominic asked.

William struck him once, hard on the cheek. "Don't ever lower your guard. I will be the best because I've earned it. I don't need you to hand me my victories."

He turned and walked out of the practice arena. He had not raised his voice or lost control of his colour, but Dominic had felt the force of his anger whipping through the air.

If William's skill had increased as much as his height, he might earn a victory today, and Dominic had just the weapon for him to use. He opened his trunk and removed a layer of neatly folded clothing—plain tunics and jerkins, as befitted a soldier in the field—to uncover the gift that lay beneath.

There was really no way to make a sword unrecognizable. With a grin of delight, William pulled it free from its scabbard and took a few enthusiastic swings before holding it horizontally in one hand to test the balance.

Dominic turned the sword so that William could see clearly the four star-shaped gems laid in the gold hilt. "Now there's one place where the four of us are always together."

William laughed. "You sound as though you're dying. Or perhaps you've met an accommodating Welsh miss and wish to change allegiance?"

With a grin, Dominic shrugged off his sentimentality. "You'll be the first to know."

As she entered her mother's outer chamber, Elizabeth straightened her shoulders, ensuring that the green and gold brocade of her dress did not ripple across the stomacher but flared perfectly from tiny waist to wide skirts. Elizabeth had heard her mother cut a lady to shreds with her tongue for an uneven hem or a slight stain, and she did not doubt that Anne would subject her own daughter to the same.

A dozen of her mother's ladies were grouped in threes and fours around the ornate presence chamber. Several were working on a tapestry while others wrote letters or talked quietly amongst themselves. One lady, with a straight fall of rich brown hair, played lightly on a lute. As Elizabeth passed her, the young woman looked up and her fingers missed a chord.

She returned to playing almost at once, but not before giving Elizabeth a hostile glance. What was her name? One of the de Clares, she thought, but not from an important branch or Elizabeth would know her better. Almost she stopped to speak to the woman, but her mother was waiting.

Queen Anne sat in a gilded wooden chair placed next to a tall window, a Tyndale Bible open on her lap. As Elizabeth curtsied, she wondered how much longer her mother would be able to see the fine print of the books she loved so well. These days she could read only in brightest sunlight.

Rising with a seductive grace that was still the envy of every woman in England, her mother said, "Will you join me within, Elizabeth?" Despite the intonation, it was not a question.

She followed her mother to the door in the north wall that led to the intimate but no less elegant privy chamber. Only one lady of the privy chamber was inside—one who flung herself at Elizabeth in a most inelegant manner.

"Elizabeth!"

Minuette hugged Elizabeth with unrestrained delight while the queen, who would have frozen any other woman with a stare of ice for such behaviour, smiled upon the pair. Beneath her own delight, Elizabeth felt a brief spasm of pain. Minuette had always had charm—not the studied, showy type, but natural as breath and as much a part of her as her honey-coloured hair. Elizabeth could clearly remember her father visiting the schoolroom in the year before his death. She had spent an hour translating Latin and Greek for him, doing mathematics, and discussing theology. Though he'd complimented Elizabeth's mind, it was nine-year-old Minuette who had disarmed him. When the formidable, enormous King Henry had left, it had been Minuette whom he'd hugged goodbye.

Elizabeth might have hated her for that charm, if Minuette weren't so utterly without guile.

Queen Anne's beautiful voice broke into Elizabeth's memory. "I take it that you are both pleased."

Beneath the words lay a hint of perplexity, as though she could not imagine why. Truthfully, Elizabeth would have been hard-pressed to name a single woman whom her mother considered a friend. She had always preferred men.

Feeling almost sorry for her mother, Elizabeth said, "I could not be more pleased. It is generous of you to allow her to return to my household."

Her mother might like flattery, but she was never stupid. "Considering that you have been pressing the king for months, you cannot be surprised. She is a trifle young still—as are you, Elizabeth."

"I will be twenty in September," Elizabeth said mildly.

As if she hadn't heard, her mother went on, "But your brother is determined to allow you an unusual measure of independence."

It was Minuette, naturally, who had something complimentary to say. "And how could he do otherwise, with the example of his great father before him? Did not King Henry give you the right of *femme sole* over the objections of his council?"

Anne smiled slightly. "And I trust he never had cause to regret it. See to it, Elizabeth, that your brother never has cause to regret your independence."

Elizabeth met her mother's eyes, biting back the impulse to argue. Independent? She couldn't even sell one of her farms without the council's approval, let alone travel abroad or marry whom she liked.

With a steadiness to match her mother's, Elizabeth said, "I will act in all ways as you would."

And then came one of those rare and disconcerting flashes from her mother, as though she could read every shade of meaning in Elizabeth's careful words. "That is what worries me." Then Anne waved her hand at the girls. "You may go," she said. "I will see you both this evening."

Elizabeth drew a deep breath as they left her mother's rooms, unsure if it was regret or relief that she felt. She looked at Minuette, walking beside her in a passable imitation of demure restraint, and said, "Do you think there will be any difference between being my friend and being my attendant?"

"Do you?" Minuette's directness was disarmed by her smile.

Without waiting for a reply, she tossed her head. "At least it means that I am finished with tutors and teaching. Now my duties will be considerably more to my taste."

Elizabeth could not resist teasing. "Your duties will be at my discretion. Perhaps I will require you to translate a page of Greek each day."

But Minuette knew her too well to take her seriously. "I am to translate people, not books—to discern who is making a bid for power, which diplomat should be seen and which snubbed, who amongst your ladies can be trusted in the privy chamber. And, perhaps, who is in the best position to claim you as a bride."

"You think me incapable of seeing such things for myself?"

With a look of mingled amusement and scorn, Minuette said, "Of course not. Everyone knows you are far more clever and subtle than I am. I've no doubt you see things that go by most of the men at court. I am to be your foil. The lighthearted, merrymaking girl who is thought to be less discreet than her mistress."

Elizabeth laughed from the heady sense of mischief that Minuette carried with her. "I think you and I will do very well together."

William was annoyed to find his uncle and the Duke of Northumberland waiting for him when he returned from the morning's exercise. He was sweating after two hours in the practice yard, but when he asked sharply, "Can't this wait?" his uncle merely gave him a measuring look and answered, "If this were a courtesy call, Your Majesty . . . but we must discuss the French situation."

He changed clothes rapidly, wincing at the bruise on his upper arm. Though he had forced Dominic to work hard, William had still been disarmed in the end by a spectacular and unexpected kick to his hand that had sent his wooden practice sword flying. Afterward he had made Dominic show him just how he'd done it, and then practiced the move himself for twenty minutes.

Dominic had always been sought after as a sparring partner, and he'd had plenty of competition this morning aside from William. After more than a year spent honing his skills against the Welsh, he had faced little serious competition from the men at court, some of whom were not as careful as they should have been. Giles Howard, Lord Norfolk's youngest son, had suffered both a clout to the head and a slash to his doublet.

William rejoined his uncle and Northumberland in his privy chamber, where he once again picked up his sword. No matter what palace he stayed in, the privy chamber was always his favorite, because he could keep out the hordes that buzzed around in the more public rooms. While listening to his councilors discuss the latest proposed treaty with France, he paced the room, refighting the morning's exercise and perfecting each move. It wouldn't be long, he vowed, before he and Dominic were evenly matched.

Northumberland flinched when the sword came within a foot of him and, as was his custom, spoke bluntly. "Your Majesty, if you could stop roaming and pay attention . . . This is serious."

William came to a dead stop and stared at him. "Do you imagine I can do only one thing at a time?"

Rochford intervened with a touch of amusement. "Lord Northumberland imagines that he can persuade you out of this treaty, or at least the provision for your sister's marriage."

William had been expecting this from the staunchly Protestant Northumberland, and his reply came easily. "King Henri and I meet in Calais in September. I support France against the

Hapsburgs in exchange for a thousand pounds in gold and French support of England against Spain. This to be sealed by the betrothal of my sister, Elizabeth, to Henri's brother, Charles."

William locked eyes with Northumberland and went on quietly, "Are you saying you would rather ally with the emperor? Because it's one or the other. And Elizabeth married to Philip of Spain would be far more dangerous."

A man of both great temper and high humour, Northumberland was not easily cowed. He looked like what he was—a newcomer to noble ranks—and standing next to the sleek, elegant Rochford only highlighted his imposing figure. "I would rather that an English princess honour her father's legacy and not tie herself to a Catholic prince."

"My father's—"William made himself stop until he was sure he could go on without anger leaking through. "My father's legacy is practicality. When Elizabeth marries Charles, English Catholics are appeased and my choice of a bride widens."

Though Northumberland was less subtle than Rochford, he was no less clever. More, possibly, except that he always let people see what he was calculating. "So Princess Elizabeth marries a Catholic and you marry . . ."

"Whomever I wish," William said shortly. "Which is also my father's legacy."

He could practically hear the turning of Northumberland's mind. If he could persuade the king to marry the partly royal and wholly Protestant Jane Grey . . . well, that would be worth sacrificing Elizabeth for.

Even if Northumberland's son, Robert Dudley, objected.

The door to his privy chamber opened and William saw Dominic hesitating beyond the guards. "We're finished," William said. "The French treaty must be presented to the full council. But not today."

He turned away as they bowed themselves out of the room. Dominic spoke behind him. "You really shouldn't bait them."

"Do you think my father would have put up with insolence?"

"Your father wasn't ten years old when he became king. The regency council is to help you learn, Will, and to protect England while you do."

William replaced his sword in the scabbard and tossed it on a table. "I'm not ten years old anymore."

He stalked past Dominic, ignoring the pressing crowds in the presence chamber. His guards could read his moods and kept the people well back. William was aware of Dominic following him down the arched corridor, but his friend had the good sense to keep quiet. Even in his anger, William knew he was acting in precisely the childish manner that his councilors seemed to expect.

Dominic caught up to him and spoke carefully. "I'm sorry, Your Majesty. Sometimes I forget which one of you I'm addressing. I speak to my friend when I should be speaking to my king."

That brought William to a halt. Shaking off his injured pride, he turned back to Dominic, glad that the guards had closed off the ends of the corridor so that the two of them were briefly alone. "Don't you know that's why I value you? Because you I can always trust to speak honestly—even when you shouldn't. That's more than I can say for any of my councilors. They speak what they think I want to hear, or only as much as they want me to know."

Pausing for breath, William grinned. "One year, Dom. Then I can dispose of the regency, if not of councils altogether. When I am eighteen, they'll see I've been paying a good deal of attention. They think they are molding me to be biddable when older. They will learn better."

Throwing an arm around his friend's shoulders, he pulled him forward. "Let's go see what the women are up to. You must have missed them this last year."

As they reached the stairs that led down to Clock Court, they heard voices drifting up from below. Amongst the chatter of the court, two voices were nearer and damningly clear. "So the king's agreed to your marriage with the Wyatt girl?"

William knew the voice that answered: Giles Howard, Norfolk's son, the one Dominic had disarmed rather brutally this morning. "Father's determined on it. She's poor, but as the queen's ward, she's well connected. And now that she'll be in the princess's household, someone will use her. Might as well be the Howards."

As though they were discussing a London doxy, the first voice said, "A bit skinny. Not much to sink into."

Howard's reply was even coarser. "Genevieve will breed well enough. And my uncle claims that her mother was less than a lady in bed. Besides, the girl is rather like a colt—all eyes and legs and spirit. It will be no hardship to break her in."

"Genevieve? She's called something else around court, I thought."

"She's got some pet name from the royals. Thinks it makes her important. She'll learn humility quick enough when I get hold of her."

William jerked his head at Dominic, who had gone utterly still, and they went noiselessly down the steps. They interrupted Howard and his friend in raucous laughter, which died instantly at the sight of the king.

Giles Howard managed an awkward bow. "Your Majesty."

William could invest a great deal of contempt in a single word. "Minuette."

Howard looked at his friend, who seemed determined to

melt into the bricks behind him, then back to William. "I'm sorry, Your Majesty?"

"Her name is Minuette. You, of course, will refer to her as Mistress Wyatt on the very rare occasions when it is necessary for you to refer to her at all."

Howard's face flooded with colour until even the tips of his ears were red. "Of course, Your Majesty."

William stepped back, satisfied with the effect of his words.

Dominic, apparently, was not satisfied. He stepped right up to Giles Howard and, in a voice William had never heard before, said, "If you refer to the lady in such terms again, I'll take more off you than a strip of fabric."

The two men stared at each other until William could almost feel the hatred pouring off Howard's skin. But Howard was not fool enough to fight the king's nearest friend in the king's presence. Never mind that Dominic could probably beat him senseless without even breathing hard.

It was Dominic who broke the tension by turning his back and walking away. It wasn't often that William had to scramble to catch up to someone.

Keeping his voice deliberately light, William said, "You surprise me, Dom. I thought you disapproved of impulsive violence."

"And I rather thought you preferred it."

"Howard's easily managed with words, so why waste the effort? He'll not insult Minuette again."

Of that he was sure. He was not so sure that Howard wouldn't come after Dominic. He had seen the quality of his stare at Dominic's retreating back. It was the look of a man who has revenge on his mind—and revenge was something the Howards did impeccably.

CHAPTER TWO

ELIZABETH SPENT THE early part of the afternoon with her personal secretary, leaving Minuette to her own devices. She went straight out of doors, through the royal privy garden—to which William gave her unlimited access—and, after looking around to make certain she was unobserved, climbed nimbly up to sit on the low brick wall enclosing the knot garden. With her back to the river, she gave her full attention to the palace spread before her.

The smooth green of turf, the jewel-bright colours of primrose and clematis, the scent of roses heavy in the air—and beyond, the unshakable permanence of redbrick walls, turrets, and chimneys. Hampton Court was Minuette's favorite palace. She and Elizabeth would be leaving next week to accompany William on his summer progress, and after that they might go on to any of the half-dozen manors owned by Elizabeth herself. Though Minuette knew she would return here often in the coming years, she couldn't shake the feeling that it would never be the same.

It seemed likely that Elizabeth's betrothal to the French king's brother would take place before the end of the year. The princess could not be delighted at wedding a man more than ten years her senior and twice a widower. Still, married or not, odds were she would remain in England for some time. Until William had a queen and children, Elizabeth was his successor and the council would want her near. But the thought of her friend's marriage made Minuette wonder what her own future would be. Would she stay in Elizabeth's service, forever single and devoted? Or would she marry away from court and leave the closest thing to a sister she'd ever had? Perhaps she would follow her mother's example and marry a man also tied to royal service, giving her the best of all worlds.

Marie Hilaire, French from the top of her blonde head to the tips of her petite fingers, had befriended Anne Boleyn more than thirty-five years ago when both had been in service at the French court. As different in temperament as in looks, Anne had nonetheless come to trust "my Marie" as she had trusted very few in her life. When Anne had found herself embroiled in the most tangled love affair in history, she had sent for Marie, and the Frenchwoman had left her home without a moment's complaint. Even marriage did not separate them, for shortly after Anne was crowned queen, Marie married Jonathan Wyatt, a gentleman lawyer who served in the Exchequer. The old king had been effusive in his thanks, rather less so in material goods, and when Jonathan Wyatt died of the sweating sickness in 1541, all that had been left was a modest manor house and farm. It was then that Minuette—at five years of age—had been introduced to Elizabeth's household, and within a year her mother had married again. But this time the marriage meant leaving court and Anne, for her second husband was brother to the Duke of Norfolk and he took his wife to the country. Minuette had often wondered if her mother's spirit had been broken by being removed from the royal circle she had always known.

Minuette was shaken from reverie by the sight of several yeomen of the guard approaching. She stood upon the wall and shaded her eyes. She recognized William's customary springing step—and there was Dominic, half a pace behind and exuding watchfulness. She always thought of the two of them as looking alike until she saw them together. Though both had dark hair, only Dominic's was truly black. William's had more red to it, and his eyes were the clear sea blue of King Henry's. Also, though nearly of a height, William was like a greyhound, where Dominic had broad shoulders and the build of a soldier. Picking up her heavy skirts, she walked lightly along the top of the wall feeling so perfectly happy to see them both that she wondered how she had ever endured the separation.

"Seventeen years old and you haven't outgrown climbing walls?" Dominic called as they neared. She had never been more happy to be reproved, so familiar was the tone of weary patience behind which laughter lurked.

"I haven't climbed a single wall while you were away. Who would catch me when I jumped?"

Suiting the action to the words, she jumped into Dominic's arms. He caught her automatically, as he had a hundred times before. Minuette lifted her head, pleased by the fact that she didn't have to look up nearly so far as she used to.

"Happy birthday, Minuette." William's voice seemed to shake Dominic out of himself, and he released his hold on her.

She smiled at William. "And to you." Of Dominic, she demanded, "What did you bring me?"

He laughed. "You two could not be more alike—'Where is it? What did you bring me?' What makes you think I brought you anything?"

Undaunted, she held out her hands. Dominic shook his head. "I sent it to your room. Your new one, near Elizabeth's."

"It had better be worth the wait."

William grabbed her hand. "You don't have to wait for my gift. Come see it now."

The king's gift turned out to be in the stables—a beautiful snow-white palfrey that surprised Minuette into silence. She had never owned a horse before, let alone one as elegant as this.

As the silence lengthened, William chanced a question. "Don't you like her?"

Hearing the hurt in his voice, Minuette said, "I love her. I'm just . . . I never expected something so grand."

It was the right note to strike, for William loved to be generous—and to be seen to be generous. His satisfaction was evident through the next quarter hour in the stables. Minuette stroked the velvety nose of the horse, which she promptly named Winterfall, while William chattered on about her breeding and gentleness.

Dominic said only one thing: "A very grand gift indeed."

Minuette fretted about that remark afterward as she returned to her room. Dominic had sounded almost disapproving. Minuette was not naive, however open her face and manners. She knew what might be said of a woman to whom a king gave such a costly gift. But no one would say such things about her. Everyone knew she and William were nearly siblings.

So why did Dominic not approve?

When she reached her new chamber, she found Dominic's promised gift lying atop the carved chest at the end of her bed—a small linen square tied with ribbon, and a sealed letter beside it. Not fabric, she thought, disappointed. But not a book, either.

When she untied the ribbon, the linen unfolded to reveal a pearl and sapphire necklace. It was so lovely—and so completely unexpected—that it took her a few minutes of admiration before she realized that the filigree pendant that hung from the jewels was in the shape of a star. When the realization came, she broke the seal of the letter with sudden eagerness.

There, in Dominic's bold handwriting, was the story. The one he had imagined for her sake, on a particularly lonely birthday nine years ago. Her mother had died in childbirth some months previously, but Minuette had felt only a distant sort of grief at the time, for her mother had been living in the country with her new husband for two years, and Minuette had seen her only a few times since then. It wasn't until her birthday that Minuette had felt the force of the loss.

That particular day had passed at Greenwich, where the entire court had gathered to celebrate Prince William's eighth birthday. As the hours passed, Minuette realized for the first time that, with her mother dead, there would no gifts for her this year—nothing more than a hug from Elizabeth. Though her mother's gifts had always been of a practical nature—a prayer book, new embroidery needles—they had at least been for her alone, a measure of someone's remembrance that she had come into the world and been loved.

She curled up in a corner of the rooms she and Elizabeth shared at Greenwich and cried. Elizabeth grew exasperated when she could not calm her. Minuette wished she could halt the tears, if only to stop worrying her friend, but it seemed beyond her control. She thought she might just huddle in this corner forever—arms around her knees, head buried in her skirt—and cry until she turned to dust.

When Elizabeth had departed for her audience with her parents, Minuette thought she was all alone and her tears increased. She didn't realize someone was sitting next to her until a hand came to rest on her back.

She knew Dominic by his voice, just beginning to deepen. "Cry as much as you like. It's a sad thing to have lost both your parents."

The kind understanding had startled her into lifting her head off her knees. His dark green eyes were sympathetic as he said, "Elizabeth cannot understand why you are grieving now. Your mother has been gone some months."

"But . . ." She'd stopped, feeling all at once ashamed of her display. "But today's my birthday," she whispered.

"I remember."

She'd looked away. "Because William was born the same day."

"Yes, he was. But don't you find it fascinating that you were born in the same palace at the very same hour as the prince when you had not been expected for another six weeks? Surely that must mean something."

Interested in spite of herself, Minuette had said, "Do you think so?"

"I do. I think it means that we are all connected. You and William are closer than even twins would be, for you drew your first breaths in the same minute. And now you share Elizabeth's life as I share Will's. Dozens of noble families would give anything to have their children in such a position. But it is you and I, Minuette, who are here." Dominic had let out a long breath. "You've heard of the falling stars that were seen in the sky in the hour before William's birth?"

Minuette had nodded. "It meant that a boy was coming who would be a great king. A sign from heaven of his importance."

"Perhaps. And perhaps it was something else." He'd looked at her and smiled. "Perhaps it meant that we are all important. Even you and I."

And then Dominic had begun to tell her a story.

Once there were four stars who shone very near one another in the skies over England. They danced and laughed and twinkled as stars do, until the time came for them to jump into the world and become human.

The biggest, boldest star went first, promising to catch those who came after. The next star to go was the quietest, though she shone with the clearest light.

The last two remained together for a time, until the day came for the brightest star to go on. He prepared to jump into this world, and hesitated. For the last star—she who was sweetest and merriest of them all—was weeping, her tears streaking in flashes of light across the sky.

"Don't leave me behind," she begged.

And so, though it was early for her yet, the brightest star enveloped her in his light and they jumped together.

Pleading tiredness from travel, Dominic excused himself and left the stables pondering his reaction to William's unexpectedly generous gift to Minuette. He wanted to believe his discomfort was because of what the court might say. But beneath that entirely practical reason, Dominic felt something less laudable: he could not help comparing the magnificence of the horse with the star pendant he'd left in Minuette's room.

As he came through the entrance into Clock Court, a page presented him with the message that Lord Rochford wished to see him at once. It was not a request. George Boleyn, Duke of Rochford, was not only Queen Anne's brother but Lord Protector of England until William became king in fact as well as in name. Rochford was the most powerful man in England—and well he knew it.

Dominic had never liked the duke much, though he'd spent his childhood as Rochford's ward. It had been an honour accorded Dominic because of his blood—Boleyn by his mother, royal by his grandmother. But the year Dominic turned seven, his blood seemed likely to be his undoing. His paternal uncle, the Marquis of Exeter, committed treason and the estates that had made Exeter the largest landholder in England after the king were confiscated. The marquis himself went to the block, while his wife and twelve-year-old son were imprisoned.

Dominic had known nothing of his own father's subsequent arrest until Rochford had come to see him a month after Exeter's death. Young as he'd been at the time, Dominic had never forgotten it. Rochford's black stare could make grown men sweat, let alone a seven-year-old boy.

Rochford had not troubled to be gentle. "Your father is dead. He died of a fever in the Tower."

Dominic had felt his lower lip tremble, but he'd met Rochford's gaze unblinkingly as the duke continued. "It is fortunate for you, for nothing had yet been proven against him. Better the son of a possible traitor than the offspring of a proven one. But not much better. You would do well to remember that."

For a time Dominic's future had hung in the balance, though he had not been aware then of how close he'd come to being sent away. But King Henry, ever unpredictable in his enthusiasms, had taken a liking to Dominic. Thanks to the old king, Dominic was placed in the Prince of Wales's household and thus had begun his friendship with William. Rochford had not been pleased, and Dominic knew the duke had watched him closely ever since—presumably to ensure he was not another Exeter, just waiting to betray his king.

Dominic's spine straightened automatically as he approached Rochford in the long gallery outside the chapel. The Lord Protector was speaking rapidly to a clerk, no doubt giving orders related to one of the hundred projects in his control. He jerked his head in acknowledgment of Dominic's presence but did not stop talking.

Dominic wondered how Rochford would adjust to his diminished role when William turned eighteen and the regency council was dissolved. He would retain a place as his nephew's advisor, likely the most important, but it wouldn't be the same as ruling England in all but name.

"Courtenay." Rochford dismissed his clerk abruptly and turned to Dominic. "You've done good work in Wales. Will the peace hold?"

Dominic chose his words with care. "For a time. But when border lords are unduly harsh, they create enemies where there need be none."

"You do not approve of our measures."

"I am neither the king nor a member of the council. It is not for me to say."

Eyes dark with amusement, Rochford nodded. "Which brings me to my purpose for speaking with you."

Rochford led him into the chapel and straight through to the queen's pew. Dominic was curious about his obvious desire for privacy—and a little wary. One could never be certain just what the Lord Protector might be going to say.

He waved to Dominic to sit and did the same, leaning forward with hands clasped and elbows on his knees. "I have a proposal for you, Courtenay. I would like to train you as my personal envoy to the Continent. It would require you to travel and meet with various political and religious leaders. You would take your orders from me alone."

In the dead silence that followed, Dominic scrambled for an answer more sophisticated than *Are you mad?* "I'm not sure I understand."

Rochford raised one eyebrow. "I believe I spoke plain English."

Dominic felt the colour rise in his cheeks, and the humiliation of it made him blunt. "Why me? There are plenty of men older and better qualified for such a position."

"Yes, there are. But none who has the ear of the king the way you do. In one year, the regency ends. William will then choose his own council—and you will be on it. Do I think that, at twenty-two, you are too young to advise the king? I do. But as it appears you will be advising him whatever my opinion, I intend to make you as fit for the position as possible."

Dominic had to admit the wisdom of Rochford's reasoning, even if he left out the part about using Dominic for his own ends. And, in spite of himself, he was flattered.

Rochford said smoothly, "It is a proposal, not a command. I prefer an envoy who wants to serve, not one who is compelled to."

Dominic stood when Rochford did, surprised when the duke offered his hand and said, "To be honest, you've turned out better than I expected. You are a steadying influence on His Majesty. I only want to increase your ability to serve him."

How did the man do it? Just when Dominic thought he had him figured, Rochford turned around and did something so genuine and unexpected that Dominic was taken completely off guard. Although he would never understand Rochford, neither could he entirely dislike him.

After William's embrace, Elizabeth made him stand back so she could look at him. He had passed her in height two years ago, and the difference had only increased in the last few months. Where Elizabeth had the fair skin and red-gold hair of their father, William was undoubtedly a Boleyn, with his mother's darker colouring and sulky, sensual mouth.

Alerted by the turn to that mouth, she asked, "What's wrong?"

"Nothing." He attempted to stare her down but was soon grinning. "When are you going to teach me how to read others like you do?"

"As soon as you have learnt how to control your countenance."

"Fair enough," he sighed. "Dominic was displeased with my gift to Minuette."

Elizabeth tilted her head in query, and William continued. "A Spanish jennet. If she's to be your lady, she needs a horse of her own, not whatever she can borrow at stables along the way."

As mildly as possible, Elizabeth said, "I could have provided her a horse myself."

"Why may I not do the same?"

"Because people will talk. Minuette is young and pretty and orphaned. If you destroy her reputation with thoughtless gifts, she will not thank you for it."

Elizabeth felt her brother draw into himself, channeling irritation into arrogance. "She is nearly as much my sister as you are. I cannot control people's opinions, but I can control the expression of them. If anyone is fool enough to hint at anything improper between us, they'll have severe cause to repent it."

He bowed haughtily to his sister and swept out, taking some of the pleasure of the day with him. Unsettled, Elizabeth waved off her attendants to a far corner of the room and perched on the window seat.

She amused herself for a time watching people pass below her in Clock Court. There were the Dukes of Norfolk and Northumberland clearly arguing with each other. The Catholic Howards and the Protestant Dudleys were long enemies—both personally and religiously—and the two lords did not often agree on anything. Elizabeth wondered what this particular disagreement was about. If she was lucky, Northumberland was protesting her betrothal to the French Catholic prince.

Several of the younger men of the court were grouped around a figure in one corner, whom it took her a moment to identify as Giles Howard. He was worked up about something—he kept gesturing violently. Elizabeth stifled a laugh when she realized he was moving as though he held a sword and fought an unseen opponent. No doubt he was embellishing some tale of his mediocre abilities.

In the circle around Howard, she found at last what she had not admitted looking for—a young man standing toward the back, disdain writ clearly in the slouching lines of his body. Robert Dudley did not care much for Giles Howard. Then again, Robert Dudley did not care much for most anyone.

As she studied him, Robert lifted his head. Whether he identified her by the brightness of her hair or simply knew which window was hers, Elizabeth did not know, but he saluted her with a nod of his head and a quirk of his lips that made her heart beat faster than it should have. She drew away from the window and willed herself to composure.

Her marriage was a matter of state, not of liking. She had known that since she was old enough to talk. Kings may indulge their desires apart from marriage—but she was a woman, not a king. Her reputation was even more delicate than Minuette's, and she could not afford to tarnish it with a man she could not marry. Robert was Northumberland's fifth son, not a promising prospect for any woman of ambition and certainly not for a royal princess.

But for all that, Elizabeth knew she might have been severely tempted to plead with her brother to consider such an uneven match—if not for the simple fact that Robert was already married.

CHAPTER THREE

"HER MAJESTY, QUEEN Anne, presents the Three Graces. Long may they shed their light on England and our king."

Applause rippled through the great hall as the steward retreated and three white-robed maidens took his place. Though this particular pageant was his mother's birthday gift to him, William let his mind wander as a poet declaimed on the wonders of his reign and the glories still to come.

Elizabeth sat straight-backed, head held high in a manner he knew was unconscious. His eyes flicked from his sister to his mother, sitting next to him, and back to Elizabeth. Though their colouring could not be more different, he had always seen a great similarity in the two. Something about the set of the chin and the expression of the eyes—and, as intelligent as their father had been, William thought Elizabeth's mind owed more to Anne's quicksilver wit than to Henry's stubborn shrewdness.

As he watched his sister, Elizabeth smiled at one of the dancers and William followed her eyes. He had not realized Minuette was part of this pageant. She was draped in white, arms bare and honey-coloured hair worn loose, and she moved with an assurance that surprised William—he was more used to seeing her jump off walls and scramble up trees. How had she changed so much in just a year?

As though his mother could read his mind, she leaned in and said softly, "Genevieve was so quick and impatient when she came to me, but she has learnt to control herself and turn her energy to elegance."

"You have taught her well, Mother," William said, and meant it. There did seem to be something of his mother in the way Minuette held herself, as though aware of everyone watching her.

"She is a good girl. Elizabeth must see to it she remains that way."

"Of course she will," William said sharply, indignant at the thought that Minuette could be anything but entirely good. Mischievous, yes, but never a hint of ... whatever his mother was implying. But beneath his denial lurked uneasiness, as he remembered Giles Howard on the staircase earlier. Minuette's virtue would never falter, but the men around her might not be so cautious. He would have to keep an eye on her.

The Graces finished their performance in a swirl of white silk. Through the applause, William turned his attention to Eleanor Percy, seated across the room. She was eighteen and newly come to court as an attendant to Lady Rochford. He had been watching her for the last month, at the way she moved as though wearing the thinnest nightdress rather than layers of stiffened fabric, at the way she looked at a man through lowered lashes, all warmth and promise. Tonight he stared at her until her cheeks coloured faintly, but she did no more than flick a single glance his way and catch her lower lip with her teeth—a gesture that made William want to bite it in turn.

His father had married for the first time at seventeen, but

William did not find that idea appealing. Marriage was about politics, and what he wanted at the moment was not a matter for negotiations and treaties. He wanted someone soft and pliable—a woman who would share his bed and his company when convenient, and willingly retreat when not. Eleanor was of the perfect social standing: sufficiently below him that her father and brothers would gladly accept any honours offered while she shared the king's bed, not so low that he would feel guilty about damaging her future.

He continued to stare at her until she at last met his gaze fully and smiled—an inviting smile that decided him then and there. He would have to find her a husband. That was a necessity, for he knew that ambitious families still remembered his own mother's elevation from lady-in-waiting to queen. He could not afford to let the relatives of attractive women dream of a throne.

He would wed for practicality, and take his pleasures where he could. For all the unorthodoxy of his parents' marriage, that was the way of kings.

Elizabeth spent nearly all her waking hours weighed down by the responsibilities of her life: how she should dress, what she should study, whom she should speak to, where she should go.

Dancing with Robert Dudley teetered on the very edge of those responsibilities, and she was aware of how quickly she could fall over the edge into scandal. Tonight she didn't care. William was ogling Eleanor Percy, her mother had retired to her chambers, and the French ambassador was busy with Northumberland. To hell with what anyone else thought.

Robert knew every aspect of her—especially the rebellious, temperamental part, which he delighted in bringing out. And not just in her. Robert seemed born to stir up tempests.

Tonight he said what everyone else was thinking but was too circumspect to say aloud. "Lady Mary is going to get herself in trouble one of these days. Even a half sister can only defy a king for so long."

Elizabeth shrugged, annoyed at having Mary dropped into the conversation. Even absent, her half sister had a dampening effect on everything around her. "William knows perfectly well that Mary will not attend any court function at which my mother is present. He invites her because he must, but he does not care that she does not appear. She would only take the pleasure out of it anyway," she added peevishly.

"Pleasure being the operative principle of governments and courts," Robert said drily.

Elizabeth refrained from pouting, just. "Your father is surely pleased at any sign of discontent from Mary. It means the court is safely out of reach of the Catholic faction. If Mary were wise, she would realize that and swallow her pride. Decisions are made by those who are present. Her idealism will leave the Catholics nothing but their pride."

"Why do you dislike her so much?"

Because she thinks my mother is a whore and I'm a bastard, and for all her apparent submission to Will she thinks the same of him . . . "Because she's a fanatic. She would see England burn rather than compromise. And that sort of belief I will never understand."

Robert sighed. "I do not disagree, but I also do not think it wise to ignore her as the king does. Fanatics breed followers, and Mary free will forever be dangerous."

"What are you suggesting?"

He shook off the introspection and smiled lightly. "Me? I am not serious enough to suggest anything. Leave that to councilors. My job is to entertain."

"And you do it so well," she replied. Sometimes she marveled that Robert should be Northumberland's son—though the physical resemblance was there, Robert seemed to belong to the court in a way that his father never had. Northumberland used his size and forceful presence to get what he wanted; Robert came at things more subtly.

As he escorted her off the dance floor, a woman in a dark red gown appeared so suddenly in their path that Robert nearly collided with her. She didn't move even when he put his hand out to stop himself, just stared him down with an impertinence that would have done royalty proud. Elizabeth recognized her: the sullen lady from her mother's presence chamber.

"Yes?" Elizabeth asked sharply, uncomfortable despite herself when the woman met her eyes.

Slowly enough to be rude, the woman dropped into a curtsy. "Pardon me, Your Highness. Sometimes it's all a woman can do to look to herself."

She addressed the last part to Robert, and Elizabeth wondered why, then told herself she didn't care. If the woman had made a fool of herself over Robert Dudley, she was neither the first nor the last.

Robert remained polite, but there was an undercurrent to his reply. "You would be wise to watch your step, Mistress de Clare. You might have disturbed the princess."

Once more the woman met Elizabeth's eyes, but this time the hostility was moderated by something softer that Elizabeth couldn't place. "That was not my intention. I apologize, Your Highness."

Elizabeth accepted with a nod and pulled Robert back to the dance floor. At least there no one would interrupt them and she could pretend that Robert's wife did not exist—and nor did any other woman who might have caught Robert's eye.

By the time Minuette returned to the great hall after the pageant, the dancing had begun. She stood and watched from the shadow of a corner, letting the music rush through her like the surge of a waterfall. There was something about the Greek costume she still wore—the loose white silk pleated at the shoulders to leave her arms bare when she moved, the lengths of fabric caught beneath her breasts by a simple gold cord and then skimming around her body in flutters like butterfly wings—that made her feel light and joyous and just a little reckless.

Elizabeth was dancing with Robert Dudley. Minuette approved, for Robert could nearly always cajole the serious-minded Elizabeth into something approaching lightheartedness. She liked the smile she saw on Elizabeth's face as she danced, though an image crossed her mind of a widowed French prince who might not approve if he were here.

William stood on the low dais at the front of the hall, in the company of a young woman who had recently come to court. Minuette could not recall her name, only that she was in Lady Rochford's employ. William looked rather like a sleek cat as he bent his head to listen to the lady. His eyes were not on her face, and he was slow to remember himself when another woman, in a dark red dress that highlighted her figure, interrupted.

Alyce de Clare. Minuette frowned. What could Alyce have to speak to William about, important enough to interrupt his obvious flirting? *Could it be . . . could her trouble . . . is it Will?*

No, Minuette told herself immediately. If Alyce had been in the king's bed, the entire court would know it.

"Can it be that one of the Three Graces does not have a partner?" The voice in her ear was low and familiar, and she turned from her worries about Alyce to greet Dominic.

"Not unless you choose to honour me," she said.

He hesitated for the barest moment before taking her hand. "It's been a long time since we've danced together. You've grown taller."

As he led her out, her free hand came up to touch the star pendant around her neck. "Thank you for this, Dominic. It's lovely. All of it. I . . . thank you." She felt his eyes on her, a dark, jewel-hued green, but for some nameless reason could not meet them.

"You're welcome," he said, pulling her into the opening steps of a pavane.

Although Minuette had long ago learnt the patterns of many dances, the last two years had taught her to move without thought. Every posture, every cadence, was instinctive, and Dominic partnered her perfectly, which was perhaps not surprising in a man who had known her all her life.

When the dance ended he escorted her off the floor, and she waited for him to say something. She waited so long that she finally opened her own mouth in a question, only to find him speaking at the same time.

"Tell me about—"

"You've become—"

They both stopped. Feeling unaccountably shy, Minuette said, "I'm sorry. I only meant to ask about Wales."

She could see Dominic relax as he answered her. "The border country is beautiful. And the Welsh mountains . . . far more rugged than anything I've seen before. Being a soldier suits me perfectly. I don't think I have any talent for diplomacy, whatever Lord Rochford might say."

"What has Lord Rochford to do with you?"

He shook his head and said lightly, "Never mind. It's nothing."

Minuette did not think it was nothing. But before she could

press her point, Giles Howard was asking her to dance. Smiling as graciously as she could manage at the unappealing prospect, she let him take her hand and lead her away from Dominic, who scowled at the interruption.

In spite of the fact that Minuette's stepfather was also Giles's uncle, Minuette hardly knew the young man at all. He was a familiar figure, of course, his peacock clothing contrasting sharply with his solid build and sallow skin. In spite of his appearance, he was of some importance, and Minuette knew how to be effortlessly polite even while dancing with a man an inch shorter than herself.

When he caught hold of her fingers at the end of the dance and asked her to walk with him in the courtyard below, Minuette thought wryly that she might have been too polite. There was nothing improper about the request—there were plenty of people about, both inside and out—and because she didn't like him, she agreed out of guilt.

To her relief, Giles didn't try to hold her hand or quote poetry to her, just boasted a bit about his prowess at fencing and jousting. He seemed in no hurry to reach the courtyard, however, leading her through the far entrance of the great hall and down the gallery by the chapel. The stairway on this end was deserted, and Minuette shivered as they reached the stone steps, wishing that she wore more than the thin layers of her costume.

Because she had been listening to Giles with only half her mind, it took a moment for the last thing he said to sink in. She stopped at the top of the stairs and looked at him. "What did you say?"

He repeated himself, his expression a mix of satisfaction and condescension. "Our betrothal. It's all but done."

Her bewilderment turned to fear. "Betrothal? No one's said anything to me."

"Well, they wouldn't, would they? My father spoke to the queen about it some time since, and it awaits only final approval by the king and council."

"But . . ." She tried to think, to ignore the stab of betrayal that William was arranging a marriage for her without her knowledge. The hurt made her less than gracious. "But I don't want to marry you."

Giles gripped her arm with surprising force. "Your fortune is small. If it weren't for your personal ties to the royal family, you'd be of no use to my father. The Howards are the closest thing you have to family. It's time you make it worth our while."

Minuette tried to free her arm while retaining her dignity, but she was beginning to feel a faint sense of panic. The stairway was dark and empty, and Giles's eyes were glittering strangely. He not only ignored her efforts to free herself but wrapped his other arm around her back and pulled her close.

"There's really no need to wait for the formalities. I've a mind to see just how spirited you are."

At that point she would gladly have thrown off her dignity and screamed, but his mouth was on hers so quickly that she nearly choked on her own breath. Then she nearly choked on his, thick and rancid in her throat. She struggled for all she was worth, but it served only to arouse him further.

And then, with a suddenness that made her lose her balance and sit down hard on the ground, Giles was off her and she could breathe. Angry to feel herself shaking, she inhaled deeply several times, though it would take more than that to cleanse her mouth of the taste of him.

She stared up to where Giles stood perfectly still, his right arm twisted sharply behind his back and the point of Dominic's dagger pricking the underside of his chin.

Dominic's voice was a purr that raised the hair on the back of her neck. "Did you not listen to me earlier? That was a mistake."

Giles gurgled, and Minuette swallowed a laugh of pure hysteria. The dagger moved slightly, and she saw a pinprick of blood slide down its blade.

"Don't," she said.

Dominic turned his face to her, though she wasn't sure he could see anything through the haze of fury in his eyes.

From behind Dominic, a voice of undoubted authority rang out. "Let him go, Dom." William strode into view, flanked by two of his guards. He extended a hand to help Minuette up without taking his eyes off the two men locked together in a threat of violence.

At first it seemed that Dominic would not obey. When he did release Giles, it was with a shove that sent him staggering. In an instinct of violence, Giles raised a fist, but William's voice stopped him cold. "I shouldn't do that if I were you."

Giles wasn't so pompous that he didn't recognize the danger in his sovereign's voice. Mumbling halfhearted curses, he retreated down the corridor with less grace than speed.

William touched his hand to her cheek. "Are you all right?"

Minuette was staring at Dominic, who sheathed his dagger with an energetic thrust that frightened her—as if he imagined it to be Giles's body. "I'm all right."

William let his hand drop, and Minuette seized it impulsively. "He told me . . . he said that you're arranging a betrothal between us."

His lips tightened. "You needn't worry. He'll not come near you again."

"But you were considering it?"

Shifting from one foot to the other, William said cautiously, "It had been mentioned. But it hadn't gone any further than talk. I would have told you if it had."

"Then you won't—I won't have to marry him?"

"No."

Dominic had turned away as if she weren't even there. Trying to focus on the matter at hand, Minuette wrenched her eyes back to William. "I know that I can't marry without permission. But I should at least like to respect my husband. Promise me, William, that you won't force me to marry against my wishes."

His right hand came up to cup her chin. "I promise."

Dominic refused to let Minuette out of his sight—he insisted on escorting her until she was safe behind the thick door of her quarters. But William would not let them leave until Dominic gave his word that he would not go looking for Giles Howard afterward.

"A beating is too simple," William had said softly before sending Dominic off with Minuette. "I've much better ways of making a man pay."

Dominic didn't doubt it, though part of him still ached to smash Howard's face. As he walked beside Minuette, he considered that he had only promised not to go looking for him. If he should happen to come across him by chance . . .

Had William not stopped him earlier, Dominic was in little doubt that he would have killed Giles Howard. He was less disturbed by that than he would have liked, for he was not an especially violent or impulsive man. But when he had seen Howard with hands and mouth on Minuette, Dominic had given in to a red rush of fury.

He would have been displeased to find Howard assaulting any young woman, and he tried to convince himself that his reaction would have been the same even if the woman involved had been a stranger. But he was too honest to believe it. From the moment Minuette had jumped into his arms this afternoon, a trembling, half-formed suspicion had hovered in the back of his mind.

When he had come upon her in the gardens with William, he had not known her. And in those few seconds of nonrecognition, he had found himself appraising her as if she were a stranger—tall, lithe, and with a touch of joy in her movements that was very pleasing.

And then, like a shifting prism, it was Minuette on that wall, jumping to him as if she were still ten years old. But it had been the body of a woman he'd caught and held for longer than he'd meant to. And in that brief embrace, he'd heard a voice in his mind that had thrown him out of all countenance: Giles Howard's crude but accurate assessment—*rather like a colt, all eyes and legs and spirit.*

He'd almost forgotten that Minuette walked next to him until she said softly, "I'm sorry, Dominic."

Startled, he said, "What on earth for?"

"You should not have had to see me like . . . I should never have been there. I should have known what to do. It's so humiliating. . . ."

That stopped him in his tracks, horrified at how he had been brooding on his own injuries and completely ignoring Minuette's. She would not look at him, and he wanted desperately to make her do so.

"Your only sin is too great kindness," he said firmly, "and who can fault you for that? You would not be Minuette without it. I only hope that tonight has not driven kindness from you."

Finally she looked at him, a liquid glance that rearranged his insides. "You are not angry with me?"

"Never with you."

"This was not how I imagined it would be when you came back to court."

"What did you imagine?"

He told himself that he was wrong about the hitch in her breathing, that he was tired and fanciful and the whole day was becoming increasingly unreal. He needed to sleep, he told himself firmly. And when he woke up, the world would right itself and Minuette would be—

A scream knifed through the air, abruptly cut off with a sickening thud. Some things Dominic could do by instinct; he was moving toward the sound before he knew it, Minuette on his heels. He almost told her sharply to stay behind, but he didn't want to abandon her in an empty corridor.

A woman lay in a fatally unnatural sprawl at the bottom of a staircase, the rich red of her dress pooled around her; in the torchlight he could not tell where the blood began and the fabric ended. Dominic threw out his arm to stop Minuette, but she had already seen. More than just seen—recognized.

"Alyce!"

CHAPTER FOUR

MINUETTE WAS SOMEWHAT startled to wake up the next morning; she had been so certain that she would never be able to sleep. Still, when she opened her eyes she saw not only the narrow chamber around her but Alyce's crumpled body and dented skull from last night.

She sat up and pressed her hands to her face, but blacking out sight didn't change things. Alyce was dead—and it was Minuette's fault. She should have told someone about the pregnancy, even though Alyce hadn't wanted it. Her friend had been in despair and not thinking . . . why else would she have thrown herself down the stairs? And why hadn't Minuette realized how desperate Alyce was?

An accident, Dominic had soothed her last night. No light at the top of those steps, and so easy for a woman to stumble with the heels and the skirts . . .

Minuette didn't believe that for an instant. Court women were accustomed to their heels and skirts; otherwise, there would be tripping in corridors and slipping on steps every day. Alyce had not stumbled last night, except on purpose. Maybe she had not even meant to kill herself. Maybe she had only been trying to lose the baby.

Then why did she scream? a little voice niggled. *If she did it on purpose . . .*

She opened her eyes and brought herself back to the now. It was her first day in Elizabeth's service, and she could not begin by being late.

Swinging out of bed, she almost hit the opposite wall with her knees. The chamber she had been allotted was tiny, but for the first time in her life it was all hers—a rare luxury for any nonroyal lady, and a mark of how high she stood in Elizabeth's household. Minuette might hold no objective power, but she would be a gatekeeper to the princess.

She stood up, already making a list of things to do: choose a dress, find someone to help with her hair (she might be more important now, but that didn't mean she had any more money to hire a maid of her own), pretend that she had not watched Dominic nearly kill a man last night (*for your sake,* a little voice whispered).

Giles Howard was vile and dangerous, true. But Dominic had stopped him with an intensity that had penetrated her own fear, and William . . . William had promised he would let her marry whom she chose. She still felt a jolt of triumph that she held that kind of sway with the King of England—a jolt that turned uneasy at the memory of Alyce speaking to William last night. Surely that meant something; she could not recall Alyce ever speaking with him before. And that she had died soon after . . . Minuette shoved the thought aside.

She chose her simplest gown of white underdress and blue linen overdress embroidered with ivory leaves along the hem. As she tied her hair back with a silver ribbon, someone knocked on the door. She opened it to a young page, expecting to hear that Elizabeth had summoned her, but instead the page said, "Mistress Wyatt? I have a letter for you."

He handed over a thick sheaf of paper—it was more a small book than a mere letter—and she looked at the plain wax seal. "From whom?" she asked.

"Mistress de Clare." He bowed himself away in the moment of Minuette's shock.

Alyce de Clare. Alyce—who was dead. But apparently still sending letters.

She broke the wax and read the first page, dated yesterday.

Minuette,

You are right, of course. I am in trouble, though I do not think you could begin to imagine what sort. I believe I can find my way clear. But in spite of my protestations, I find I need your help. Will you keep the enclosed for me and not tell anyone? They are my assurance. When I am clear of this trouble, I will let you know and you may burn the enclosed.

Alyce

Postscript: Thank you for the loan of Petrarch. If I forget to return the volume, you may retrieve it yourself from my chest.

Unnerved, Minuette sank onto her bed. What did Alyce mean, that Minuette could not guess her trouble? She was only too clearly with child. And what were these assurances of safety? Love letters, perhaps, meant to force a man to take responsibility and help his lover? But then why throw herself down a staircase if she thought she knew her way clear?

Scanning the enclosed sheets, her bewilderment grew. There were eleven in all, but they were completely unreadable. There weren't any words, just strings of nonsense letters in short blocks of text. Ciphered? Her confusion gave way to fear. Alyce had been right: Minuette could not begin to guess what sort of trouble her friend had been in.

She folded the ciphered pages together with Alyce's covering letter and put them inside her sparsely tenanted jewelry casket. She was in over her head and needed to think about who best to help her. Her first thought was Dominic—probably because he had been with her last night when Alyce had died. Also because he was the steadiest man she knew and she needed someone steady to tell her what to do.

But first she had a princess to report to.

William prowled the perimeter of the council chamber, empty except for Dominic, who said, "Don't you ever sit still?"

"I think better when I move."

"Any chance you're thinking about Alyce de Clare?"

William drew a momentary blank, then remembered and shrugged it off. "You're overreacting. So she spoke to me last night. So I agreed to meet with her today about whatever she wanted to talk about. No doubt it was about something trivial like taking a leave from court."

"Then she would have been speaking to your mother, not you. Are you sure you've never spoken with her before?" He asked it casually, but William heard the unspoken accusation and resented it, the more so because it came from Dominic.

"I will swear it on my throne, if you like. I do remember women's faces, if not always their names."

"Still," Dominic pressed—and this time the casualness was overdone, making William's nerves twitch—"I think there is something more to this."

"The girl fell down the stairs . . . and that's the charitable version. I've already heard from four people this morning that she was pregnant. For her family's sake we should leave it alone. Why give the gossips more to talk about?"

"Why would she ask to speak with you and then throw herself down a staircase?"

William stopped prowling and stared at his friend. "What aren't you telling me?"

Dominic hesitated, and in that moment the door was thrown open and the regency council entered by twos and threes, only Lord Rochford keeping to himself amidst the babble of male voices. William braced himself to argue with his uncle about Dominic's presence at today's meeting. Dominic was staying—William would make him a secretary or clerk on the spot if he had to; hell, he'd make Dominic a bishop if necessary to keep him in the room. But Rochford merely went to his customary seat to the right of William's and waited for his nephew to take his place. In the flurry of the eight councilors arranging themselves at the long table, Dominic quietly sat against the wall behind Rochford as though he had always belonged there.

So his uncle had anticipated him. William couldn't wait to hear what that was all about. He would have to ask Dominic—at least if he wanted more of an answer than "I think it's best for the kingdom."

Not the *kingdom,* William always wanted to retort. My *kingdom.*

The topic of this meeting was, of course, the French treaty. No one said a single unexpected word—in fact, William was certain he could have written out the entire discussion himself, complete with repetition and petty disagreement and mind-numbing boredom. It didn't matter in any case; Rochford wanted this treaty as much as William did, and now that Northumberland had been persuaded, the debate was a matter of form.

As Lord Protector, Rochford gave the final orders. "I'll speak with the French ambassador and send word to our ambassador in Paris. We will continue plans for a September meeting outside Calais."

Why am I even here? William wondered as his uncle looked around the table and asked, "Anything else?"

Amazingly, William heard Dominic clear his throat. Every head at the table swung in his friend's direction. Curious, he waited for Dominic to bring up Alyce de Clare's death (what else could he have to say? Something about the Welsh border?), but instead Dominic shook his head and said, "Sorry. It's nothing."

Rochford didn't look as though he believed Dominic any more than William did, but he dismissed the councilors. As they rose Northumberland asked sardonically, "I suppose the Lady Mary is ill once more and unable to attend the celebrations this week?"

"She is," William said, since his uncle didn't seem in any hurry to answer. Rochford usually let William deal with his troublesome half sister—at least in public.

Northumberland snorted. "Not ill enough to keep from holding mass."

The aging Duke of Norfolk—the leading Catholic lord in England and William's great-uncle—said stiffly, "This council has granted her permission to hear private services as she chooses. It is little enough to allow her."

"Private, are they?" Northumberland said bluntly. "With dozens of worshippers who don't even pretend to be part of her personal household?"

William wanted to hit something. Mary was a never-ending flash point, one he did not wish to argue about today.

His uncle, sensing his mood, cut across the quarreling councilors. "No doubt the Lady Mary is truly ill," he said smoothly. "Unless you believe Henry's daughter is a liar?"

Not a liar, William thought. *Never a liar—just inflexible.* Religiously, emotionally, historically . . . Mary did not bend, she did not forget, and she did not forgive. And never would she come near a palace where her mother's replacement was in residence. In the twenty-one years since Anne's coronation, Mary had not once acknowledged her stepmother as anything other than "the person" or "the woman."

But Northumberland was not willing to let it go. "Your Majesty, your leniency does you credit as a brother. But as a monarch, every leniency you allow your sister is pushed fourfold by those who continue to adhere to Rome."

"You cannot expect the king to upset the delicate feelings of either Lady Mary or the queen," Rochford said.

And that was one condescension too many for William—especially in front of all his councilors. "Northumberland has a point. I believe someone once told me that mercy is only effective once strength has been established."

He could swear he had made his uncle twitch, and the pleasure of catching him off guard made William bold—and impulsive. "Send word to Lady Mary that I expect her to attend me at Hampton Court this night. I will brook no excuse." It wouldn't be that hard on her; she had spent the week at Whitehall, which was only a few miles upriver. She could come by boat and hardly be disturbed.

"If she will not be moved?" queried Norfolk.

"Tell her that she will either spend tonight in my court or I will arrange lodging for her farther east."

Had he really just threatened to send his half sister to the Tower? Apparently he had, for no one said a word more. William himself was so surprised that he almost forgot to detain

Lord Norfolk. It was Dominic who stopped the duke and looked at William questioningly.

"Right." William snapped back to himself, carrying the satisfaction of power used and respected. "I am not to be interrupted for anything," he commanded a guard, then flung himself into a chair.

Studying the slight but still erect figure of the man who had been a child in the last days of Richard III, William did not mince words. "Your son is a disgrace to my court."

Norfolk's eyes flickered, and William realized he had expected to be lectured about his partisanship of Mary. But despite his age, Norfolk was quick and had ears everywhere. "You speak of young Giles."

"You will see to his removal at once. He may return to the country while I . . ." William tapped his fingers on the arm of his chair. ". . . consider his punishment."

"Yes, Your Majesty," Norfolk answered, not anxious to expend political capital on defending a son of minor importance. Once before he had stood by a son, and he had been condemned to death for it. His eldest son had been executed, and only the death of William's father—the day before Norfolk's scheduled execution—had saved the duke. After languishing in the Tower for the first two years of William's reign, Rochford had suggested a pardon and a restoration of Howard's title. Northumberland had also been made a duke at the same time, in order to balance any Catholic sentiment on Norfolk's side.

"Also," William continued, "you've held the patrimony of Mistress Genevieve Wyatt since her mother's death. After the grave insult offered her person, I will not subject her to any dealings with your family in future. I have sent a messenger to her estate at Wynfield to apprise them that I claim her holdings for the crown."

That did not sit well with Norfolk, property being more important than sons, but he managed to bow stiffly. "As you wish, Your Majesty."

After just four hours as Elizabeth's principal lady, Minuette was exhausted both physically and mentally. Elizabeth was not a decorative princess. She was a serious scholar who kept up a voluminous correspondence with Continental philosophers and religious figures, a powerful landholder who knew every animal and outbuilding in her control, and a primary avenue of royal influence. She had secretaries and ladies and clerks in plenty, and she threw Minuette straight into the fray without blinking.

"The only way to learn is to do," Elizabeth commanded. "Hastings won't you let stray too far."

And so with her own secretary from Elizabeth's household (Minuette had known Oliver Hastings since childhood), by midafternoon she had dictated two dozen letters in answer to the most pressing complaints, ranging from a boundary dispute on one of Elizabeth's farms to abased pleas for preferment at court. It had barely touched the surface of what waited. As Minuette separated letters into appropriate stacks for future work, she directed a steady stream of commentary at Hastings.

"Another request for a place at court from a friend of a friend of a relation," she sighed. "Do these people really think a princess royal has nothing better to do than look after their candidates for sheriff or priest or clerk?"

Beneath his formidable graying eyebrows, Hastings's eyes met hers levelly. "As long as the king is unmarried and childless, the princess is next in succession. People will take of her what they can."

Minuette sighed and placed the last letter on the smaller

stack, those she would write herself. Handing over the larger stack, she said, "Be polite, Hastings, but firm. Make it clear that she is more likely to respond favorably to their requests if they refrain from making them quite so shrill."

"I know my business, girl."

Minuette smiled at the secretary, who had always treated her with a sort of fretful indulgence, as one would treat a puppy that could be trusted only so far.

"And I know mine," she said briskly. "You can trust me to compose my own replies to the diplomats. Discretion is best hidden behind the mask of candor," she said, repeating a favorite maxim of his.

He eyed her with mock gravity and shook his head. "Yes, well, mind you keep your wits about you. There's many looking to take advantage of the princess, and their eyes are upon the newest—and most influential—lady in her household."

A sharp voice cut in. "Don't go flattering her, Hastings. She's still only a girl."

"Kat!" Minuette stood and enveloped the older woman in a hug. "I've missed you."

Kat Ashley stepped back and surveyed Minuette critically. "You look well enough," she sniffed.

Minuette grinned. Kat had been Elizabeth's governess in childhood, which meant she had been as good as Minuette's governess. Round-faced and rather plain, Kat possessed a good mind and an excellent education and had trained both girls well in everything from sewing cambric shirts to choosing their words with care in tense political situations. "Have you missed me?"

"There's no time in this household for sentiment," Kat said. "You need to change. Put on something finer. I'll send a girl to do your hair. And hurry—you're needed."

"For what?"

"To help the princess keep the peace. The king is receiving Lady Mary in the great hall in one hour."

Minuette could not speak for shock. Mary, coming here? Where Queen Anne was? As far as she knew, the two of them had not shared breathing space in twenty years.

Keep the peace, indeed.

On the surface Elizabeth was calm when Minuette joined her (in a cleverly remade cloth-of-silver gown that had once belonged to the queen), but her tense voice betrayed her. "I can't imagine what William was thinking, threatening Mary," she said, sweeping Minuette along to the great hall.

"He threatened her?" Minuette asked.

"He did. But why now? Why provoke a confrontation today and not last year or last month or next week? What purpose is served today?"

"The French treaty," Minuette mused aloud. "Lady Mary will be unhappy with it."

"Mary will always be unhappy because she cannot turn back time and make life the way she thinks it ought to have been," snapped Elizabeth.

One could hardly blame Mary for that. Minuette had great sympathy for the once-princess who had lost her mother, her title, and her future when her father married Anne Boleyn. She was thirty-seven years old now, with nothing to occupy her but memories and politics. If she had been allowed to marry, things might have been different, but William could never risk her having children.

The crowd in the great hall was not, Minuette was glad to see, as large as it might have been. Some effort had been made to lessen Mary's humiliation—and certainly Queen Anne was not present. Minuette could not imagine William ever being so deliberately cruel. But there were curious courtiers aplenty, buzzing softly in a manner that was more felt than heard, and both the French and Spanish ambassadors were present—the latter with lips pressed tightly together as though he was restraining a protest with some effort. The emperor was always pressing for Mary's better treatment—not to mention her restoration to the line of succession—and his ambassador was clearly angry.

Elizabeth apparently was thinking along the same lines. "At least William does not intend to provoke an utterly irresponsible scene," she murmured to Minuette before joining her brother on the dais. Minuette looked for Dominic and found him watching her, unmoving. She went to his side and whispered, "What was he thinking?"

"Whatever the immediate motivation may have been, make no mistake—William will turn this to his own purpose."

"Which is?"

"A show of authority followed, I would wager, by a gesture of generosity. I suppose we'll see."

The crowd hushed as there was movement at the far end of the hall. Tall as she was, Minuette still had to twist and turn to catch a glimpse of Mary.

A handsome woman, with the erect bearing of royalty and the stamp of Henry in her features. Not as beautiful as William, not as alluring as Elizabeth—but no one who saw her could doubt that she was the descendant of many kings and queens. Minuette always felt sorry for Mary until she was with her, and then pity seemed unbearably offensive. Mary did not want pity. Mary wanted her due.

For all the attention she paid them, Mary might have had no onlookers. She crossed the length of the hall without ever wavering under her brother's gaze, and when she reached the dais she swept into a low and perfect curtsy of obeisance.

Everyone held their breath, and then William (no doubt with clear-eyed purpose) took her by the hand, raised her, and kissed her on both cheeks. "You are most welcome to my court, dear sister," he said loudly. "I could not ask for a greater gift this week."

Oh, yes, Minuette thought. *Dominic was right.* Even if the initial command had been rash, William would use it to his advantage. She marveled at this show of power, not certain if she entirely liked it.

Mary greeted Elizabeth with real affection. Despite being illegitimate in Mary's eyes, Elizabeth herself had never been a target of Mary's malice. As for Elizabeth's feelings . . . well, she was bright enough to amuse herself by running circles around her sister in a fashion that Mary could not recognize. Not even Minuette knew what Elizabeth really felt for Mary.

After the formal greetings, the siblings withdrew for a private meal. Minuette let her breath out from the release of tension and then realized that she had the opportunity she'd been waiting for.

"Dominic," she said, "something odd happened this morning."

He cocked his head, but it seemed mere politeness. "Yes?"

"I received a letter from Alyce de Clare. Twelve hours after her death."

Suddenly she had his whole attention. "What did it say?"

"You can read it if you like. And the other pages. Perhaps you can make sense of them."

"Other pages?"

"Full of nonsensical text. I can't read them."

Dominic was obviously thinking hard and fast, and Minuette felt a hint of unease. What else was going on that had him already worried?

"Do you think . . . should you let Lord Rochford know?" she ventured. "He is the one who arranged Alyce's position at court. He's known her family for years. . . ."

He hesitated before saying, "Lord Rochford has asked me to work for him. I think I should see them first. Then we'll have a better idea of what there is to know."

Although astonished that Dominic would agree to work for Rochford, Minuette was not going to argue with his logic. The Lord Protector made her intensely nervous. Far better to hand the pages over to Dominic and let him decide.

Dominic followed Minuette to a tiny rectangle of a room one floor above Elizabeth's chambers. At first he was worried about the propriety of being alone with her in such a confined space, but the moment he began to look at the pages he forgot such cares. He even sat on the edge of her bed while she perched on her closed trunk and said nothing, anxiety vibrating through her.

"What do you think?" she asked finally. "Something to be worried about?"

He wanted to say no honestly; since he couldn't, he at least wanted to keep her out of it. But Alyce had been her friend. She had trusted Minuette far enough to hand these over. Minuette deserved the truth.

"I'm worried about any correspondence that has been ciphered," he said. "At the least, Alyce was receiving letters that the sender did not want read openly. For a lady so near Queen Anne . . . well, I don't think it was a mere game."

"So how do we read these ciphered pages, then?"

"It's some form of substitution cipher, obviously. It might be as simple as one letter representing another—which could be broken with enough time and effort. But often these types of ciphers use a keyword, possibly a different one for each message. And if I'm to find these keywords, I need your help."

"I don't know anything about ciphers."

"But you were her friend. You shared a chamber for . . . how long?"

"Two years," Minuette said.

"Right. I rather hope these pages were ciphered with keywords, because in that case she likely kept a list. It would be readily available but not obvious, most likely amongst her personal belongings. We need to search the chamber."

Minuette bit her lip, and Dominic prepared to overcome her scruples about privacy and the ethical ramifications of rifling through a dead friend's belongings. But then she said decisively, "Wait here and I'll be back."

She didn't wait for a reply, and Dominic was left awkwardly alone. He did at least stand up, since he was all at once aware of sitting on the bed where she slept. When his mind strayed to a fragmented image of her thin Greek dress and bare arms, he took to pacing like William. Although, could it be called pacing when he could take only four steps before hitting the window and having to turn to take the four steps back to the open door? Maybe he should close the door. Would it not cause comment if he was seen in here?

He was still debating the matter when he heard Minuette's footsteps. They sounded triumphant, and her face, when she reached him, was bright with hope.

"Here." She handed him a book, a volume of Petrarch's sonnets in Italian. "I don't know precisely what a list of keywords looks like, but Alyce gave us the hint herself."

"She did?"

"In what she wrote to me." Minuette plucked the covering letter from Dominic's hands and read the postscript aloud. "'Thank you for the loan of Petrarch. If I forget to return the volume, you may retrieve it yourself from my chest.'" She smiled. "This book was never mine. I don't know where she got it, but it wasn't from me."

Dominic whistled softly. "That does indicate this book is the key. Alyce was clever." *And frightened,* he thought.

"Can you solve it?"

"Probably. May I take these with me?"

"Will you promise to let me know what they say?"

So much for keeping her out of all this. "Give me a few hours, and I'll let you know what I find."

It took two hours for Dominic to locate the first keyword. The volume of Petrarch—all 365 sonnets written to his adored Laura in Italian—yielded a handful of randomly underlined words scattered widely throughout the text. Working on the assumption that Alyce had kept her messages in chronological order, he matched the first underlined word—*mirabil* in the second line of the fourth sonnet—to the first message, but it yielded only more nonsense.

He sighed. It was going to be a long afternoon.

He moved on to the next underlined word (*amor* in line six of the twenty-third sonnet) and through two more unsuccessful attempts before he had it. The keyword for the first message was *venir*, in the first line of the forty-seventh sonnet. Quickly, the random jumble of letters in Alyce's message gave way to plainness: *What does she say of Mary?*

Refusing to ponder the possibilities, Dominic moved on to the second message, prepared to go through another ten attempts at trial and error to decipher them all. But as he looked at the list he'd made of the underlined words and the sonnets they'd come from, he was struck by an idea. The first keyword had been in the first line of its sonnet. Was it the line order, rather than the sonnet order, that revealed the right keywords?

He went back to the fourth sonnet and *mirabil*, which came in the second line. Sure enough, using that word the second message was easily deciphered. The remaining nine messages revealed themselves just as quickly following that pattern until he had complete translations of every ciphered letter Alyce de Clare had been hoarding.

Success gave him no pleasure. When he was finished transcribing, he put his head in his hands and rubbed his aching temples. Then he reached inside his doublet for the folded paper he'd been carrying on him since last night.

He smoothed it out gently, for it was quite old and yellowed, with hints of foxing from damp. But the broadside—the sort affixed to buildings around the city as a means of news and persuasion—was only too legible.

Surrounding the vile depiction of a naked woman were words: *witch*, *whore*, *heretic*. Those words could have applied to nearly any woman against whom public opinion had turned. But there was another title as well, one all too specific: *the king's concubine*.

Anne Boleyn.

These kind of broadsides had plastered parts of London more than twenty years ago, when the populace was furious with the woman who had replaced their beloved Queen Catherine. Why had this one been preserved all this time, and why had Dominic found it in the possession of a woman of the queen's household? He had been the one last night to carry Alyce's broken body to a nearby chamber. He had heard the rustle of paper inside her bodice and, with more than a twinge of apology, had worked it free from her tight corset while Minuette was alerting the guards.

If Alyce de Clare had been spying on the queen . . . well, that was one thing. Everyone reported on everyone else in this court. But the ancient broadside had a new addition. Scrawled across the bottom in large, angry letters was nothing less than treason: *England will not have a Boleyn king.*

He would have to tell William. And Minuette would never let him forget his promise to tell her what he'd deciphered, so he might as well tell them together. And if it was the three of them, then it should definitely be the four of them. *Honestly,* Dominic thought, *Elizabeth will likely be the calmest of us all and with the most practical suggestions.*

And yet, as he wrote the messages that would set in train a private meeting tonight, Dominic knew it was a mistake. He should be reporting even this minute to Lord Rochford, laying out the broadside and the letters and the key. Rochford was the queen's brother and Lord Protector of England; Dominic was nothing. Only a king's friend.

William's triumph at having brought his oldest sister to heel lasted through only one course. Then he remembered why he was perfectly content to let Mary go her own way—she was a crashing bore. She never laughed, she never let up, and she never stopped pressing her point. Politely, of course. Mary was every inch royal and well bred to a fault. But she had never learnt to use charm as Elizabeth did, and William privately thought that her greatest failing. If she knew how to flatter men, how to lead them on and implicitly promise and inspire . . . just as well for William that she did not. Mary with the ability to rally men to her personally rather than just to a bloodless cause would be extremely dangerous. As it was, William mostly found her a nuisance. He thought wryly of his mother's cold anger at being asked to stay secluded in her rooms tonight so as not to upset Mary and wondered how he always seemed to be caught between temperamental women.

Tonight Mary chose to be temperamental over the French treaty. Proof that secrets were difficult to keep—she seemed to know all the pertinent details.

"You are reconciled to this marriage?" she demanded of Elizabeth.

"We all do what we must for England," Elizabeth said drily. "Marry . . . or not. As the king wishes." She raised her glass to William with a mischief that their sister entirely missed.

"But is this truly your wish?" Mary asked him anxiously. "Or that of your councilors? I fear they do not always look to your interests as much as to their own."

"So do all men," William answered.

Beneath the irritation and boredom, he filed away every word Mary spoke. As long as she lived, William could never be entirely at ease. Just by breathing, she was a focus for rebellion. In the seven years of his reign, at least a dozen Catholic plots had been uncovered. Several of them had involved little more than a comment made at the wrong time and place. But there had been two or three that could have been disastrous—like the Aylmer plot.

Even now, the thought of his former tutor was enough to tie William's stomach in knots. He had liked Edward Aylmer, a gentle scholar who had made the schoolroom a place of intellectual adventure. Aylmer had been part of his household when William was still Prince of Wales, and he'd been a familiar and comforting presence during the bewildering transition to king. No one had not known Aylmer was an unrepentant Catholic—

not until the night he was dragged out of William's bedroom with a dagger in his hand.

Aylmer had claimed he meant no harm to his king, that he only wanted to take William away from the Protestant regent, Lord Rochford, and into the care of less-hated men. In the week following Aylmer's arrest, four minor members of the Catholic nobility had been implicated in the plot. They were arrested, tried, and executed before anyone could draw a deep breath. Aylmer's death was the last—and the bloodiest. Where the others had been neatly beheaded, Aylmer's middle-class status was not enough to protect him from the full weight of the traditional sentence. He had been hung, disemboweled, and beheaded.

Though he was years distant from the memory, William could hear his uncle's unbending voice echoing in his head: *You must sign the warrant, Your Majesty. You are as yet too young to be merciful. Mercy is appreciated only when strength has been established.* So he had signed, and Aylmer had died.

By the time a page entered the dining room with a message in Dominic's handwriting, William's head ached and he wondered what he had been thinking, demanding his sister's presence. He seized gladly on Dominic's request for a private meeting (*Bring Elizabeth if it pleases you,* he had written) and dismissed Mary to her chambers with near rudeness.

She began to protest at spending the night under the same roof as his mother, but William cut her short. "I do not require you to meet with those unpleasant to your sentiments. Tomorrow you may return to Whitehall. But I will not trust you to the river after dark. You would not have me trifle with your safety, would you?"

What could even Mary say to that? It wasn't as though she would have to stay anywhere near Anne—William had made sure their rooms were separated by as many wings of the palace as he could manage. She curtsied and bade him a sour goodnight. No doubt she would not sleep, but rather spend the night in prayer against the influence of his mother.

Dominic and Minuette were waiting for them in the privy garden, a secluded honeysuckle arbor that William and Minuette had often escaped to when avoiding lessons as children. They had always been the ones straying—with Dominic and Elizabeth always the ones dragging them back to duty.

Tonight looked to repeat that pattern. If William had thought escaping Mary meant relaxing, one look at Dominic's face told him differently. "What's wrong?" he asked as Elizabeth joined Minuette on the bench.

"Minuette received a letter this morning from Alyce de Clare," Dominic said.

William let out a disbelieving laugh. "The dead Alyce de Clare?"

"Yes."

"You're going to tell me you were right, aren't you? That there is something to worry about in her death."

"Alyce asked Minuette to keep for her some papers until she saw herself clear of her trouble. Obviously she intended them as some sort of hold over whoever wrote them."

"Who did write them?"

"I don't know, but whoever it was is no friend of yours."

"How do you know that?"

"Because the pages were ciphered, and I broke the cipher."

Dominic passed the translations to William, who in turn passed each one as he read it to Elizabeth and then Minuette. There was silence in their little corner until the last one had been read and given back to Dominic.

"A spy," Elizabeth said flatly. "For whom?"

William said, "Does it matter? I appreciate your concern, Dom, but this hardly seems worth skulking in private gardens over. Alyce was asked to report on my mother's reading habits, on those she corresponded with, on her religious devotions. It's petty and intrusive, and if the woman were alive, I would take pleasure in dismissing her from court in the most public manner possible. But she's dead—and no matter what you're thinking, I don't believe she was killed over something so petty."

"Spying on your mother is petty?"

"You know as well as I do that my mother is not well liked. There are many with long memories who like to prick her, but what more can they do? She is the widow of one king and the mother of a second. She cannot be touched."

Dominic sighed, and Elizabeth said sharply, "There's something else. What have you not told us?"

From inside his doublet, Dominic pulled out another paper and, without a word of explanation, handed it to William.

The broadside hit like a sword blow. William knew about the attacks on his mother before his birth, but he had never seen the evidence with his own eyes. Fury rose like bile in his throat at the vicious words and the caricature of a naked Anne calling upon Satan to help her seduce Henry. He almost missed the words freshly scrawled across the bottom, but when he read them his chest burnt with the venom of the phrase.

Elizabeth took the broadside from him, her face paling when she read it. William wanted to pull it away before Minuette saw it, but he knew that would only make her more determined. He looked away, not wanting to see his revulsion mirrored in her eyes.

"I found it on Alyce de Clare's body last night," Dominic said. "Hidden away in her bodice. I suspect . . . The last ciphered letter, it commanded her to 'plant this to be widely seen.' I think the writer must have meant this." He waved his hand at the paper Minuette held gingerly away from her.

"So no longer just reporting," Elizabeth mused, "but acting. Alyce was about to become more than merely a pawn."

"I knew she was in trouble," said Minuette numbly. "I thought it was only because of the child. But this . . . Alyce would never have agreed to this. She may have supplied information, but planting this in public? She would not have done that. She respected Queen Anne too much."

"Perhaps that was why she wished to speak to you, Will," Dominic said. "She knew she was in trouble and wanted to warn you. Only she died before she could."

Red tinged the edges of William's vision. "Someone wants my throne," he spat. "That's what this is, right? Raise old questions about my parents' marriage and my legitimacy so as to get rid of me?" A bolt of anger shot through his control. "Am I king or am I not king?" He slammed his left palm against the wooden support of the arbor. "Is this another Aylmer?" he ground out through his tight throat.

Minuette shot to her feet and pulled him around to look at her. "No," she said decisively. "This is not at all like Aylmer."

"And why is that?" he asked. "Because you say so?"

Elizabeth's voice held both irritation and affection. "Because she believes so. And because Minuette is assured that whatever she believes must be true. Rather like you, Will."

"This is not at all like Aylmer," Minuette repeated, to Elizabeth this time. "He used his friendship to betray from within. Will learnt his lesson then—do not trust so easily. Those he trusts today are fewer, but absolute in their loyalty."

"Absolute loyalty," William murmured. "Is there such a thing?"

Minuette faced him. "We are absolute in our loyalty. Do you not remember what I said to you six years ago?"

Of course he remembered. He remembered it all, not just Aylmer's betrayal and death, but the aftermath. He remembered hiding away with Minuette. In this very arbor, actually.

They had been meant to be studying Greek, but with Aylmer arrested there was no tutor expecting them. So William had commanded his guards to allow them in the garden and not to stand too near. They had allowed the first part, but there were still two guards near enough to snatch him if danger threatened.

"What is the good of being king if even my guards won't listen to me?" William complained.

"Everyone is worried about your safety these days."

"What is there to worry about? Aylmer is dead. This very morning."

Minuette's face did not change; she continued looking at him without flinching as William went on ruthlessly, "The others behind the plot were beheaded, you know. Because they were important, or at least related to those who are. But Aylmer . . ." He swallowed hard. "First they hung him from a gibbet. Carefully, you understand. They didn't want to break his neck, for the rest is no fun if he's dead. Then they laid him on a table and ripped into his stomach with hooks. He could feel every pull and thrust of it until his entrails were spilling out. Only then did they cut off his head. You must have heard the Tower bell toll—it was just this morning."

When his voice would no longer hold, William looked down and kicked at the smooth, raked gravel of the path. He knew he should not have told all that to a girl, but whom else could he tell? His sister cut him off every time Aylmer's name came up, and Dominic . . . well, William did not want Dominic to know how much this execution bothered him.

Minuette, though, always knew what to say. "It hurts because it was someone you trusted. You thought Aylmer was your friend."

"Kings don't have friends." William flung out the challenge, daring her to disagree.

But he should have known he could not daunt Minuette. She laid her hands on either side of his face and drew his forehead down to kiss it. Though they were of an age, the gesture made her seem much older.

"I am your friend," she had said simply. "I love you. Not because you're king, but because you are Will."

William had never forgotten that. Tonight, both so much older, he could see the same unwavering friendship in Minuette's eyes. "Because I am Will," he whispered to her.

Dominic interrupted, sounding slightly harried. "Protestations of loyalty and friendship are all well and good," he said. "But what do we do next? We must tell Rochford."

"Must we?" Elizabeth, usually so certain, actually sounded as though she wanted an answer.

Dominic rounded on her. "Oh, no," he said. "Not you as well. One rebellious Tudor is quite enough to deal with."

"How can I possibly be rebellious?" William asked. "I am king. I am also a loving son. The more people who see this, the greater the chance my mother will hear of it."

"Lord Rochford would hardly tell his sister—"

"But he might tell someone who would. Besides, who can guess exactly how my uncle's mind works? For all we know, he would find some perverse way to twist this to his own advantage. No," William said, certainty growing. "This is ours to deal with. The four of us."

"How?" Elizabeth asked, but William knew from her tone that she agreed. For all her scholarly gravity, his sister also liked to have her own way.

"By doing what we each do best," said Minuette. "Elizabeth with her correspondence and knowledge of every political faction in England; William with his ability to go anywhere and ask anything he wishes and expect an answer; Dominic with his new post in Lord Rochford's employ and his talent to make anyone nervous enough to babble simply by staring at them."

"And what do you do best?" William teased.

"Minuette is the foil," Elizabeth said, sounding as though she were quoting. "The lighthearted, merrymaking girl who sees far more than most give her credit for."

Minuette laughed. "So I do. And I think there is no secret that the four of us cannot discover."

Dominic alone looked reluctant, but William knew him well enough to see that it was partly feigned. Even he had the light of adventure in his eyes. "I will agree, with the condition that Rochford be told at once if any of the secrets we discover are immediately dangerous to William or the realm."

"Secrets?" Minuette asked. "You think there is more than one?"

William spoke for Dominic, who met his eyes with a shared memory—a motto, of sorts, that his father had imparted to both boys often before his death. "There's always another secret."

CHAPTER FIVE

WILLIAM HEARD HIS mother's voice when he was still well down the corridor from her rooms at Richmond. The court had traveled upriver the first week of July to this palace, which his grandfather had built fifty years ago. It was less than ten miles west of London and considerably more comfortable in the summer months, though that didn't seem to have calmed his mother. The court never stayed in any one palace for long. After a month or two, the refuse of a thousand people required moving someplace new while the last place was cleaned. With the French visit looming in September, William expected they would continue to move eastward by small degrees over the next two months until they reached Dover and the sea.

His mother was shouting quite loudly. He nearly turned around when the furious shouts were punctuated by the crash of things being thrown hard against walls, but continued on with a sense of sacrifice. He had always been able to soothe her rages, and from the sound of things that skill would be appreciated today.

What had set her off this time? he wondered as he strode into the presence chamber, where most of her women were safely out of reach of the crashes that could be heard through the inner door. A bow that was slow in coming, an expression that she interpreted as disdain, a letter that did not praise her as effusively as she'd hoped . . . William knew all about his mother's vanity. But he also knew her history and how hard it was for a woman as intelligent and opinionated as she was to always be second-guessed by her past. She had one of the best minds in the kingdom, but despite a long precedent of dowager queens advising their young sons, Anne had not been allowed any official role in the regency. Even the fact that her brother was regent didn't erase the humiliation of being shut out of state affairs.

Whistling softly, William stepped into the privy chamber and surveyed the pieces of what looked to have been a matched set of pottery vases scattered around the fireplace. His mother stopped in midpace, skirts swirling around her, and he said, "Whose head shall I have off this time, Mother?"

She didn't lose an ounce of fierceness; if anything, her face darkened. "Is it true?" she demanded.

"Is what true?"

"That you are taking your whore to France with you for the treaty signing."

"I . . . what?" He didn't know which surprised him more—that she was angry with him or that she already knew he was sleeping with Eleanor.

"The Percy slut. How could you be so stupid, William? You cannot take her to Calais without raising old stories. You know the associations that will arise."

Of course he knew the associations. Calais was where his mother had finally succumbed wholly and where Elizabeth had been conceived, months before his parents' secret marriage. He knew it, but that didn't mean he wanted to think about it—

especially not with his mother looking at him like that. Damn it—why couldn't his mother be more conventional?

"I have no intention of taking Eleanor to Calais."

That appeased his mother not at all. "She should not be at court. I would never allow a single woman in my household to conduct herself in such a way."

"What about Alyce de Clare?" he said, and was instantly sorry. It had been six weeks since her death and they still didn't know much at all. And having to keep his mother from finding out that Alyce had been spying on her had made the investigation even harder.

Before his mother could follow him onto that tricky ground, William added, "And in any case, Eleanor Percy is not in your household. She is in Lady Rochford's."

Her sniff was supremely contemptuous. "Jane Parker only has a household at court because I permit it. One word to George and he would divorce her like that." She snapped her fingers.

William's anger, always slower to be roused than his mother's, began bubbling. "No, he would not divorce her at your command."

"He most certainly—"

"It is my command that matters, not yours."

That finally broke her tantrum. She was no less angry, but her mind was working once again. "I am your mother," she said, as though testing the effect of it on him.

"And your brother is my regent. For yet a little while. But that time is coming to an end. He would do well to remember that."

He would have been shocked by her slow, satisfied smile if he were not long accustomed to her various sudden moods. "And what would I do well to remember?"

Taking hold of her hands, he leaned in and kissed her cheek. "You would do well to remember that I am as you and my father made me. You can trust me, Mother."

Which was true. He had never been going to do anything so stupid as take Eleanor to Calais. Then again, he hadn't meant to take her to bed before he'd found her a husband, but Eleanor was ... persuasive. He had thought of taking her as far as Dover, but now he knew he wouldn't. Just because he had the right to choose didn't mean he wanted to be yelled at by his mother. He would leave Eleanor behind and spend the next few weeks deciding whom she should marry.

That should please his mother. And despite any irritation she might cause, William was never so happy as when he pleased his mother.

19 September 1553
Whitehall Palace

After three weeks of delay at Dover, the court has returned to London. It's a relief to be away from the English Channel. Everywhere I went the sound of water followed, whispering of how dreadfully ill I would be the moment I set foot on board ship. It never came to that. King Henri kept putting us off—first because his wife was ill, then he himself, then something about the weather that sounded suspect even to me. Lord Rochford went about for a day or two with a very black look, and William was in council meetings for nearly twelve hours straight.

That was five days ago. Four days ago we left Dover behind— along with all thoughts of a French treaty. It appears the French were more interested in playing with William than in actually making peace. They will learn soon enough that Will is not to be mocked. But for now, selfish being that I am, I am merely grateful that I shall not have to cross the sea anytime soon.

I am not the only one relieved. Elizabeth went so far as to blink three times when informed that we were to make for London. It's as much emotion as I've seen from her in a month. As the time drew near for Calais and the treaty and her betrothal to Charles, she seemed to pull ever more into herself. She would never say so, but I am sure she is glad not to have to marry just yet.

While at Dover, Dominic went everywhere Rochford did. It seems an unlikely pairing—Dominic has always been so straightforward. But he has picked up on Rochford's trick of blanking his eyes so that one has no idea just what he might be thinking. I suppose that will be useful in diplomatic situations. It's rather irritating for the rest of us.

I do enjoy being in Elizabeth's service. Not all has been smooth, for there are many who covet my position. But Mistress Ashley has eased the way with her unhesitating acceptance of me. She has known me nearly as long as she's known the princess, and sometimes I catch her about to scold me or send me running along to bed before she remembers that I am quite grown and have responsibilities of my own now.

We are beginning well enough in our autumn pleasures, for there is to be a wedding tomorrow. Eleanor Percy is to marry Giles Howard, and we are bidden to attend. A wedding is always festive, even if . . .

Minuette paused, searching for a polite way to end that sentence. *A wedding is always festive, even if* . . . *Giles Howard is a horrid man whom I wouldn't wish on any woman. Even if* . . . *I suspect William of arranging things for his own advantage.*

It doesn't concern me, she told herself sternly. *What William does is his own affair.*

But *affair* was a poorly chosen word and set her off again

wondering what it was that William saw in Eleanor Percy, a woman incapable of sustaining any conversation longer than five minutes.

It's not conversation he wants, her treacherous mind whispered. And when she found her mind wandering to the shadowy details of what he did want, Minuette shut her diary emphatically. Biting her lip, she eyed Elizabeth. The princess appeared totally absorbed in her account book, and Minuette hesitated to interrupt her for something as trivial as a vague sense of discontent.

Without looking up, Elizabeth said, "What is bothering you, Minuette?"

"Well, now it's the fact that you can read my mind without effort."

Elizabeth made a last entry, wiped her quill, and laid it down. "Truly, what is it?"

Since she still could not come up with a polite way to express herself, Minuette said it plainly. "Are you not bothered by this wedding tomorrow?"

"Why would I be?" Elizabeth asked in genuine surprise.

"It just seems so ... cold-blooded. Eleanor Percy cannot possibly care for Giles Howard. And it is so rushed."

"I am quite sure Eleanor is content. With the rush, as well as the marriage."

Minuette weighed pouring out her true fear, but Elizabeth spoke first. "You need not worry. Eleanor will serve a particular purpose in Will's life ... but she will never be his friend."

She picked up her pen once more and turned back to her work. "And all the better for Will. If he is content with a woman like Eleanor, then he is unlikely to ever do anything so disastrous as fall in love."

William was relieved to be at Whitehall—away from Dover and his uncle's black mood and constant arguments about Henri's intentions. For three weeks Rochford had kept William busy from dawn to dusk with discussions of policy and the implications of the upcoming treaty. Now that the treaty appeared lost, William knew there would be continued debate by a council that seemed more anxious to talk than to act. He was prepared to endure a great deal of boredom in the coming days.

But not today. He had flatly refused to meet in council again until tomorrow, reasoning that they were all tired and would do better after a day or two of rest. Somewhat surprisingly, Rochford had agreed and William had enjoyed an afternoon of doing not much of anything—reading, gambling with some of his gentlemen—while his mind danced to Eleanor. The last three weeks of separation had only burnished her allure. Give her one night with her husband, and then she would be all his.

As he considered it, William felt a twinge that he smothered with righteous argument. He was doing nothing that had not been done a hundred times before by kings long dead—his own father's first acknowledged son had been borne by a woman married to someone else. (He had never known his half brother; Henry FitzRoy had died the month after William's own birth.) And it wasn't as though Giles Howard were being secretly cuckolded. He knew the price of his return to royal favor.

When Dominic entered the privy chamber, William brightened and waved off everyone else. Weeks of tension had left their mark in the lines etched around Dominic's eyes. Shadowing Rochford couldn't be an easy task when the Lord Protector was in a rage.

"Why didn't you tell me?" Dominic demanded, in a tone reminiscent of William's mother.

"Tell you what?"

"That Giles Howard is back at court—and being given a lavish wedding at your expense."

"It was hardly a secret. I assumed you knew."

"If I had known, I would have stopped it."

William gave a short laugh. "This marriage has nothing to do with you, Dom. Why do you care?"

"Have you forgotten what he did to Minuette?"

Why was it that Dominic could so easily make him defensive? "I have not forgotten."

"Then why . . ." Dominic searched him with probing eyes.

He forced himself to look steadily back, knowing that Dominic could read him almost as easily as Elizabeth did.

At last Dominic shook his head. "Neatly done. Tell me, does Howard know the price of his return?"

"He's pleased with his advancement. And I imagine he'll be kept busy administering affairs on his new estates in Cumberland."

"While his wife remains in Lady Rochford's service."

"Naturally."

"Have you given any thought to the lady, beyond what you desire?"

William hovered on the point of real anger before shrugging it off. "I assure you, Eleanor is quite content with the arrangement. No matter how long she . . . however long we . . . she will be the daughter-in-law of one of the premier dukes in England. It's more than her family ever dreamed."

But Dominic placed the matter in more candid terms. "You mean she's willing to sell herself for her family's sake."

Exasperated, William stood up ready to pace. "If you think I've bought Eleanor, you're mistaken. She is no innocent and she needed no inducements. Eleanor's only virtue is devotion to her own interests. Not the quality I would wish in a wife, but she will do nicely for now."

He put his hands on Dominic's shoulders and noted with satisfaction that their eyes were at last level. "Tonight is for pleasure, Dom. Get some sleep and then come dance with the bride. You've kept to yourself too much these last months. Find a woman—that's what you need."

Dominic attended the wedding as William had bidden him, but he did not dance with the bride. Arms crossed, he leaned against the linenfold paneling that adorned the walls of the chamber and considered the spectacle playing out before him.

It seemed that William had been right. Eleanor Percy—Eleanor Howard, now—looked remarkably content. She behaved impeccably toward her new husband and even coaxed the old Duke of Norfolk into dancing with her. Giles, dressed in the gaudiest bright blue doublet Dominic had ever seen, preened as he watched his wife and father. But before long his eyes wandered, and Dominic's chest constricted when Giles's hungry gaze lit on Minuette and stayed there.

She sparkled in a gown of shimmery shades of pink and white, deep in conversation with a young man Dominic did not recognize. Perhaps more than conversation, he thought. Her smile, the way she lowered her lashes demurely, the silver of laughter . . . Minuette was flirting. And Dominic was not the only one to notice. Every man within eyesight seemed to subtly orient himself to her.

He had seen this sort of feminine power before—despite her age, Queen Anne could still command any room of men she chose. It seemed Minuette had learnt more from the queen than just dancing and diplomacy.

Flirting is part of diplomacy, he told himself, but his feet did not listen. He strode to Minuette and interrupted with only the barest attempt at civility. "If I might have a word?"

With surprised pleasure, she said, "Dominic, may I introduce Jonathan Percy? And this is Dominic Courtenay."

Jonathan started to stumble out a greeting, but Dominic cut him short with a nod and an abrupt "Excuse us."

He steered Minuette by the elbow to a window embrasure where they could be somewhat private. "What's happened?" Minuette sounded genuinely worried.

Instantly he felt foolish. "I just . . . I wondered if you had made any progress amongst the queen's ladies. Any information about Alyce de Clare that might help us?"

"That's why you dragged me away from poor Jonathan? You were really quite rude."

"Was I?" For the first time, Dominic registered the young man's surname. "Percy—is he a relative of the bride?"

Minuette sniffed. "He and Eleanor are twins. Though one would never guess—Jonathan is quite cultured. He's a musician, currently with the Bishop of Winchester. I think I'll ask William to bring him to court."

It seemed she was as unhappy with this marriage as Dominic. Because of William's willingness to let Giles return to court so soon?

They both looked round as the music stopped. But William immediately clapped for more and went straight to Eleanor, standing next to her new husband. William did not even ask—simply took possession of her hand. Then the music struck up and they were dancing.

In spite of himself, Dominic was impressed by Giles Howard's self-control. Only a flicker of his eyes betrayed possible discomfort. Whatever he had agreed to—unspoken or not—it could not be pleasant to stand by and watch your wife smiling radiantly in another man's arms.

Dominic knew this was as close as William would come to publicly shaming Howard. Affairs in the English court were conducted circumspectly; gossip might run riot, but the only ones who would know for certain where Eleanor spent her nights were the gentlemen who escorted her to the king and then stood guard outside the door. For once Dominic was heartily relieved to be working for Rochford—there was no way he meant to stand twenty feet away while William bedded any woman.

Though Dominic had not been precisely celibate in the last two years, campaigning left little enough time for dalliance, and Rochford now drove him with an intensity that left no energy for anything else. When he wasn't attending the Lord Protector, he was studying foreign affairs and the history of English diplomacy. In truth, watching Rochford work was the greatest tutorial. It had been a revelation to see what could be accomplished with the raise of an eyebrow, a few judicious words, and an occasional veiled threat.

"She is very lovely." Minuette's voice made him jump. Her gaze was fixed on William and Eleanor. "I imagine he'll be happy with her."

Dominic turned sharp eyes to her, wondering which "he" she meant. Surely she didn't realize . . . surely she did. The entire court knew what was being enacted here tonight.

Before he could think how to change the subject, Minuette did it for him. "I have been speaking to the queen's ladies, but they have told me nothing I did not already know about Alyce. It's just that I didn't want to know some of it."

Since a dead woman seemed a safer subject just now than a living one, Dominic asked, "What do you know?"

"That she was ambitious, and poor, and not in the least sentimental. She used to laugh whenever I would talk about love or even kindness. 'No one marries for love,' she'd tell me. 'That's just a story we tell ourselves to cover our own natures.'"

Dominic didn't ask if Alyce was ambitious and poor enough to be bought—clearly she had been. "So how did a woman so hardheaded fall pregnant?"

"Perhaps she knew herself less well than she thought," Minuette said. "Perhaps she was surprised by love. She may have been reckless—but she could never be stupid. Whatever she did, she did it knowingly."

"Any idea with whom?"

She shook her head and smiled ruefully. "I could have sworn that she didn't look twice at any man. But then, I could have sworn that I would never again be in the same room with Giles Howard."

"Minuette—"

"And when shall we be dancing at your wedding, Dominic?"

The abrupt change of subject left him floundering. "What wedding?"

"I hear the women talking. You have only to look around you to find any number of willing brides."

Unable to bear her direct and unsuspicious gaze, he looked over her head to the painting of Henry VII hanging behind her. The miserly face of William's grandfather helped him speak sparingly. "I'm sure you're wrong. I've nothing to recommend me but the rather precarious gift of royal favor. No title, no land, nothing but the king's goodwill."

Her voice was untroubled. "I think the recommendation of your person is quite enough for any lady. And if marriage isn't to your liking, it isn't necessarily required."

Startled into looking at her again, he saw that she was staring at Giles Howard. "Never mind me." She waved a hand and turned toward him. "You are a favorite amongst the ladies. That is all I meant."

Dominic smiled slightly. "It's kind of you to say. However, with the treaty in shambles, I expect at any moment to be sent off and who knows when I'll return. Now is not the time to begin an affair of the heart."

It was an eminently practical and reasonable answer and Minuette accepted it with a nod. As Dominic watched the rise and fall of her breathing beneath the star pendant she wore almost continually, he repeated it silently to himself. *Now is not the time.*

The morning after Eleanor's wedding, Elizabeth summoned Dominic to attend her and Minuette riding. Though there were also grooms in attendance, the three of them could converse with much less chance of being overheard while on horseback.

Once they were well away into the fields, Dominic asked, "Is this simply checking in or do you have something definite to report?"

"Nothing definite, just hints of provocation. Mary has increased her letters to the emperor—sometimes three a week. And her household is seeing an increase in visitors."

"I've heard," Dominic said. "Rochford keeps telling Will he should tighten his control of her household. But I'm not convinced Lady Mary has anything to do with Alyce and the broadsheet. It was a man who fathered Alyce's child and wrote those letters."

"But a man working for whom? This was not an idle game. You said yourself there was purpose behind it. And I doubt that purpose was so inconsequential as ruining Alyce."

"She's not ruined," Minuette said sharply. "She is dead."

"I know," Elizabeth sighed. "But that broadside and its slogan argue a political purpose. There is only one group who wants my brother gone—the Catholics. And the Catholics look to Mary. She may not have known particulars, but wherever there is smoke, there is Mary as the tinder."

Minuette interrupted. "Dominic, why don't you have Lord Rochford send you to question Mary? Surely he would do it if you asked."

"And if I asked, he would want to know why I am suspicious. Aren't we meant to keep this secret?"

"So we are, which makes my next move all the better. No one could ever suspect an ulterior motive."

"An ulterior motive to what?" Elizabeth asked warily.

"I've been writing to Alyce's sister. Emma de Clare married a gentleman farmer named Hadley about the time Alyce came to court. It was Emma that Alyce would visit whenever she had leave."

"Do you think Emma knew her secrets?" Elizabeth asked.

"It's not the sort of thing one can ask in letter without rousing suspicion: 'Do you know whom your sister was sleeping with? And might it be the same person who asked her to spy on the queen? Oh, and are you secret Catholic sympathizers, by the way?'"

Dominic pulled his horse to a halt, and Elizabeth followed suit. Minuette kept going for a dozen paces before she swung Winterfall's head round and walked the horse back to them. "What?"

"What," Elizabeth enunciated carefully, "is your plan?"

"Didn't I say? Emma has extended an invitation to her home. She would like to speak in person to 'one who knew my sister well' these last years. William has given me leave to go."

"William has given you leave?" Elizabeth let her annoyance leak out. "You are a member of my household."

"And you would never say no to me." Minuette smiled triumphantly, then heeled Winterfall round and gave the horse her head. "Try and catch me," she called over her shoulder.

Elizabeth grumbled, "Why does this feel so familiar—Minuette and Will doing whatever comes into their heads while you and I pick up the pieces afterward? I'm going to have to learn to say no to her before she does something irredeemably reckless."

"She's not reckless. Just . . . willful," Dominic said. "And you're not the one who needs to say no to her."

He kicked his horse into motion and Elizabeth followed suit, foreboding playing along her nerves.

Two days after Eleanor's wedding, William sat in his privy chamber with his grim-faced uncle waiting for Dominic to arrive. He had been pulled out of the most private of his bedchambers at midnight—from Eleanor's arms—straight to an emergency session of the regency council.

The treaty with France was indeed lost. Earlier this evening, the French ambassador had finally deigned to wait upon the Lord Protector and inform him that King Henri's brother, lately betrothed to Elizabeth, had married the niece of the Holy Roman Emperor. England's greatest fear had come true—France was allying itself with Spain.

Rochford had proposed sending a delegation straight to the Netherlands in response. If the Catholics were aligning themselves against England, then it was in England's best interest to come out in open alliance with the Protestant nations of Europe. The Duke of Norfolk debated the idea—more for form's sake than because he really disagreed, William thought—but in the end, the vote was unanimous. Not that it mattered. Rochford's vote was the one that counted.

But William was king, and it was his voice that had given the order for Lord Sussex to head a delegation to the Queen of the Netherlands and open negotiations for a formal treaty.

William had risen with relief as the council departed, anxious to return to Eleanor.

But his uncle had stayed him and sent a page to summon Dominic. As Rochford seemed disinclined to explain himself, William sat in silence and let his mind wander away from the tangle of European politics.

Eleanor was everything he'd hoped for. She had proven that she could read his moods and knew instinctively how to meet each one—soothing when he was angry, sympathetic when he was tired, and playful when he was eager. And he had not mis-remembered her skill in bed. What more could he want?

When Dominic entered the room, he looked straight at his king and William had the disconcerting sense that Dom could see right into his thoughts. He didn't know why that bothered him. Dominic was five years older and had certainly enjoyed any number of women.

Rochford was terse even for him. "Courtenay, I need you ready to ride in an hour. There's a ship at Dover ready to weigh anchor on tomorrow's tides. You are to tell no one where you are going."

"Where am I going?"

"France."

Dominic didn't look particularly surprised. "Shouldn't you be sending a larger delegation?"

"I'm not hoping for a treaty from this. I'm hoping for … insight."

"You want a spy."

"I want an envoy."

The two men stared at each other until William grew impatient and broke in. "For heaven's sake, sit down, Dom."

He took over the explaining, trusting his uncle to interrupt him if he got any of it wrong. He knew he wouldn't. "A delegation will leave within the week for the Netherlands. We can't afford to overlook obvious avenues of alliance. And I don't mind putting pressure on Henri. He thinks he can overawe me because I'm young. This is a bluff—Henri doesn't want war. All we have to do is show him that his best interests lie in a treaty with England."

"And how am I supposed to accomplish that?" Dominic asked with pardonable skepticism.

Rochford took over. "You aren't. I am. I need you at Henri's court to give me eyes and ears into the situation so that I will know where and when to apply pressure."

"He will suspect that."

"Of course he will. It doesn't matter. This is a game, Courtenay, and you're a pawn at the moment. Go where you're told and leave matters requiring intelligence to the masters."

Dominic nodded and rose. "Within the hour? I'd better pack."

William said, "Wait."

Both men stopped, his uncle looking impatient. It gave William pleasure to say, "I agree that Dominic will be of great use in France, but I have work for him this week. There is no need to send him off tonight."

"There is a need," Rochford said. William could almost hear what he wanted to add: *Because I said so.*

He stared his uncle down. "I require Dominic's service. He will be available to you six days from now. Make whatever plans you like, but Dom does not sail until then."

It wasn't often he made his uncle this angry. But there was, as always, calculation to it. And tonight his uncle's calculation decided that this was not a point worth fighting over. Icily Rochford bowed and said, "As you wish, Your Majesty."

"I'll speak with you in the morning," William said, dismissing him.

If Dominic resented being fought over like a woman, he didn't show it. But he did ask, once Rochford had left, "Am I truly required, or was that a convenient excuse to spread your wings?"

"I do require your service . . . or at least, Minuette does."

Dominic's expression sharpened. "For what?"

"She told you of the invitation to visit Alyce de Clare's sister?" When Dominic nodded, William said, "The woman lives only five miles from Minuette's estate, Wynfield Mote. Now that I have reclaimed it from the Howards, I thought it would be convenient for her to visit and see how things are in hand. I want you to go with her."

"You do not trust her?"

"Her intentions? Absolutely. Her good sense . . ."

At last Dominic relaxed. With a laugh, he said, "Are you really the one to criticize her good sense?"

"And that is why you are the perfect escort for her, as you are the perfect counselor for me."

"I'll do my best." He bowed and turned for the door.

"Dom?"

But when Dominic looked at him, William found that he didn't know what he wanted to say. He settled for, "I wish I didn't have to let you go to France. But if my uncle is going to use someone, I'd like it to be someone I trust."

"Don't do anything rash while I'm gone."

Disarmed by the familiar banter, William said, "You think I still need a nursemaid?"

"I think you're likely to get yourself into trouble without me around to stop you." Dominic paused. "Don't marry anyone else off without letting me know."

"I promise, if any of my sister's ladies are asked for, I'll check with you first."

And then Dominic was gone and William felt momentarily as empty as the chamber in which he stood. There was an element of truth to Dom's teasing—he had always been the one to steady William in both his anger and his enthusiasm. William wondered how long it would be until he saw Dominic again.

Thoughts of Eleanor broke through his melancholy, and desire returned with a rush as William pictured her, warm and eager. He set off for his bed, where nothing need be debated or measured or calculated.

CHAPTER SIX

26 September 1553
Wynfield Mote

I have been at Wynfield only one day, and already I feel myself home.
The house is unchanged and I find in every room and corner a
memory of earliest childhood, both bitter and sweet, for I have not felt
the presence of my parents so strongly since their deaths.

I was worried about my reception from my father's steward. I
thought Asherton old and forbidding when I was six, and I expected
him to resent my presence after all this time running the estate by
himself. But when I met with him last night, I found a man who
cannot be above fifty. And though he is taciturn, he is not unkind. In
all, a man whose good opinion I should like to earn. I am determined
to learn everything about running an estate this size, and I shall defer
to his judgment and knowledge wherever it exceeds mine. Which is
everywhere.

27 September 1553
Wynfield Mote

I have been busy from morning till night. I never could have imagined
I'd find such pleasure in simple domestic tasks. I begin each day in

consultation with Mrs. Holly, who has kept the interior of Wynfield spotless all these long years. She is almost giddy now that she has someone to actually serve. Even court banquets pale next to the ceremony with which Dominic and I are served our meals. I would prefer to dine in a smaller room, but Mrs. Holly insists we use the hall, where the long table is set, somewhat pathetically, for two.

In the afternoons I have ridden out with Asherton. I have now visited every tenant farm and cottage on the estate. It is only twelve in all, but I quite delight in the pretty households and the healthy faces of my people. My father was born at Wynfield, and I can judge the respect in which he was held by the reverent manner in which he is spoken of to me. Though my mother's tenure here was short, she was also loved. I have been told numerous times how much I resemble her. I wonder if they know there is nothing I would rather hear.

Mrs. Holly delights in telling me stories of my early years. And not all the stories are flattering. She claims that I once screamed three hours straight because my father rode off without me. Not for me the ladylike tears of a broken heart, she said, but full-throated shouts of pure rage.

I think her memory is not as good as she claims.

She said she has one or two of my mother's personal belongings that she will search out for me. Most of her things, naturally, are in Howard hands, as that is where she died. I shall be interested to see what she left behind when she remarried.

Tomorrow is our last day at Wynfield, before Dominic must return me to court and take himself to France. I shall spend the morning with Emma Hadley, prying out her sister's secrets. I can only hope they are useful.

Within five minutes of meeting Alyce de Clare's sister, Minuette was desperate to get away. Emma Hadley had the same rich brown hair as her younger sister, but her figure had grown stout with childbearing and her expression was all discontent and greedy curiosity about the court.

"Alyce was always so sparing in her stories," Emma said, eyeing Minuette with an unnerving hunger. Though they were seated across from each other in a shabby parlour, it felt far too close.

"One learns to be discreet, especially in the queen's household," Minuette said politely. She had come here to pry secrets from Emma, but how much would she have to give in return?

"Oh, yes," Emma sniffed. "Naturally. But still, I was her sister and all I could get from her was the most general of information. What the queen wore for Christmas mass or the weather when she went riding. Never anything about the king himself. Is he as handsome as we hear? What sort of women does he like?"

Repressing her revulsion, Minuette said, "The king is very handsome." Not for any amount of secrets could she bring herself to talk about William and women. Not when he was probably with Eleanor at this very hour.

"Alyce told me you were raised with Princess Elizabeth, that you were only in the queen's household to be trained for her service. What is the princess like?"

A woman who would reduce you to silence with a single blazing look, Minuette thought. "She is her father's daughter and noble in everything she does."

Before Emma could launch another inappropriate question at her, Minuette noted, "I know how much Alyce enjoyed her visits to you. If she did not speak much about court, surely she spoke about her own life away from you."

Emma harrumphed. "Oh, she enjoyed coming here, right enough. To lord it over me, show off her fine dresses, and look down her nose at us. No country gentleman for her, she said. She had her sights set on marrying well and staying at court."

Minuette could not dispute that picture—Alyce had always had a self-contained manner that just missed being superior. "Did she ever mention anyone in particular?"

"Got herself in trouble, did she?" Emma's eyes sharpened. "They didn't say, when they told us she'd died, but it only makes sense. No, she never said a word to me about any particular gentleman. But then, I hadn't seen her for more than a year."

Minuette stopped in midquestion when she realized what Emma had said. "Not for more than a year? Are you certain?"

"I'm certain. We saw her August last year, and then not again. Said the queen wouldn't release her. She said maybe Christmas this year. But of course—"

Emma stopped talking suddenly, and for the first time Minuette saw grief in her eyes as she realized she would never see her sister again.

But even as Minuette murmured the appropriate words of comfort, her mind was spinning. Alyce had claimed the queen would not release her in this last year—but twice in that twelve months Alyce had left court. November last, for two weeks. And for the whole of March this year. A month when she had told Minuette she was going to her sister's . . .

Wherever Alyce had been in March, simple arithmetic made it likely that she had been with the father of her child.

Excited by the news, Minuette stood abruptly. "Thank you for seeing me. I liked Alyce very much. I miss her." *And those are the truest words either of us has spoken yet,* she thought.

Emma talked all the way to the door, and this time her conversation was more than just inappropriate—it was incredibly rude. "I suppose you will marry well," she said enviously. "Not likely to see you around your farm in future. You'll be like your mother—off like a shot the day she was free to marry a duke's brother."

"I beg your pardon?"

It was a mistake, for Emma's instincts sharpened to the question. "Didn't you know? Everyone round here knows the story. Your mother only married Wyatt because she fell pregnant with you. It was the younger Howard she'd always had her eye on. But he was married at the time, so she did what she had to. By the time your father was dead, so was Howard's wife. From queen's household to country gentleman to the nobility . . . she planned it as sure as anything."

"My mother married because she wished to," Minuette managed to say.

"Easy to indulge your wishes when you have royalty as friends," Emma muttered. "You're as spoiled as she was."

Minuette arranged her features into an expression of contempt that would have done Queen Anne proud. "A word of advice, Mistress Hadley—it is not wise to speak so freely of those in power, or their friends. The royal temper can so easily be excited."

From the moment they'd arrived at Wynfield Mote, Dominic had seen Minuette bloom like an exotic flower returned to its native soil. The manor house sat in a hollow of land edged by the remnants of great woods, with a stone bridge that crossed the moat into a cobbled courtyard. Newer timbered wings added by Minuette's father nestled comfortably next to the fourteenth-century great hall; orchards and gardens ringed the outside of the moat; and everything from dovecote to stables to kitchens was neat and pleasant.

Despite William's warning, Minuette's good sense had been

very much in evidence as she negotiated her way with a wary steward and a smothering housekeeper. She had visited her tenants, addressed them by name, listened to endless memories of her parents. Dominic had been impressed—not by her kindness, which he knew well, but by her patience and astuteness. She was more herself here than he had ever known her, and it made him almost sorry to return her to court.

Not that he had been idly watching her all this time, for even in the country he had work to do. Dispatches from Rochford arrived daily—leaving Dominic to marvel at the cost in time and money expended on lecturing him—and he always had a stack of recommended reading.

On their last day at Wynfield, Dominic sent Minuette off with Asherton and then shut himself up in what had been her father's study to puzzle out the latest reports from Rochford's spies in the emperor's court. It would be useful to know what was being said in Spain about their new alliance with France.

But after several hours, it was almost a relief to turn from Continental politics to the more personal kind. Amongst the latest dispatches from Rochford was a letter from Queen Anne complaining that not enough money was being allocated to the college she had founded at Oxford with funds from the dispossessed monasteries. *Deal with this,* Rochford wrote him. Dominic knew he did not mean *Find the money* or *Give her a precise accounting of funds* but rather *Flatter her out of her temper.*

Dominic had known the queen all his life, and yet she still made him uncomfortable. This hadn't always been the case. He had once been in and out of her presence without a second thought except to mind his manners. But around the time he turned sixteen and gained his full height, growing into something more than just a boy with too-large feet and hands, the queen had begun to speak to him differently. She drew his name out, letting it linger in the air while she studied him. She would touch him briefly, lightly, on the arm. It was never any one thing that made him nervous, but an awareness that she reflected back at him—that he was young and attractive and she knew exactly how to play him.

But she was his best friend's mother, and he would not play that game with her. Instead he avoided her when possible and spoke (or, as in this case, wrote) as formally as though he were a priest and she were an importunate child. He very much doubted that anything he sent back to her by this letter would flatter her out of her temper—more likely it would only increase it.

He didn't realize how late it had grown until Mrs. Holly brought a tray to his room for dinner.

"Is Mistress Wyatt not back yet?" he asked, concerned.

"She is, sir. But she asked not to be disturbed."

Interesting. Did her withdrawal mean that she had learnt nothing from Alyce's sister? Or that whatever she had learnt was too upsetting to be immediately shared?

He tried to keep away. He finished his letters and then checked that his trunk was neatly packed for tomorrow's departure. But when he couldn't help it any longer, he went looking for her. Her room was empty, as were the solarium and the great hall. As he came out the front door, a voice said, "The young miss is in the rose garden."

Dominic jumped and swore at the sudden voice from behind, and rounded on the speaker. "Someday you will have to teach me how you move so silently for such a big man."

Harrington—three inches taller than Dominic and three stone heavier—didn't even blink. "The rose garden," he repeated, then padded away toward the stables.

For a man supposed to be my servant, Dominic thought, *Harrington behaves as though he is in charge.* Rochford had put the man at Dominic's disposal when he left court, with orders to take him to France. "He's useful," Rochford had said, "in more ways than one."

Rochford hadn't elaborated, and Harrington hadn't said more than ten words at a time to Dominic all week. Was his usefulness confined to moving like a shadow and knowing without asking whom Dominic was looking for?

Minuette was indeed in the rose garden, already bare of blooms, leaves shriveling in the early autumn frost. It was pleasantly symmetrical, with four quarter circles bounded by a low brick wall, and Minuette sat on the single wooden bench in the center of the garden. She had an embroidered shawl around her shoulders and her hands twisted at something in her lap.

Jewels? he wondered. They dimly reflected light back. "What do you have?" he asked.

She blinked as though coming back from a faraway thought, and used one hand to hold up a strand that was not jewels, but . . .

"Minuette," he said sharply. "Is that a rosary?"

He did not need an answer. The jet beads with a heavy silver cross at the end were quite clearly that banned item of Catholic devotion.

"My mother's," she said conversationally. "The housekeeper gave me a casket my mother left behind when she married Howard. Though I don't know why she didn't take it with her—the Howards being Catholic. Supposedly it was a gift to her many years ago in France." Minuette looked at him. "A gift from the queen, back when she was just Anne Boleyn in the French court. Ironic." She let the rosary beads fall into a pool in her lap. In spite of her conversation, she didn't seem to have come all the way back from wherever her thoughts had taken her.

"What did you learn from Alyce's sister today?" he asked.

"Besides the fact that she is a nosy, bitter woman who thinks everyone she meets owes her something?"

The bitterness did not sound like Minuette at all, but before he could probe she added, "She did have some useful information, at least. About Alyce's absences from court. I will discuss it with Elizabeth and William when we return and it should lead us somewhere."

So it wasn't Alyce that was bothering her. "What are you thinking about, Minuette?"

It wasn't just politeness. He really wanted to know, with an ache that he told himself he imagined.

In an instant she had a court smile on her lips. "Oh, about fabric and ribbons and young men asking me to dance."

William would have teased along with her, maybe even Elizabeth, but not Dominic. Not tonight, when tomorrow he would have to say goodbye to her for however long Rochford wanted him in France. "Tell me the truth."

The smile slipped away like a shy child ducking behind a door. "I was thinking about friendship and love and marriage. And if those three can ever come together."

The imagined ache grew. "And what prompted such philosophical thoughts?"

"Oh, the wedding last week." Her voice strengthened. "Honestly, Dominic, I cannot understand Eleanor Percy. Not even a crown would have induced me to marry Giles Howard."

"You are not Eleanor."

"It's not just her," she said, so softly it was as though she didn't want her words to make it into the world at all. "Giles Howard is not so much like his father—but he is very like his uncle."

"Your stepfather."

"I've always believed that my mother had no choice but to marry when Stephen Howard wanted her. But what if . . . I was only six when my father died and eight when my mother died. How do I know who she really was?"

Dominic let the question hang, though she hardly seemed to expect an answer. It was that vagueness that disturbed him, for Minuette was usually as clear as a swift stream. Feeling his way toward whatever her true worry might be, he finally said, "Whatever choices your mother made, they don't alter you. I know who you really are, and you have nothing to fear."

"How do you know? I am part of the court. I am trained to reflect back whatever a man expects to see. And I'm good at it, Dominic. Don't pretend you haven't noticed. You pulled me away from Jonathan Percy quick enough last week because you thought I was flirting. So I was. And if you did not like my be-haviour . . ."

She turned to him with eyes that in the fast-falling darkness were troubled. "You are my conscience, and you are going away again. William never reproves me, and Elizabeth just sighs and lets me go along. What shall I do without your always-right voice to tell me when I'm losing myself?"

Somewhere in her tumble of words, which left Dominic wanting to jump to his feet to expend his nervous energy, there were questions he had to answer. But not strictly honestly. If he were to be honest, he would tell her, *No, I did not like your flirting. But not because you were improper or making a spectacle of yourself. I did not like it because . . .*

Even silently, he dared not finish that thought. And still Minuette appealed to him, with wide eyes and furrowed brow, for help.

"I think," Dominic said carefully, "that if you are asking these questions, then you are quite safe. You only stop questioning when you know you don't want to hear the answers."

Finally Minuette laughed; though small, the laugh was real. "I shall simply have to imagine that you are my shadow, watching over my shoulder everything I do and say. Though I would rather it was you yourself."

So do I. The words stuck in his throat, and he had to stand up then, because if he didn't, he would touch her, and he didn't dare touch her when he didn't have himself in perfect control.

If he'd needed proof that Minuette did not feel the same way about him, it was there when she easily threw her arms around him in a hug. "I shall miss you dearly. Promise you'll write."

"I promise."

CHAPTER SEVEN

My visit to Wynfield was brief but fruitful—personally, in addition to the visit with Alyce's sister. No longer will I have to make shift with what maids I can find wherever I am in residence. Elizabeth has been urging me to take on an attendant, not seeming to understand how limited my purse is. Being a companion to royalty is expensive and I have always had to scrimp merely to pay for my clothing, let alone a woman to care for it.

Thanks to my visit home I have a maid of my own now, one who seems quite content with the little I can pay her. Truthfully, I had to insist she accept payment at all, for she appeared willing to serve me for nothing more than her food and a place to sleep.

Her name is Carrie Prescott. She was born at Wynfield and, upon my parents' marriage, my mother took her into the household and trained her as a lady's maid. She followed my mother to the Howards' when she remarried. After my mother's death, Carrie returned to Wynfield, married one of my father's tenants—one of my tenants, I suppose—and had two children by him. But they are all dead now— her husband and daughter in the plague two years ago and her little boy to the sweating sickness last autumn.

I did not recognize her at once. She is older, of course, nearing thirty, but she is still as neat and pretty as a wren. The change is in her eyes and in the gravity of her countenance. I remember Carrie as cheerful and with a merry laugh that could always tease me out of any childish mood. She does not look cheerful any longer.

Still, she seems genuinely pleased to come to me, and I find pleasure in helping a woman who served my mother with such loyalty. Surely whatever she can tell me of my mother will be much nearer the truth than anything claimed by Alyce's spiteful sister.

7 October 1553
Greenwich

I have told Elizabeth and William about Alyce's unaccounted-for leaves from court in the last year. After checking that my memory was correct—and that she had indeed left court and lied about her destination—William had his secretary compile a list of gentlemen of the court who were also absent at the same times. There are fifty-four names on the list. And as William does not wish to alert a possibly guilty party to inquiries, he's leaving it in my hands. Whom should I begin with? The Duke of Northumberland, with his devoted wife who has given him thirteen children? Might as well begin with him because not only is he incredibly unlikely but he's Robert's father. All I need do is ask Robert if he remembers his father accompanying him home in March—and that will strike two names from the list.

Giles Howard is also on there. I'm trying not to let my own opinion prejudice my investigations.

29 October 1553
Greenwich

Queen Anne left court this week to return to Hever. Her eyesight is growing worse, though she covers it well. Her Majesty takes care to walk only in bright sunlight or in rooms she knows well. She is beginning to avoid crowds, and I suspect it's because she cannot always see to whom she is speaking. At Hever Castle she will be surrounded by those who have known her since she was a child, and she will be able to rest more easily.

And Elizabeth and I leave for Hatfield tomorrow. As Hever was her mother's childhood home, Hatfield is Elizabeth's. It was given to her at birth, and her earliest—and happiest—memories are there. Though William is normally anxious to retain our company through the winter, he seems not to mind our leaving this year. Indeed, I wonder how long it will take him to realize that we are gone.

15 November 1553
Hatfield

I received a letter from Dominic today, the first he's sent me from France. It was brief and general. Honestly, if I wanted a weather report, I'd go to France myself.

3 December 1553
Richmond Palace

Our respite at Hatfield was brief. We arrived at Richmond yesterday to keep Christmas with the court. I suppose I should be flattered that William sent for us.

We dined with him last night. Elizabeth and I, Lord and Lady Rochford—and Eleanor Howard. Giles is in Cumberland, overseeing the manor that William gifted him upon his marriage.

It was an uncomfortable dinner. As intimidating as the Lord Protector can be, I've always thought Lady Rochford far the more frightening of the two. I don't think she likes me—but then, I'm not sure she likes anyone. Certainly not her husband. They've never had *children, and one can only imagine Lord Rochford would rather not bed a woman with the eyes and tongue of a snake—which is saying something, since everyone knows he'll bed almost anyone else.*

Oh, dear, I'm becoming rather shrewish. I'm sure I don't know why.

4 December 1553
Richmond Palace

I do know why—I just don't want to admit it.

I am jealous of Eleanor.

I spent the afternoon watching William play tennis with Robert Dudley. I was seated next to Eleanor, and she kept saying things to me, things about William. About the horses he favours and the people he detests and his worries about the negotiations dragging on in the Netherlands. It wasn't what Eleanor said so much as the way she said it—as if she were confiding great secrets about a man only she understands. I wanted very much to say, "I've known William far longer than you have." But I held my tongue.

Perhaps pettiness would have been better. As if determined to break my silence, Eleanor began to insinuate things—intimate things—that I'd rather not know. And I cannot escape the fact that she does know William better than I do, or at least more fully. When one is unclothed with a man, one is certain to learn things others do not.

7 December 1553
Richmond Palace

I have been asked for as a bride.

When I heard that Thomas Seymour wished to marry me, my first impulse was to wonder what a widower thirty years my senior could want with me. I have but a very small fortune and no family ties to speak of. But the truth is, I know perfectly well what Lord Thomas wanted. He is very fond of young women—his indiscretions have been a source of gossip for some time. Unlike many gentlemen, he is not afraid to flaunt his affairs. I suppose I should be grateful that he was willing to marry me rather than persuade me into something less respectable. But all I can feel is a shiver of disgust when I think of him wanting to touch me.

William remembered his promise and spoke to me in private before giving Lord Thomas an answer. Thankfully, William accepted my quick refusal, but he did ask if I had any definite ideas of my own about marriage. What could I say? Although he is my dearest friend, William is a man, and so I could not say, "I should like to feel my heart beat faster at the sight of my husband. I should like to marry a man whose touch I crave in the night, and whose company I crave in the daytime. I should like a friend and a lover in one."

At any rate, I don't want Lord Thomas and William has told him so.

12 December 1553
Richmond Palace

Eleanor is with child. The only pleasure I take in the news is that custom—and discretion—will force her to retire from court after Christmas.

I have heard from Dominic only three times since he went to France. Perhaps he has a pregnant mistress as well.

Four days before Christmas, Dominic woke at dawn with the closest thing to anticipation that he'd felt since arriving in France. Today he was leaving court with Vicomte Renaud LeClerc, a relative of King Henri's and the only genuine friend Dominic had made here. Renaud had invited Dominic to spend Christmas with his family—a wife and two small sons—at his home in the Loire Valley. After weeks of endless talk, Dominic would have accepted any invitation that removed him from political circles for however short a time, but this invitation was truly welcome.

He slid carefully out of bed, but not carefully enough. As his weight shifted, the woman beside him stirred and woke. "Dominic?" she purred in a way that made him very conscious she was naked. "Where are you going?"

"I ride out in an hour," he reminded her. "With LeClerc."

"An hour," Aimée said, with the kind of smile that said everything about her intentions. "It does not take you an hour to dress."

He considered for the space of one breath. "No, it doesn't."

Aimée's very best quality was her boldness, a quality Dominic appreciated every time he wrapped himself around her and let his mind take flight. Indeed, she was in his bed now because one night, after several weeks of hints and innuendos, she had finally waylaid him—there was really no other term for it—in a darkened corridor. He had been homesick and lonely and had taken some liberties and in the heat of her eager response he had brought her to his room.

That had been eight weeks ago. And though Aimée's allure had not waned, Dominic had been growing steadily more restless. Even now, as his hands found her curves and his mouth tasted hers and his body roused to her own confident caresses, his eyes played tricks in imperfect flashes. For one moment he thought Aimée's dark hair shone gold, then her blue eyes warmed to hazel . . . Dominic forced away those disconcerting imprints and let himself be swept into forgetfulness.

After a satisfying three quarters of an hour, she propped herself on one elbow and watched him dress. "I do not see why you wish to spend Christmas elsewhere," she sniffed. "Would you not rather stay here with me?"

"You will never miss me," he said, truthfully. Aimée was not known for her fidelity.

"But you will miss me—every night that you are alone."

Perhaps. All right, yes, part of him would miss her very much. But Dominic was beginning to think that he'd given free rein to that part of himself for long enough. The previous women in his life had been warm and kind and self-effacing and it had all felt very natural, not as though every encounter was a skirmish to be won or lost.

If this were a skirmish, Dominic knew he was losing. Which meant he was glad to be joining Renaud this morning and riding away from the Louvre. He rather thought he needed a break.

When he was dressed, Dominic grabbed his woolen cloak for riding and leaned over Aimée. "A joyous Christmas," he said, and kissed her.

She teased at his mouth, almost making him wish he wasn't leaving, then shrugged away, letting her hair fall around her bare shoulders. "*Au revoir,* Dominic. Think of me while you are gone."

Something in her seductive, possessive tone called to his mind an image—of Eleanor Howard dancing triumphantly in William's arms while her husband watched from the sidelines. What was it Dominic had said to his friend that day? *Have you given any thought to the lady, beyond what you desire?*

Dominic was many miles away from Paris before he could shake that uncomfortable image, but gradually his heart lightened with each mile he put between himself and the French court. Leaving aside the issue of Aimée, being a diplomat, even an unrecognized one, was more difficult than any battle Dominic had fought. He did well enough, he supposed—Rochford had not complained—but his heart wasn't in it. In the midst of drawn-out debates on theology or the significance of Salic law in Anglo-French relations, Dominic often found himself wanting to smash his head against the nearest wall. No wonder treaties took so long to negotiate—no one could stop talking long enough to come to a decision.

Renaud, at least, was a man he understood instinctively—a soldier who was more comfortable campaigning than negotiating. But he was also French, which made him naturally more devious, and he had taught Dominic a few things about the uses of flattery in building relationships. And between coding letters to Rochford and learning which French ministers would be most open to peace with England, Dominic had a little time for things he did enjoy, such as jousting or swordplay with Renaud and his men.

As they approached a village snuggled in a wide loop of the Loire River, Renaud pointed out his boundaries. "My land, Dominic," he said, pronouncing his name with the lengthened vowels of the French. "From river to hills. This prospect I take with me wherever I go."

A moment later a rider came into view, dressed in the scarlet and gray of Renaud's livery. He stayed his horse only long enough to salute them, then turned and rode rapidly ahead.

"Nicole likes to have warning," Renaud said. "It is superstition with her that she always be in the courtyard when I return."

The vicomtesse was indeed waiting in the courtyard as they rode in, wrapped in a fur-lined cloak, her eyes going straight to her husband. From the way Renaud had talked about his wife, Dominic had expected . . . something different.

She was short and a little plump, with mouse-brown hair and ordinary features. Dominic wondered what could possibly keep her husband as entranced as he'd always sounded. But just then she smiled at Renaud as he swung down from his horse, and Dominic caught his breath. Her smile completely transformed her face, and the charge between husband and wife made the courtyard pale by comparison, as though all the light and energy of the winter sun had concentrated on these two people, embracing fiercely in the open air.

By the time dinner was over that evening, Dominic had no remaining doubts about Renaud's attraction to his wife. A wordless glance, a brief clasping of hands at table—it all served to reinforce the picture of a marriage Dominic had not known could exist. After a brief introduction to the LeClerc sons, a shy four-year-old and a rambunctious two-year-old, Nicole bade the men goodnight and swept off with her boys.

Renaud settled back with a cup of wine, basking in the contentment of home and family. Dominic could not keep from asking, though he endeavoured to be subtle, "Your wife's family, they are well situated?"

Renaud laughed. "You mean did I overthrow all caution in marrying for love? Nicole is of the proper background, and my family was pleased with the match. Not that it mattered to me. From the first time I laid eyes on her, I thought only of Nicole herself."

"And if she had been ..." How to finish that sentence without rudeness?

With a lift of his eyebrows, Renaud finished it for him. "A peasant? A serving maid? Would I still have taken her, if everyone around me had disapproved?" Renaud twisted his face in a wry expression. "Who can tell? She is who she is. I cannot imagine her different. All I can say is that Nicole, as she is, is the only one for me."

Dominic stared into the fire, at the blue flames leaping into crackles of orange. There were images in those flames: the sheen of honey-coloured hair, the scent of a dying rose garden, and the appeal of hazel eyes.

"And what of you, Dominic? You are restrained with the women at our court."

Remembering Aimée's adventuresome nature in bed, Dominic thought "restrained" was not the word he would use. He parried the question. "Not as restrained as you are."

"I am married."

"So are most of the men at court. It doesn't seem to bother them."

"Ah, but I am deeply in love with my wife. Which causes me to wonder who you might be in love with. Is there a betrothed waiting for you in England?"

"No." Dominic blinked hard, and the fire became once again just a fire.

Something in the tone of his voice must have warned off Renaud, for he declined to pursue the subject. "Shall we speak of your king, then? What manner of man is this William? One to bring King Henri to terms?"

Snatching the opportunity, Dominic said, "Surely that depends partly on Henri as well."

"True enough." Renaud studied him. "Is William his father's son?"

"In some things." As Dominic looked at Renaud's curious face, a suspicion came to him that perhaps this invitation had not been entirely for friendship's sake. Renaud served his own king, after all.

Choosing his words with greater care, Dominic continued. "William is quick and has a perfect memory. What he hears once, he remembers. He has learnt well from his uncle how to see the larger picture, how history is woven together out of seemingly random people and events. He is not as subtle as the Lord Protector, but he knows how to use the strengths of his advisors."

"Lord Rochford, yes." Renaud drew the name out in a way that made Dominic smile. The French had always been ambivalent about George Boleyn. "He will continue to be powerful after the regency is ended."

"Yes. But William is his own man. He is young and impatient, but he has not been idle. He is prepared to rule—and he means to rule well."

"And his temper? His father had a most notorious temper."

Dominic held Renaud's gaze steadily, letting him know that he recognized the drift of these questions. "He does not act in anger, nor does he let passion overrule his practicality. His temper will never get the best of his ambitions."

"A paragon, then?" Renaud lifted his cup in an amused salute. "Perhaps you confuse your king with your friend."

"Cannot he be both?"

Renaud's lips tightened, and with a shake of his head he set his cup down. "Let us speak frankly, as becomes men-at-arms. You know why I ask about your king, and I hear how cautiously you answer. It is the game of diplomats, and we will play it as we are ordered. But it is not our natural environment."

He laced his fingers together, his voice gathering conviction as he spoke. "Kings are not men like us, Dominic. Their world is one of distrust and intrigue. They talk and twist and look always for their own advantage. So do we seek advantage, but only on the field of battle. And that is never personal. If you and I were to meet in the field, we should fight with every weapon at our disposal and we should not stop until one or the other of us had won the day. And when it was done, we could meet afterward without malice. Our fight would be honourable, and so would be defeat or victory."

"And kings do not have honour?" Dominic felt defensive on William's behalf, though he recognized himself in Renaud's assessment.

Renaud shrugged. "Of their own kind, yes. But make no mistake, it is not of a kind we understand. Kings are devoted to their own interests—always. It is a little like the religious heretics. They do everything driven by the belief that they are right and they alone know God. Kings are just as fanatic. They are true believers—in themselves. And true believers are always dangerous."

"What is your point?"

"It is good to serve your king," Renaud replied, reaching for his cup once more. "Just don't imagine he will ever return the favour. Friendship with kings is always one-sided."

"No more," Elizabeth protested as Robert tried to pull her into another galliard. She moved nimbly out of his reach and sat next to Minuette on a trestle bench across the table from William.

It was the day after Christmas, and there were three dozen men and women gathered for a private celebration with their king. Not one of them was older than twenty-five. Elizabeth had heard Lord Northumberland grumbling in the courtyard earlier about the bad influence of the "young and flighty."

Elizabeth scanned the ambitious and flattered guests. Eleanor was here, of course. Pending motherhood had not lessened her obvious appeal—if anything, it had enhanced her generous curves in a fashion the men seemed to find pleasing. Even Robert's eyes rested briefly on her cleavage as she crossed the room and seated herself cozily next to William.

Minuette was absorbed in conversation with Eleanor's twin, Jonathan Percy. Of all the guests he looked the most ill at ease, too serious and shy to relax in such close proximity to his king.

Elizabeth's eyes drifted back to where Robert stood, Gypsy-dark and smiling as he spoke to Jane Grey. After this week's festivities, Robert would be leaving court for at least a month. It should not trouble her—he had a home, after all. But she was all too aware that Robert going home meant Robert seeing his wife.

She realized with a start that Eleanor was addressing her. "I beg your pardon?"

"Forgive me, Your Highness. I did not mean to divert your thoughts from something more ... intriguing." Eleanor's eyes flicked ever so quickly to Robert and back again. "I only meant to ask about the pageant you and your ladies have prepared for Twelfth Night. Is it quite ready?"

Elizabeth knew very well that Eleanor was inquiring out of spite. She had been hinting for an invitation to participate. "All is quite ready. Thank you for asking."

Which would have been the end of it, but for Minuette jumping into the exchange. "Do you not miss your husband? I would think families should be together at this season."

Eleanor's smile sharpened as she struggled to compose an appropriate reply. Apparently an appropriate reply included laying claim to William, for Eleanor leaned against his shoulder until he stopped speaking to one of Robert's brothers and looked at her.

Smiling into his eyes in a manner that made Elizabeth want to roll her own, Eleanor said, "One does not argue with His Majesty's wishes."

"Really? I argue with his wishes all the time." Minuette positively dazzled as she added, "And I always win."

Turning laughter into a polite cough, Elizabeth wondered what her brother would do. She expected he would pull Eleanor into a dance to stop the exchange—there was nothing William liked less than women sniping—but after a long and thoughtful look at Eleanor, he said, "I believe Mistress Wyatt has the right of it. To argue with royalty and win—it's a rare gift. I wouldn't try to cultivate it if I were you."

The table fell silent, every eye fixed on Eleanor to see how she would handle the rebuke. Her lips trembled, but Elizabeth thought that was from rage rather than hurt. Eleanor managed an airy tone in answer: "I could never wish to argue with you, Your Majesty."

William heightened the tension by standing up abruptly and extending a hand to Minuette across the table. "Care to dance?" With a glance at Jonathan Percy next to her, he added casually, "You don't mind, do you, Percy?"

"Not . . . no, not at all."

With a snap of his fingers, William commanded the musicians, "Play a volta."

With visible effort, Eleanor addressed Elizabeth. "If there was some way I could be of service to you, Your Highness . . . Your brother listens to you in all things. I'm sure you could persuade him . . ."

Elizabeth watched William and Minuette, dancing the seductive volta in perfect harmony. The only thing that saved it from impropriety was their laughter. "I know only one person who can persuade my brother to all of what she wants. If you need an advocate, you've chosen the wrong woman."

In the two months since Christmas, Dominic had grown increasingly irritable as each day came and went without any apparent progress toward peace. On the last day of February he sent off a curtly worded message to Rochford before joining some of Renaud's men for the evening meal. Renaud himself was in attendance on his king this night, and in his absence the men were unusually boisterous. Dominic drank more than was wise and fell into bed some hours after midnight.

Harrington woke him early the next morning. The light from the uncurtained window pounded through Dominic's skull in a rhythm of discomfort as he took the note Harrington held out for him.

It was from Diane de Poitiers, King Henri's mistress, requesting Dominic's presence in her rooms as soon as convenient.

Dominic presented himself in under an hour, his head and stomach still somewhat fragile. Madame de Poitiers accepted Dominic's salute graciously. "Please, seat yourself."

He took the empty chair before her and endeavoured to look as if meeting privately with the most notorious woman in Europe were an everyday occurrence. She wore her customary black and white and studied him with undisguised interest.

"Lord Courtenay, it is a pleasure to meet with you *seule*. Such a presentable young man, and such a good friend to his king."

Dominic's ears pricked. He hadn't expected that this visit was a social courtesy, but such a quick mention of William confirmed that. "Madame, it is I who am fortunate in the connection. My king already bids to shine as brightly as his father."

"Indeed? He is so young, as yet—but then youth is not always a hindrance."

The gleam in her eyes reminded Dominic that this woman had become Henri's mistress when she was a widow in her thirties and Henri was newly wed—and sixteen. In spite of the king's marriage to Marie de Medici, Diane de Poitiers was the true power behind the French throne.

Forcing his mind back to the thread of the conversation,

Dominic said, "His youth and energy are devoted entirely to England's welfare."

"And you, Lord Courtenay? What has kept you from this perfect king for so long? Surely you must miss your home."

"I serve at the pleasure of my king."

Dominic waited for more—for the message that surely must be the reason for this visit—but she studied him in a long silence before abruptly changing the subject.

"I hear you are not enamoured of our women. That you keep to yourself and ignore the great beauties before you."

Dominic had to stifle a laugh as he imagined Queen Anne or Elizabeth posing such an impertinent question. Inclining his head, he said smoothly, "I am entirely aware of the great beauty before me."

She smiled complacently and, in a voice like warm honey, said, "And yet you turn away from pleasure. I hear my women talk—there have been opportunities. Opportunities declined." Nodding to the corner where her attendants sat embroidering, she said, "Aimée, there, I fear you have quite broken her heart."

Dominic wondered whether it would be less humiliating to keep looking at Madame de Poitiers's mocking smile or to acknowledge Aimée. He hadn't spoken with her since January, when he'd returned from Renaud's home and had ended their liaison. Aimée had refused to take him seriously and for several weeks had continued to appear in his room until finally he had resorted to telling her something that was almost the truth.

"There's a woman in England," Dominic had said. "And this is not fair to her." Never mind that the woman in question hadn't the slightest idea of how much he thought about her. Though he might now be lonely and frustrated, at least he despised himself a little less for taking no thought with Aimée beyond his own desires.

Aimée, unfortunately, did not seem to appreciate his thoughtfulness.

Dominic attempted to extricate himself gracefully. "Madame, such a beautiful woman has no need to worry about a poor Englishman when she could easily capture any number of more appealing gentlemen."

Diane cocked her head to the side, considering. "I do not believe, as some have hinted, that it is because your inclinations lie elsewhere. No, your instincts are those of most young men. So it must be that your heart is already engaged. You are unmarried, I know—a lover, perhaps, back in England? She must be extraordinary to command such faithfulness."

Dominic wanted nothing more than to sink through the floor. Was this the reason he'd been summoned—not as a private messenger to William but as an exhibit of English coldness? He would not, no matter how obliquely, discuss Minuette with Diane de Poitiers. Summoning up every ounce of control, he said calmly, "I simply endeavour to remember that I am here in the service of my king, not my own desires."

"Ah, yes. Your king. He will soon be eighteen. King Henri is prepared to offer him quite the gift for that occasion. He would wish to speak of it to some of your lords—it is something requiring time and much conversation."

Grateful that she had at last gotten to the point, Dominic rose and bowed. "I'm certain that can be arranged."

"It is to be a surprise, *vous comprenez*? We should not like word to leak out to those who would spoil it."

Meaning Spain or the Netherlands. "Naturally."

He kissed the perfumed hand she held out. When he would have released it, she tightened her fingers and, with a hint of enticement in her voice, said, "Give the young lady my regards."

"Which young lady, madame?" He hadn't forgotten one, had

he? He was sure Aimée was the only woman at court he'd . . . dallied with.

"The one who is not your lover." Her expression was that of a conspirator. "We shall have to return you to England soon, so you may remedy that."

The sooner the better, Dominic thought. It was already the first of March; if things progressed smoothly, he could be home in time to wish Minuette a happy eighteenth birthday.

In time to give her Diane de Poitiers's regards.

A week later, William sat in his private study with Lord Rochford, reading a copy of Dominic's ciphered letter. "You think this is a serious step toward reconciliation?" William asked.

"I do."

"I agree. Private messages, shrouded in secrecy—it reeks of the French. Henri does not want us campaigning this year. Northumberland will be disappointed not to be going to war." William tossed the paper on the desk and leaned back in his chair, thinking. "Whom do you propose sending to treat with them?"

"I thought Edward Seymour and the Earl of Surrey."

"Seymour's good, but Norfolk's grandson? I don't know."

"He is liked by the Catholics."

"And as like to support Mary as he is me."

Rochford said, "So give him a reason to support you. They are not just subjects, they are kinsmen. Tie his positions, his honours, and his wealth to your rule. Loyalty is surest when self-interest is involved."

"As my father did." William knew his uncle was not wrong. The Tudor kings were known for breaking the old hereditary nobility, with its dangerous blood claims to royalty, and elevating those of lesser birth but outstanding service. Like Rochford himself, whose father had been ennobled only when Henry grew enamoured of Anne. Or the Duke of Northumberland, who had received the title after the centuries-long Percy hold on it had been broken.

Rochford waited for an answer, which William appreciated. Perhaps his uncle was also counting the days until his majority, when the office of Lord Protector would cease to exist and he would continue to serve only at William's pleasure.

"All right," he agreed. "Send Surrey. But I want to speak with him first. Let him know personally that the trust we repose in him will guide our future generosity. Anything else?"

There shouldn't be; this wasn't a council meeting, and Rochford would want to get to work preparing Seymour and Surrey for France. In his mind, William was halfway to the grounds to watch the training of his newest hunting dogs.

He should have known better.

"What is Mistress Wyatt up to, William?"

His uncle only called him William when he was displeased. Instantly uneasy, and angry that Rochford could still make him so, he said sharply, "I don't know what you mean, nor do I see how Minuette is any concern of yours."

"Minuette." Rochford drew out her name and eyed William with an unreadable expression. "Personally, she does not concern me at all. But when she interferes with the court—"

"Interferes?"

"—by writing to men far above her rank and fortune, seeking information that is none of her business . . ."

William drew in a sharp breath. They should have anticipated this—how could they ever have thought that they could completely evade Rochford's watchful eye? Now William was going to have to tell him the truth.

At least part of it.

He chose his words carefully. "Do you remember Alyce de Clare, who died the night of my last birthday?"

"From Anne's household. Yes."

"She and Minuette were friends. You know the girl was with child. Minuette is bothered that she does not know who fathered that child. I have given her leave to search out the man. Discreetly."

Rochford grunted. "Do you think that wise? The girl is dead, the damage done. Why raise more enmity?"

"Enmity?" William said mildly. "She is not seeking to build a court case, merely to satisfy her own unhappy conscience and let the man know of my personal disapproval." He apologized silently to Minuette, who no doubt would have raged at this casual dismissal of Alyce's death.

But he was not prepared to talk to Rochford about the other aspects, the overtones of treason. That was his fight.

If it even existed any longer. They had gone months without any further outbreaks of old scandal or new threats.

He met Rochford stare for stare, and at last his uncle relented. "I would advise her—and you—to be wary. These are not men to make enemies of. Be sure the information gained is worth it."

"Thank you for your counsel," William said, and surprised himself by meaning it. Perhaps because it had truly been offered as counsel, instead of as a command cloaked in politeness. If this was what being king meant, then he looked forward even more to June.

Elizabeth arrived after the tennis match had begun, and she was glad of the rustles and whispers of disturbance as she moved to the front of the crowd. Those rustles caught Robert's attention, and he paused before serving to bow to her. William, waiting on the other side of the net, threw a brief glance at Elizabeth before turning back to his partner.

"I'm waiting," he called, in a tone that brooked no argument. It seemed to Elizabeth that lately William had become more watchful where she and Robert Dudley were concerned.

He was not the only one. Northumberland had spent a lot of time this winter being wherever she was. Today, for example. Not five minutes after she arrived, Northumberland slipped into a suddenly open space next to her. Like her, his eyes were fixed on the game—but his attention was not.

"May we speak, Your Highness?" he asked in a low voice.

"Speak of what, my lord?" Neither of them looked away from the tennis match. Robert and William were both good, keeping up long volleys between serves.

"There are whispers, Your Highness, of disturbances planned to disrupt the king's coming majority celebrations."

"Surely that is a matter for the council."

"Not those kinds of disturbances. These are more . . . subtle. Rumours, old gossip, stories that you would not like retold."

Like the broadsheet of her mother's reputed witchraft or the taint of bastardy being flung at Will . . . no, those were stories she did not want retold. But neither would Northumberland. He had staked everything on Anne's children and the English Church. He could never profit from Mary.

Which made her blunt. "What do you want?"

"Lord Rochford keeps things too close. He makes decisions alone that rightly belong to the council. This embassy to France after their treachery to us last fall—it should have been discussed openly. Rochford is Lord Protector for only a short while longer. He should be reminded that I am not his enemy. We seek the same end—a stable, Protestant England. Keeping us divided is what the Catholics want. He must trust me."

Elizabeth finally turned to him a little, enough so that she could see the pointed beard that might have concealed his expression if he'd ever cared to try. At the moment he looked crafty. "Are you seeking a matchmaker, my lord? For all your similar aims, I do not think you and my uncle well-suited for long-term happiness."

"It would be in your interests to look to my happiness." Northumberland lowered his voice. "Without the regency, your brother will make decisions based on all the counsel he receives. Do you wish that counsel to come solely from your uncle? Or might there perhaps be a matter dear to you on which my counsel would be useful?"

Northumberland gave a long look at his son, conceding graciously to William on the tennis court, then turned his shrewd eyes on Elizabeth. "Perhaps a matter to which you and I see the same end? A happy marriage, Your Highness, is not a gift to be slighted."

He bowed and backed away through the crowd, leaving Elizabeth flushed and edgy. And also, she admitted to herself, intrigued.

CHAPTER EIGHT

A s APRIL BLEW in with gusty rain, Minuette set down her
pen and stretched. She'd been working for hours and her
head spun with deciphering the spidery handwriting of European diplomats. Why could men not learn to write legibly?

But diplomacy was not her only work today. She had three
letters addressed to her personally that she had left till last. The
first letter was less than a page, and she could almost have re-
cited it word for word without even reading it. It was from
Philippa Courtenay, Dominic's mother and, as always, it contained a mix of spiritual and everyday counsel: *begin each day on
your knees . . . remember the suffering of our Lord's mother and our
own lot as women . . . never wear wet slippers . . . subdue the body to
the spirit*. Philippa was not an original correspondent, but she
was at least consistent.

In her own orphaned state, Minuette had not paid much attention to Dominic's family. She knew his mother was born a Boleyn,
first cousin to Queen Anne, and that she had remained secluded
in a country manor after her husband's death. When Minuette
was fourteen, just before joining Queen Anne's household, she
had come around a hedge corner in the Richmond gardens one
day and stopped at the sight of Dominic crumpling a letter in his

hand as though he could unwrite what was written. His shoulders were taut and he wasn't quick enough to hide the pain in his eyes.

And she, always curious, had managed to worm out of him the news that his mother had tried to set fire to her bedroom three nights before. Although he'd spoken grudgingly, Minuette had thought there was a relief for him in sharing with someone who did not recoil.

Still, as becomes a dutiful son, Dominic had not said much else, only that his mother had always been delicate and a little unbalanced.

It was Queen Anne who had told her much more, as Minuette became a trusted attendant and daughter substitute in the months that followed. She had told Minuette stories of the cousin she had grown up with, of their correspondence when Anne went to France, of Philippa's devout nature and desire to take the veil. Of her parents' promise to let her become a nun when she turned sixteen.

But when Philippa was fifteen, all had been undone the first time William Courtenay laid eyes on her. He was thirty, Queen Anne had told Minuette, and completely wrong for her. A girl who has dreamt her entire life of the solitude and contemplation of the convent is unlikely to make a good wife to a worldly and virile soldier.

In eight years of marriage, Philippa gave birth to six children; only Dominic, the firstborn, survived. When she was widowed at the age of twenty-three, Philippa might gladly have gone to a convent as a lay sister—except that convents no longer existed in England. Because of her cousin Anne.

Minuette shook her head and laid Philippa's letter aside. She would write to her tomorrow. She debated which of the remaining two letters to read first, and with a sigh decided to deal with the more difficult.

It was not her first letter from Stephen Howard, the Duke of Norfolk's younger brother and her stepfather. He had written sporadically over the years, usually when he was drunk, she thought, and missing her mother. But this wasn't that sort of letter. This letter had come in answer to one she had sent two weeks ago, prompted by Giles Howard's name on the list of possible gentleman suspects in Alyce's pregnancy.

Not that she had asked outright if Giles had truly been at Kenninghall, as he'd claimed, during March of last year. That would come later, after an exchange of pleasantries and casual correspondence. With that thought, she had asked after Stephen's own health and family (he had three children from a previous marriage, who were all married themselves and scattered through the kingdom and court) and told him inane stories of her days with Elizabeth, pretending with every word that it was normal for her to send such an inquiry.

The moment she read his answer she saw that her stepfather had not bothered with such pretense.

Am I to believe that after all this time, you are truly interested in my doings? If so, the court has altered you more than I would have thought possible. Come, Minuette, let us not play games. You write with a purpose. Why not simply tell me what that purpose is? You might find me willing to oblige you . . . for your mother's sake.

Until you send to me again (with the truth, this time), I remain yours,

Stephen Howard

Minuette had never liked her stepfather, but she felt a grudging respect as she reread the letter. Not only was he not stupid (which she had never believed any Howard to be, save Giles), he was also straightforward (which no Howard ever was). Or straightforward to a point. It did make the task easier, she conceded. She would simply write and ask him if he knew of Giles's whereabouts during the crucial month of Alyce's absence. If he asked her why . . . well, she would think of something.

She meant to write back at once, but when she opened the last letter all that changed. She thought some very bad words that Dominic would be shocked to realize she knew, then set off immediately in search of Elizabeth.

It had been a restless winter for Elizabeth. With the French marriage off, she was once again adrift in a sea of waiting. She coped as she always did—busy, composed, always ready to be whatever was needed. Except when the sick headaches struck, leaving her for hours in a darkened room at least three times a month.

Today, though, she had Robert to entertain her. As her dancing master led Elizabeth and a dozen of her ladies in practice, Robert played the perfect courtier with each—whispering to one until she laughed aloud, complimenting another on her light step, bowing deeply to a third. But it was Elizabeth he had eyes for, and she in turn knew where he was at every moment even when her back was to him.

She caught sight of Minuette entering and waved for her to join them. But Minuette shook her head and raised her hand until Elizabeth could see that she held a letter. She remained against a tapestried wall while Elizabeth clapped her hands, thanked the dancing master, and dismissed her women.

Robert lingered. "And what have you been doing this fine day, Mistress Wyatt?"

"Working. You?"

"Also working—to please our dear princess is my favourite task."

He had certainly applied himself diligently these last weeks. Every time Elizabeth so much as thought of him, there he was with a story to make her laugh, a book to make her think, or a game to make her forget herself.

And how much of that is his father's doing? Elizabeth wondered. *Does Robert know his father's hopes? Do I know his father's hopes? Perhaps I am imagining what I want to hear—that Northumberland will do whatever it takes to get Robert divorced so that he is free to marry me.*

"Elizabeth," Minuette said, breaking her thoughts, "I have gleaned some news. From the Continent. Perhaps bearing on the . . . private matter."

Not waiting to be dismissed, Robert kissed Elizabeth's hand languorously. "I know when to retreat gracefully. Until later, my lady." He drew out each syllable, making the phrase almost sensual.

Only when he was completely out the door did Elizabeth manage to turn her attention to Minuette. "What news?"

Minuette sat down on the nearest bench and waited for Elizabeth to do the same before speaking. "I've had a note from a secretary in the Spanish ambassador's household. The secretary thinks he's in love with me and shares more than he should trying to impress me. He says the latest dispatches from Spain speak of stories springing up around the emperor. About how little William looks like your father. About how much he resembles instead . . ." Minuette hesitated.

"My mother?"

"Your uncle."

Elizabeth wasn't entirely surprised. "So that's the line they're taking, is it? Not only is William a bastard, but he is a bastard born of incest. *A Boleyn king.* The Spanish want people to wonder whose son he really is."

"Anyone who's met him knows he is his father's son."

"But not that many have met him—not even in England. And even some who have would benefit from questions about his legitimacy."

"I just don't understand why it's being stirred up after all these years."

"Because William is about to take personal control of his kingdom. And precisely what he will do—well, he will not ever be a figurehead. My uncle at least was a known quantity. But Will . . ." Elizabeth trailed off.

"A Boleyn king," Minuette mused. "The stories may be in Spain for now—but that phrase was found in the very heart of William's court. The day Alyce died. Someone in England is involved."

Elizabeth closed her eyes. "Mary."

"Surely not. Mary is very fond of you both—"

"Fondness has little to do with principle, and Mary is extremely principled. Even if she does not believe William is Rochford's son, she will assert to her dying day that she is the only legitimate heir to England's throne."

"It doesn't have to mean Mary personally is involved. There are many Catholics who act in her name."

"Have you not heard that Mary has once again claimed illness as a reason not to join us for Easter? Perhaps she merely wishes to avoid a heretical service—or perhaps she is distancing herself even more from Will's court."

Minuette sighed, and Elizabeth opened her eyes. "What else was in that note?" she asked, noting the distress on her friend's face.

"He told me that the ambassador visited Mary last week and found her very ill indeed. Ill enough that he believes . . . apparently Mary hinted . . ."

"Mary hinted what?"

"She believes she was poisoned."

"Oh, wonderful." All the mischief and joy that Robert had brought her vanished. "Does she not get tired of the same conspiracies? According to her, my mother tried and failed to poison her more than once before my parents were ever married."

"We'll have to tell William," Minuette said at last.

"Do you really think he doesn't know? Whatever the Spanish ambassador is saying, my uncle Rochford has most certainly heard it. Don't worry about telling William—worry about how to soothe his temper afterward."

On April 10, the official envoys from the English court presented themselves before King Henri, preparatory to opening formal negotiations. As the Earl of Surrey and Edward Seymour were received and flattered, Dominic breathed a sigh of relief, glad to leave diplomacy in the hands of these more experienced men.

Not that he would be leaving France just yet. Rochford had sent orders by the new envoys that he was to remain as long as they did, with the cryptic reminder not to "underestimate personal influence." Dominic thought cynically that his orders had more to do with Rochford's instinct for multiple avenues of control rather than any help Dominic might provide.

It seemed he was not the only one to think so. When he met Renaud that afternoon for a desultory exercise with swords, the first thing the vicomte said was, "So Rochford keeps his favorite spy at our court."

Parrying Renaud's strike, Dominic twisted neatly away. "I'm a pretty poor spy if everyone knows me as such."

Renaud advanced in a series of quick blows. "Your honesty will drive the negotiators wild. Perhaps that is Rochford's intent."

Allowing himself to be driven back, Dominic dropped his sword at the last second, causing Renaud to falter slightly, just long enough for Dominic to plant his feet firmly beneath him and kick upward with his left foot. But Renaud was a better fighter than anyone else Dominic had tried that trick on—he managed to hold on to his sword. He stumbled backward, though, and by the time he recovered his balance, Dominic had his own sword pointed straight at Renaud's chest.

Renaud's smile was genuine, but so was the hint of calculation in his eyes. "English tricks."

Dominic lowered his sword. "Welsh, actually."

The resentment vanished in a burst of laughter and the appreciation of any soldier for a well-executed maneuver. "Bravo, Dominic. You've surprised me once. No man surprises me twice."

"No *man*?" Dominic teased.

With a look that only a Frenchman could give, Renaud said, "Women are meant for surprise."

"I'll remember that."

When a messenger pulled Renaud away, Dominic left the yard and went to his room—a small, high-ceilinged chamber that, in spite of its meager size, was more richly decorated than any room he'd ever had in his life. The French liked their comforts, and Henri, whatever his opinion of England, had been faultlessly polite to Dominic. It would need more than politeness to write a treaty, though. As he sat on his bed so that Harrington might pull off his boots, he wondered how much longer they'd be here.

Harrington asked that very question. "Any word on our return?"

Dominic shook his head, surprised as always by the sound of Harrington's deep bass. Even after their months together, Harrington spoke sparely, though he had turned out to be every bit the useful man Rochford had promised. Perhaps his best quality was that he never gave any appearance of being intimidated by vicomtes and Catholic dignitaries. Dominic had learnt to appreciate the man's quiet service and wondered what he would do without him when they returned to England.

Once again Harrington read his mind. "If it's all the same to you, I'd like to remain your man when we do return. It's more to my liking than the Lord Protector's household."

He did not wait for an answer, as though he trusted in his own view of Dominic sufficiently to know what the answer would be.

Spring had never seemed lovelier—or longer. With every day that brought him nearer to his majority, William felt perversely that time was lengthening. It might have had something to do with Eleanor's absence, he admitted. Not that he had lacked for companionship, but she really was . . . gifted.

Only two more months, he reminded himself, humming under his breath. He had retreated to Hever Castle this last week of April for a week's respite from the hectic period ahead and to visit his mother. She had spent the entire winter here and he had missed her. Usually she spent the winter in London, sometimes in residence with the court but more often in her own comfortable house at York Place. On the south bank of the Thames, just across from Whitehall, York Place had always been a symbol of her power. But as her eyesight worsened, she preferred the seclusion of private residences, none more so than her childhood home.

When she had requested a visit, William had agreed instantly. There was nothing he would not grant her—especially now, when ancient rumours swirled below the surface and Mary's illnesses continued to give the Catholics a point of attack. Rochford had not wanted him to come to Hever, but William had assured him that he was not ignoring threats, nor was he hiding from them. Hever was a chance to plan while reminding the court that to attack his mother was to attack the king himself.

Minuette studied the chessboard intently, the tip of her tongue protruding slightly from her lips. He hummed louder.

"That's not fair," she said, still staring at the board. "I did nothing to distract you while you were thinking."

"Your beauty is distraction enough."

She raised startled eyes to him and, realizing what he'd said, William laughed. "Sorry, I spoke out of habit."

"It is your habit to speak flattery you don't mean?" She looked back to the chessboard, her hand hovering over a knight.

"I can't be the first man to have said such a thing to you."

She moved her knight and sat back in her chair. "And no doubt they mean it as little as you do."

"So you don't deny you have been flattered. Am I to know by whom, or have you decided to take matters entirely into your own hands and inform me only after the marriage vows have been spoken?"

"My beauty may move men to flattery, but not to self-destruction. No one would marry the queen's ward without royal permission." She lifted her chin dismissively. "And what of you? You have only to point a finger to claim whomever you wish. Will it be a Protestant princess from the Low Countries? A French Catholic? Or perhaps you wish to consolidate power at home. Jane Grey is being pushed on you quite shamelessly."

With rueful acknowledgment, William said, "Poor Jane. She's pleasant enough if one can talk to her away from her family, but she has no personality to speak of. And too devout for my tastes."

"So you will choose a wife based on your own preferences?"

Something in her cool questioning shook William's temper. "I don't think England could endure another royal love match. We're still feeling the effects of the last one."

Minuette let that hang in the air before saying lightheartedly, "Well, then, I shall continue to back Jane. I quite think she has the best chance, seeing as she's already here. What is it they say about possession?"

She was teasing him now, as shamelessly as she had when they were children. William let it soothe the edges of his irritation and turned his attention back to the chessboard.

"How are your inquiries coming along?" he asked. "You haven't given them up simply because my uncle was asking about it, have you?"

"Of course not." As he moved a rook out of harm's way, Minuette sighed and went on, "It's tedious. There were more than fifty names on that list. Even eliminating those least likely— I honestly don't believe that Alyce was besotted with the Bishop of Winchester; not only is he sixty years old, but he weighs more than two men put together—that still left nearly three dozen to track down. It has taken time to write letters and approach the matter discreetly."

Though her words were nonchalant, William knew every expression in her store. She had something—she just wanted it teased out of her. "So how many of these men did you have to allow to proposition you before you had your name? And how many deserve my wrath for that, if not for Alyce?"

He loved her laughter—it was summer and childhood and freedom in one. "I'll never tell. However, my stepfather sent me a letter this week, a most intriguing one. Not only was a certain kinsman of his not at the family seat, as he claimed to be, the first time Alyce was away from court . . . but said kinsman also stayed in a remote country manor the entire month of March a year ago."

"The month when Alyce was got with child."

"Quite."

William allowed Minuette her moment of triumph as she studied the board and moved her king to box in one of his bishops. Finally he was forced to say, "Do tell, Minuette."

"Can you not guess?" She sounded truly surprised. "You know my stepfather."

He did, but only after making himself remember. After her father's death, her mother had married a younger brother of the Duke of Norfolk.

And a Norfolk kinsman meant . . . "Giles Howard."

"Yes."

William wasn't quite sure what he felt. On one hand, he didn't like Giles Howard. On the other hand, he was Eleanor's husband.

"What's your next move?" Minuette asked, and he knew she did not mean chess.

He had an answer she would not expect. He had only been waiting for the right time to tell her. "My next move is—you."

"I'm intrigued."

"I have decided that the quickest way to mend matters with Mary is to require her attendance at mass on my birthday. An English mass."

"To mend matters—or bring them to a head?"

"Mary's feelings have been indulged too long. I intend to begin as I will go on—and that means that she and her supporters will recognize that I am king. She will make me her submission, and she will recognize my mother."

"And how do I come into it?" Minuette asked skeptically.

"I am sending you to Mary's household within the week."

Minuette studied him with the same care she had given the chessboard. "She will not like it."

"She will not."

"She will think I am sent to spy on her."

"And so you are."

With exasperation, Minuette said, "William, what exactly am I meant to discover?"

"Whatever you can—I trust your intelligence to alert you to oddities. But that is not your most important task."

With dawning comprehension, she shook her head. "I am not a messenger, I am the message. 'Don't trifle with me,' you're telling her. 'I control even the details of your own household. And if you don't like it . . .'" Her face darkened. "If she doesn't like it, then what?" she asked. *How far will you go?* she meant.

"I will not let my kingdom be divided. If the Catholics force my hand, they will regret it."

"And what of Giles Howard and his involvement with Alyce?"

"I'll put Elizabeth to work on that. The Duke of Norfolk has always liked her. She'll know how to play that."

Before she could say anything more, a page crossed the room and presented William with a letter sealed with Eleanor's initials. He read it conscious of Minuette's assessing gaze.

"All is well?" she asked neutrally.

William tossed her the letter. "Eleanor delivered safely three days ago. A girl."

He felt a twinge of disappointment that it was not a son, swallowed up in a larger relief. A boy would have been trickier to deal with in the future. A girl, though, could be safely left in the Howard household. *Providing her father of record is not a traitor,* he thought. *Better get Elizabeth to work on Norfolk without delay.*

With the clarity and edge of glass, Minuette said, "Congratulations . . . to Eleanor. I'm sure she's delighted that her child is safely delivered almost two months early."

William met her eyes. "I'm sure she'll welcome your congratulations when she returns."

Her gaze flickered as she hovered on the edge of speech, and he wondered if she would forget discretion long enough to tell him that she despised Eleanor Howard and always had.

But she merely laid aside the letter and smiled sweetly. "Your move."

Elizabeth sat in the solarium at Hever Castle, reading aloud in the unseasonably warm May Day afternoon. She read Latin as fluently as she spoke English, and the mellifluous syllables spilled from her tongue to her mother's ears. Anne sat with eyes closed in concentration—and also, perhaps, as a defense against the many things that she could no longer see even when her eyes were open.

A slight nod from her mother stopped Elizabeth at the end of the essay. "A pity more women do not trouble to learn Latin."

Elizabeth darted a quick glance at the gaggle of waiting women embroidering near the window and stifled a smile. "A great pity."

"It is good of you to spend this month with me. A pleasant pause before the ceremonies of this summer."

Why, Elizabeth wondered, *are the two of us incapable of making any but trite conversation?* As she felt the beginnings of a headache, which always signaled frustration, she could only say lamely, "I doubt we'll see anything this fine again, not until a queen's coronation."

Her mother's smile was wistful, and Elizabeth thought she

must be remembering her own coronation. "And have you any idea when that might be?"

"William does not seem anxious to make a decision. Marriage, after all, has so many unforeseen consequences."

Perhaps it was that last barb, veiled though it was, that moved her mother to ask smoothly, "And you, Elizabeth? Shall you ever be wed?"

Elizabeth stiffened into formality. "That is a matter for the council or the king, my brother."

Her mother's glance was quite penetrating for a woman who could see only outlines and shadows. "Indeed it is."

She rose, and instantly two attendants were at her side to guide her unobtrusively across the room. But her mother had one last caution to deliver, in an offhand, even slightly amused, manner. "Robert Dudley, charming though he is, can never be anything but a diversion. I trust to your intelligence, Elizabeth, to remember who you are."

The room emptied in the wake of her mother's departure, while Elizabeth sat with lips pressed tightly together, restraining the retorts that had risen so easily to her tongue. *And you, Mother, how well did you remember yourself when a married man threw himself at your feet? When all of London called you whore and witch? Tell me, Mother, what is the difference between a diversion and a crown?*

She curled up in the chair and laid her aching head in her arms. Before she knew it, Minuette's soft voice pulled her out of the dreamlike state she'd slipped into. "Elizabeth? Can I do anything for you?"

Elizabeth opened her eyes and smiled. "Come sit and talk to me before you go away. We must have a good gossip—heaven knows you won't get any of that with my sister. Tell me about Jonathan Percy and the sonnets he keeps writing you."

Minuette blushed. "I'm sure you know as much about him as I do."

"I'm sure I don't. He's never said two words to me, but you he can talk to for hours. A musician and poet—I never expected you to find such a scholarly young man appealing."

"He's a nice boy," Minuette said. Elizabeth raised her eyebrows in question, and she laughed. "All right, he's not a boy. But he *is* very nice. He talks to me as though I am a person, not just a woman."

"Very different from his sister." Elizabeth could never resist teasing Minuette about her dislike of Eleanor.

"Indeed. I find it hard to remember that he and Eleanor are not only siblings but twins." Her face hardened a little. "You've heard that she's been delivered of a daughter."

"Will is pleased, though no doubt Eleanor would have preferred a son." She studied her friend's averted face. "Tell me true, Minuette: could you bear to be her sister-in-law?"

Minuette hesitated. "I . . . it's not a question of that."

"Isn't it? The only reason Jonathan hasn't asked for you yet is that he lacks the arrogance of most males. He may actually be unsure of your answer." She studied Minuette closely—the troubled eyes that would not quite meet hers. "You would say yes, wouldn't you?"

Minuette did not precisely answer. "He's a good match for me. He's a court musician, so I could continue in service to you. He would be kind to me and to . . . any children." Her blush deepened. "I do not find him unattractive. That is more than most women can expect in a husband."

"Certainly more than I can expect."

Minuette must have caught the edge of despair in her voice, for she went straight to the heart of Elizabeth's chaotic emotions. "Have you spoken to William about your future? He cannot wish you unhappy. If you could tell him how you feel, make him understand ..."

Elizabeth aimed for sarcasm but didn't quite bring it off. "What do you imagine, Minuette? That I confess my wildly improper love for Robert and hope the king and council would approve a royal princess marrying an ambitious man who would divorce his wife for that sole reason? Brotherly affection will never overrule William's practicality." But wasn't that the very thing she hoped? Wasn't it, more or less, what Northumberland had hinted at?

"Your parents married for love."

Throat painfully tight, Elizabeth stared at the tapestry on the far wall, an image in deep shades of russet and green of Judith cutting off Holofernes's head. "My father, perhaps. But if you have managed to uncover my mother's heart enough to know why she married, it is more than I have ever done."

"You do not think she loved him?"

Elizabeth took her time answering, though it was a question she had long debated. "I think she loved him as well as she was able considering she had no choice in the matter."

4 May 1554
Beaulieu

I arrived yesterday before noon. I have yet to see the Lady Mary. She has kept to her privy chamber all day while I sit amongst her women in the presence chamber. No one seems at all likely to speak to me, and I'm beginning to wonder what precisely William expects me to do. Interrogate the women? Force myself into Mary's presence? At least I have Carrie with me—she insists she is only my maid, but I tell her she is my friend. And here at Beaulieu, she is my only friend.

At least I can report that I have unsettled everyone. I suppose that's something.

5 May 1554
Beaulieu

I was summoned to speak with Mary's private chaplain today. Father Hermosa was a confessor in Catherine of Aragon's household and, though greatly aged, he is intelligent and—surprisingly for a Spaniard—practical.

He apologized for Mary's continued confinement, alluding to repeated bouts of weakness since her great illness in April. And just as he knew I wondered if the illness was real, I knew that he wondered if I'd heard the supposed cause of it.

"You are a ward of the king's mother?" he asked. If it weren't for the disdain behind the words, I would be entertained by the convoluted ways they speak of Anne, since they will never call her queen.

"I am."

"And a companion to the Princess Elizabeth?"

I simply inclined my head, since he obviously knew all about me. Perhaps that is what they've been doing behind closed doors for two days—gathering information about me.

"Elizabeth would dearly love me to give her best wishes to her sister," I said smoothly. "As would the king, her brother. I am here to see her for myself, so as to send my personal assurances to those who cannot visit."

"I shall let Her Highness know."

He used that title deliberately, to see how I would respond. Mary is not a royal highness, not even inside her own walls. But then they are not her walls, are they? The walls, like every other thing in her life, belong to William.

8 May 1554
Beaulieu

I was at last granted an audience with the Lady Mary this evening. I arrived just after what was undoubtedly a private service of vespers in her makeshift oratory. Clearly William is not the only one of Henry's children to know how to send wordless messages.

But she was kind enough to me, if naturally wary. She asked with genuine goodwill after Elizabeth and William, and seemed pleased when I asked with intelligence about her latest project—writing a rebuttal of Martin Luther's heresies (much as her father did more than thirty years ago).

"I remember you," she said suddenly, apropos of nothing. "In the gardens at Hampton Court. You and Elizabeth were walking with my father. He liked you—you made him laugh."

"I am glad to have known His Majesty, even a very little."

Mary is not good at dissembling. Her efforts to decide what to do with me were all too apparent from the tightness of her hands on the chair arms and the tension around her eyes. She knows she cannot send me away, but she could choose to stay behind private doors while I am here.

Her face softened slightly, though not anywhere close to a smile. "I am honoured that the king, my brother, has sent you to me for a time. I look forward to speaking with you often of his health and happiness."

I made a deep curtsy and was then dismissed to bed. I cannot possibly be duplicitous by nature, or I would not care whether she welcomed me or not. I do care—it would be awful to spend the next seven weeks trapped in a house with a woman who hates me.

Though if she hated me, I might not feel quite so guilty about spying on her.

CHAPTER NINE

"MORE WINE, LORD Norfolk?" Elizabeth asked, and when the old duke nodded, she motioned forward an attendant to pour.

Elizabeth was doing William's bidding in hosting the duke for dinner in her presence chamber. Though there were two of her women and four of his men in attendance, she and Norfolk sat alone at the small round table. *He'll be less wary of you,* William had said. *Soothe him and sympathize with him . . . and see what he might spill about Mary. And Giles.*

Just as well he had asked her to do it, Elizabeth thought, for William was in a chancy mood at best. Beneath the surface enthusiasm and energy devoted to his coming majority lurked a temper that had been flaring more often than usual these last weeks. Just yesterday William had shown himself mightily displeased at losing a tennis match to Robert. Though truly, it was when he stopped throwing tantrums that William was most dangerous.

Norfolk might be charmed by her, but he was too canny to believe this dinner was to flatter him. "What is our topic this evening, Your Highness?"

"Must we have a topic?"

"I knew your mother at your age—don't tell me you don't have a purpose."

"My brother would like assurances that his looming majority will not precipitate a domestic crisis. I'm sure you'll agree that we have quite enough to deal with on the Continent just now."

"And I'm sure you would agree that the king's first responsibility is to his own people. Many of whom have been hunted and repressed for years."

Elizabeth had her marching orders, and she delivered them smoothly. "In return for your personal assurance that all His Majesty's subjects will respect his throne, he is prepared to return the Lady Mary to the line of succession—after his own future children and myself, naturally."

Of course Norfolk would accept. He could not hope for more. The Protestants would be furious, but sometimes balance was maintained by keeping both sides discontented.

"And my assurance will take what form?"

"An act of Parliament, to which you will give vocal and written approval."

Norfolk steepled his fingers. "May I ask what the king envisions for the Lady Mary in his reign?"

"Our dear sister may continue with the attendants of her choosing and the ability to hear mass privately from her own chaplain. How privately is up to the king—but I daresay he will not countenance attendance above two or three at a time."

"She will be allowed to travel?"

"At the king's discretion—and certainly not abroad."

Elizabeth knew that the Catholic powers were divided on this point. Some had pushed for years for Mary to quit England and return to her mother's Spanish home in order to rally support. But others cautioned that once Mary was gone, she might never return, and thus would die the last hope of Catholics in

England. William was of the opinion that an enemy, especially one in your own family, should be kept close at hand.

"Your Highness," Norfolk said, "principle demands that at the very least I demand a return to your father's Act of the Six Articles"—meaning dismantling the heavily Protestant changes led by Rochford and Northumberland. Norfolk continued, "If the king can assure me that he will consider—seriously consider—doing so, then I am prepared to support such an act of Parliament as has been proposed."

Even Elizabeth was impressed with how well William had predicted Norfolk's response. Of course Norfolk had to ask, and of course he knew it would never happen. No matter; they would observe the formalities. "He is prepared to so consider, and will indeed appoint a commission for that purpose on the day after his majority is reached."

Norfolk bowed his head, but Elizabeth was not finished. "On the condition that our beloved sister, Mary, attends the king at Hampton Court on June twenty-eighth, to make her personal recognition. And also upon the condition that, in that same visit, she attend service in the Chapel Royal."

She quite enjoyed the play of emotion rippling across Norfolk's face. *You may think you can outmaneuver my brother because he is young,* she thought. *But so what if you knew Richard III as a boy and have outlived four kings? You won't outlive William . . . and you can't beat him, either.*

Anything but stupid, Norfolk managed to get a handle on himself. "I shall write the Lady Mary."

"Thank you." With a brilliant smile, Elizabeth raised her glass to him. Then, just as he began to relax, she said, "I've heard some disturbing reports about your son Giles. Only gossip, I hope, but perhaps you can set me straight."

His whole body seemed to tighten. "What reports have you heard—that I have not?"

"Public drunkenness, gambling beyond his means, lechery—"

"As might be reported of many gentlemen at this court. Robert Dudley, for instance."

"Rape."

"There has never been a claim laid of such."

"Treason." Elizabeth let the last word fall into the startling silence.

Norfolk might have thrown something at her if she were a man. But he knew too well the dangers of raging at royalty. "What evidence have you?"

"As I said, these are only reports. I should be glad to have them proved wrong—the last, at least, since the others are only too true." She sipped from her goblet, then faced him squarely. "The king is not a fool. If Giles has indeed gotten himself caught up in something . . . dangerous . . . then he is being used. By someone with both more wits and more influence than Giles could ever have. As his father, no doubt you will wish to discover if your son is indeed being used." *Unless you are the one doing so,* she thought, *in which case you are being given fair warning.*

"Are we finished?"

"For now."

Elizabeth rose from the table and Norfolk followed, looking older than he had when they sat down to dinner.

He bowed to her and began to walk out. She stopped him with a voice pitched for his gentlemen to hear as well. "Lord Norfolk, my brother expects a full accounting of your investigations within a fortnight. If he is not satisfied . . ."

Finally his patience gave way, and his age, authority, and bone-deep dislike of having to submit to a woman released themselves in speech. "Do not think to threaten me, girl. I understand the king perfectly—and I will welcome discussing the issue with him. But if he tries to send you to interfere again, he will not be satisfied."

And that, thought Elizabeth, was exactly what William had predicted. Now they had only to wait and see what Norfolk did next.

Days at Beaulieu followed an inflexible pattern: Lady Mary spent the morning closeted with Father Hermosa, two secretaries, and one or two of her most trusted women; the afternoon was given to reading and needlework in the presence chamber and an hour's walk outdoors; then came a simple meal followed by a private mass.

Except that Mary did not seem to appreciate the meaning of the word *private*. The mass was held in her privy chamber, true, but there were never fewer than two dozen in attendance. On this warm evening in early June, Minuette counted twenty-seven bowed heads as Father Hermosa chanted. She wondered how many of those were true believers, how many were simply loyal to Mary, and how many were council spies passing every name on to the Protestant lords.

And how many, like Minuette herself, did not know why they were at a Popish mass. Though Minuette attended to make Mary content, she could not bring herself to go so far as to take communion. She had already been treated to several intense lectures on the state of her soul from both Lady Mary and Father Hermosa, to which she had listened with outward politeness and inward unease. The rigidity of their beliefs frightened her, and for the first time she realized why so many feared the thought of Mary on England's throne.

After the Latin benediction, Mary rose to withdraw but was

stopped by a servant who came in and spoke to her in a low voice.

"Of course," Mary replied to whatever had been said. "I will meet him in my presence chamber. Father Hermosa, will you join me?"

"Milady," the servant added, speaking up a little, "the gentleman also requests the presence of Mistress Wyatt."

Minuette started. Who on earth would want to speak to both Mary Tudor and herself? For a breath's hope she thought of William. Mary turned to her and said, "Mistress Wyatt, this way."

The gentleman was leaning against a paneled wall in the presence chamber, clad in dark riding clothes that should have looked plain but somehow suited his powerful figure. When he saw Mary, he straightened with an air of not-too-much-bother and bowed.

"Your Highness," he said, and it was the voice that cracked Minuette's shock. She had not seen him in years, but she knew that voice.

Stephen Howard favoured Minuette with a look that made her stomach rise. "Well, stepdaughter, clearly I have let you alone for far too long or I should not be surprised by how much you are like your mother."

She could not have answered if she'd wanted to. Fortunately, one didn't have to answer when a Tudor was in the room. With glacial politeness, Mary said, "Lord Stephen you are welcome, as are all of your family. The Howards have been better friends to me in recent years than our earlier years might have indicated."

Minuette forced herself to follow the conversation, knowing that this was precisely the sort of laden encounter that she had been sent here to discover. But it was hard to concentrate on even the spoken words, let alone their unspoken meaning, with her stepfather there reminding her forcibly of Giles and that night at Hampton Court, and also stirring memories of her mother's wedding . . . she had not thought of that wedding in ages. Around the time of her mother's wedding Minuette had spent a month at Framlingham, one of the Norfolks' homes, slipping away from supervision and wandering the corridors . . .

"My brother, the duke, sends his regrets," Stephen said. "There are events in play that require his attention in London. But he has sent me with a letter for Your Highness, and with counsel that I will deliver to you alone."

Mary regarded him coolly. "I shall be interested to hear of these events that keep him away from me. I will receive you privately in the morning. Mistress Wyatt, will you show your kinsman to a chamber?"

Minuette curtsied and her stepfather bowed as Mary's heels clicked out of the room along with Father Hermosa's softer tread. Looking straight ahead, Minuette led the way to the opposite door. "I shall see where the steward has put your things," she began, but he stopped her with a hand on her arm that made her swing away with a sudden, drowning fear.

He dropped his hand. "You need not shy away. I only wished to ask how you are."

"Quite well, thank you."

"Enjoying your role as the king's spy?"

She would not let him unnerve her. "Why?" she asked. "Do you have something secret to tell me?"

"I've done you one favour already in answering your question about Giles," he said. "If you want something more . . ."

The look he gave her as his voice trailed off was tantalizing, clearly meant to invite questions. Minuette wanted to turn on her heel and walk away, possibly after slapping his face, but she had been sent to play this type of game. At least here was someone willing to play, unlike the close-mouthed members of

Mary's household. And she could not dismiss the possibility that beneath the banter he held real information.

"What do you want?" she asked, remembering his preference for bluntness.

"Peace, pleasure . . . prosperity."

"I don't buy information."

"And I'm not stupid enough to try and sell any to a Tudor king. Some of us remember Henry only too well." He shook his head, gravity mixed with cunning. "I want an assurance from you that whatever happens, you will speak for my good intentions toward the king."

"My assurances?"

"The king will listen to you, so I've heard. And he must trust you, or he would not have sent you here. I want you to tell him what I'm about to tell you, and I want you to promise that he will know the information came from me."

"I promise."

"Tell the king that my brother is searching for a document, known as the Penitent's Confession. It is an affidavit said to have been sworn and signed years ago. An affidavit stating that Henry VIII was not the father of Anne Boleyn's son."

"Who swore this?"

"Someone in Anne's household—a clerk, a lady-in-waiting . . . the story changes in details. But not in essentials. Whoever swore it was supposedly in a position to know whose child William was."

When Minuette said nothing, her stepfather added urgently, "This is not mere gossip, child. This is the sort of legal maneuvering that could set England on fire and lose your friend his throne. If he wants to stop a rebellion, he'd best find that affidavit before the Catholics do."

"You are Catholic."

"I am English before I am Catholic—and I am an opportunist before either."

William stood at the window of his presence chamber at Hampton Court, his back to the regency council. As the heated words and angry inflections rose, he stared absently before him, his hands ceaselessly turning the piece of stained cloth in his hands.

Although he missed nothing that was said, not a word of it influenced him in the slightest. He had known what to do as soon as the weary, travel-stained rider had appeared late this afternoon, just hours after William's own arrival. But it cost him nothing to let his councilors talk, so he let them roll on while his own anger burnt out in silence and hardened into ice.

It was Norfolk, naturally, who voiced caution, though not as vigourously as he might have. He was on edge, William knew, for today was the end of his two-week grace period. After today's council meeting, he would have to report personally to William about his investigation. "Border raids are a way of life. One might as soon stop the tide as stop the reivers. Berwick has been burnt before and no doubt will be burnt again. The people had sufficient warning and no lives were lost."

He spoke with the authority of a man who had guarded the Scots border in earlier days and whose grandson's troops guarded it now. The Earl of Surrey was presently in France, but his men knew what they were about. "It would be foolish to walk away from French negotiations because of a few burnt-out cots and trampled fields."

"It's neither cots nor fields at issue here, and well you know it," countered Northumberland, already twitching with the desire to fight. "It's the French soldiers who marched with the reivers."

Norfolk's reply held an edge of disdain. "You'll wreck the chance of peace upon a fragment of muddy cloth?"

"And the testimony of your grandson's troops," Northumberland retorted. "Are you saying they planted evidence against the French? Because trying to provoke a war would be perilously near to treason."

Rochford intervened at last, with the inflectionless voice of command. "The evidence cannot be gainsaid. There were French troops in Berwick. As our envoys are treating with Henri, he sends his soldiers across our border."

Once his uncle would have finished the matter, issuing orders in that same neutral voice. But today he paused, and William knew it was for his sake. In ten days he would turn eighteen and Rochford would no longer be regent. It seemed his uncle was prepared to step aside and let William rule.

Aware that every word and movement would be closely scrutinized, William turned slowly to face his council. He let the muddy cloth unwind until it draped down in the unmistakable shape of a tunic. There was a long streak of dried blood surrounding the gaping slash where an English sword had driven into the wearer's shoulder. In spite of its condition, the colours were unmistakable—bright azure and three gold fleurs-de-lis. French royal colours.

William looked from face to individual face, until the eight men were taut with concentration. Only then did he speak.

"My lord Rochford, recall the envoys. All of them."

His uncle didn't hesitate. "Yes, Your Majesty."

They waited for more, their eyes fixed on William, but he said nothing.

Northumberland made a mild protest. "That seems an . . . inadequate response. If you will not treat, you should fight. Withdrawal and silence accomplish nothing."

William bared his teeth in a smile that he knew was like his father's. "By all means hold your men in readiness, but I intend to give Henri every chance to hang himself. He thinks he can play me because I am young. He thinks I will overreach in my eagerness to avenge an insult. I think, if I can possess my soul in patience, he will make a mistake. And then we will see what silence may accomplish."

Northumberland paused, his mouth open, then looked at Rochford. William felt a flash of hot anger when his uncle nodded discreetly.

Swallowing his temper, William said, "Send to France today. I want our men home."

Only Norfolk remained when the council filed out, though he stood now in deference. William was tempted to leave him standing, but the man was old and there was no need for discourtesy.

"Sit," he commanded. When Norfolk had, William asked, "You have a report for me, my lord duke?"

Norfolk didn't waste any time. "I have found no evidence at all that my son Giles is involved in anything remotely treasonous."

"Would you tell me if you had found such evidence?"

"Listen to me, boy—I served your father and his father before him. You might even be said to owe your existence to me—it was I who brought your mother to Henry's attention. Why would I allow anyone to jeopardize all that I have worked for since I was a young man?"

"Perhaps because you are now an old man and the next world begins to loom larger than this one. Men will do nearly anything for religion."

Norfolk shook his head. "My conscience is clear. I have never forsaken my beliefs for convenience's sake. The Lord will require to know what I have done, not what England has done."

William wanted to believe him. It would certainly make his

life easier. But there was still the problem of Alyce de Clare's death and Giles's likely involvement. He drummed his fingers on the table while he thought. With the ambassadors being recalled and French troops in Scotland, the next step was war. He didn't need this hanging over him. But neither did he have the resources to cope with every problem at once.

His solution was imperfect but workable. "Lady Mary will attend our majority celebrations on June twenty-eighth. I know that she would enjoy a stay with your family afterward. At Framlingham, I would suggest. Of course, I will provide additional men for her protection and comfort." *And to keep you from getting up to anything dangerous,* he silently added. Putting Norfolk and Mary in one place was either brilliant or utterly mad.

Norfolk gave no clue as to which he thought it. "As it please Your Majesty. My family is ever at your service."

I hope so, thought William. *I truly do hope so.*

Four days before William's—and her own—eighteenth birthday, Minuette departed the Palace of Beaulieu with Lady Mary on their way to Hampton Court. On the first day of travel, Minuette rode. To her surprise, on the morning of the second day she was asked to ride with Mary inside her coach. Though she preferred horseback, Minuette took this last opportunity for a private conversation.

After nearly eight weeks with the former princess, Minuette's sympathy was tempered by impatience. She had been subjected to hours of gentle lectures on the need for England to return to the Holy Church and put away the heresies running rampant through the kingdom. "His Majesty is young, and thus easily blinded by evil councilors," Mary had said.

His Majesty is young, thought Minuette, *and yet years more pragmatic than you will ever be.* There was no going back. Catherine of Aragon was dead, and Henry as well, and no one could pretend that Anne Boleyn and her children had not happened.

Though straightforward in many ways, Mary showed an advanced ability to refer to her love for her half siblings without ever acknowledging their mother. Even when Lord Norfolk had come in person to repeat the king's command to attend him upon his birthday, Mary had listened stonily and then bade him tell the king that, as she loved him, she would do all that he commanded . . . within her conscience.

At least her conscience allowed her to be driven to Hampton Court today. If nothing else, Minuette was desperate to see her friends once more. Especially Dominic—she'd had word from Elizabeth that he had been recalled from France. She could not wait to have people to speak to freely again. She had not even had Carrie with her for the last two weeks. As soon as her stepfather had left Mary's house, Minuette had sent Carrie back to court carrying on her person a message to be hand-delivered directly to Elizabeth.

They rode for hours without speaking, and Minuette wondered why Mary had wanted her at all. Only when the lanes began to show the familiarity of the approaching palace did Mary speak.

"Mistress Wyatt," she said. "Will the king allow the woman to humiliate me?"

"Never. And I assure you that the queen has nothing but care in her heart for you. She would be your friend if you would let her."

The downward curl of Mary's lip reminded Minuette of William when he was displeased. "You are too young to know of what you speak," she said dismissively. "However she may appear to you, that person is the cause of all the misery in my life.

She turned my father's heart away from me. She rejoiced when my mother died, and she would be happy to see me follow."

Minuette felt a great pity for the resentful and, yes, wronged Mary. But she was also weary of her inability to recognize what would be in her best interest. "And as you loved your mother, my lady, so does the king love his. He does not ask you to betray anything—only to be civil. Surely we can all manage that for the good of England."

When Mary turned stubbornly to look out the window, Minuette added, "It would have pleased your father greatly."

"Do not presume to tell me about my father!" Mary snapped, and this time it was Elizabeth she resembled.

Fortunately, Minuette was too used to Elizabeth's anger to be intimidated by Mary's. "I seek only to serve His Majesty. He wishes peace at home. You have the power to give it to him."

Then she turned away herself and shut her eyes, calling up images of Hampton Court to soothe her. She could not wait to arrive and hand over this responsibility to William.

Dominic rode into view of his mother's house just before sunset on June 26. He had landed in Dover the day before and, though anxious to return to court, he could not in conscience overlook the opportunity to visit. He came alone, having sent Harrington on ahead. There were things waiting here too personal to be shared with anyone.

His mother stood on the steps as Dominic dismounted in the courtyard, her slight figure dwarfed by the double-width oak door behind her. The dark blue gown she wore was unadorned, her hair completely covered by a white headdress. She looked like nothing so much as a mother abbess.

Which, some days, she thought she was.

But today, it seemed, was one of her good days. She greeted Dominic with a smile and even stood on tiptoe to kiss his cheek. In spite of that, Dominic could not relax entirely—he was too busy searching her face and voice for clues as to her state of mind. She knew who he was, she knew he'd been in France, and, most important of all, she spoke with a soft lucidity that indicated her mind was as calm as her face.

After a hot bath and fresh clothing, Dominic escorted his mother to the low-beamed hall where a long table had been set for four. They were joined at dinner by Dominic's old nurse, Grace, who now cared for his mother through both good and bad. The other guest was a short, powerfully built man in dark robes who was introduced only as Michael, his mother's clerk. It was a charade one played in Protestant England. Michael was only the latest in a long line of Continental priests who had taken refuge in his mother's house.

It didn't take long for the first danger signs to appear. Dominic grew increasingly uneasy as his mother questioned him about his personal life and attachments. Not that the inquiries themselves were unnatural—it was what mothers did, after all, and he usually welcomed any sign that Philippa was normal.

But with each probing question, his mother's voice grew higher and more rapid and her green eyes began to glitter unevenly. Dominic was spare and neutral in his answers, hoping by his reserve to keep her anchored firmly in the present. But he could not avoid answering a direct question and he was forced to admit that, no, he was not as yet betrothed.

Philippa smiled. "I've been corresponding with Margaret Haywood in Devon. Her husband is sheriff of the county. Four sons and one daughter. The girl's quite lovely . . . they sent me a miniature—"

"Mother, please. I don't need you to find me a wife."

She perched on the edge of her chair, chattering on as if he had not spoken. "She needs the right kind of husband, of course—it is such an uncertain time for those of the true faith. But you are both kin and friend to the king. The girl would be quite safe with you. Her name is Katherine, and her mother assures me she's as sweet-tempered and biddable a girl as ever there was. Just turned fourteen, but a woman. You would not have to wait for children—"

"Mother."

She blinked.

Caught between anger and despair, Dominic did not measure his words. "You speak out of turn when you consider me of your faith. I do not follow Rome. And when I choose to marry, it will not be to some child I've never laid eyes on. I'll not bed a girl of fourteen, willing or not."

In that brief pause that followed his outburst, hope flared in Dominic that maybe it would be all right. Maybe this time she had heard and understood him and would treat him as any other indulgent mother, laughing off his unpardonable manners and retreating to a safer subject.

Her voice, when it came, was brittle and cracked, like ice rotting from beneath. "You prefer a reluctant wife? But of course. You are a Courtenay, after all."

Dominic could not answer, his throat tight with self-disgust. It was Michael who saved them, by the simple expedient of taking Philippa by the arm and raising her from the chair. Like a docile child, she let him lead her from the room. With a shake of her head, Grace followed.

He never should have come here. It was too late to leave for Hampton Court now, but at first light he would be on his way.

Provided that his mother didn't burn the house down around them in the night.

When Grace returned to the room an hour later he was still sitting at the table, pondering the unpleasantness of filial duty, while the servants cleared up around him.

With the gentleness of long affection, Grace said, "You make things worse, you know. The tone of your voice, the turn of your countenance—it's no wonder she sees him in you."

"Pity I wasn't born a girl," Dominic said lightly.

Grace continued to gaze at him, eyes wide and mild. For some reason, the very lack of judgment in her face made Dominic want to defend himself. "I can't help how I look."

"It's not only that. You are your father's son, Dominic. You have his ideals and his ambitions and his passion. Such intensity frightens your mother, for it made her own life a misery."

"Then why is she pushing the Haywood daughter on me? I'd expect her sympathies to be entirely on the girl's side."

"They are. According to Margaret Haywood's letters, her daughter is willing and eager to marry. No doubt she's been fed romantic stories of your looks and your skill at arms, not to mention your friendship with kings. It's enough to turn any girl's head."

Dominic snorted. "So it's all right to marry me off to a stranger as long as the bride is convinced she herself wishes it?"

"Odd as it may seem, your mother wishes this marriage for your sake. She would not have you marry after your heart as your father did. She did not love him, but there were moments when she could pity him. His life was no less bitter than hers, loving a woman who flinched every time he touched her. Better, she thinks, to leave your heart out of it altogether, for then you cannot be hurt."

She rose and kissed him on the forehead. When she had gone, Dominic could not bear the closeness of the house another minute. The half-moon gave enough light for him to wander across the lawn to the perimeter of the kitchen garden. He could hear the lowing of cattle from a distant field, and he tried to lose himself in the pastoral serenity.

As he leaned against the trunk of a knobby oak tree, random images tumbled before his eyes: his father showing him how to hold a sword, his large hand swallowing up five-year-old Dominic's fingers; his mother standing before his father's tomb with dry eyes and compressed lips; a girl of fourteen somewhere in Devon, her features soft and unformed, waiting in a church for a husband she'd never met.

Dominic kicked at a clump of grass and swore. Why was this so difficult? Men married every day for reasons far from romantic—for land, for family, for connections. When he'd troubled to think about it, he had assumed he would do the same. After all, his heart had never entered into his affairs before, only considerations of pleasure and good company.

He had followed his own strict ethics—no virgins, no wives, and no force—and had thought his detachment a point of honour, a means of avoiding entanglement. Now, as the summer darkness closed around him, with the seductive smell of warm grass and sleeping flowers almost tangible against his skin, Dominic forced himself to dive into the icy center of his heart and admit the truth.

He was afraid of being his father. He feared falling so desperately in love that he would ride roughshod over anyone, even the woman herself, to get what he wanted. By that measure, his mother's suggestion was sensible—if Dominic was going to marry for reasons of logic and practicality, the Haywood daughter was as good as any other. And it wouldn't be so terrible for the girl. He would be kind.

But Dominic choked at the thought. He didn't want to marry Katherine Haywood. He didn't want a biddable girl or a needy widow or a calculating mistress.

He closed his eyes and allowed thoughts of Minuette to creep through the barriers in his memory. The unexpected feel of her in his arms when she'd jumped to him at Hampton Court. Her pale face, turned to him in appeal the night he'd pulled Giles Howard off her. The lilt of her laughter as she'd flirted with another man.

In the darkness of his mind, he let his control slip. He imagined her before him, trembling a little as he ran his fingers down her cheek to her throat. He imagined her eyes closing and her chin tilting up, bringing her mouth closer to his own, her lips parting as they kissed . . .

His eyes snapped open. God in heaven, he was in trouble.

William slipped out of bed and shivered once at the night air on his bare skin before he slipped a robe over his shoulders. Moonlight poured across the floor and he padded silently to the window, looking over the shadowy courtyard and the moon-bleached gardens to the silver glint of the river beyond the walls.

Hampton Court slumbered below him, though he knew many were still awake at this hour—laundry maids scrubbing, cooks working through the night to ensure that the court and its many guests were well fed. And surely more than one couple engaged in breathless intimacy.

Hitching himself onto the window ledge, he stared absently back at his empty bed. Eleanor had returned to court this week with her husband and had not missed a chance to remind William of her charms. But her charms came with a price, and he hadn't felt like listening to her subtle persuasions that he increase her allowance or acknowledge her daughter. He wasn't married yet—he should be allowed some peace.

Of course, the council would change all that if they had their way. William's marriage had been a topic of every council meeting for the last six months, with opinions on an appropriate mate ranging across the map of Europe, plus several serious contenders here at home.

Jane Grey was the nearly unanimous choice of the Protestant faction, with more than just religion in her favor. Royal blood, for one: Jane's grandmother had been his father's beloved youngest sister, and it was always wise to co-opt any future threats to the crown. Her age, for another: at sixteen, she was ready to take her place as England's queen without delay. The only Protestants who disliked her were those who had fallen foul of her difficult mother, the Duchess of Suffolk, and didn't want their king in his cousin's debt.

The most serious Catholic candidate was the French princess Elisabeth. As King Henri's oldest daughter, she was quite valuable, and a marriage to her would enhance William's standing in Europe. The largest drawback, though by no means insurmountable, was her age. Elisabeth de France was only nine years old, and her father likely would not permit her to solemnize a marriage before she was twelve. Though once word got out that French soldiers were loose in Scotland, the girl's age wouldn't matter at all. There could be no betrothal without peace.

Throughout the long and contentious debates, only two men had kept their opinions quiet—William himself and his uncle Rochford. Although they had not discussed the matter openly, William was certain that they were thinking the same thing.

Mary Stuart, Queen of Scotland.

She was perfect. Like Jane, the granddaughter of a Tudor

princess. Like Elisabeth de France, a Catholic. And as a queen in her own right since she was six days old, Mary had a stature that no other woman could match. That she was Scotland's queen only enhanced the temptation. To be the English king who united the island was an inducement far greater than Mary's personal charms, which were many.

William had been betrothed to Mary Stuart at one point—when he was seven and she was an infant queen. But Marie de Guise had smuggled her daughter away to France five years later and the English betrothal had been succeeded by a French one. Now eleven years old, Mary was only a few years from becoming the wife of the dauphin, Francis. The Scots themselves seemed content, no doubt trusting that the future Queen of France would spend her time in Paris, leaving her religiously independent subjects to their own devices. An English marriage would be far too close to home.

The only way to secure Mary Stuart was on the battlefield. But William could feel it in his bones—his chance was coming. He would know the moment and he would seize it. And then he would have what he wanted.

He sighed and ran his hands through his hair. Sometimes he envied his people—not the nobles and courtiers who surrounded him at all times, but the staunch, worthy everyday Englishmen who worked the land and served in the background and never had to trouble themselves about politics or treaties. They married for love—or at least for choice—rather than assessing every possibility without consideration for personal feeling.

Not that William's personal feelings had ever moved him to want more than what he had with Eleanor. He supposed, if he had not been king, he might have married Eleanor last year for desire alone. *Just as well I am king,* he thought wryly. A marriage based solely on desire was certain to be a disaster.

Minuette rode out of the forecourt the next morning conscious of the pleasures inherent in being once more amongst friends. She rode Winterfall, the white palfrey that William had given her a year ago. William himself rode next to her, with Elizabeth and Robert and a dozen others behind. She felt a petty satisfaction that Eleanor had not been invited, and tried not to dwell on what she wanted it to mean. After all, it was natural that a woman who'd given birth two months before would not be prepared to ride.

Jonathan Percy's was another face missing from this morning's hunt. He did not care for blood sport, and he'd needed to rehearse with the choir for tomorrow's service in any case. But he had not seemed to mind her going, only kissed her hand and bade her be safe.

Winterfall was aching to run this morning, and Minuette could feel her own blood pulsing in response.

Calling over her shoulder to William, she issued a challenge. "I'll wager I can reach the river before you can."

She didn't wait for a response, but let Winterfall have her head. Some might think it cheating to begin the race while William was still talking to Elizabeth, but as Minuette was handicapped by a sidesaddle and long skirts, she thought it only fair. She knew the path by instinct, having ridden it for years. Winterfall was responsive to her slightest touch, and soon Minuette could see the main road to London running alongside the Thames.

It was as well that she slowed before pounding onto the road, for a lone horseman had just come round the bend. It took all

Minuette's strength to pull Winterfall's head round to the right and even then she felt the whoosh of the large black horse passing so close that her blue skirts billowed up.

"Good girl," Minuette said shakily, patting Winterfall's neck as she slowed the horse to a walk and then a stop. Being mangled in a riding accident was not what she'd meant when she'd thought of an exciting morning. Perhaps she should be a little less careless in her enthusiasms.

It seemed the other rider thought so as well. She heard him pull his own horse around and canter back to her. Even the horse sounded displeased. Minuette adjusted herself in the saddle, prepared to apologize prettily.

She never got the chance.

As Dominic drew near Hampton Court, he moved his palfrey into a gallop. He was looking up at the turrets, just visible above the parkland trees, when he heard an approaching horse. Because he knew the lanes of the park well, he was able to swing aside in time to avoid being hit by the careless rider. But it spooked his horse thoroughly, and he had to struggle to get the black Barbary under control.

He wheeled round in the road, prepared to deliver a scathing criticism, when he realized the rider was a woman. That was enough to make him pause and look her over more closely.

For the space of a fleeting thought, he hesitated, and so he barely had time to dismount before Minuette was upon him. Then she was in his arms and he was aware of nothing but the feel of her against him.

He was home.

CHAPTER TEN

28 June 1554
Hampton Court

The sun has just risen on my eighteenth birthday. This is likely to be the only time of the entire day when even I remember that. This day is for William—and England.

When I was young, I thought of eighteen as a mystical age, a time when I would know my future and myself. But I find this morning that I am sure of nothing. I know that Jonathan spoke to William yesterday. I know what Jonathan will ask me today. I thought I knew what I would answer him.

I will say yes. Of course I will say yes. There is no reason I should not. But why, then, did I avoid him at last night's banquet? For I took care that Jonathan could not catch me alone. I spent my evening flirting discreetly with the Spanish ambassador, feeling him out as to a possible marriage for Elizabeth with Prince Philip.

I avoided Dominic last night as well, though I was aware of his every movement. From the moment he pulled me against him on the road yesterday, I have felt almost shy. It's ridiculous—me, shy of Dominic? Might as well be frightened of William. But the fact remains that Dominic seems all at once a stranger to me. Perhaps it is only his appearance. He has let his hair grow while in France, until it brushes against his chin. And a thin mustache and the hint of a beard, which make him look . . . older. Darker.

I'm being silly. Dominic is the same as ever he was. All I need do is speak to him and I will feel myself again.

Elizabeth stood perfectly still as Kat Ashley surveyed her from head to toe, then circled the wide-skirted cloth-of-silver gown that to Elizabeth felt almost like armour. Today was about acknowledging William without completely fading into the background. The silver shimmer of Elizabeth's dress, complemented by the Tudor roses embroidered on her sleeves and kirtle, marked her as royal without staking the first claim to power. Though her women would cover their hair in snoods for church, Elizabeth merely had a length of gossamer silk attached to her small silver crown. *It's always my hair,* she thought. *The people want to be reminded that I got this red-gold hair from my father.*

After smoothing a nonexistent crease and tweaking a ribbon that edged one wide trumpet sleeve, Kat nodded once. "You're ready."

For chapel? Yes. For Mary? Elizabeth sighed.

"Mary will come," Minuette said confidently from over Elizabeth's shoulder.

"Because you say so?"

"Because I believe so. Didn't you say that whatever I believe must be?"

"You are terrifying in your certainty—you know that? You and William both."

"And that is why you love us. In any case, Mary would not have come all the way to Hampton Court only to balk at the last minute."

Don't be so certain, Elizabeth thought. *Mary is quite capable of doing what she wishes.*

The Chapel Royal was easily reached from the royal apartments—thanks to Cardinal Wolsey's connecting gallery—and although they were entering the Royal Pew from above and behind the main floor, the crowds were still enormous. Elizabeth began to appreciate Rochford's planned celebrations in London next week. Hampton Court had sentiment on its side, but it was not built for entertaining on quite this scale.

The Royal Pew—divided into two chambers, for king and queen—was already nearly full, though naturally Elizabeth had a seat waiting in the arch of the bowed window that overlooked the main floor of the chapel. Despite its name, the queen's box was empty today of her mother. "One submission at a time," Anne had agreed with William. "First Mary attends church. My acknowledgment comes later."

Courtesy dictated that Elizabeth sit next to the Duchess of Suffolk, her most unpleasant cousin. Frances Brandon Grey had never liked Anne Boleyn's children, her own mother having been a great partisan of Catherine of Aragon, and she generally kept her distance. But her ambition was greater than her sentiment, and so she was here with all three of her daughters, no doubt still angling to catch William for her oldest, Lady Jane Grey. Minuette squeezed onto the end of a bench nearest the door at the back, leaving the remaining empty seat in front for Mary.

Elizabeth loved the Royal Pew, for it brought her closer to the exquisite blue of the ceiling, with the golden pendants and cornices commissioned by her father; the height of the box also allowed for the greatest musical appreciation. But its best quality was that it allowed her to look down on the mass of the court rather than being in the midst of it.

From her position, Elizabeth could see a fair part of the chapel proper below. It seemed every eye was fixed on the empty seat next to her. *Half have come to watch William,* she thought, *and half to watch Mary. And that divide is at the very heart of our troubles.*

A ripple of movement and then people were on their feet and bowing. Elizabeth stood with the others and turned to see her brother framed by the doorway into the queen's box. As she breathed in, she almost thought she was back in Westminster Abbey nearly eight years ago, the day of William's coronation.

Ten years old he'd been, and the very model of a grave boy king. He had not fumbled once, in word or action, and when St. Edward's crown was placed on his head, he did not stir in spite of its weight.

She could remember the restraint of the audience and, beneath the pomp, the uneasiness. From a king who had dominated Europe for decades to an untried boy in the blink of an eye—no one had known what the future held for England.

Elizabeth felt a rush of pride as she watched her brother today. Now, at last, England had an independent king—handsome and merry and well loved. With the eyes of his people and most of Europe upon him, he moved as though he had been born for it.

As he had.

Only when she heard a wordless pressure of pent-up sound around her did Elizabeth realize that William did not stand alone. With one hand resting lightly on his arm stood Mary, with her royal pedigree blazing from her figure. She did not look happy, but she did not falter as her brother—head of a Church she considered heretical—led her to her seat next to Elizabeth.

As she swept up from her curtsy, Elizabeth caught Minuette grinning at her from the back of the room. She could almost hear her friend's voice in her head: *See? I'm always right.*

Throughout the celebration mass, Dominic did not hear a word of worship or a note of music, and he was only dimly aware of the press of people in the Chapel Royal. Even William was little more than a figure glimmering in gold and silver and jewels somewhere at the front. Dominic had never been so glad to be unimportant, for that meant he did not have to sit farther forward but could stand at the back of the king's pew near the open doorway. By angling his body to an uncomfortable degree, he could catch glimpses of Minuette in the queen's pew.

He kept his gaze fixed on the front of the chapel as much as possible, for he did not wish to make her uncomfortable. But his eyes kept returning to what he could see of her—the straight back inside her ivory damask gown, the slender neck wrapped in the sapphire star pendant, the great mass of hair confined in a jeweled net attached to the rounded headdress in an ivory that matched her dress. Though he missed the sight of her honey-warm hair, it did have the effect of heightening the outlines of her profile, the straight lines of nose and chin softened by the curve of cheek and lips.

Once, she turned her head to him, as if she could feel the weight of his stare, and Dominic looked hastily away. His heart skipped a few beats, and he almost shook his head at his own foolishness. From the moment Minuette had flung herself into his arms yesterday, Dominic hadn't drawn a deep breath. He had hardly spoken to her as yet, for she had busied herself at last night's banquet with the Spanish ambassador, making even that hardened cleric smile with the brightness of her personality.

He had not slept last night, merely lain on his bed while inside him raged a debate of body and mind, desire and discretion. Even now, he could feel Minuette's every curve imprinted against him, and he wondered fleetingly if this was how his father had felt when Philippa Boleyn claimed his heart without even wanting to.

The prudent thing, the expected thing, would be to speak to William at once and ask formal permission to marry Minuette. But prudence warred with familial demons. He wanted her, but he would not take her by arrangement or without consulting her wishes. He wanted her to come to him willingly—joyfully, even—and that would take time. He would be patient and persuasive, and when her desire matched his, they would go to William together.

He turned his head and, this time, caught Minuette's eye. She smiled—an oddly tentative smile that made his breath catch. Today was for celebration. A perfect day to coax her into the glories of falling in love.

As the Te Deum rose to its conclusion, William had to refrain from a sigh of relief. He was accustomed to working through church services, not sitting perfectly still while watched from all sides. After Archbishop Cranmer's final prayer, William led the way out of the king's pew and waited for both of his sisters. Offering an arm to each of them, William made the short progress to the great hall, where Mary had one final part to play.

Beneath the soaring hammer-beam ceiling, the great hall was packed with people, the rich fabrics and bright colours of their clothing merely a continuation of the tapestried walls. He noted several in particular: Jane Grey looking fair and neat next to her formidable mother, Robert Dudley winking at Elizabeth, Northumberland standing at a slight remove from the rest of the council.

Those in the room lowered as one into bows and curtsies as William took his place on the dais. A gilded and cushioned throne waited for him beneath the canopy of state, the rich cloth hung above to signal his authority, and to one side of it stood his mother. William left his sisters flanking the opposite side of the throne and went to Anne. He took her by the hand and raised her up. He could have sworn that the great hall vanished for a moment and it was just he and his mother acknowledging what the two of them had wrought. He had meant only to kiss her hand, but on impulse he kissed her on both cheeks instead.

"Rise," he commanded the audience as he sat. For perhaps the first time in his life, not a soul was looking at William. Mary had all the attention she ever could have asked for. *Will she balk?* William wondered. *Will she refuse to submit? Will she faint to avoid it?* He hoped not. Fainting women were not his specialty.

It was the slightest movement that could almost have been imagined, but everyone was so intent there was no chance of missing it. Her expression like stone, her eyes looking far beyond this room, Mary turned just enough so that she might be said to have been facing in the general direction of Anne and lowered her chin.

The crowd let out its collective breath. It was done. William smiled warmly at Mary in thanks. She looked tired and perhaps legitimately ill. He would make this next part quick so that she might retire with dignity.

In the arched imperial crown of the King of England, Ireland, and France, with the jeweled collar over the crimson velvet and ermine state robe he had worn to the church service—with Henry's queen on one side and his two daughters on the other—William had never felt more ready to take his father's place.

He began with the announcement of what had been already widely rumoured. "Lord Rochford."

William counted it to his uncle's credit that he managed not to look complacent as he stepped before William and bowed low.

"My lord Rochford, we are grateful for thy service to our crown and kingdom. Thou hast kept our realm safe and prosperous through our tender years." At the edge of the dais, he saw Minuette's lips quirk.

Repressing the urge to wink at her, he continued. "We appoint thee Lord Chancellor of England. Long may your wisdom aid us."

As William presented his uncle with the Great Seal of England, the mark of his new office, there was a slight murmur from the crowd, though no great surprise.

"Master Dominic Courtenay."

Unlike Rochford, Dominic did look surprised, and the interest of those watching sharpened. He stepped forward and bowed graciously enough, but William did not miss the question in his eyes.

"Thou hast long served us well. Thou are first amongst the knights of England, rightly renowned for both prowess in arms and honest diplomacy. Thou hast earned what we freely give."

William extended his hand, and his steward was ready, laying in it the sword Dominic had given him last year. "Kneel."

William touched him lightly on each shoulder. "Dominic Courtenay, Marquis of Exeter."

Whatever the crowd had predicted, it had not been this. That title had belonged not to Dominic's father but to his traitorous uncle. For fifteen years the crown had held Exeter's land, though his wife and son had been released from the Tower four years ago. William knew that some had expected him to return the title to Exeter's son, who, at twenty-seven, had shown none of his father's inclinations to rebellion.

But he had determined some time ago to pass the title and

estates to Dominic. Not quite all of the estates—he had left the dispossessed Edward Courtenay several lesser manors—but the bulk of the wealth, along with the hereditary rights, was now Dominic's.

In the surprised silence of the great hall, Dominic proclaimed his fealty to William and England. When he stood, there was just time for William to clasp his hand warmly before Dominic was surrounded by a surge of well-wishers and power seekers. William's lips twitched again at the look on Dominic's face as men and women alike sought to speak to him at once. With the official ceremonies ended, everyone was anxious to assert his or her own position.

A soft hand slipped into his, and Minuette's voice was in his ear. "That was generous."

He grinned at her. "What is the point of being king if one cannot be generous to one's friends?"

Eleanor had wound her way through the press of people and now took possession of William's free arm while speaking to Minuette. "Wasn't it a wonderful surprise? I always think these gestures are best when only a few people know beforehand."

William wondered why she made it sound as though she were one of those who had known before. Removing his arm from Eleanor's grasp, he said, "Minuette, I haven't forgotten it is your birthday as well as mine. I thought I would let you name your gift from me." He leaned forward and pitched his voice in a conspiratorial whisper. "Perhaps, once you have spoken to Jonathan, you will have a better idea what you might desire."

She blushed prettily, and William knew he'd been understood. Minuette could have the grandest wedding in the kingdom at his expense—she need only name when and where.

Refusing to be snubbed, Eleanor thrust herself into the conversation once more. "A Christmas wedding, perhaps? Although you may not wish to wait that long. I'm certain my brother would name the earliest possible day."

Minuette freed her hand from William's, looking unnaturally flustered. "If you'll excuse me, I'm needed elsewhere."

With a warmth that William did not believe for an instant, Eleanor said, "Take care how you treat my brother's heart. It's quite fragile."

"Is it?" Minuette said. "Not at all a family trait."

Before William had absorbed her rudeness, she was gone. With the merest nod of his head, he made to leave as well, but Eleanor caught him by the arm once more. He could feel the points of her fingernails even through several layers of fabric.

With a seductiveness that had never failed to stir him before, she said, "I do hope your entire week won't be taken up with public ceremonies."

Allowing his eyes to wander the length of her body, William said, "No, I don't imagine it will." He let complacency settle in her expression before adding, "As a matter of fact, I'm going to dine in private later with my closest companions."

Already gleaming with gratification, Eleanor looked ready to purr.

William leaned closer and said, "With your husband at court, I wouldn't dream of keeping you away from him. Perhaps I'll see you at the dancing tonight."

He could feel her fury burning into his back as he walked away, and for a moment he was disconcerted. He didn't like the way she had talked to Minuette, but was that reason enough to dismiss her out of hand? She was the mother of his child, after all.

He would think about it later. Perhaps after a glass or two of wine.

It took nearly an hour to be released from the crowds, but

finally William retreated to his privy chamber with Dominic in tow. Elizabeth and Minuette were there waiting for them. With a wave of his hand, William dismissed the attendants. "Leave us. We will serve ourselves."

A table had been laid with smoked salmon, artichoke pie, glistening pomegranates, and gingerbread stamped with the lion of England. And wine, both red and white. William was very glad of that wine—he had the beginnings of a headache.

When the door shut, he was suddenly aware that he was standing alone, with the other three grouped together. The weight of his state robes and crown seemed to emphasize the heavy silence that settled into awkwardness.

Is this what being king means? he thought desperately. *Always standing alone?*

But then Minuette did precisely the right thing. She curtsied deeply, raised her head to him from her lowered position, and winked.

In a moment, the four of them were laughing together and all was once again simple. Minuette approached William and began to untie the thick cord holding the state robes in place across his shoulders. "Now that we have done our duty to our king, we can dispose of this at least."

"Let me," Dominic said, as Minuette pulled the robe free and nearly collapsed from the staggering weight of it.

"Good heavens," she said. "However can you stand it?"

"I'm trained for it. Like riding—begin small and work your way up. I suppose the robe I'll wear in twenty years will be twice that weight." William poured himself wine and drank.

Dominic stood still in the doorway to William's bedchamber, frozen in place with the robe still in his arms.

"Dom? What's wrong?"

He said nothing. Elizabeth moved first, William and Minuette together behind her. As they moved, Dominic continued into the bedchamber and laid the robe on William's bed. He still did not speak. He did not have to.

Scrawled in paint on a linen sheet was a vicious message: *The Penitent's Confession is true—Long live Queen Mary!* It was pinned to the bed by a knife.

Heedless of the women, William breathed out an oath. "Where will this end?"

Dominic answered, "I think our own counsel is no longer sufficient. Rochford must be told."

"I quite agree," drawled Rochford's familiar voice from behind William. He turned slowly and found his uncle watching them from the doorway. "I wondered when the four of you would come to that conclusion."

"You knew?" Elizabeth asked bluntly.

"I know everything that goes on at court, and most everything that goes on outside of it. Did you never consider that these kinds of attacks would not be confined to you alone?"

William was getting good at reading his uncle. "You have been targeted as well?"

"I have."

"And you did not tell me?" He felt his anger growing and reminded himself to use it rather than be swept away by it.

Rochford raised one insolent eyebrow. "You did not tell me, either."

"I am king!"

William thought someone jumped—probably Minuette—when he shouted, but Rochford seemed almost pleased. "So you are, Your Majesty. What do you command?"

"That you tell me everything. Now."

"Of course. Would you care to withdraw to greater privacy?"

Rochford's gaze scanned Elizabeth, Dominic, Minuette, dismissing each of them with his eyes.

"I would not. We will speak together—all of us."

That displeased Rochford; it was obvious in the tightening of his jaw. William did not give him time to object. Leading the way back into the privy chamber, he pulled out a chair and said, "Would you care to join us, Uncle? I would appreciate your . . . insights into this matter."

"By all means." Rochford held a chair for Elizabeth; Dominic did the same for Minuette.

When they were all seated tensely around the circular table, Rochford said, "Perhaps we might begin with that message. The Penitent's Confession—you have all been dabbling in this matter for some time, so I presume you've heard of it?"

William nodded. "Elizabeth and I have, from Minuette. Sorry, Dom, there hasn't been time to tell you everything."

Rochford leaned back in his chair and drawled, "I'd wondered if that was the reason for Stephen Howard's visit to Beaulieu. So he's feeding information to his stepdaughter. Interesting."

"You know about that?" Minuette asked.

With surprising sharpness, Dominic said, "Does someone want to tell me what the Penitent's Confession is?"

"A Catholic rumour," Rochford said. "A claim that one of my sister's household had, on his or—more likely—her deathbed, sworn an affidavit that Henry was not William's father. It's a tissue of lies wrapped in whispers."

"That is not a whisper pinned to the king's bed," Dominic said flatly, meeting Rochford's stare with one of his own. "Minuette, how did you come to hear of this?"

"As Lord Rochford said, while I was at Beaulieu the Lady Mary was visited by my stepfather, Stephen Howard. He spoke to me privately and offered warning that the Catholics are looking for this affidavit. He wanted me to . . . well, to speak for him. To assure the court that he personally has no ill intentions toward the king, whatever his family might do."

"So Norfolk lied to us." Elizabeth spoke softly, but William heard the steel in her words. He nodded at his sister to go on, and she said to their uncle, "Can one falsely sworn affidavit truly be that dangerous? Surely it has been so long ago that everyone would greet it as the mere ravings of the discontented, even if it is not an obvious forgery."

"I do not think you appreciate how deeply resentment of your mother still runs. Make no mistake—religion may be the driving force, but Anne has always been the flash point. If William had not been born a boy . . . if Henry had not been so taken with his healthy son—" Rochford broke off, his face dark with anger and—could it be fear? William wondered. Or the memory of fear? "Anne came perilously close to losing more than just her crown in the year before William's birth. Henry was always unpredictable and easily persuaded in his tempers. So yes, niece, this affidavit could be truly dangerous—and I assure you that the forgery will not be obvious—dangerous enough that we must keep it out of Norfolk's hands at all costs or it will be used to raise an army for Mary and drive us out once and for all."

"Why can't Norfolk simply create his own false affidavit that meets these criteria?" Elizabeth replied. "We're allowing him the opportunity, what with Mary being in his household the remainder of the summer."

"He's always had the opportunity," William said. "Mary being there won't change that. But if Minuette's stepfather is correct that his brother is searching for it, that implies that Norfolk believes it's a true document, one not currently in his possession. And if he has evidence for his search . . . that might lead us to further conspirators."

In the silence that fell, Dominic alone moved. He stood and walked to the bedchamber. "What are you doing?" William asked.

"I'm going to lay a fire and burn that message. And if I might make a suggestion?"

William nodded.

"Keep your bedchamber guarded even when you are not in it."

Dominic didn't have to say why. Only a very limited number had access to William's bedchamber in any case.

Which meant that whoever had left that message—and the knife—was someone he knew well.

CHAPTER ELEVEN

I N A LIFETIME of long days, Dominic thought, this one was the longest. He was late into the great hall for the dancing. By that time he was so keyed up from lack of sleep, long days of travel, and the events of the day that he had to keep blinking himself into reality. Every time someone called him Exeter, it took a breath or two for him to answer. He kept expecting someone to tap him on the shoulder and tell him it had all been a mistake.

He felt he had accomplished little enough in Europe, and so he had claimed last night at the final gathering of the regency council. But in spite of the general resentment of the French, the lords had been gracious in their thanks, and even Rochford had unbent so far as to shake his hand and say softly, "Never underestimate the power of backstairs diplomacy."

Dominic suspected that the next encounter with France would have little to do with diplomacy, backstairs or not. He had seen the look in William's eyes and knew his king was itching for the opportunity to fight the French. The next move was Henri's—and Dominic planned to keep in good fighting condition until then. Like William, he preferred the thought of an open battlefield in France to the twists and uneasiness of the

Penitent's Confession and Catholic conspiracies. Better to face off against a known enemy than brood over a hidden one. Rochford could do the latter well enough—as he had pointed out earlier. "Let me monitor conditions for a few weeks," he'd concluded after Dominic had burnt the banner. "I am not certain it is wise to allow Lady Mary to continue on to Framlingham with Norfolk."

"I think it is," William had said with conviction. "Most important, I gave her my word. She came to chapel with me—and managed to acknowledge my mother without throwing anything. Her reward is a stay with Norfolk. And if we wish to draw out the enemy, we must give him space. If we give her a measure of liberty in this, the traitor may very well be drawn out. Especially if it is Norfolk."

He's starting to think like Rochford, Dominic thought, and didn't know if he was pleased or not. Normally he would celebrate any restraint from William—but while restraint was one thing, cold-blooded calculation could be turned to something else entirely.

When he at last entered the great hall, his eyes went straight to Minuette with the unerring instinct of a man besotted. She positively glowed in a dress of shot silk that swirled through every shade of blue and green when she moved. She spoke to a young man that Dominic recognized as Jonathan Percy, her head tilted to the side in a manner that made his chest ache.

"How is the newest peer of the realm?" William came up next to him, sounding remarkably pleased with himself.

"I'm not sure I'll ever learn to answer to Exeter." Dominic smiled a little. "Thank you. It was as generous as it was unexpected."

William shrugged, but Dominic did not miss the satisfaction in his eyes. "It was for my sake as much as yours. I need you independent. You now rival Norfolk and Northumberland as a landowner."

"And you don't mind tweaking their noses a bit."

"Not at all." William grinned. "But that doesn't take away from the fact that you've earned it. There is no man on this earth I trust more than you."

William uttered the words easily enough, but they struck Dominic with a force he would not have expected. For the first time since his father's death, he felt the weight of his family's disgrace slip away, and in that moment it was not William he saw before him but his king.

"I live only to be worthy of that trust, Your Majesty."

William clapped him on the shoulder. "Now, tell me about France—and not the boring diplomatic details. Plenty of pretty women at Henri's court, I'll wager."

Minuette rushed back into Dominic's mind, and he answered automatically while his eyes searched the room for her. "Very pretty."

There was a long silence, broken by William's unregal snort. "That's it? Really, Dom, it is possible to take discretion too far."

But Dominic's roaming eyes had lighted on Minuette, dancing now. "Does Percy spend a lot of time with Minuette?"

"Still playing big brother? Jonathan Percy is harmless enough. A musician—I stole him away from the Bishop of Winchester. He composed the music for this morning's service."

Dominic, who had not the faintest idea of what this morning's music had been, nodded vaguely while William continued. "He spends all his spare time writing sonnets to Minuette."

Feeling a trickle of ice along his veins, Dominic asked, "Is he serious?"

"He's asked for her, if that's what you mean."

It was as though all the colours in the room had dimmed suddenly. "They're betrothed," Dominic said flatly.

"You'd have to ask Minuette that. I told Percy he'd need her permission before he gained mine. But she seems to like him well enough. Young, poor, poetic—yes, I imagine she'll take him."

The fog that seemed to have descended on Dominic spread, deadening both sight and sound. He was hardly aware of William moving away, and if the king said anything else before leaving, he did not hear it. The only thing he could see clearly was Minuette's coronet of burnished hair as she left the hall on Jonathan Percy's arm.

No doubt they would walk in the gardens or somewhere else a little more private. No doubt Percy had things of a personal nature to say to her. No doubt he was as certain of her answer as William was.

In an instant, the adrenaline that had buoyed Dominic through this day vanished, and he was left feeling exhausted. He had thought only about himself. He had never considered that she might fall in love with someone else.

As he stared unseeing across the hall, he felt a near overpowering urge to follow her. No, not just follow her—stop her. He need only ask to speak to her. She would not deny him that.

And then . . . what? Dominic knew he could be persuasive. He had titles and wealth and royal kinship on his side. Any other woman would gladly dismiss Jonathan Percy in favour of a marquis.

But Minuette wasn't any other woman. Oh, he might be able to convince her, for he knew her weaknesses—already he could hear sentences forming in his head, the effortless manipulation of her emotions and loyalties. He could do it, he thought; he could tear her away from Jonathan Percy.

But he wouldn't. Though he felt as though his bones might crack beneath the burden of jealous desire, he would not override her choice. If she wanted Percy, she must have him. William had left her free to answer for herself—Dominic would do no less.

Minuette knew she could not avoid Jonathan forever. So, determined not to let nerves get the better of her, she sought him out as soon as she reached the great hall. He greeted her as he always did—with a mix of awe and gratitude that she had always found pleasing. But tonight she could not help contrasting his shy and halting words with the easy conversation of William or Dominic.

Such a comparison was laughable. William and Dominic were her friends, the nearest thing she had to brothers—of course they conversed easily with her. They didn't even think of her as a woman.

She smiled and laughed and danced with Jonathan and acquiesced when he asked her to walk in the gardens. It was only when they reached the quietness of the riverbank and Jonathan turned her to look at him that she grew nervous.

He told her of his audience with the king and of William's permission to proceed. Minuette kept her eyes modestly lowered while Jonathan's voice strengthened. He spoke of her beauty, and her kindness, and her virtue, in words that flowed ever more easily as the poet in him took over. And when he grasped her hands in his and asked her to marry him, she looked up, prepared to make him happy.

But as she looked in his eyes—a light, clear blue that surprised her for some reason—the ready words died away and she felt again that faint panic closing off her throat.

"I . . . I don't know what to say." That much, at least, was true. She saw his hurt, deep and immediate, and hastened to ease it. "I do care for you, very much. And I thought I was ready for this. But . . ." *I'm frightened,* she wanted to cry, *and I don't want to hurt anyone.*

He released her hands and said stiffly, "I would never presume to offer any addresses I did not feel were welcome."

Stricken by the look in his eyes, Minuette said, "They are not unwelcome. It is myself I am unsure of, not you. Would you give me a little time to think? A day, even?"

She fixed him with a pleading look. When he moved away, Minuette clung to his arm and tilted her head in appeal. She could not bear for him to leave unhappy.

He hesitated, then reached out one hand to cup her chin. "You look just like a bird when you do that. A most enchanting bird."

Minuette had wondered what it would be like to be willingly kissed. She closed her eyes as Jonathan's lips, soft and dry, brushed against hers. It was not quite what she'd expected—her breathing did not falter and her heart continued to beat its normal rhythm—but it was pleasant enough.

They did not linger by the river. Jonathan escorted her back to the great hall, where he bowed himself away with a kindness that only increased Minuette's guilt. She nearly went after him, but her nerve failed her. She was not prepared to say yes. Not yet.

She looked around the crush of courtiers, wondering if she should find Elizabeth and excuse herself for the night. There was an ache behind her eyes and she felt a great need for quiet.

She found Dominic, watching her unsmilingly as he leaned against the far wall. In an instinct she did not stop to analyze, she headed straight for him.

"Come dance with me, Dominic," she said, her heart pounding an unfamiliar rhythm.

Dominic shook his head. And when Minuette laid a hand on his arm, he stepped away and made a bow in her general direction before turning and vanishing into the crowd.

All at once, her confused emotions crystallized into clear anger. What did he mean, ignoring her like this? What had happened to his earlier happiness?

It was easy to track his dark head, as he was taller than almost everyone around him. He moved rapidly, and Minuette had to catch up her skirts to keep pace. He went down the stairs and wound his way through courtyards and doorways and arches until they were in a part of Hampton Court she'd never been before. Narrow lanes carved between brick buildings that, by the smell of things, housed kitchens and storehouses. The pastry house was all right, with its heat and scent of bread and sweets, but soon she was wrinkling her nose at the overwhelming smell of fresh game and fish. Servants brushed past with platters of sweetmeats and trays of comfits. Minuette ignored the stares directed at her, though she did look up at the rumble of thunder overhead. It was too dark to tell if rain was imminent.

Dominic turned a corner, and Minuette thought she'd lost him. But when she rounded the corner, he was waiting, with arms crossed and a scowl that would frighten off most women.

"What do you think you are doing traipsing around these lanes in a dress that cost more than these people will see in their lifetimes?" Dominic had always liked to lecture.

The tone of his voice called up her own combative instincts. "I wouldn't be traipsing around if you hadn't run away from me as though I had the plague."

Something flared in his eyes. "I didn't ask you to follow."

"Dominic, why are you angry?" His mouth opened, as if to deny it, and she rushed on. "Yes, you are angry at me. What has happened?"

"You're imagining things."

Her temper increased at the flat denial. "You're a rotten liar, Dominic. However did you manage as a diplomat?"

Even in the shadows of the torchlit alley she could see his cheeks darken, and she was momentarily sorry.

But only momentarily, for he said, "I hear you're betrothed to Eleanor's brother. I imagine you'll quite enjoy family gatherings with Giles Howard."

Minuette let out a gasp, feeling as though he had hit her. Almost at once Dominic apologized. "That was unforgivable. My temper got the better of me."

"Then you admit you are angry."

At last he let out a long sigh and shook his head. "Only with myself. I wanted something and, in my arrogance, made no effort to secure it. And now it is too late."

Minuette searched the face she knew better than her own and felt a faint prickling at the ends of her fingers. "What did you want?"

Dominic uncrossed his arms and moved forward until Minuette was forced to step back. She stopped only when her back came up against the wall. She spared a thought for the condition of her gown, pressed up against the smoky yellow brick, but she couldn't concentrate. Rain began to fall, cool against her flushed skin.

He put his hands flat on the wall on either side of her shoulders and leaned in so near that she could feel his breath. His eyes were like liquid emeralds and his hair fell in curved wings around his face.

His voice came soft and clear. "Do you love him?"

"What?" Minuette had to scramble to think what he meant. "Who?"

"The Percy boy. Do you love him?"

The thought of Jonathan Percy seemed unbelievably distant, as though she were struggling to remember a mere acquaintance, not a man who had kissed her in the dark a short time ago.

Dominic stepped back so suddenly that, although he had not touched her, Minuette felt that a support had been withdrawn. Beneath the yards of heavy silk, her legs quivered and she had to will them to keep her upright. The wall at her back helped a little.

When he spoke again, it was with the distant courtesy of the court. "Forgive me. You need not answer that. He, of course, is in love with you. A desirable quality in a husband."

She swallowed hard and tried to think of a sensible reply. Just then a servant bustled into the lane and stopped cold, his expression comical as he looked between her and Dominic. No doubt the poor man was wondering what he had interrupted.

Minuette was wondering quite the same thing.

In that same infuriatingly remote voice, Dominic said, "Do you wish to return to the dancing?"

"No, I . . . my chamber will do."

It was just as well Dominic walked with her, for Minuette still had no clear idea of where she was. But for all the company he gave, she might as well have asked a servant to escort her. He did not so much as take her arm.

When they reached her door, Dominic bowed and turned away. She could not bear it—she could not let him leave without even a word. She took a step forward and laid her hand on his arm.

He turned slowly and she bit her lip, waiting for his eyes to meet hers. But he did not look at her face. He stared at her hand as he lifted it off his sleeve into his own. She shivered as her fingertips went from the velvet of his doublet to the warmth of his skin.

Why was she breathing so hard? She was quite accustomed to having her hand kissed, and it had never roused in her anything but amusement. Certainly not the trembling that had now seized her entire arm.

With exquisite care, Dominic turned her hand so that it rested palm upward, cradled in his. He raised it and Minuette drew in her breath, waiting for the touch of his lips against her palm.

His mouth came to rest, soft and gentle, on the inside of her wrist.

The sensation was so completely unexpected that Minuette thought her heart had stopped. How was it that a touch on her wrist could send waves through parts of her body completely unrelated to either hands or arms?

And now, finally, he was looking at her. Caught in his dark, insistent gaze, she realized how she must look—hair curling damply from the rain, cheeks burning, lips parted. Above her self-consciousness, she felt the tension of opposing wishes—to stay in this moment forever, or to plunge headlong into whatever it was that came next.

The bell's toll sounded sharp and loud, shattering the silence in which they'd been wrapped. At the first peal, Dominic dropped her hand and jerked away as if he'd been burnt. The bell continued tolling, slowly at first, and then with a rising urgency.

He swore softly. "I have to go."

She managed a nod. Dominic opened his mouth, then tightened his lips, as if restraining words he wanted to say. She watched him stride firmly away to whatever emergency the bell was signaling. He did not look back.

William paced the length of his privy chamber, the beat of temper in his head matching the rhythm of the sounding bell. Rochford watched him in quiet stillness, his eyes hooded.

Within a quarter hour the gentlemen of the council were assembled, Dominic amongst them. The men were grim-faced and silent as they faced their king, and in spite of the seriousness of what he had to say, William felt a brief shiver of pleasure that not one had looked to Rochford.

He had rehearsed his words while he waited. "I have received a message from the French. Henri's armies have taken possession of Guînes."

Guînes was a town long ceded to the English, and, looking from one lord to the next, William could see the same sweep of emotions he'd been through in the past hour. Northumberland was outraged, Norfolk was angry but already calculating what came next, Dominic . . .

Dominic looked blank, and William wondered if he'd even heard him.

He let his voice rise a notch. "I have expelled Henri's ambassador. At dawn he will be on his way to France. And so shall we."

It was an exaggeration, of course, for the kind of expedition William planned could not get under way in less than a month.

But he could send a small coterie ahead immediately, and he wasted no time giving orders.

"Lord Northumberland, you have charge of the muster. A thousand knights on horse and ten thousand men-at-arms assembled and ready by mid-July. Lord Sussex is your second."

He looked next to Dominic. "Lord Exeter, you will command the advance. Choose two dozen men. I want you in Calais in one week."

There would be further orders, of course, more precise instructions on what he wanted accomplished and when. But William knew by instinct that the best thing was to send them off roused and ready and not to cool their blood with details just yet.

He felt again that rise of triumph as the lords bowed and took their leave. Rochford was amongst the last to go. Bestowing one of his rare smiles on William, his uncle said simply, "Well done, Your Majesty."

Only Dominic was left, still looking rather stunned. "Dom? I need you moving now."

His eyes cleared. "Yes, Your Majesty."

"Dominic?" William's voice stopped him at the door. "If you were any older, I'd have given you charge of the entire campaign. I can't push Northumberland too far—not yet. But yours is the advice I'll be listening to."

Once he was alone, William could feel the anger he had leashed beginning to threaten his restraint. If Henri thought he would be cowed by the threat of battle, he was wrong. The blood pounded in his ears, and he felt as though he might jump out a window just to unleash some of his tension.

With a clap of his hands, he summoned a page hovering outside the privy chamber and sent him to tell Mistress Howard that the king wished to see her.

29 June 1554
Hampton Court

It is dawn, and once more I'm writing by the first light of morning.
How could I have known that between one sunrise and the next,
everything would change?

I didn't know I could feel like this. I didn't know anyone could feel
like this. I've been so superior this last year, wondering how Alyce
could have been so weak as to get with child. But if the bells had not
rung last night . . .

I watched Dominic ride out an hour ago. We are at war, it seems,
and naturally Dominic will be in the midst of it. He looked up just
before leaving and seemed to see straight through the shadows to the
window where I stood. It can only have been my imagination that his
mouth softened into a smile, for I could not see that clearly in the
darkness.

It was not my imagination. I know he smiled.

CHAPTER TWELVE

Dispatches from Dominic Courtenay, Marquis of Exeter,

to Henry IX, King of England

5 July 1554

We are keeping to the security of Calais while our numbers are few. The officials here have little more knowledge than do we—that the French took possession of Guînes ten days ago with no warning and meeting only a minimal resistance. I will ride out tomorrow and see for myself. I cannot imagine that the population is happy about the change of control. I know that the citizens of Calais are unhappy about the French armies being only six miles away.

7 July 1554

Calais

The French give every appearance of being firmly en-trenched at Guînes, but I suspect their troops are not deep. The banner over the castle is that of Michel St. Pierre, a man of more bluster than skill. I cannot fathom why Henri would entrust such a man with command—unless this occupation was a casual idea that Henri never expected to succeed. If so, he will have been almost as surprised as we were when Guînes fell, and he will be less prepared for war than we expected. All to our advantage, if we can move quickly.

11 July 1554
Calais

I believe Guînes will fall quickly and we should know beforehand what we mean to do after. If you wish to press Henri, you will never have a better opportunity. Guînes has received no reinforcements, which tells me Henri is scrambling for troops. Best weigh your options now, so you can issue commands without delay.

18 July 1554

The first of the light cavalry disembarked yesterday and the heavy cavalry is expected with Northumberland tomorrow. We have left Calais for our preliminary encampment, two miles north of Guînes. We will be ready to lay siege within days. I expect Northumberland will be able to inform me of your intended arrival. Until then ...

Dominic

The wind, hot and relentless, tugged fitfully at Dominic as he strode across the encampment. As far as he could see were men and tents and horses, banners whipping bright colours across the hard blue sky of early August—the green and gold of the Dudleys, the sable and silver of Sussex, the gold wings of the Seymours. And above them all, flying proudly from Guînes castle itself, the English royal banner.

St. Pierre had proven himself as incompetent a commander as Dominic had predicted. After ten days of siege, rather than wait and see how far he could test English resolve, the French commander had sent his garrison outside the walls to try to fight their way through to reinforcements. The encounter had been short and sharp, and the townspeople of Guînes had cheered when William rode triumphantly through the gates.

As Dominic walked up the short incline from the outer wall to the castle gate, he could see the signs of undisciplined soldiers all around him—from the smashed glass of looted shops to the wary glances of the populace. Though they had welcomed William, they no doubt feared the English troops as much as the French ones.

The forecourt of the small castle was thick with riders carrying dispatches to the ships that sailed between Calais and Dover. The weather had been with them thus far, and communication had been straightforward. Dominic was escorted to the utilitarian hall where William stood at a table with Northumberland, overlooking maps and discussing terrain. Though they had narrowed the possibilities for attack down to two, William had still to make the final decision.

Dominic joined in the debate, deferring to Northumberland. John Dudley, or "Black Jack," as he was often known, was a talented field commander, clear-sighted and canny. Also, Dominic happened to agree with Northumberland in this case. One option was to push forward out of Guînes and teach the French a lesson by taking some of their towns along the path to Paris. It was what the English had done for a century in the last war—there were towns within forty miles of Calais that had changed hands a dozen times during the Hundred Years' War. Which meant it was expected.

The unexpected option was to leave a small force of men to bolster the Guînes garrison, sail away with the rest—not to England, but just far enough off the French coast so as not to be spotted—and head south to the new port city of Le Havre-de-Grâce. It was an extension of Harfleur, a city that Henry V had once famously captured. Besides being unexpected, Le Havre had the great advantage of lying on the Seine. If they could hold that port, they could move upriver to Rouen and thence to Paris.

William liked that option because of the romance and glory of his ancestor's victory. Dominic liked it because it meant not getting bogged down in sieges, which brought all the dangers of supply lines and disease to their camps. So it wasn't a huge surprise when, after an hour of dutifully weighing the advantages of each action, William chose Le Havre. Northumberland left with orders to begin the loading of the ships first thing in the morning.

William sat back beneath the hastily arranged cloth of state. Eyeing Dominic, he asked, "Assuming we catch Le Havre off guard and take it quickly, what will we face at Rouen after?"

"Depends on how quickly we move and how quickly the French figure it out. They'll make a stand at Rouen if at all possible."

"Under whose command?"

"It has to be Renaud LeClerc. They have no one who can touch him."

"Have we?"

Dominic shrugged. "I know him, and that helps. A bit."

William nodded and stood up once more, restless with unspent energy. "I have something for you. Percy brought it with him from Greenwich."

Dominic thought he had heard wrong. "Jonathan Percy?"

"He arrived an hour ago."

Dominic chose his words with care, trying not to let personal displeasure colour his arguments. "Why? Your army needs men who can fight, not those who may or may not stand their ground."

"Percy can fight." William must have seen the flare of skepticism in Dominic's eyes, for he said emphatically, "Truly, he can fight. Not as well as you, but then few can. He's sturdy with a lance and he doesn't flinch—I made sure of that. He'll do well enough."

"I'm surprised Eleanor didn't beg you to leave her brother behind." Dominic dared not think of another woman pleading for Percy.

"I would have left him—to be honest, I hadn't even thought of him—but there he was, laying a sword before me and begging to offer his service. It will be good for him," William said. "Find a place for him, won't you, Dom? There must be room amongst your own."

William had at last located what he was looking for in the pile of letters and maps—a parcel wrapped in plain cloth. "From the girls," he said, tossing the soft weight into Dominic's hands.

The first item Dominic pulled out was a tunic, sized loosely to fit over armour, the padded gold silk embroidered with the red discs and blue lions of the Courtenays. The second piece was thinner and longer—a pennon blazoned with the same colours. His father's colours.

Dominic found it unexpectedly hard to speak. "Thank you, William."

It took him a moment to realize that something was missing—something he had expected to see. He picked up the tunic once more and inspected it closely. "There's no crescent."

William shook his head. "You are no longer the cadet branch of the family, Dom."

But the cadet branch sprang from the younger sons, such as his father. Even though Dominic's uncle was dead ... "My cousin Edward still lives. He is the oldest heir to the title."

"And has been granted new arms as Viscount Lisle. You are Marquis of Exeter, and you bear no mark of cadency. Nor will your son, when one day he flies those colours."

Before Dominic could think of an appropriate reply—any reply—William handed him something else. "A letter, as well. From Minuette."

With the sealed letter burning in his hand, Dominic left. He nodded as he passed the squires standing guard outside the hall; then his eyes went to a figure, sitting still and braced on a bench in the corridor.

With a curt gesture, Dominic motioned Jonathan Percy up. "The king has placed you in my service, Percy. Walk with me."

As they passed through the darkening town, Dominic glanced sidelong at the shorter, younger man and said, "What possessed you to come to France? You're a musician, not a soldier."

"I ask only to render what service I can."

"You think to return home covered in glory? Have you ever even seen a battlefield? Precious little glory in mud and death."

Percy's voice remained measured. "One wonders, then, why men such as yourself continue to seek it out."

Dominic stopped walking and faced Percy straight on. "You want to see battle? Fine. You may carry my standard. Wherever I go, you follow. That should cure you of your fantasies."

"Fantasies, my lord?"

"I've no time for a man who thinks only of impressing his betrothed. You want to impress Mistress Wyatt? Return home in one piece."

Even by firelight, Dominic could see Percy's jaw tighten. "Is that all, my lord?"

"For now. Find a spot with my men. I'll see you at dawn."

Alone in his tent, Dominic rolled his head, easing the knots of tension in his shoulders. He needed to give Harrington orders, to start the process of packing up his men and horses and weapons to take ship once more. But first . . . He laid the tunic and pennon on his bed, and the single candle picked out shards of colour as he moved—gold, red, and azure. Atop the tunic lay Minuette's letter, the oval of the silver seal seeming to watch him like a great, unblinking eye.

Since riding out from Hampton Court, he had refused to dwell on what had passed between them, since there was absolutely nothing he could do about it while he was campaigning. And also because he wasn't sure how much importance he could attach to it. Nothing had been said or done that could not be ignored. Only a moment in time when everything vanished and they two were alone in the world.

Never had Dominic been nearer losing his head completely than while standing in that corridor with Minuette. He had been unable to stop himself kissing her wrist where the fine blue veins traced their path beneath the white skin. He had felt her tremble, her hand shivering in his. He had not dared think of it since, partly because it was too precious a memory for everyday handling, and partly because he didn't know how morning's light had affected Minuette. He would stake his life that she had seen his desire that night. And he wanted to believe that, in that moment, she had been willing. But when morning came and he was gone, and she was brought up against the promise she had made to Jonathan . . .

He took up the letter and broke the seal.

The first page contained a drawing, an exquisitely shaded rendering of his entire coat of arms. The gold escutcheon, quartered and bearing the red torteaux of the Courtenays and the azure lions that sprang from his grandmother's royal blood, surmounted by an earl's coronet and a rising dolphin. And beneath it all, the motto.

When Dominic read the Latin words, he closed his eyes and smiled. He should have known she would remember.

He could see her face, bright and eager before him—eleven years old and chattering like a magpie after Dominic's first tournament. He'd been tired and sore and ridiculously disappointed that he hadn't won. Minuette's voice had flowed around him in a stream of words he did not bother to decipher.

At last she'd plucked on his sleeve. "I asked you a question," she said.

"Sorry. What was it?"

"Why do you not use your father's coat of arms? Why wear plain gold with no decoration?"

"I am not head of the Courtenay family. My cousin Edward is that."

Minuette let out an impatient breath. "And your father's arms carried the mark of cadency. This is nothing to do with your cousin. It's because of your father himself."

He turned back to his horse as Minuette hurried on. "Nothing was ever proved against him. And even if it had been, you were not at fault."

He stared at nothing while he answered her. "Do you think I take pride in the fact that my father managed to die before he came to trial? Even a whisper of suspicion is too much. Do you know what he wrote to King Henry from his imprisonment? *Ubi lapsus? Quid feci?*"

He could see her trying to work out the Latin in her head, and he translated impatiently. "It means 'Whither have I fallen? What have I done?'"

She saw at once what he meant. "That isn't necessarily a confession. He might have been truly asking what offense he had caused."

Dominic took the reins of his horse to lead him back to the stables. "Perhaps. It is not good enough for me. If ever I can bear his arms in honour, I will take that as my motto. I will blazon it for all the world to see, so that everyone will know I am not my father. I keep my fealty."

He opened his eyes and was once again in his tent on a hot and windy plain in France. Laying aside the drawing, he read the brief note on the second page.

I am not betrothed.

Elizabeth sat in her brother's presence chamber at Greenwich Palace, listening to Sir Oliver Lytle complain about his men being mustered to guard the Scots border. As he droned on about his crops going to waste if he and his men were not released before September, Elizabeth let her mind wander away from the sunny chamber in which she sat to the more pleasant memories of Robert's farewell three weeks ago.

"Regent?" Robert had said, laughing. "What a blow to Rochford. The Lord Chancellor must answer to a woman while William's away."

With that narrow, focused gaze that always made her feel as if Robert saw straight through her, he'd asked, "Your brother values you. Are you never tempted to find out how highly? To ask a favour of him that no one else could grant?"

She had forced herself to look away from those probing, knowing eyes and said, "My only desire is to serve my brother and England as best I may."

Robert had slid along the garden bench, until she shivered at the touch of his breath along her neck as he whispered, "Not quite your only desire."

"Your Highness?" Lytle's rough voice startled Elizabeth out of memory and back into the ornate presence chamber.

"Yes, Sir Oliver." Elizabeth did not wait for him to begin his complaints all over again. "I shall review your demands with Lord Rochford, but I remind you that we are at war and not inclined to any request for release of fighting men."

His round cheeks went scarlet with temper and he opened his mouth, no doubt to argue some more. Elizabeth cut him off. "We will inform you of our decision tomorrow."

He had no choice but to bow and leave, though even his back looked affronted as he stalked out. Elizabeth turned to her steward. "Is that all, Paget?"

"Lord Rochford is waiting for you without."

"Very well."

With a perfunctory bow, her uncle entered and handed over a sheaf of papers. "Dispatches from Surrey."

Elizabeth glanced quickly through them. The Earl of Surrey was charged with holding the Scots border and had been sending daily dispatches with his outriders. "No movement?" she asked.

"No. It seems the Scots are biding their time—or perhaps they've learnt discretion."

"Speaking of discretion," Elizabeth said, laying aside the papers and fixing her uncle with a steady gaze, "what news from Framlingham?"

The day after William's birthday, Mary had departed Hampton Court in company with the Duke of Norfolk for his castle near the eastern coast. Preoccupied as he had been with planning a war, William had passed the burden of watching the Catholics to his uncle. There had been little word thus far, but

Elizabeth knew that if she were in charge of a rebellion, this would be precisely the time she would choose, with the king and his army out of the country.

Rochford huffed in irritation—at the situation, she thought, rather than at her. "The lady spends her days in prayer and study, and Norfolk spends his in solitude. He is aging fast, I hear, and we can only hope that is a result of his fading hopes."

"Then they do not as yet have the Penitent's Confession?"

"Unlikely. I've had no hints of men gathering anywhere in Norfolk lands or in other Catholic strongholds. If they had the Penitent's Confession, I would expect them to use the king's absence as the perfect opportunity to strike. As it is, most of them have turned out soldiers for France. The war seems to be temporarily uniting us."

"Are we any nearer to tracking down the Confession?" Elizabeth was curious about her uncle's network of spies and how they worked, but he was generally vague.

"Your mother had quite a number of women in her household, even during the relatively brief time before William was conceived. The records the court holds are not always complete, so it's taking time to check through each name—and then widen the net to see who in that lady's web of relationships might have put her name to evil use."

Elizabeth tipped her head, curious. "You do not think it quicker to ask my mother for her records and perhaps her own knowledge of the women who served her?"

The black stare she got in return was answer enough, but Rochford said anyway, "This does not reach Anne's ears. Ever. Do I make myself clear?"

While wondering what William would say to such a command, Elizabeth merely nodded. "You are very clear, Uncle."

Rochford jerked his head in acknowledgment. "As for Scotland, I've prepared a dispatch for Surrey, telling him our intelligence sources are quiet and he should continue as he's begun along the border. Have you anything to add to that, Your Highness?"

He was already turned to the door as he asked, clearly expecting her to say no. Piqued by his easy dismissal, Elizabeth made an instant decision. "Yes. Tell him Sir Oliver Lytle will be returning to the front lines to lead his men. Tell him Lytle's forces are to remain in the muster as long as the crown so pleases."

One of her uncle's best qualities was his sense of humour, sardonic though it may be. The corners of his mouth lifted. "Shall I inform Sir Oliver, or will you?"

"You may do so."

Rochford bowed himself away, and Elizabeth waved her steward out of the room as well. She had never appreciated that ruling meant being surrounded by more people than even she was accustomed to. No wonder William delighted in hiding away in his private bedchamber with only Eleanor for company. It was the solitude he craved.

Still, in spite of the drawbacks, she admitted to herself that ruling also had its pleasures. Though she had long ago assumed control of her own household, there was something intoxicating in making decisions for a wider realm. She was not immune to the charms of power.

Not that this particular power would last for long. William would come home and Elizabeth would return to her own domestic affairs. A pity, for she could see that she had a talent for rule. If she was lucky, William would marry her off to a man of power, one who might be generous enough to share it—or could be influenced to do so. She would not mind that.

And yet, in spite of that wish, her desires betrayed her ambition every time she thought of Robert, every time she worried for his safety in France. Every time she closed her eyes and felt his hands and his lips as he'd bidden her an indiscreet goodbye six days ago, murmuring in her ear, "I like powerful women."

Elizabeth's eyes snapped open when Paget cleared his throat in the doorway. "Forgive me, Your Highness. A most urgent message for you from Hever."

"A message for you, milady," the boy said, bowing so low Minuette could not see his face.

She had long ago given up trying to correct the younger, more nervous of the servants, who seemed convinced that any woman who spent as much time as she did with royalty surely must have a title.

The boy gave his message without raising his eyes from the floor. "Her Highness, Princess Elizabeth, asks that you join her at once in His Majesty's presence chamber."

She left the room on the boy's heels but, for his sake, slowed her pace slightly to allow him to escape her. As she walked through the sparsely populated corridors, she marveled at how empty Greenwich seemed without the men. Many of the women had left court as well, seeing little point in spending money to impress young men who were absent.

Eleanor, at least, was still here, in the apartments William had set aside for her use last year. If Minuette had been regent, she'd have locked her out and sent her straight back home. But Elizabeth seemed unconcerned about Eleanor's continuing presence. "Let William deal with her as he wishes," she'd warned Minuette in their one and only conversation on the subject. "He would not thank either of us for interfering." Elizabeth was right in that, so Minuette had held her peace and avoided Eleanor as thoroughly as possible.

Which was why she breathed out a silent curse when she heard a door open before her, from Eleanor's apartments. She had only an instant to compose herself to haughtiness before a man stepped into the hall directly into her path. It was Giles Howard, straightening his tunic and looking for all the world as though he'd just come from something more than conversation with his wife.

It was the nearest she'd been to Giles since that night at Hampton Court when he'd—before Dominic—

But Giles didn't give her a chance to think long on Dominic. "Mistress Wyatt," he said, managing to make even her name an insult.

She stared back evenly, as she had learnt from Queen Anne. Giles was dressed for riding and Minuette remembered that he was supposed to be in the North, supporting his nephew, the Earl of Surrey, along the Scots border.

He seemed in no hurry to return to the Scots. "Must be lonely for you with all your young men away. Jonathan being the least of them."

She was surprised into replying. "You need not concern yourself with my affairs."

"Affairs?" His smile was cold, and Minuette realized that he had hardened in the last year—his features were sharper and his stance more confident. "What a well-chosen word. I'm afraid I can't help but concern myself with the . . . affairs of a woman who will shortly be my sister-in-law."

Minuette nearly told him that she had refused Jonathan, but she swallowed her retort. Her personal life was none of his business.

In any case, he seemed more interested in talking than listening. "Jonathan is such an innocent. He's probably never imagined just what it is you do with your dear friend William behind closed doors."

He took half a step nearer, until his face was only inches from her own. "And what of the bold new Marquis of Exeter? Tell me, do they take you in turn, or is it both at once?"

Without pausing to consider, Minuette slapped him with all the force she could muster. Giles's face snapped to the side, the imprint of her palm stamped against his cheek.

"Little hellcat," Giles said, catching her still-raised arm.

She had not even time to feel afraid before footsteps and a commanding voice came from behind Giles.

"Is there a problem?" Lord Rochford asked, surveying the two of them with what appeared to be absolute indifference.

Giles released her arm and stepped back. "Not at all."

"Mistress Wyatt?" Rochford turned to her.

Not for anything would she have repeated those vile slanders to that cool, composed face. Curling her lip in a practiced manner, Minuette looked at Giles and said, "A misunderstanding. He had me confused with his wife."

As Giles turned scarlet and Rochford assessed her, Minuette heard the door open once more. Wishing she had the nerve to curse aloud, she held her chin high. Damned if she would cower before either of the Howards.

But it was not Eleanor in the open doorway. It was Lady Rochford, staring straight into her husband's eyes with a bitter humour she did not bother to mask. Lord Rochford held his wife's gaze with a hint of a smile playing across his lips.

It was he who spoke first. "You found your own rooms unsuitable?"

Lady Rochford raised her eyebrows, the only movement in the smooth whiteness of her unlined face. "A change of locale does add a certain spice to things."

Minuette had to clamp her mouth tight to keep from gaping. What did they mean? Was Lord Rochford implying . . . Lady Rochford and Giles Howard? But she was so old. And, stupid as Giles was, surely he wasn't stupid enough to seduce the wife of the most powerful man in the kingdom.

But Giles seemed . . . Minuette had to look twice to be sure. Where she expected to see fear, she found only grim amusement and that unnerving confidence. Rather, she realized, like Rochford himself.

And Rochford did not seem disposed to make an issue of it. "Howard, I have dispatches for Surrey. We'll have you on your way within the hour."

Thoroughly bewildered, Minuette stared after them as they walked away. What was going on between Lord Rochford and Giles Howard?

Or, for that matter, between Giles and Lady Rochford, who said now, "You needn't look so shocked, girl. A woman has one power in this world. If you're wise, you learn to use it to your advantage."

With a gaze that was disconcertingly like her husband's, Lady Rochford looked Minuette over before shutting the door behind her and walking rapidly away.

Shaken by the encounter, Minuette withdrew into the nearest convenient alcove and perched upon a window ledge. Elizabeth would have to wait until she could present herself without any trace of distress.

It had been a miserably sordid encounter all around. Giles's questions, Lord Rochford's veiled barbs, Lady Rochford's unwelcome advice—all had left Minuette feeling contaminated and uneasy.

With one insult, Giles had managed to insinuate his nastiness into the most precious of her memories—that moment in the corridor at Hampton Court, when she and Dominic had looked at each other as though they alone existed. After Dominic had left her that night, she had flung herself onto her bed in her rain-ruined gown and hugged the sweetness of that feeling tight. It had remained with her ever since, a spark of warmth and light at every turn.

And now Giles Howard and Lady Rochford between them had managed to make her doubt. Was that the sum of Dominic's interest in her? Was he no better than any one of a dozen lords, interested only in the pleasures her body could provide?

She could not believe it. Not of Dominic. There were too many of the other memories—the stories he had told, the games they had played, and even the flares of anger at her impatience or recklessness. Someone so fond of lecturing her must be interested in more than just bedding her.

That, she told herself firmly, *is quite enough thinking for today,* and turned her mind to duty. When she entered the presence chamber several minutes later, Elizabeth looked up from the table where she was writing. Her expression was enough to make Minuette forget all else.

"What's wrong?" she asked, fear clutching at her stomach. *Not France. Please, not France.*

"I need you to go to Hever," Elizabeth said calmly, folding up the letter she'd been writing. "My mother has had a fall. She is conscious and does not appear to have broken anything, but I'm sending a physician and I'd like you to go as well. She'll want a familiar voice around her."

"You cannot come yourself?"

"If there's any change, send word at once." Elizabeth paused, and a flicker of worry crossed her face. "As regent, I have responsibilities here, and the government is not so easily moved. As long as there's no immediate cause for concern, I must stay."

Minuette crossed the room and planted a kiss on Elizabeth's cold cheek. "Of course you must. No one will understand that better than your mother. I'll write as soon as I arrive."

CHAPTER THIRTEEN

Two weeks after their deliberate retreat from Calais, the English armies were in possession of Le Havre and Harfleur and, with the port firmly held, had laid siege to Rouen. The good weather of July had given way to a rainy August that made both men and horses miserable, as did the long and boring work of wearing down a town's defenses. Rouen was decently provisioned, and each day's delay was nearly as dangerous for the English as for the town. Campaigning had a season, and Dominic knew if they did not get moving, they would have to fall back for the winter. Already the first few cases of illness had been reported in the camp.

There were those who felt they should hold what they'd taken, garrison Le Havre and Harfleur for the long term and leave that thorn in Henri's side to fester. Others wanted to press forward the advantage they hadn't had in a century. And while the debate continued, every day was a gift to Renaud LeClerc inside Rouen, allowing him time to plan and prepare for any eventuality. Dominic chafed at the inaction.

No more. He finally had a plan, one that even Northumberland might be persuaded to accept, though Dominic was less concerned with persuading the Earl Marshal than he was with persuading William. As long as the king was in the field, the king would decide.

Dominic ducked inside the tent where Northumberland and Sussex were engaged in their daily reports. William sat at a table, reading and signing letters and apparently not listening at all. Dominic knew that was an illusion. William was quite capable of doing ten things at once and still recalling word for word any conversation held in his hearing.

He motioned Dominic near while the others continued to discuss supply lines. Looking at Dominic's mud-splashed plain gold tunic, William said, "Tell me again why I bothered to make you a marquis. Any other man would gladly flaunt his new rank and colours."

William's teasing had been going on for two weeks, ever since the day they sailed from Calais and William first saw him still dressed in his familiar plain gold. Dominic had not been able to articulate why, offering fumbling responses about not wanting to wear his new colours at sea. The truth was vaguer— he simply hadn't felt that the time had come for him to don his Exeter colours. He looked at them every day, the tunic and pennon laid neatly in his tent, and felt that they were saying to him, *Not yet*.

Then, late last night, Jonathan Percy had come to him with some question about horses and armour. Dominic really couldn't remember what it was he'd wanted to know, because the first thing Percy had said was, "I'm sure Lord Robert will mention that I was talking to him about this earlier. That's the third time I've mistaken him for you and got halfway through a question before I realized. You're both so dark it can be hard to tell you apart without paying attention."

Percy had kept talking, but Dominic hadn't heard a word of it, for his mind had caught hold of that—*the third time I've mis-*

taken him for you. And he thought of a story that one of Renaud's men had told him once, about a campaign in Italy and a daring move by Renaud to surprise the enemy.

And all at once, Dominic had it—the unexpected, the twist that would throw Renaud off-balance and give England the edge in open battle. Renaud might claim no man had ever surprised him twice, but Dominic knew that with this plan, he could more than surprise Renaud.

He could beat him.

He answered William's taunt with the same reply he'd given every time. "I want to wear my new colours in battle, not waste them in the tedium of attrition."

"Le Havre and Harfleur were battles."

"Over so quickly there wasn't time to change tunics."

"Sieges are as much a part of war as battles."

"Don't tell me you're content sitting on this muddy plain waiting for a break in either weather or siege."

Indeed, William looked more each day like a warhorse that had been relegated to a farm. Dominic could almost see the pulse of his desire, the wish for action beating beneath his skin.

"I'm not content. But there seem to be no viable options other than pulling back."

"There are always options," Dominic answered. "One has only to recognize them."

With a quizzical expression, William waited.

"All soldiers share the same dislike for sieges, whichever side of the wall they're on. And the leaders of Rouen will not want an army camped inside indefinitely. They want open battle as much as we do. Let's tempt them outside the walls to fight."

"You cannot give the French the advantage of numbers and expect to win," Sussex said.

"We can," Dominic said, "if we have the advantage of choosing the ground. Move now, and we can pick our battlefield and make the French come to us."

"What are the benefits?" William asked, prudent as a king should be even when prudence is against every instinct.

"The unexpected will always give the advantage of surprise."

"Northumberland?"

The duke shook his head. "Surprise or not, we cannot escape the fact that in head-to-head battle, our army will be outnumbered."

"Which is why," Dominic said promptly, "I have one more surprise in store. What if Renaud looks to our line on the field and sees the colours of all our leaders arrayed against him—Northumberland, Sussex, Exeter . . . and the king?"

Sussex snorted, and Northumberland narrowed his gaze as he said, "Put the king in the line? That's madly dangerous."

"It will bring out the French."

"Of course it will!" Sussex exploded. "A chance to capture the king? Do you know what that ransom would cost England? And what if he's hurt or—"

"That's enough," William said. "There's more to this, Dom, isn't there? Something to do with your previously unworn colours as Exeter." William leaned forward with a gleam in his eye. "What are you thinking?"

Dominic smiled. And then he told them the outlines of the story Renaud's lieutenant had shared months ago. Of a battle against the Italians, when Renaud's men were tired of a long siege and it seemed retreat was the only option. Renaud had created another option, using a decoy dressed as himself to lead his army away while he and a small force of handpicked men slipped into the Italian city in plain clothes. Renaud's "retreating" army circled back around in the night and attacked from without at the same time Renaud and his force set off explosions from within. The surprise of sabotage, coupled with the surprise of Renaud being where no one had expected him to be, turned the tide, and the French won back the city.

Northumberland eyed him with a glimmer of hope that reminded Dominic of just how clever a commander John Dudley was. "But you are not counseling a retreat and sabotage; you want to advance openly, let them know we're coming."

"I want them to know *you* are coming," Dominic said. "You, Sussex, the king—and, yes, myself. Dressed in the gold I have always worn in tournament or battle. Renaud will count the colours before him and never think to look behind."

Slowly Northumberland smiled and nodded. "Unconventional."

Sussex was less impressed. "Some might call it cheating."

"Not cheating," William answered. "Winning." He looked straight at Dominic, eyes glinting in a manner that made the latter unaccountably nervous, and said, "It's perfect, except for one thing—I will command the covert force that comes in behind."

The tent was silent, save for the sound of rain hitting the sodden fabric above. *I should have seen this coming,* Dominic thought. *He is aching to prove himself. How the hell do I tell him no?*

Because of course William could not do this—and Dominic would have to tell him so. No one else wanted that task. As Sussex and Northumberland exited the tent, Dominic thought he saw sympathy in the duke's eyes.

Dominic wasted no time in evasion, and he emphasized his seriousness with formality. "Your Majesty, you cannot lead this force. You must take the field here, surrounded by the full weight of your army."

He could almost have given William's answer, word for clipped word. "I decide what I can and cannot do. Let Henri sit safely at home—I do not ask my men to take risks I will not."

"Which is why I allow you to take the field at all—but this I will not allow. Might I remind you of what happened to the last English king who charged an enemy headlong? Surely a Tudor remembers Bosworth Field. Richard made a brave end, but an end nonetheless. Your grandfather, on the other hand, was wise enough to hang back, and he ended the day as king."

William's cheeks were flushed with temper, and his voice slipped a little. "Why not tell me the truth, Dom? You don't want me leading the covert force because you don't think I can do it. At the least, not as well as you can."

"You can't," Dominic said simply. "I am the last man in the world to underestimate you, Will, but this situation requires experience. We cannot afford to fail. You need me to do this—and I need you to do as I ask. Stay here. Stand with Northumberland and Dudley. Be the symbol that will draw out the French. And trust me to do the rest."

Enthusiastic acceptance was too much to hope for, but William did manage to nod and even clasp Dominic's hand in his. "If you fail, I'll never let you forget it," he warned.

"Fair enough."

18 August 1554
Hever Castle

We arrived after nine o'clock last night and found the queen sleeping. I stood quietly nearby while the physician asked questions of her household. He pronounced himself satisfied with what they had done and did not seem inclined to wake her.

It was her eyesight that betrayed her. Since her vision has darkened,

Her Majesty has taken to descending stairs with even more studied grace than normal, one hand always trailing lightly along a balustrade or against a wall to steady her. At last, her precautions failed. A misplaced step, a momentary loss of balance—the briefest unsurety was all it took to send her tumbling to the bottom of the stairs.

It is her head that is the great concern, for according to her attendants, she struck the stone floor quite sharply. But the local surgeon who saw her first assured us there was no break in the skull. Other than a quite natural headache, she complained of no pain. The royal physician will see her again this morning when she wakes. I sat with her through the night, and she seemed to sleep peacefully enough. I shall hope for encouraging news to send Elizabeth later today.

23 August 1554
Hever Castle

The queen is not progressing as we had hoped. After our first morning here, when she seemed no more than irritable and uncomfortable, Her Majesty's condition has declined. She has been restless and feverish, and the least light brings on blinding pain in her head. The physician seems of little use—but perhaps that is only my fear speaking. I am certain he is doing all he can. If not for the sake of the queen, then for his own reputation at least.

I have been with her nearly every waking hour and for much of the nights. She is worse during the day, for the heat of summer and the necessity of keeping her room dark and shuttered does nothing to ease her fever. We keep her cool as best we may, with wet cloths and even damp bed linens, trying to reduce her temperature.

At night we can throw open the shutters and allow the cool air to circulate in the room. Within an hour or so of sunset last night, Her Majesty began to breathe more easily and the hectic flush in her cheeks cooled. And then it was that she began to talk.

I have never heard the queen speak so candidly. She told me stories of her childhood here at Hever, of the games she and her brother would devise, with their sister, Mary, never quite able to keep up. It gave me pause to hear Lord Rochford spoken of with such casual warmth.

She spoke also of her marriage, occasionally in terms that threatened to make me blush. Her Majesty does not mince words, either in praise or in condemnation. Her marriage could never have been serene, but hearing her talk, I wager she found more pleasure in arguments with Henry than she ever would have found in a placid existence with a less dominant husband.

I shall give it another day before I write again to Elizabeth.

24 August 1554
Hever Castle

I have sent a messenger for Elizabeth, requesting that she come as soon as possible. Her Majesty refuses all food, and only laudanum eases her enough that she can sleep—and even drugged, she twitches and moans.

But it is her mind that worries me. She did not know me this morning. She called me Marie, thinking I was my mother. It was only for a few minutes, but it was unnerving to have the queen speak to me so familiarly, calling me "chérie" and "pet" and asking me what I thought of the latest letter from Henry. I hardly know what I said in return, but eventually her eyes cleared and she came back to the present. I almost wish she hadn't, for the present meant also a return of pain. The physician dares not increase her laudanum, for fear of putting her into a sleep from which she will not wake. He claims he has done all he can. Perhaps Elizabeth can motivate him to something new.

26 August 1554
Hever Castle

Elizabeth arrived after dark the day after I sent my message. Since then, she has alternated between sitting with her mother and doing what government business is necessary. I do not believe she has slept at all.

Though we have kept the castle itself as empty as possible, the outbuildings and surrounding farms are crawling with government functionaries. At least we have been able to keep out the useless members of court, who could serve no purpose but to be in the way.

The queen is no better, but she is also no worse. There are hours when my heart sinks, afraid of what I will not name, even to myself. But there are also long periods when she is lucid and somewhat eased in body. The physician has bled her and dosed her until he can do no more. It is a matter of time alone, he says. Until she is better, Elizabeth adds. She will believe no less.

We have not written to William, not yet.

Soon we may have to.

28 August 1554
Hever Castle

We have dispatched a rider to Dover with a letter for William. Though she appeared composed as she wrote it, Elizabeth's elegant script was less tidy than normal, and the postscript was barely readable: "Do not delay."

"Marie?"

Minuette stirred instantly at the sound of the queen's voice. She had learnt to doze easily on a pallet these last nights, as she stayed with Anne almost constantly. Elizabeth she had sent to bed with her own dose of laudanum tonight, and though Lord Rochford had arrived two days ago, he could not bear to stay long in the sickroom. Minuette was the chief mainstay, with Carrie and two of the queen's women doing most of the heavy nursing.

"Marie? Are you here?"

"I'm here, my lady." The lie came easily to Minuette, as did the use of Anne's long-outdated title. The queen spent a lot of time wandering in the past, and Minuette did whatever she could to let her stay there.

She leaned forward in the chair she kept next to Anne's bed until the queen's fingers closed around her wrist and her head turned in the direction of her voice. "Don't leave me tonight, Marie. You can't leave me. The blood . . . I've been bleeding since yesterday. Since the moment of Catherine's internment—"

She gave a twisted laugh that ended in a spasm of pain. Even that kept her firmly in the past. "If I lose this child—the very month of her death—the people will say it is God's will. That it is God himself denying me. Denying my marriage. They will turn Henry from me. His eye wanders . . . does he think I cannot see it? I know him. If I lose this child . . ."

"You will not," Minuette said firmly, with all the assurance of present truth. "You will recover and you will give the king a healthy boy. England will love him and love you for his sake. You will have done what no one else could do. You will see your son crowned king and you will marvel at the goodness of the Lord."

Anne gave a shuddering breath. "You will stay with me until the end?"

"I will stay."

"No," Anne said sharply. "No, I remember now. You are already gone, Marie. You are bound to your Henry. You tried not to be—you married your nice Jonathan—but in the end . . ."

Minuette's head, already dizzy with lack of sleep, whirled with Anne's words. *Your Henry*? What did that mean? Her mother had married Jonathan Wyatt, Minuette's father, and then he died and she married Howard.

"Your Henry," Anne murmured. "I named him that. Because I know what it is to love a dangerous man. A man you should avoid. A man you love and hate in the same breath. A man you cannot do without as much as you sometimes want to."

"Stephen Howard."

Minuette only knew she'd spoken aloud when Anne agreed. "Howard, yes. Go to your Henry. Genevieve will be safe at court. Between us, we will keep her happy and away from the attention of dangerous men."

The queen patted her hand, then slipped back into an uneasy sleep. Minuette stayed in the chair, wide-awake and finding it hard to swallow. *Your Henry*—was that how her mother had felt about Stephen Howard? If anyone would know, it seemed that the queen would. But she was not the only one. There was Carrie, silent at the end of the bed, who had heard it all. Who had known her mother with both of her husbands.

Carrie must have sensed her mood, for she came on quiet feet to Minuette's side and crouched down to eye level. "Don't fret yourself tonight, miss. The dying do not always know what they are saying."

"Is she right? Did my mother love Howard?"

"And if she did?" Carrie shook her head with pity. "Whatever she felt for him did not touch what she felt for your father. I saw her with both, remember? And I tell you true that she was never more at peace than when she was at Wynfield with your father and you."

Minuette nodded in acknowledgment and thanks, but still she did not sleep. In the hour just before dawn, the queen woke again, and this time she did not call for Marie.

"Genevieve?"

"I'm here, Your Majesty."

"Is William coming?"

"Yes, he is coming." *I hope soon enough,* she thought.

A long series of shallow breaths, then the queen said, "I am glad you are here, Minuette."

Only much later did she realize that it was the first time the queen had ever called her by her pet name.

CHAPTER FOURTEEN

WILLIAM SAT HIS horse at the top of a rise two miles west of Rouen, watching the French formations moving slowly, steadily toward him. He was a little forward of his own line here, but there was no hurry—the royal archers were between him and the enemy line, and it would be some time before the French could break a way through those deadly volleys. There were no better bowmen in the world than the Welsh. Besides, they were flanked by cannons.

The weather was perfect—blue sky and a freshening breeze—and so was the terrain. Northumberland had chosen their battlefield well. The English held the high ground, such as it was, and the French were coming at them hemmed in by trees on one side and the Seine on the other. There was little room for artillery that wouldn't cut down one's own forces, and the low spot that the French were moving toward was still boggy from weeks of rain, enough to cause hesitation in both horses and men.

William withdrew just as the archers were beginning to fit shaft to bow, running expert hands the length of their arrows and calmly leveling their aim. The master bowman stood behind, his eyes fixed to the line of mounted knights; when the

French shifted from deliberation to speed would be the moment to loose.

With his squire following near behind, William walked his horse the length of his own mounted line. Northumberland was in the center, leading the vanguard that would burst into motion as soon as the French managed to break through the archers. William's personal forces were on the river side to the right, the most protected position of the day. He had argued long and loud about that but had given way in the end. He would not have done it for anyone but Dominic.

He reached the far left flank and wheeled his horse round to make his way back. As he did so, he saluted Robert Dudley with a nod and a quick twitch of his lips. His eyes went from the borrowed plain gold tunic that Robert wore, deliberately flaunted, to the dark line of trees that cut off any sight of Rouen. He wished briefly that Dominic were next to him. Nothing had been harder than watching him set out with his men last night, having to trust that all would be well. Not, as everyone assumed, because William had wanted to lead the covert force himself. He had, but that was not why he had prayed twice as long as usual last night. It was not jealousy that had prompted his devotions—it was fear and a memory of the time his own willfulness had nearly cost Dominic his life.

It had been in January 1547, when William was nine. He'd been staying at Hever with his Boleyn grandmother, and he'd dared Dominic to sneak out of their room before the sun rose. It was the coldest winter in decades and he'd wanted to see if it were true, as a maid said, that it was cold enough to freeze running water.

Any other time and place and they never would have gotten as far as the river. But his father was dying at Windsor Castle, and in the disruption of a smaller household, they were able to slip away with vague lies about watching the sun rise for an astronomy lesson.

William had been disappointed to find the river still running, though tendrils of ice snaked out from the banks, winding white fingers through the black water. Dominic, fourteen years old and cautious by nature, wanted to go straight back. William might have listened if Dominic hadn't made the mistake of calling him a foolish boy who took too much pleasure in flouting the advice of his elders.

William hit him. Well, almost hit him, but Dominic was bigger and well able to predict his moods. He saw William's arm move and stepped back to avoid it.

He had forgotten that his back was to the river.

Before he knew it, William was in the water after him, screaming his name. The water was running high, but Dominic was able to hook an arm round the limb of a fallen tree. He was quick enough to grab William's hand and awkwardly shove him into the crook of the limb, William's body as far out of the water as possible.

Even nine years later, William could feel the ache of the cold that seemed to come from inside his bones and spread outward. Dominic kept talking to him while his legs, in water up to the knees, grew numb. He didn't know how long it was before he realized Dominic was not talking anymore. Shaken out of himself, he saw that though Dominic's arm remained twisted around the branch, his eyes were closed and a rim of frost iced his wet hair.

It was the next part that still gave William nightmares, the memory of his own desperate pleading: *Dom? Dom, wake up. Don't do this to me. Don't leave me alone. Everyone wants something from me but you. My father's dying and I have to be king and I'm afraid. I can't do it without you.*

They'd been plucked out of the river in time, but William had never forgotten his fear of being left by the only friend he knew he could count on. But this wasn't Hever and he was no longer a child king. Prepared for battle, William heard the surge of the French line before he saw it—the brief last hush, broken by a rumble of hooves that vibrated through the earth, making his own horse pick up his feet in recognition. He risked one more look behind the French to the trees. There wasn't even a glimmer of steel—not that he had expected there to be. Dominic knew what he was doing. And so did William.

The archers set about their work with deadly accuracy. Hole after hole opened in the French line, men and horses going down in a tangle of flesh and blood, with the worst damage done to those who could not rise quickly enough and were trampled by their own forces.

It might be as long as an hour before the archers could be bypassed, but William stayed mounted so as to view the field clearly. Although he was aware of the entire battlefield, with its individual swirls and eddies, he kept his attention fixed on the bright scarlet and gray banner that floated constantly above the driving wedge of the French.

Renaud LeClerc was a formidable fighter. He kept his men ordered and methodical, and soon William could see that the archers wouldn't be able to hold off this man as long as an hour. Already he was advancing—not carelessly or without thought to his own losses, but with precision and accuracy.

Northumberland saw it as well, for he called sharply to his men to be mounted and ready. The chaplain made a brief benediction before withdrawing behind the line. The English army readied itself, squires doing their office to mounted knights, unmounted men-at-arms sturdily gripping pikes. William drew in a cleansing breath as he saw the tip of the French army wedge itself into a point decidedly to the right of middle. They were heading for Robert Dudley. Dom had been right. LeClerc had set himself straight for the foe he most wanted to meet in battle.

Robert was ready for them. As his father brought the vanguard into movement, Robert surged ahead of his own men, with a yell that set William's heart alight with pleasure and a wish to do the same. But William's job was not to dive into the heat of the fighting. He was the distraction—the royal prize that would keep most of the French occupied in attempting to reach him and draw their attention away from what might be happening behind.

Northumberland and his son bore the brunt of this battle, and they met it well. Though William was busy enough keeping the fight turned inward so that no one slipped behind their lines, he could track Northumberland's figure, ferocious and commanding in his armour. He kept his men tight about him, and even his banner looked disciplined.

In contrast, Robert Dudley romped through the field, fighting with a careless joy that William well understood. He wheeled and circled on Daybreak, Dominic's own favoured charger, and the horse followed his movements perfectly. No one could touch them.

Two things happened almost at once—in a moment of time that seemed to slow until it nearly stopped. As William pulled his sword free of some unlucky squire who'd been wearing only leather armour, he looked to his left, where he saw Northumberland erect on his horse, sword raised high.

He seemed to hold that position forever, until William wondered just what enemy he was trying to intimidate. The sword fell first, out of a hand that William could see was suddenly senseless. Before he could even think what that meant, Northumberland himself fell, his armoured body hitting the ground hard and his horse shying away. A French arrow stuck out of the shoulder joint where his armour plates met.

The French had seen Northumberland's fall as well, and they took it as a sign and a motivation to press harder. Even as he was swept into this new and more dangerous fight, William saw what he had been waiting for: Renaud LeClerc, achingly close to the plain gold banner and the man who fought beneath it, checked and hesitated.

Though William was not near enough to distinguish individual sounds, he thought LeClerc might have given a shout of laughter. Without a second look at Robert Dudley, LeClerc wheeled his horse around and called his men to him. In that turning motion, he looked straight at William.

For half a second it seemed LeClerc might forget the threat to Rouen and his own rear guard and make a dash for William instead. Capturing the king certainly would undo any advances the English made today. But after that one brief look, LeClerc decided. With what might have been a salute to William, he led his men back the way they'd come, not in retreat, but to meet the covert force that he now knew lay behind him to cut him off from Rouen. Between facing William and facing Dominic, it seemed there was no choice.

William fought his way through to where Northumberland lay stunned and swearing. Standing tall in his stirrups, William let out a great yell of command. "St. George! St. George!"

His squire was as quick as he was. "To the king!" he called.

From all around, the men caught the phrase and threw it back in an echo that grew in size and intensity with each utterance.

"To the king! The king! The king!"

His blood pounding in his ears and singing through his veins, William dove into the heart of the fray, ignoring the little voice that whispered, *Dominic will be angry.*

Over the heads of the French army, he could see at last a great reflection of sunlight on steel as men and horses swept into sight in a movement that meant England's victory. Above the glitter of arms, William's eyes went straight to Dominic's banner—the colours of Exeter, floating free and defiant and heading straight for Renaud LeClerc.

The worst part for Dominic was the waiting. He had led his men into position after midnight, then sent them to what rest they could find. It had been a long march through late summer darkness, a thousand men and two hundred horses moving as swiftly and silently as possible. They had picked their way with care through the thick trees, blessing the clear skies and full moon that made this night movement possible. They traveled light, with only their weapons and what was needed for a morning battle, and most men rolled themselves up in their cloaks and slept without murmur on the ground.

Dominic made no pretense of sleep. He set scouts around the camp and walked its perimeter himself. These were Courtenay men—knights and squires who had long followed his father and his uncle, and his grandfather before that. They were unquestioningly loyal to the banner of Exeter, and it left Dominic even more careful than he was wont to be.

An hour or so before dawn, Dominic checked through his armour one last time with Harrington's help. Then there was nothing to do but sit. So he sat on the edge of the camp, staring straight ahead, as though he could see through the trees that cut off the field of battle from his eyes. He knew the ground by heart, and in his mind he was imagining what would come in the next few hours.

A quiet figure seated itself next to him. Dominic glanced briefly at Jonathan Percy before concentrating once more ahead.

William had been right—Percy could fight. He had carried himself well through the brief, sharp encounter outside Harfleur. He had not faltered at either sight or smell, and he had never been more than five feet away from Dominic, which wasn't as easy as it sounded when one considered the weight of holding a banner aloft while maneuvering a horse through the chaos of battle.

At last Percy drew a deep breath and said softly, "Is it always like this?"

"The waiting?" Dominic replied. "Yes."

"I'd rather fight than think about fighting."

"So would I."

There was another silence, broken once again by Percy. "My lord, thank you for giving me a decent chance. I shall never be a career soldier, but this experience will pour itself out into the music I write. I'll never forget it."

And then, swiftly, as if afraid he'd stop himself if he had a chance to think about it, Percy rushed on. "You were right. When I came here, I was thinking of impressing ... someone. You obviously know that I had asked Mistress Wyatt to be my wife."

Dominic sat perfectly still, not certain if he wanted the boy to keep talking or not. He had no idea if Percy knew that Minuette had written to him. Or why.

But Percy did not elaborate, merely stood up and looked to the east. "The sky is beginning to lighten. Shall I wake the men?"

Dominic kept his voice even. "The chaplain first. Give the men another quarter hour. Then we'll hear service and move into position."

Percy nodded. And then, completely unexpectedly, he looked straight at Dominic with penetrating eyes. "She said no."

Dominic was caught in Percy's gaze, the younger man studying him intently as though trying to divine something. Then he turned on his heel and set off for camp.

By the time the sun had risen fully and the men had been shriven clean, Dominic moved them into position with his mind cleared of everything but the coming battle. He sent a single scout north along the tree line to where he could see the battle plainly. As soon as the French broke through the archers, Dominic's force would begin to move, pouring silently out of the trees beyond sight of the armies and coming up behind.

The scout alerted them before they had time to grow impatient. Dominic had known Renaud would break the Welsh line fast, but this was faster than even he'd expected. All the better. He was aching to fight, and so, to judge by their expressions, were his men.

The road and surrounding fields were empty as they formed up and began marching west. Dominic kept his horse reined in, setting a deliberate pace that would not tire any of them before reaching the field. Behind the mounted knights, Harrington commanded the foot soldiers. In light armour and carrying a two-handed sword, Harrington was even larger than usual, and Dominic pitied any man who got in his way.

They heard the battle before they saw it. That was the purest agony—to hear the cries of men and horses, the clash of arms and the ring of steel. To hear and not see was a purgatory. Dominic urged his borrowed horse forward, his tension communicating itself to his mount until the horse was as ready to run as he was. He did not look behind him as he went—his men knew their work.

With a cry of pure pleasure, he burst onto the field. This was the moment he loved, when all was clean and the body and mind worked as one without troubling itself over past and future.

He took in several sights at once: William, fighting far deeper in the middle than he should have been; Robert Dudley's borrowed gold flashing as he pursued those of the French who had turned back toward Rouen; and, right where he'd expected, Renaud coming straight at him. Dominic ignored everything but the flash of scarlet and gray that marked his man. Renaud seemed just as anxious to meet, and they cleared their respective paths with ruthless efficiency.

They drove at each other as though they were in the lists, and the first clang of sword on sword rang through Dominic's head in answering vibration. They were past each other in an instant, both moving too quickly for more than that one blow, but already Dominic was checking his horse, turning it sharply to wheel round and meet Renaud again. But this borrowed horse was not as swift as Daybreak, and in the precious seconds it took him to get the animal to do what he wanted, Renaud was upon him, striking from his undefended side.

Dominic managed to get his sword up and deflect the blow, but his arm was at an awkward angle and the force of Renaud's strike set him off-balance. He kicked his foot free and let himself fall from the saddle so that his not-quite-good-enough horse was between him and Renaud.

Renaud sprang down from his own horse in response, and now the two of them were truly in their element, aware of nothing but each other, bringing swords together in a dance of constant attack, neither one giving way to the other, both using the force of the other's thrusts to power their own movements. Dominic felt his blood singing through him as he twisted and turned and sidestepped in harmony with Renaud, not slowing his reflexes with plans or tactics. His body knew what to do.

It might have gone on much longer—to a draw that could only have been broken with the utter defeat of one army or another—but for a lucky blow from an English foot soldier who couldn't have duplicated it if he'd tried. The man was inexpertly swinging an old-fashioned mace, and he wasn't even aiming for Renaud. But his clumsy swing swiped Renaud across the head, staving in the back of his helmet.

Dominic shoved the man out of his way and grabbed Renaud as he went down.

"Help me!" he commanded.

It was Percy who responded, lighting down from his horse and dropping the Exeter banner into the mud before helping Dominic dismantle the dented helmet so that Renaud's pale face lay free to the sun. Dominic ran his hands over Renaud's head and gradually his pulse slowed as his fingers found no evidence of a broken skull.

Renaud's eyes flickered open and, incredibly, he laughed. "You've surprised me twice, Dominic. I had not thought that possible."

With an answering laugh born of relief, Dominic said, "Good thing your French head is so hard."

Renaud's right hand moved slightly in the grass, fingers searching until they found the hilt of his sword. His voice, though hoarse, was steady. "To none else would I surrender."

Dominic hesitated, feeling an unaccountable reluctance to accept this surrender. Renaud's defeat owed more to chance than to any skill on Dominic's part, and though he knew fairness was a luxury he could not afford in battle, he disliked beating his friend in this way.

As though he could read Dominic's mind, Renaud gave what might have been a snort of disdain. "Take your victory as you find it, Dominic. There is no dishonour in seizing upon good fortune. Do you think I would not do the same?"

With a nod, Dominic accepted Renaud's sword, knowing as he did so that the battle was won. Renaud was the heart and spirit of his men, and his fall and surrender spread defeat quickly. Within half an hour, all that was left was the clearing away of the wounded and dead. Leaving Renaud in the custody of Harrington and several Tiverton squires, Dominic mounted once more and rode out to meet William. Even from a distance, he could see the flush of victory setting a sheen of gold on that bright face. Closer up, William was dirty and his hair curled damply from sweat. He was obviously untouched and as shining as a victorious king should be.

He shouted his congratulations while Dominic was still twenty paces off. "Perfect, Dom. This will make Henri sit up and take notice."

Yes, Dominic thought, *so it will.* And fair enough, too, since Dominic was certain that the original threat to Calais had never been more than a feint designed to draw William to the field of battle. Henri had wanted to test this young king. Well, he had got his test, and Dominic wondered if he would count the loss of lives and cities worth the knowledge he had gained of William's nature.

Dominic waved a salute to Robert Dudley, grinning broadly in his borrowed tunic. He was about to head over to thank him for his part in the victory, and to ensure Daybreak was in good condition under his borrowed rider, when the sound of a galloping horse caught his ears.

A running horse in the aftermath of battle was odd enough—even odder was the sight of the royal chaplain riding it. He pulled up to William and made a hasty bow in his saddle.

"Forgive me, Your Majesty. There's a rider just come from Le Havre." He handed over a sealed letter. "From Her Highness, the Princess Elizabeth."

The sun was still an hour from setting when William gathered what he had of his council in the great hall of Rouen's castle. Northumberland was absent, lying on a bed in the infirmary with a sword wound in the shoulder. Looking at the handful of men around him, William spoke with quick authority—the best way, he had found, of giving orders and conveying unwelcome information. "A ship weighs anchor from Le Havre tomorrow. I will be on it."

"What of the fighting, Your Majesty?" It was Sussex who asked, expectant beneath his grim face. With Northumberland down, the army needed a new commander.

"The fighting is finished. I expect negotiations to commence quickly. We have, after all, the king's relative and most prized soldier securely in this castle. Henri will pay dearly to ransom Renaud LeClerc."

William looked straight at Sussex and dashed his hopes. "If military need arises, I leave you in the hands of Lord Exeter as lieutenant general."

Sussex could not quite keep his face from disappointment, though he controlled himself so far as to say nothing.

To the rest of his lords, William added simply, "Thank you for your work today."

Dominic walked with him to the courtyard, waving off the anxious grooms. William stood next to a fresh horse, rubbing it absently on the neck while giving his last instructions. "You have the archbishop for diplomacy. Use him, Dom. He's better at it than you are. He reports to you until I return."

"When will that be?"

William shrugged, unable to think calmly about how long his mother might linger and when he might be free of mourning. "Henri will wait. He can't have peace without me."

Dominic nodded and offered him his own hand up into the saddle. Looking down, William gave his final command. "LeClerc is dear to Henri. He'll offer a generous ransom. You and Cranmer are free to conduct negotiations as you see fit— with one condition: LeClerc goes free only when Henri agrees to meet me face-to-face. No more negotiating in shadows. We do it ourselves this time."

"Agreed. Safe travel, Will." He hesitated, and William could see the beginnings of sympathy in his eyes. "I hope . . ."

William jerked his head once in acknowledgment of a hope he could not bear to have put into words.

I hope she's still alive.

CHAPTER FIFTEEN

1 September 1554
Hever Castle

The queen is dead.

Elizabeth and I stayed with her through all this long last day of seizures and purgings and ravings, as physicians and attendants did any number of useless things. So still was Elizabeth that I almost would have thought her insensible to my presence—save for her hand, clutching my own so tightly I can still feel the imprint of her nails in my palm.

Lord Rochford stayed longer at his sister's side than I would have expected, staring at her while she slept after a prolonged convulsion. Before he left he laid his hand on her cheek and kissed her lightly on the forehead.

I have sent Elizabeth to her own bed, and watched until she slept. Tomorrow there will be things to do—arrangements to make and business to carry on. Tomorrow we will lock away our personal loss and move upon the stage of public mourning.

Tonight is the hour of private grief.

Somewhere between Hastings and Hever it began to rain. William rode on, driving straight through Sussex for hours as rain and wind buffeted them and early shadows fell in the gray twilight.

It had taken longer than it should have to cross from Le Havre. The winds had been all wrong, and when William had ordered the captain to set out of harbour regardless, they had been forced to put straight back in. While they waited for more favourable weather, William had paced the length of the ship more times than he could count, measuring his memories with every step. Although he had hero-worshipped his father, it had always been Anne who inspired him, who urged him to study hard, know his role, and rule wisely. Though her sight had weakened, her personality had never diminished, and he wondered what he would do without her.

Action drove memory away, so on this sustained dash from Hastings his mind was clear of everything but movement. He almost wanted to keep riding forever, if only to continue in this state of clean blankness.

An hour after sunset, the first straggling cottages of Hever village came into view. He turned his horse toward the castle, his anxiety rising at the sight of the familiar square towers. He was a quarter mile from the castle when he heard the first bell. He checked his horse, which complained with a whinny at having his head jerked hard to the side but came to a quick halt. William sat motionless in the middle of the lane, surrounded by his guards and focused on counting each toll of the bells, as though he could make it be wrong through sheer force of will.

The bells rang fifty-one times.

The courtyard of the castle swarmed to damp, dark life when he rode in. He dismounted and moved with a single thought. Shrugging off the innumerable people surrounding him, William went straight to Lord Rochford.

"Where is she?" he asked.

His uncle hesitated. "Should I summon Elizabeth?"

William flexed his hands at his sides, as if the action would help control his words. "I didn't ask for my sister. I didn't ask to be shown my room or to be given time to change. I know I'm too late. Now I want to see her."

Rochford led him to his mother's rooms. When he opened the door he paused, as if debating whether to enter with William. He thought better of it.

The room was empty of the living. The shutters stood open to the rain, and beneath the fresh, cool air, William could smell the lingering remnants of illness. He swallowed and moved nearer the bed.

His mother lay with a rigidity that never could have been mistaken for sleep. Her face and hands were the marble white of a statue, as if death had drained not only spirit but blood from her. Her dark hair, with the strands of silver that had appeared only in the last few years, was brushed neatly back from her forehead.

He felt only an echoing emptiness where surely thought and emotion should be. He closed his eyes hard, but when he opened them she still lay there, motionless and silent forever. Stumbling to the window, he breathed in shakily, letting the rain fall on his face, cooling his hard and swollen eyes.

An increase in light caught his attention. He looked over his shoulder to the half-open door where Minuette stood. They stared at each other over the trembling, flickering candle she held. Then she gave a sudden cry and set the candle down upon the dressing table near the door. Wax had dripped on her hand.

William watched as she rubbed her hand where the wax had fallen. When she looked back up, she said softly, "I'm sorry, William."

He had to turn away from her then—from that voice and those eyes that knew him too well. He put one hand on the stone edge of the window. He heard her footsteps moving across the room. She stood at his shoulder, so that he could just see the top of her head out of the corner of his eye.

"How bad was it?" he asked.

She must have anticipated this, for her answer came quick and steady. "She was mostly unconscious at the end. Had you been here, she would not have known."

"Did she ask for me?"

The answer was in her hesitation. "Yes."

He tilted his head to meet her eyes. Slowly he looked beyond the familiar green-gold swirls in her hazel eyes and saw the purple shadows of exhaustion, the lines marking her forehead and mouth.

"Why are you wandering the halls alone?"

"Elizabeth is asleep. I heard you ride in and didn't want you to be alone."

To his surprise, William found that he could still feel a little happy. "What would we do without Minuette to watch over us?"

In a tone that aimed for briskness, she said, "You're soaked through. You must get into something dry at once."

"I will. I just . . . I had to see her first."

Her face softened into sympathy once more, but William could see the tremble in it, the effort to subdue her own grief in the face of his. Reaching her hands to his cheeks, she pulled his head down.

She kissed his forehead, brief and warm. When she would have stepped away, William caught at her wrists with his hands, to keep her long, cool fingers curved on his face, and he rested his aching head against hers. It took him a minute to realize that Minuette was crying. Only the shaking of her hands alerted him, for she cried soundlessly. Ignoring his wet clothes, he wrapped his arms around her while she clung to him, her hands moving to grip the front of his shirt.

It was impossible to say what happened next. All William knew was that, as he held her, he became gradually aware that she was wearing only a loose gown of thin silk that did little to disguise the contours of her body.

He tensed—a slight movement, but it penetrated Minuette's tears. She raised her face to his.

It might have been as long as two minutes that they stood there, staring, though William was in no condition to notice time. With her hands clinging to his wet shirt and his arms locked around her, he studied her face as if he had never seen it before. The straight line of her nose, the arch of her brows above hazel eyes that looked back at him unblinking, the fullness of her mouth, so achingly near his own.

He moved without thought and came to himself in the midst of a kiss. And suddenly he was aware of everything, every inch of him alight with her touch. He kissed her again, his hands moving up her back to twine into her heavy, loosely plaited hair. She returned his kisses with a hunger that might have started in grief but changed rapidly to desire—he knew the signs well enough. Her hands swept through the tangle of his wet curls, keeping his head pulled firmly down to hers.

As his body stirred into fierce life, he pulled his hands free of her hair and trailed them down the curves of her waist to her hips. He shifted her against the wall and at last released his lips from hers, but only to kiss her throat while one hand found the neckline of her gown.

"William."

He froze when he heard Elizabeth's shocked voice, one hand on Minuette's hip, holding her fast against the wall, the other resting on the curve of her breast.

With a control greater than any he had ever exercised, he managed not to jump guiltily. Minuette buried her head in his chest, like a little girl who thinks that covering her own eyes will keep her unseen by others.

Moving both hands safely up to her shoulders, William met his sister's gaze. There was no judgment in her eyes, only shock and exhaustion. She glanced briefly to the bed where their mother's body lay and back to William.

He thought he sounded remarkably normal considering the situation. "Go back to bed, Elizabeth. I'll see you in the morning."

He half expected her to refuse to leave the room, at least until Minuette was gone as well. Instead, very slowly, she shook her head once. She could not have been more plain if she'd dragged Minuette away by the arm.

She did not close the door behind her.

Uncurling his hands from Minuette's shoulders, William stepped away to the other side of the window. He kept his back to her, struggling to get himself under control. Over the sound of the rain and wind, he could hear his own breathing, harsh and uneven. He was flooded with a mix of shame and revelation—at what he had nearly done and at what the wanting of it might mean.

When he had achieved the nearest thing to calm that he could manage, he drew a deep breath and turned around.

Minuette was gone.

Minuette shut her door with shaking hands and leaned against it, as if her weight would help lock out the memory of what had happened. Her entire body trembled violently.

Feeling her way across the dark room, she found the bed and pulled the velvet coverlet off to wrap around her. Sitting on the bed with her back to the wall, she buried her head in her knees and squeezed her eyes shut. But complete darkness only made it easier to feel the aftereffects of William's touch, the buzz along her skin where his lips and hands had strayed, leaving lines of fire in their wake.

At first, when he had so surprisingly and thoroughly kissed her, the intoxication of it had dizzied her out of all thought and she had welcomed the blotting out of sorrow and exhaustion. When he had slid practiced hands down her body—just how practiced, she did not care to consider—she had known that she should stop him, but her body seemed to have a will of its own, one that wanted desperately to know what came next.

She covered her face with her hands and felt her cheeks burning with shame. What kind of woman was she, to allow William such liberties? Not just allow—she had positively encouraged him. She had always loved William. Had she now fallen in love with him? Part of her said, *Yes, of course, I must be in love or I never would have behaved so shamelessly. I am no Eleanor, ready to hand over my body to any man.*

But another, more insistent voice, whispered, *No, I cannot possibly be in love with Will.*

I am already in love.

She had not dared name it before, but the hope of it had sung through her every day since Dominic left. Was it not love she had cherished since he'd walked away from her, leaving the touch of his lips imprinted on her wrist? Was it not love that had steeled her to tell Jonathan that, much as she cared for him, she could not possibly marry him?

Despairing, she lay down, keeping the velvet cover wrapped around her like a cocoon. Maybe this was her punishment for having refused Jonathan. Perhaps God preferred that she live a placid, restrained life, without any of this trouble and turmoil.

Perhaps, she thought with a twist of humour, *if I flutter my eye-lashes just so, I can get Jonathan to propose again.*

But as she drifted into sleep, it was not Jonathan she thought of, but the two men she had always loved best in this world.

It was still raining at dawn when William went downstairs and ordered his horse readied within the hour. His uncle was sitting before the fireplace in the hall, looking as if he'd spent the night in his chair. With a wine bottle for company.

Rochford received his orders without comment, though William could see the question in his uncle's eyes. It was, to say the least, highly unusual for William to be leaving less than twelve hours after his mother's death, but he didn't care for appearances this morning. He wanted away from Hever.

He had thought he would be well away before the women stirred, but he had underestimated his sister. She found him in the courtyard, with several men already mounted and ready to ride with him. His jaw tightening at the sight of her, William took Elizabeth by the arm and steered her out of earshot to the edge of the damp and forlorn-looking rose garden.

In spite of her drawn face and shadowed eyes, Elizabeth sounded perfectly herself. "Leaving so soon?"

He met her eyes steadily but did not answer. She gave a little shake of her head. "William, what are you doing?"

He deliberately chose to misunderstand her. "I need to be in London. I need diplomats and couriers. Rochford will see to the details at this end. He knows what to do, better than either of us."

"You can't avoid her forever."

After a heartbeat's pause, in which he decided further evasion would be pointless, William said, "I don't intend to."

"What do you intend?" Elizabeth shot back, as if she were

interrogating some clerk caught overreaching himself with a lady.

The flare of anger overrode a little of his guilt. "This is nothing to do with you."

"Minuette is everything to do with me, particularly if you intend on setting her up in Eleanor's apartments as quick as you can empty them of your former whore."

If she had been a man, William would have hit her. As it was, he had to clench and unclench his hands several times before he trusted himself to speak. To her credit, Elizabeth looked nearly as shocked as he felt at the word she had used, but she did not apologize.

Pronouncing each word with even emphasis, William said, "If you know me so little as to need assurances, very well. You may trust that I will do nothing to insult Minuette or our long friendship. She is as dear to me as you are, and I would not injure her for the world."

In a gentler voice, Elizabeth said, "Then why not stay and set it right at once? It will not be easier for waiting."

Finding her sympathy harder to face than her judgment, he turned away and said roughly, "I can't see her yet. Not yet, Elizabeth. I need time to . . ." *To forget the smell of her hair and the taste of her skin and the feel of her body against mine. To forget that I wanted her so desperately I'd have overthrown all honour to have her at that moment, with my mother lying dead not ten feet away.*

He shook his head to clear it and said in a stronger voice, "I need to concentrate on France. With our victory, we have the best chance we've ever had of breaking Mary Stuart's French betrothal. She is the only woman I can think about just now."

Elizabeth touched his shoulder. "You cannot afford to fall in love with her, William." She did not mean Mary Stuart.

Almost he asked about Robert, and the expense of loving

where one should not. But there had been enough discord for one morning.

As he took her arm to escort her back, he thought bleakly, *I'm not certain that falling in love is entirely in my control.*

8 September 1554
Tower of London

Over a period of two days, Queen Anne's hearse was brought from Hever to the Thames, and today we continued by river to the Tower. As Elizabeth and I arrived by boat ourselves, she murmured to me that the last time her mother had rested at the Tower was the night before her coronation. "She was pregnant with me at the time," Elizabeth added, her eyes far away.

I can still see every detail of the journey—the black-draped church fronts, the press of people lining the river, the flat-bottomed boat atop which the queen's hearse rested, draped in her colours and her falcon badge.

Once the procession had arrived, her ten days of lying in state began with a solemn mass in St. Peter ad Vincula. The orations were fulsome but not genuine. I would swear not one person in a thousand truly mourns Anne Boleyn.

I saw William only from a distance. I am not certain he even knew I was there.

11 September 1554
Tower of London

Elizabeth and I will remove tomorrow to Greenwich until the funeral. I am glad—though the Lieutenant's Lodging is comfortable, I do not like the Tower. There is violence here, sucked in by the stones. The ghosts of Richard VI and Lady Salisbury and even the first King William, the conqueror who planted his White Tower as a fortress five hundred years ago. I cannot get warm while I am here.

William left for Windsor yesterday.

I have written to Dominic. I wish he were here. It would be better for all of us if he were.

But would it be better? Minuette wondered as she closed her diary. Or would it merely increase her feeling of unreality, the sense that she had become detached from her own life? And how could she possibly face Dominic with the memory of what had passed—not just between the two of them, but between her and William?

Tell me—do they take you in turn, or is it both at once?

As Giles's voice sounded in her head, Minuette uttered a most unladylike word, then jumped guiltily when Lord Rochford said, "Am I interrupting?"

"Not at all. Shall I fetch the princess for you?"

Hooking a chair with one hand, he sat facing her. "I was looking for you, actually."

That could not possibly be good.

Instantly dread skittered across her mind. He knew about Hever, and had come to scold her—or worse. What were the limits of his power, anyway? Could he send her out of Elizabeth's household? Banish her from court? Surely not if William protested. But what if William had sent his uncle to do it for him?

"Mistress Wyatt, I believe you are somewhat familiar with the Duke of Norfolk's household."

Caught off guard, she stammered, "F-Familiar? I don't ... why?"

Rochford had a way of speaking to her as though she were an idiot child. "Your mother was married to the duke's brother; you spent time there when you were younger."

"Only three times, and only for a few weeks. My mother died when I was eight."

"That alone makes you very useful to the king at present. I'm sure you recall that the Lady Mary has been allowed to stay at Framlingham while we gather evidence. As you are one of the few with at least some information on the matter, I would like you to join the Howards for the next little while."

"I thought you had informants with the Lady Mary."

"And no doubt she sees them as such. You, however, have a legitimate reason to visit your family, of a sort. Besides, she likes you. And she knows you are a great friend to her siblings. She will not be able to resist thinking of you as her ally."

She likes me? Minuette was oddly flattered, but also distressed. "If Elizabeth does not wish to release me? It is such a difficult time. . . ."

"Mistress Wyatt, do I need to impress upon you the importance of the Penitent's Confession? Elizabeth knows the path of duty. If you wish to help her, you can do no greater service than to find this document before it falls into the wrong hands. I would rather not entrust this to you," he added dubiously, "but I dare not let word of the Penitent's Confession spread further than the four of you who already know. William will return to France as soon after the funeral as possible, where Lord Exeter remains, and Elizabeth would never be overlooked at Framlingham the way you will be. There is no one else."

"And if I do not wish it?"

And there was the Boleyn temper—different from the Tudors', and in some ways more frightening. "Your position here rests on the fragile base of personal regard. I can tell you, from experience, that regard can twist ever so easily to dislike and distrust. And where would you be without my nephew and niece to aid you?"

If she had to give in, at least she would do so gracefully. "I will go, as soon as Elizabeth tells me that I might."

But I'm not doing this for you, she thought defiantly as Rochford left. *I'm doing it for England—and William's security.*

And to prove that I also know the path of duty.

CHAPTER SIXTEEN

D OMINIC FINGERED THE letters in his hand—one each
from William, Elizabeth, and Minuette. After three weeks
of nothing but official communiqués from England, he had
been feeling more isolated than ever before. Because he could
not be with his friends in their hour of mourning, he had
thrown himself into his command as the only means of offering
help. With Sussex as his second, the English army had been partially disbanded and those remaining in Rouen kept under tight
control. The last thing Dominic wanted was a resentful populace.

With a word to Harrington, Dominic took himself to the
quietest corner of the castle, high atop the crenellated defense
wall. The view swept the horizon from east to west, the rooftops
of the medieval city crowding beneath him, spilling outside the
city walls in ever-lessening clumps until they gave way to the
harvest-gold fields.

William's letter was short and to the point, dealing mostly
with diplomatic matters. It was a letter that could have been
written to almost any of his advisors, and it left Dominic de-
pressed. Only the final lines contained anything personal, but

they were so oblique as to be almost meaningless: *I am most anxious to speak with you. I need the opinion of a man who is honest when he should not be.*

Unable to puzzle out William's meaning, he turned to Elizabeth's letter. She wrote as she spoke—with elegant economy and the occasional turn of phrase that was so vivid as to make Dominic think he could almost hear her.

She wrote only of public people and events—the funeral, her uncle's rigid control in the face of his sister's death, the crowds ("vultures who cover their triumph in ostentatious displays of sorrow," she called them) who had descended to see the end of the controversial queen. *Though there have been many prayers offered for the repose of my mother's soul, I am quite sure that many in England wish that she may know nothing but torment in the next world.* There was not a word in her letter of her own feelings.

With some misgiving, he opened the letter addressed to him in Minuette's distinctive hand.

Dominic, I have so wished for your company these past weeks. Grief is supposed to be lessened when shared, but sharing mourning with the masses is not at all comforting. One must not give way in public, so I have gone about with raised chin and dry eyes and I have felt every second a hypocrite. The woman who has been memorialized and eulogized in the last month bears little resemblance to the queen I knew. Indeed, the two have nothing in common, save their name. Why do we make of our dead a figure of either worship or contempt? It cheapens the complexities of human beings and makes of us all either saints or sinners. And yet one rarely meets either one or the other, but a mixture of the two.

Oh, dear, I've become both maudlin and philosophical. You cannot wish to read that. I shall say only that I hope matters in France are resolved speedily.

Yours, Minuette

She wished for his company. But only as she would wish for any friend in a time of crisis—or dare he hope something more personal? She was masking her own grief. He could easily read into her words the struggle to keep herself composed for both William and Elizabeth. Minuette would always do what she must to ease the burden of those she cared for.

Most telling was the rushed quality to her words. She was not naturally deceptive—her speech always gave her away. How many times had he seen her, eyes wide and guileless, the only clue to her discomfort the rapid flow of her words? Dominic read each word of the letter again, but confirming suspected evasion was not as simple with the sea between them.

And what of that ending? The word *yours* had a crowded, out-of-place look to it and Dominic allowed his imagination to conjure an image—Minuette signing her name to the letter, and then sitting quite still in silent debate, her tongue protruding slightly as she wrestled with that final word. *Yours.*

The sound of footsteps pulled Dominic out of that pleasant picture. He just had time to fold up Minuette's letter before Renaud appeared, looking at him quizzically.

"Were we not to ride today?" he asked.

Dominic had quite forgotten. "We can go now."

"Letters from home?" Renaud asked, falling into step beside him.

Dominic merely grunted acknowledgment, though he knew Renaud was quick enough to read a great deal into that unsatisfactory answer.

Renaud had healed quickly and had been allowed the run of the castle. A gentleman who had given his word not to attempt escape would never break his parole, and it was customary to allow them a measure of freedom even while held hostage. Indeed, Renaud was allowed to ride outside the city walls as long as Dominic and several guards were with him.

Their ride this morning took them, for the first time, west—though Dominic was distracted enough not to realize where they were headed. Renaud set the course, subtly urging Dominic on until the two horses were engaged in a flat-out run that swept personal matters from his mind.

They reined up—Dominic a close second—at the eastern edge of the battlefield, where Northumberland, Dudley, and William had led the way. The ground was still churned up, with dried mud formed into long grooves and tracks, but already grass was working its way valiantly upward. By spring this would once again be a pleasant spot, and the only evidence of the Battle of Rouen would be that fixed in treaty.

His eyes on the horizon, as if seeing the ghost movements of his own troops, Renaud said, "Dressing another man in your colours—one more Welsh trick?"

Dominic answered the unspoken question. "Your men are not always discreet, not when they've been drinking."

Renaud grunted. "A lesson they will learn from now."

"They gave me hints. I did the rest on my own."

With a wry smile, Renaud said, "I do not grudge your victory, neither to you nor to your king. It was well earned." With a spark in his eye that belied his matter-of-fact tone, he added, "Next time, the victory will not be yours."

With a laugh, Dominic turned his horse away from the field and started back to Rouen at a comfortable walk. They rode in companionable silence for a few minutes.

Renaud spoke first. "And the matter of ransom? It proceeds quickly?"

"You are anxious to leave my hospitality?" Dominic teased.

"If it were myself alone, I could keep you company for some time. But Nicole . . ."

"She knows she need not worry for your safety. She can trust me for that, I hope."

"It is not trust. Or fear. And it is not even Nicole who frets. Myself, rather." Not looking at Dominic, Renaud said, "I, too, have had a letter from my home. Nicole is with child once more."

"Congratulations."

A smile of pride, tenderness, and intimacy warmed Renaud's face. "I should like to be there and not here." And then his smiled turned outward. "Even you can understand that, cold-hearted English though you are."

"Nothing would give me greater pleasure than to send you home to your wife."

"And you? Will your king leave you here to command, or keep you near him to advise?"

Dominic shrugged. He didn't know what William would do. Dominic had his own preference. Though talent and experience made him a good commander of men, he wanted nothing so much as to return to England and never leave again.

30 September 1554
Hatfield

Hatfield is such a serene house—I think that is why Elizabeth loves it. Arriving here the evening after the queen's funeral was like burrowing beneath warm covers on a cold morning—a respite from the outside world.

But the world will not stay outside. Elizabeth leaves tomorrow for London. The king is returning to France and she will be regent once more. And I will go straight from here to Framlingham and Lady Mary. It will be good to be busy.

The only drawback to the seclusion of Hatfield is that one has too much time in which to think.

Minuette closed her diary, not daring to confide to paper the nature of her thoughts over the last month. She had always been impulsive by nature, quick to act and quicker to forget, but these last weeks had taught her a degree of introspection she had never thought possible.

During her month of pondering, she had reached two conclusions. First, that what had passed between her and William had been nothing more than grief taking comfort in a convenient manner. He would have reached for any woman that night. That it had been her was a complication, but one that would mend with time and perhaps a hint of humour.

Her second conclusion was that she wanted Dominic in every way she could imagine. In her mind, she could recall perfectly the look in his eyes when he'd pressed his lips to her wrist. If those few minutes with William had done nothing else, they had left Minuette certain of what it was she had seen in Dominic's eyes. She wanted very much to see it again.

Restless, she rose from her desk and wandered to the window overlooking the gardens. The warmth had lingered through September, but the gardens were beginning to show signs of autumn, with leaves curling in on themselves and the last blooms of summer drooping tiredly to the ground. The sky itself had changed in the last day or so, the blue faded and the clouds a dull pewter.

Matters still needed mending with William, no doubt of that, but with his return to France for negotiations she had another month or so to think of what to say and how to say it to smooth over uncomfortable memories. Another month to remember how to be his friend and to make it easy for him to treat her as such.

Another month until Dominic returned.

As she looked south, a cloud of dust caught her attention. Riders, three or four of them. Elizabeth had not spoken of visitors. Through the haze, Minuette saw the standard carried by one of the riders, and her heart stopped beating at the sight of crimson and blue, lions and lilies.

William.

William was inside Hatfield, halfway through the great hall, before Elizabeth came hastening to meet him. Her face showed her utter surprise.

"Has something gone wrong? Are you not going to France?"

"I am on my way to Dover."

"By way of Hatfield?"

"I have instructions for you."

"Instructions you could not commit to paper?" she asked with pardonable skepticism.

"And to see Minuette."

There was a long, neutral silence. William did not look away from his sister's probing expression. She was the one who had urged him to deal with Minuette sooner rather than later. She could hardly criticize his wish to do so now.

Her reply, when it came, was amused. "Do you truly have instructions for me, or shall I consider my role as your pretext duly fulfilled by saying hello?"

His lips twitched in spite of himself. "I truly do have instructions."

She gave orders for fresh horses to be readied for his continued journey and provided refreshments for his men in the kitchen. Then the two of them retreated to her study overlooking the knot garden with its meticulously groomed curves and smooth paths.

Elizabeth had been right—everything William told her now either already had been covered or could have been dealt with by letter. But she did not remind him of it again, merely asked an intelligent question or two about the state of the exchequer and the handling of a land dispute between a local baron and the crown in Suffolk. They were finished in just over a quarter of an hour.

Tidying her desk and papers, Elizabeth rose. "Shall I send for Minuette? She might prefer it if I was with her."

William knew he should accept Elizabeth's presence. No doubt Minuette would prefer it. But he wanted to see her alone, if only to prove that he still could. "No, I'll . . . I shall be in the gardens. Alone."

Her face hardened. "Will you tell her about your plans for Mary Stuart?"

"Do you imagine she does not already know?" William shot back.

With a sigh, Elizabeth said, "I'll send her to the garden. And I will remain here." *Where I can see you,* she did not have to add.

He paced the raked gravel paths from one end of the knot garden to the other, trying to keep his head clear and his mind on what he had to say. But when he heard Minuette's light footsteps behind him, his carefully rehearsed words vanished.

He had seen her only twice in the last month—distant and formal at his mother's funeral events. She had seemed almost a stranger to him then. Today she looked herself, though with a stillness about her like a bird threatened by capture.

That stillness unnerved him. He had prepared himself to face down her anger or scorn—but not silence. He could not begin to guess what it meant.

He said what had to be said first. "I apologize, Minuette, for my behaviour at Hever. I was distraught, or I would never have insulted you in such a fashion."

Her reply was so quiet he had to strain to hear it. "I know."

He waited for her to say something more—to look at him, even, for she kept her eyes firmly on the path at her feet. Fumbling for words, and hating himself for it, William said, "I fear I have offended you. I pray you might forgive me."

At last she lifted her eyes, and William felt the tightness in his chest ease as she said tremulously, "I feared that the offense was mine. I thought you might not wish to remember how shameless I was."

William nearly laughed aloud from relief. That was her fear—that he had been offended because she had proven that she could render passion for passion? Her response while in his arms had not been an offense. It had been a revelation.

But he could hardly say that to her, not when he was on his way to France with every expectation of a formal betrothal. He must forget what had happened and focus on Mary Stuart. He could not afford to be distracted by sentiment.

You cannot afford to fall in love with her, William.

He had not intended to see Minuette at all until after he returned from France, safely betrothed. He had thought to leave her a letter, perhaps, an easy method of smoothing things over without the awkwardness of referring to it in person. But yesterday, on impulse, he had opened a coffer taken from his mother's chambers at Hever: a small, carved chest containing, not jewels but his father's love letters.

There were three dozen in all, most written before their marriage. They were beautiful, a mingling of passion and tenderness that William had not yet felt for any woman. He had never doubted that his father had wanted his mother, but as he read the letters signed Henry Rex, he realized for the first time that his father's love had gone beyond desire. With each endearment—*my mistress and friend, mine own darling, wishing myself in my sweetheart's arms*—William had felt increasingly troubled. He had whispered plenty of sweet words into women's ears, but they had never matched the fervent simplicity of his father's declarations.

He dragged his attention back into the Hatfield gardens and said the first thing that came to mind. "When you return to London, you will find that . . . I have . . . that is, Eleanor has left court."

As he saw the flare of surprise in her eyes, he wished he could take back his words. He remembered Elizabeth's warning about empty apartments and whores and felt the colour rise in his cheeks. Please heaven Minuette would not read into it what Elizabeth had feared.

But she seemed as determined as he to keep the conversation on commonplace ground. "What of France? You expect King Henri to meet your terms?"

"Yes."

"Including Mary Stuart?"

When William did not answer, Minuette pressed. "She is your principal demand, is she not?"

It was getting harder to speak calmly. "Yes."

She seemed aware of his discomfort, or perhaps it was her own that prompted her to say, "You have a long ride ahead. Safe journey, William."

How could he ever have thought he could see her and talk with her and not want her? The long weight of her hair, her slender figure and steady eyes . . .

France and his future were waiting. He knew what he must do.

"Minuette."

He found himself staring at the peak of her hair, the point of gold in the perfect center of her forehead. All at once he could see his parents standing before him. He must have been little at the time, but he could recall it clearly—his tall, forbidding father reaching out one hand to smooth his wife's dark hair in a gesture of infinite tenderness.

Henry had cast off a queen and a daughter and a religion for Anne, and all of Europe had been asking ever since if he had found her worth it in the end. The answer was yes—in that moment, William was sure of it. Henry had loved her, and he had let nothing stand in his way.

He touched his right hand to the silk of Minuette's hair and said the only honest thing he dared. "I will miss you."

An hour after William rode away from Hatfield, Elizabeth finally went out to Minuette. She had stayed in the knot garden, perched on a bench and staring at nothing, and she only blinked when Elizabeth laid a cloak around her shoulders.

Elizabeth had determined from that first night not to ask about William. Minuette had always been politely reticent about Robert, and she was owed the same consideration. But the surprise of his visit and the deepening twilight seemed to unlock Minuette's reserve.

"I had thought," she said, "that I had lost his regard. I am glad to know my behaviour has not made him despise me."

Elizabeth bit back her first response—that her brother had

enough to despise in his own behaviour—and merely murmured a neutral acknowledgment. But Minuette seemed to know by instinct Elizabeth's opinion, and she rushed to defend him, as she always had.

"He apologized quite thoroughly, Elizabeth. It was awkward, but now it is past."

"What else did he say?"

"We spoke a little of France and Mary Stuart."

How Elizabeth wished she could ask Minuette how she felt about that, and whether she was truly in danger of being hurt by William. For as simple and open as she had always thought her friend, Elizabeth realized, she had no idea what Minuette was feeling.

After a pause, Minuette added, "What happened at Hever was an impulse, born of grief and strain and convenience. It will soon be forgotten, and all the better for us both."

Elizabeth knew that tone of Minuette's voice—it meant she was trying to persuade herself as much as her listener. For her part, Elizabeth was entirely unconvinced. *We Tudors are notoriously stubborn where our hearts are concerned,* she wanted to warn.

Leaning her head against Elizabeth's shoulder, a gesture from childhood, Minuette said, "I must finish preparing for Framlingham."

"Did you tell William where you are going?" Elizabeth asked.

"No more than you did. He thinks I will be in London with you, and he must go to France thinking of peace, not fretting about things he cannot control here."

Those are my uncle's words, Elizabeth thought. But she could not disagree.

Sensing her concern, as Minuette always seemed able to do, she said, "You must not fret, either. We each of us have our duties. And when they are finished, we will come back together and all will be well."

Minuette stood in a sudden movement and said into the shadows as she walked away, "When he comes home, all will at last be well."

There was something about her voice that made Elizabeth wonder whether William was the "he" she meant.

CHAPTER SEVENTEEN

B Y THE FOURTH day out of Cambridge, Minuette was
ready to run mad. They had left Hatfield a week earlier,
she and Carrie headed for Framlingham while Elizabeth returned to London. They traveled with a dozen royal guards and
Rochford had suggested she take a closed carriage as well. Minuette had flatly refused—if she was going to travel for a week,
she was going to ride rather than be jolted about like a parcel.
Carrie had to ride pillion behind a groom, but she had not
complained. Not about the riding, at any rate. But as Framlingham drew nearer, Carrie grew quieter.

It had taken three stormy days to reach Cambridge, but even
the rain had not deterred Minuette. If she had to do this, she
wanted to get started. The longer it took her to reach Framlingham, the more time she had to think about all the things that
could go wrong. Fortunately, the skies had cleared a bit after
Cambridge and on this last afternoon, though it was windy and
cold, it was dry.

They stopped briefly at an inn just four miles from the castle.
Minuette tried to spark conversation with Carrie as they walked
around the inn yard to stretch their legs.

"I'm beginning to remember the road," Minuette remarked. "I wasn't sure that I would after so many years."

Carrie said nothing.

"It must be even more familiar to you," Minuette prodded. "You were here nearly two years with my mother."

"So I was," she said at last.

"I hope you remember your way around the castle. I have only vague memories of a bewildering array of walls and towers and corridors." Even as she said it, an image sparked in her head of a particular corridor and a room opening off it—old stone, cold and empty. Or nearly empty . . .

The image vanished as Carrie said sharply, "I remember that one should not wander alone. Promise me that, mistress. The castle cannot be trusted, no more than those inside it."

It was the first negative comment she had ever heard Carrie utter. The surprise of it stayed with Minuette as they remounted and rode the last miles to Framlingham.

The flint walls rose out of the surrounding fields like a shield piercing the low sky. Minuette felt she was seeing it with doubled eyes—one set here and now, approaching on horseback with the might of the Lord Chancellor at her back, the other set those of a six-year-old girl seeing her mother's new home and knowing it would never be hers.

By the time they reached the walls the gates were open, alerted by the guards on the wall walks. Unlike most castles of its age, Framlingham had no keep, depending instead on its formidable curtain walls and towers to defend the sprawl of domestic buildings across the courtyards. They were greeted by men in the red, gold, and blue badges of Norfolk, and a soberly dressed man introduced himself as steward and offered to take Minuette to her room.

"I'll do it," drawled a voice Minuette had hoped not to hear. It seemed her stepfather was at the family residence as well.

She allowed him to lead her with a hand tucked through his arm into a wing that jutted at a sharp angle from an outer castle wall. "Near Her Highness," Howard said. "At her request. You don't mind that we use her title, do you?"

"Would it matter if I did?"

"You might report it."

"Do you think William does not know what your family calls her?"

They reached a door that Howard opened. "Yours," he said, and dropped her hand. "I think William knows what we call her. I think he doesn't care. Perhaps he should."

"Dear me," she said sweetly. "Do you have something to report?"

He gave her a somewhat savage smile. "You're in Norfolk territory now. I won't do your spying for you. However, I will give you one piece of advice."

"Yes?" She expected a warning about the duke or Mary's temper, or even a repeat of Carrie's advice not to go wandering alone.

"My nephew Giles and his wife are in residence. They've spoken of you, both of them. From their words, I'm not sure which one is the greater danger—but I tell you this: you have enemies here, girl. And I don't mean political. Their enmity is personal. I would take care if I were you."

He walked away, whistling as he went.

Dominic was surprised when he arrived, as summoned, to find William alone. The king had been in Rouen for two weeks now, and their encounters had been all business, surrounded by councilors and soldiers and diplomats. He had tried not to take it personally—he knew how critical this treaty was—but there had been a mean part of him that had wondered if William as an unfettered king meant no more Will as his friend.

Tonight William looked to be his friend. He had discarded the heavy jewels and jerkin and sat in an armchair with his legs stretched out and a cup in one hand. He nodded to the table, where another cup and a jug of ale sat. "Help yourself."

Dominic filled the cup, then sat in a matching chair at an angle to William's. "You look tired," he commented.

William laughed. "You are the worst courtier ever. Sitting alone with your king, and the first words out of your mouth are a criticism, or possibly an insult."

His tone made Dominic's shoulders ease. He sighed and leaned back in a similar pose. "I've missed you."

"Hmmm." William looked into the fire, necessary in the October chill. "I've been . . . busy. Distracted."

"Yes, I'm impressed. I never thought to see you quite so dedicated to work."

"Your lessons," William said. "You're a better teacher than you thought."

There was more than tiredness there, more than the distraction of politics. Dominic knew William through and through, and there was something bothering him.

"What's wrong?" he asked.

"I have a favour to ask."

"Anything, you know that." Why did William sound so hesitant? If he wanted, he could command Dominic to anything.

"I want you to return to England. Immediately."

Even as he said, "May I ask why?" he was thinking, *He really doesn't want to be anywhere near me. What has he done?*

Finally William met his eyes. "Because I cannot go, and you are the only one I trust for this."

"Mary?" he hazarded. "Is she still with Norfolk?"

"At Framlingham, yes. My uncle wrote to me, says there's possible movement by the emperor's fleet."

"Maneuvering to get her out of the country."

"Right."

Dominic ran a hand through his hair. "Troubling, yes, but Rochford is much better suited to this than I am. Why send me back to court?"

"Not to court. To Framlingham."

"Will, you're not making any sense."

"Mary is at Framlingham, with the Duke of Norfolk."

"I don't know what you want me to do."

William went on as though Dominic had not spoken. "Giles and Eleanor are also there—"

"So you want me to get your mistress safely away in case of trouble?"

"—and so is Minuette. It appears my uncle sent her there."

Blank silence settled in his chest with a weight that stopped his breath. He was surprised by how calm he sounded. "What in the name of God is Minuette doing in the same house as Giles Howard?"

"Rochford sent her to look for the Penitent's Confession."

Dominic was on his feet before he knew it, ready to wrap his hands around someone's neck. Rochford's, preferably. "Has he lost his mind? He has no right to put her in danger. What was he thinking, launching Minuette into a world where men kill to keep their secrets? You must get her out of there, now—"

"Why do you think I'm sending you?" William shoved the chair back and was on his feet as well, staring him down.

Dominic forced himself to breathe slowly. "Right. I'm sorry, I was just . . ."

"Worried. So am I. Ride light; get to Le Havre as fast as you can. I'll send letters to free a ship for you. When you land, don't head to London. Go straight on to Framlingham."

"How much danger is she in?"

William turned away, so all Dominic could see were his shoulders, braced tight. "Just get her out of there."

"I will."

He was halfway down the corridor when he heard footsteps. He stopped and let William catch him up.

"Will you give her a message for me?" William asked. He sounded, once again, unusually diffident.

"Of course."

"Tell her . . ." He paused, and in his eyes Dominic saw something hovering, something that his friend seemed almost ready to share. But he just smiled and said, "Tell her I have missed her."

When she was six years old, Minuette had spent the week of her mother's wedding at Framlingham, lost and unhappy and missing Elizabeth fiercely. She had been assigned a nursemaid, a girl who had taken to her job less than enthusiastically and from whom Minuette had slipped away more than once to wander around the castle on her own. Now that she had returned twelve years later, Minuette found herself ignoring Carrie's advice not to venture out alone and began retracing her steps—and her memories—through the maze of the castle.

Today, a week after her arrival, Minuette returned to the northeast tower, a place she had last been on the day before her mother's wedding. As it had been then, it was still room after empty room, some furnished with odds and ends but many more with only dust and the occasional mouse nest. Minuette remembered tracing her name several times in the grime of a low windowsill before deciding to go in search of her mother, who had promised that her daughter might sit with her while she finished the embroidery on Minuette's dress for the wedding.

She followed the trail of memory along the echoing corridor to where, all those years ago, a sound had caught her attention—an almost laugh that turned into a sigh. Curiosity had led her then to the half-open door ahead of her. She would never dream of walking into a royal room uninvited, but she had no such inhibitions in this house. Standing in the gap where the door had been left ajar, she looked in.

Her mother stood with her back against the far wall, eyes closed and skirts in an untidy heap. Her arms were locked around the neck of the man before her. Frozen in fascination and disgust, Minuette watched until the man groaned and buried his head against her mother's chest.

The moment her mother opened her eyes she let out a little cry, and the man pulled away from her and turned around. Minuette stared at her almost stepfather, waiting for a roar of words or even a slap. But when he moved, it was only to adjust his clothing and, surprisingly, he laughed.

"How long before some man has you against a wall, sweetheart?"

Minuette had run away then, back to her own quiet corner of the nursery, and when her mother tried to talk to her later she had kept her face still and nodded submissively that yes, she understood that some things were between grown-ups. She had attended the wedding the next day and gone gladly back to Hatfield afterward, burying the memory so deep she had forgotten it until now.

As Minuette stood in that still-empty room all these years

later, she knew it wasn't just Framlingham that had stirred up the memory. It had been coming at her for months, pricked into life by the nasty words of Alyce de Clare's sister: *It was the younger Howard she'd always had her eye on.* And Queen Anne's ramblings: *Go to your Henry. I know what it is to love a dangerous man.* And Hever, where a man had indeed had her up against a wall and she had not stopped him.

Minuette walked out of the empty room, not sure if her melancholy was caused by the fact that her mother was dead and thus could never explain her complexities to Minuette or if it was her own complicated emotions that were haunting her.

That uncertainty continued to stalk her over the next week, alternating only with her violent wish to be elsewhere. She did not like Framlingham, she did not like spying on Lady Mary, and she most definitely did not like being in the same place as Giles and Eleanor Howard. At least Eleanor had not brought her daughter along. That would have been one indignity too many for Minuette to bear. But still, every waking hour was tense and unhappy and every sleeping hour filled with fragmented dreams. She did not think she had truly rested at all since leaving Hatfield.

The only saving grace were the letters. Elizabeth wrote daily, and today she had forwarded five letters that Dominic had sent from France. His letters were like him: practical, steady, a rock of sense in the waves of turmoil. She wished she could ask him what to do—about Giles and Eleanor, about her mother's mysterious heart, about Mary's intentions—but the last thing she wanted him to know was where she was. He would be angry if he knew—probably with her for letting herself be manipulated into such a situation.

As Minuette tried to compose a letter to Dominic one afternoon, Carrie asked abruptly, "Should you be doing something that you are afraid to tell Lord Exeter about?"

Not entirely truthfully, Minuette said, "I am not afraid of Lord Exeter. I am doing what I have been asked to do, and there is nothing wrong in that."

"There is something wrong in it," Carrie said. "And if you will not see it, then I will see it for you."

As Carrie did not know the whole of why they were there, Minuette was curious. "What do you think is wrong?" she asked.

With a startling fierceness, Carrie said, "You do not belong at Framlingham, nor anywhere near the Howards. Why do you think your mother wouldn't have you with her when she married Lord Stephen? She wanted you kept safe, and there's no safety in this nest of vipers."

"Carrie—"

"She hated the old duke and she hated Framlingham. This is where she died, and heaven knows I would never have come back here but for you."

Minuette let Carrie's breathing even out and her high colour fade to normal before she asked, "And Lord Stephen? Did my mother hate her husband as well?"

"No," Carrie said grudgingly. "But that doesn't mean she was comfortable with him. Whatever she felt, it wasn't simple."

A woman's voice drifted from the open doorway. "Dear, dear, such venom. If I were you, Mistress Wyatt, I would slap your maid for such words."

"You are not me," Minuette said coolly, dismissing Carrie with a nod. When they were alone, she asked Eleanor, "What do you want?"

Eleanor perched on the edge of the table and plucked up one

of Dominic's letters. "'William is working hard,'" she read, "'which both surprises and pleases me. I am pressing for a quick finish, for I desperately miss England. No later than mid-November, we are promised. I send my good wishes always . . . Dominic.'"

Minuette concentrated on keeping her temper, for there was no William here to back her. Eleanor seemed a great favorite of the Duke of Norfolk, and Minuette was a guest in his home—a guest whose mission was to determine if he was about to commit treason.

"William has not written you?" Eleanor asked, a little too casually.

"I did not expect him to," Minuette replied. *I will miss you,* he'd said. She shoved that memory away.

"Really? I thought the two of you were such . . . friends." She stood up with that annoying feline assuredness and said, "He has written to me."

Not for anything in the world would Minuette ask what William had written, but she felt a strong flash of jealousy. After Hever, added to their years of friendship . . . *It doesn't matter,* she told herself. *It's not as though I want William to be in love with me.*

She stood as well, snatched back the letter that Eleanor still held, and said, "I am expected by the Lady Mary. You will excuse me."

"Of course." But Eleanor didn't move. "Have you had any word from Jonathan recently?"

Minuette had to calculate quickly in her mind—was it likely that Jonathan would have told Eleanor about her refusal? Surely not. He was kind but not stupid. This was nothing more than Eleanor fishing for information.

"I have not heard from Jonathan," she said. "I understood that he is to stay in Lord Exeter's service until the treaty is done."

"Did Lord Exeter tell you that?"

If Eleanor wouldn't leave, then Minuette would. She walked to the open door without bothering to answer, but Eleanor called after her. "Do you not wish to know why William wrote to me?"

Not if it were my last wish on earth, Minuette thought. She had just entered the corridor when Eleanor added, "He sent his congratulations. I am once more with child."

To the end of her days, she would count it to her credit that she did not react outwardly. She did not turn or exclaim or falter in her escape. But neither did she come to her surroundings until she was outdoors, in the massive enclosed courtyard. She had to stop to draw breath, to blink furiously up at the sky, to will herself not to cry. *It's nothing to do with me,* she thought. *It doesn't matter.* Who could even say that this child was William's? Eleanor had been married more than a year now, after all.

The tightness of her body eased. And just in time, for Lady Mary was walking in her direction. As she approached Minuette, she waved off the two ladies who attended her. "Will you walk with me?" she asked.

"Yes, my lady," Minuette said, falling into step with her. Mary wore a cloak over her dark blue dress, and Minuette realized she was cold, having dashed outside without any thought to the October temperatures. But "wait while I fetch a cloak" was not something one said to royalty, not even dispossessed royalty. Her light wool kirtle would have to suffice.

She waited, as one did, for Mary to launch a topic. The French treaty again, worrying away at William's matrimonial options, continued probing for cracks in the king's council . . .

"Are you a true Catholic, Mistress Wyatt?"

"I beg your pardon, my lady?"

Mary turned her handsome, severe face to her. "I have not

seen you at service above three times since you came to Framlingham. As you appear in all other aspects to be well, I must wonder if you are, in your heart, a believer."

How could she possibly answer? Those words meant something different depending on who asked them. From Mary, they meant *Do you believe in the supremacy of the Pope? Do you believe my father was wrong in claiming that supremacy? Do you believe that those who disagree are heretics?*

"I am a true subject of His Majesty, the king."

That displeased Mary. "Even kings are subject to God."

"I did not say otherwise." But whether that made them subject to the Pope . . . Theological disputes made Minuette's head ache.

"You are subtle in your words," Mary said. "I should expect that from one trained as you were, in the household of that woman."

And don't you think you might believe what you do because of your training from your mother? Minuette wondered. She thought of her mother's rosary, left safely at Wynfield, and wondered how her beliefs might have differed if her mother had not left her at court. *Perhaps all the debates have less to do with God's will and more to do with our own experience.*

Or perhaps I am wrong, and Mary is right, and I will end in hell for my support of Queen Anne. If so, she might as well be damned for her true beliefs.

"I think," Minuette said, "that God cannot love form more than He does His children. Why must England tear itself apart over this small matter of form?"

Mary hardened, and Minuette thought she must look quite a bit like her mother just now, infallibly right and royally certain. "The saving of God's children will never be a small matter. It is everything. And if the king will not see it . . ."

Every sense alert, Minuette probed, "Then what?"

"A true son of my father will shake off the evil of his councilors and do what is right."

That left some interesting possibilities, Minuette thought. Reverse that sentence and it became *If he does not shake off the evil of his councilors . . . then he is not a true son of my father.*

The only thing staying Mary's hand as figurehead of a rebellion was her belief in William's paternity. Even that was a little shaky, since William had been conceived before her mother's death and was thus, in Mary's eyes, not legitimate. But if Mary were brought to believe that Henry had not been William's father at all, then her righteousness would be a weapon used to set England aflame.

And that is why I am here, Minuette reminded herself. *Forget Eleanor, forget insults and unpleasant memories and Carrie's warnings and my ethical uneasiness. I have to find the Penitent's Confession before it can be used to start a war.*

CHAPTER EIGHTEEN

Elizabeth read the dispatch her uncle had handed her in private with an anger that increased with each word. When she finished the précis, she laid it down carefully on the table before her and said grimly, "Where did you get this information?"

"An intercept from the Spanish ambassador."

"Bring him to me. Now," Elizabeth spat.

Rochford hesitated. "I would counsel patience, Your Highness."

"Three Spanish ships are headed to our coast. How long am I supposed to be patient—until Mary can be smuggled out? Until she shows up at the emperor's court, or as the figurehead of an army? What are you waiting for?"

If he was offended, he didn't let it show. "Until we can be certain of the enemy within our gates. The Spanish cannot do this without English help. Let them play it out, think that all is well, and when they are relaxed . . . we strike."

Elizabeth sat back, considering. "Framlingham is not far from the coastline. Mary could easily be moved from there to a ship."

Rochford inclined his head.

Her anger grew. "Framlingham—where you have sent Minuette. How could you? She is the least likely spy . . ."

"Which is why she is useful. She has already shared indications that Norfolk means to move soon."

"I want her out. Today."

As he met her gaze, Elizabeth felt the full weight of her uncle's authority and years of rule. For the first time, she wondered which of them would prevail in a confrontation. Just how far would her borrowed power take her?

With a shrug, Rochford said, "The girl is not in danger. I have men nearby and she knows how to reach them."

"Why, if there is no threat of danger?" Elizabeth challenged. She thought of what William would say if he were having this conversation, and the knowledge of his anger made her even bolder. "She is not yours to use."

The struggle was all in the eyes, Elizabeth thought. *Don't look away, don't show fear, don't back down.*

Rochford spoke first. "I propose a compromise. You send a man you trust to Norfolk. A man who can be trusted with the relevant information. A man Mistress Wyatt would trust as well. Give him power to determine the situation. A man inside the house itself, who can act at once if he senses the slightest danger."

When she did not respond immediately, Rochford leaned forward and fixed her with an intent focus that reminded her forcibly of her mother. "Elizabeth, this is not a game. This is your brother's kingdom. There are those who would take it from him by violence, and though she is your sister, Mary will allow herself to be used by such men. We must know who they are. William's life may depend on it."

"Whom would you suggest?"

He shook his head. "I would prefer that you choose, Your Highness. Mistress Wyatt is your friend, and I want you to be assured that whomever you send will look after her as you would wish."

There was only one choice. "Send for Lord Robert Dudley."

Her uncle was quick—he'd been gone only a quarter hour when Robert entered the room. He bowed in the doorway, then sauntered across to her.

"You have an assignment for me, milady?" Robert kissed Elizabeth's hand, lingering to draw it along his cheek. Elizabeth closed her eyes, savouring the heady touch of recklessness.

All too soon, she drew her hand away and met Robert's intimate gaze with what she hoped was a neutral one. "I do have an assignment. A critical one."

"I'm listening."

"I need you to go to Framlingham at once."

"Sending me away? When I've only just returned from France?"

"I'm serious, Robert. Minuette is there, at my uncle's behest. She is keeping watch for him on Mary."

"And she's in over her head?"

"Possibly."

"This won't be easy. I am my father's son, after all. And the name of Dudley is not a welcome one in Catholic circles."

"You are not going at Rochford's request, you are going at mine. And I do not need you to be trusted. Rather the opposite—I would be quite glad for everyone in that house to be on their guard with you around."

It was so easy to overlook the canny and careful man behind the lightness. But it was in full evidence now, as Robert laced his fingers together and studied her with something other than flirtation. "You think they would harm her?"

Elizabeth had asked herself that, without coming to a conclusion. "I think that Minuette is too trusting for her own good. You are to ensure that doesn't get her into trouble."

"Are you certain this order comes from you?"

"Why?"

A shake of his head and the mischief was back. "I want to know that you are the one who owes me, and not Rochford." He trailed a finger down her cheek. "I'd much rather collect a debt from you."

Minuette spent the next six days in almost constant attendance of either Lady Mary or the Howard family. Her head buzzed with gossip, her skin crawled with half-told truths, and still she was no nearer finding the Penitent's Confession than she had been a month ago. She was beginning to wonder precisely what Rochford expected of her—to declare Framlingham under crown control and demand they turn out all their secrets for her? *It might come to that,* she thought blackly, *in which case Rochford did not send enough men with me.*

A headache sent her finally to solitude in her own room, but she couldn't settle to anything. Finally she sent for Carrie, merely to have someone not an enemy to talk to.

Carrie took one look at her and brought Minuette a cold compress for her head and an herbal concoction for her to sip. Then she instructed her to shut her eyes.

"I will, if you'll tell me what you've been doing with your days."

"I've been sitting with an old woman who helped nurse your mother at the end. She's served the Howards since she was a girl, and they've put her in a suite of rooms now that she's too frail to walk much. I suppose that speaks well of them."

Carrie said it doubtfully, as though admitting that even a

snake might have some useful points, and Minuette said, "Tell me about that, about my mother's death."

There was a long silence, and she forced herself to keep her eyes closed, afraid to give Carrie any reason to be distracted. Finally Carrie said, "Childbed fever, it was, you know that."

"But I don't know what it means. How long was she ill? Did she know her baby had died? Did she ask for me?" That last question brought William to her mind, and she realized that they were all of them orphans now. Except Dominic, who might as well have been, what with his mother so far away and not always sure of who she was.

"I never liked Lord Stephen, but I will say for him that he wouldn't leave her side. He told her himself about the baby, stayed with her when she wept. And when the fever came . . . he slept in a chair, when he slept at all, and he ordered us around as though he could keep death away if he just willed it hard enough."

This was an entirely new picture of her stepfather, and yet Minuette found she could believe it.

"Pity is, she didn't know he was there, not at the end."

"Like Queen Anne," Minuette murmured.

"Worse, really. Your mother . . . she didn't wake at all for the last week. She lingered longer than we thought she could, never eating, never drinking, never waking. A blessing, I suppose. She didn't know she was dying."

Carrie's tone changed to briskness. "At any rate, the old nurse was very good to her, and it's little enough I can do to sit with her for a spell. She likes to talk and has no one to listen to her. Though she said the young master was a captive audience right enough last year."

"The young master?"

"Giles Howard. She nursed him the spring before his marriage. A month they were locked up, just the two of them and someone to cook and clean. Probably he got well faster than he would have just to get away from her talking."

Minuette's attention was entirely caught. "Giles was ill the spring before his marriage?" She bit her lip. March of last year he had not been at home, despite what he had told the court. He had spent the month in a remote manor—so her stepfather had told her. She had assumed he'd taken Alyce there, gotten her with child that month. But what if he hadn't?

"What month, Carrie? Do you remember?"

"Early spring, before Easter. Had the pox, he did. Family didn't want it spread around court, so they kept it quiet."

Minuette was left speechless. She had to admit that having the pox and being discreetly nursed sounded far more like Giles than did sweeping Alyce de Clare off her feet and into a dangerous romance. Frankly, her opinion of Alyce rose if Giles had not been her lover.

But then who had?

For a frightening moment Minuette wondered if all this suspicion of the Howard family was her fault. But no, Rochford had his own spies. Her stepfather had clearly warned them of the Penitent's Confession. And just because Giles hadn't been Alyce's lover didn't mean it hadn't been a Howard. There was the Earl of Surrey, after all—he was young. There was even her stepfather himself, who was not young but did have an air of dissolute charm about him.

Still, she had been so sure it was Giles.

She didn't have long to fret about it, because just after breakfast the next morning Robert Dudley arrived at Framlingham. When he was shown in—obviously uninvited and unwanted—

Minuette didn't know whether to laugh or rage. She settled for dragging him to an out-of-the-way corner of the kitchen gardens as soon as possible.

"This is getting ridiculous," she said. "How could there possibly be anything afoot here with people popping in and out without warning? If I were Norfolk, I would simply sit back and entertain myself while everybody runs around like headless fowl."

"Finished?" Robert asked, and the fact that he was calm, that he did not tease her, brought Minuette back uncomfortably to earth. If Robert was serious, then something was definitely wrong.

"I'm finished. Why are you here?"

"The Spanish navy is on the move. If Mary's going to run for it, it will be soon—possibly days. And I have a message for you from Lord Rochford. One he would not risk committing to paper."

"What is it?"

"An informant from inside the emperor's household says that the plan might not be to spirit away Mary—if his men are presented with evidence of the king's illegitimacy, they are authorized to land and march on London."

"Then they believe the evidence is here?"

Robert nodded.

Minuette sank onto the edge of a raised planting bed, thinking of Spanish soldiers on English soil. "It might already be gone," she began, but Robert shook his head.

"If the Spanish had it, Rochford would know. It's got to be at Framlingham. Do you have any idea where?"

"The family must be keeping it near. In one of their private chambers. I've looked where I can—I've even been through Mary's rooms when she's at service—but I can hardly walk into, say, the duke's private bedchamber and start tearing things apart."

"Think, Minuette."

"I've done nothing but think!" She caught herself and said more calmly, "Robert, this is too important to be left in our hands. Rochford must intervene. Send for his soldiers, have them lock Framlingham down."

"If necessary, those are my orders." Not unkindly, Robert perched on the uncomfortably narrow edge next to her and took her hands in his. "You are not here because you're Elizabeth's friend. Rochford doesn't work that way. You are here because he believed you could do this. You have been here for a month. You can read people. You know who is keeping secrets and the ways they try to hide them. This affidavit is the most important piece of paper the Catholics could ever lay their hands on. It will be kept safe. Mary would consider it sacred. Where is it?"

She shut her eyes. *Safe. Sacred.* The most private of places—a bedchamber would be that. But Mary would know that hers was always under scrutiny. She would not risk keeping it there. The Duke of Norfolk . . . the most likely, except that he had not survived to his age by being careless. He knew he was under suspicion. He would not want such a document found in his personal possession—he would want to be able to deny knowledge.

Giles, then? Even as Minuette shuddered at the thought of invading Giles's bedchamber, she dismissed it. Giles could not be trusted—not even by his father. Nothing so critical would be left to him.

Where is it? Safe, sacred, private . . .

A thought teased at the edge of her vision.

Sacred.

Her eyes flew open, and she looked at Robert with wonder. "I know where it is."

"Good girl. Where?"

"The chapel. Well, no, not the chapel itself—too many people going in and out. But there's a lady chapel to the side, small and beautiful. And always locked. Lady Mary uses it for her private worship. Indeed, she has spent a great deal of time there these last ten days. Praying, I supposed."

"Probably she is. Mary will not take lightly to her brother's disposal, righteous though she may deem it." His eyes narrowed. "How do we get in?"

"There's only one key—and only the family have access."

"I'm pretty good at getting into places I shouldn't."

"Not this time." Minuette stood and shook out her skirts, feeling confident and terrified and elated all at once. "Giles Howard is going to let me in."

She could play him, do as Lady Rochford had said and use the one power a woman has, seduce him into letting her into the lady chapel, and then . . .

And then she could throw herself down a staircase from sheer self-loathing. *No,* she thought, *it won't go that far. Just far enough to get him close and get him distracted, and then I'll hit him with something. Hard.*

Dominic would not approve, she thought. But he worked for Rochford; surely even he had to do things of which he did not approve.

That didn't make the thought of explaining this to him any more palatable. Good thing she had time to think of how to word it.

CHAPTER NINETEEN

THE TREATY OF Rouen was signed November 1, 1554, in the great hall of Rouen Castle. The timbered hall was crowded with dignitaries, French and English, both royal retinues glittering in silks and velvets and jewels. William was the most soberly dressed, as befitted a son in mourning. He knew full well, though, that he still managed to look effortlessly royal in a plain purple doublet, ermine cloak, and jeweled collar. His head was bare, save for a circlet of beaten gold.

He looked down the long table to where King Henri of France sat, affixing his signature to the treaty. He was in the prime of life, but despite his richer clothing and the advantage of his years, he seemed to be trying too hard. It couldn't be easy, William thought, losing to a boy half his age. He tried not to let his triumph show too plainly. After all, he had gotten everything he'd asked for today.

Knowing how difficult it would be to hold Rouen, William had agreed to cede the city back to the French. However, Henri had not disputed the English plan to hold and garrison Le Havre and Harfleur. The debates had been minor and tedious, as William had guessed they would be. He was certain that Henri was prepared to give way on every lesser point, thus conserving his energy to fight the issue that mattered most: Mary Stuart.

When Archbishop Cranmer had finally raised the subject of a marriage alliance, William sensed the stiffening of the French across the room. They were prepared to refuse. Politely, no doubt, but a refusal nonetheless.

So when the archbishop formally asked for his betrothal to Elisabeth de France, Henri's nine-year-old daughter, William had nearly laughed aloud at the open mouths and bewildered expressions on every side. But he had merely continued to stare straight at Henri, daring him to refuse.

Henri did not refuse. Indeed, he appeared so relieved not to have to fight about Scotland's queen that he agreed to his daughter's betrothal with almost indecent haste. There had been no mention of securing Elisabeth's approval.

Her father had summoned her for the treaty signing, that she might at least meet her future husband. The girl stood mute at her father's shoulder with a single attendant behind her. As William rose to meet Henri in the middle of the chamber and clasp hands, the fragile-looking princess in her stiff court gown raised her head and looked straight at him. Though she had been well schooled, she was still a nine-year-old girl and she could not keep her eyes from shining.

William smiled and then, when the French king motioned his daughter forward to meet her betrothed, he bowed and kissed her hand gravely. As she sneaked another look at him from beneath lowered lashes, he thought, *I might have done worse. A betrothal composed of at least one adoring and uncritical partner is bound to be a success.*

Another thought lingered deeper, with an edge flavoured with Dominic's critical voice: *Are you sure you know what you're doing?*

But Dominic wasn't here.

At the banquet that followed, he found himself speaking to Renaud LeClerc. Dominic had been right—the French king had not demurred at the enormous sum asked for LeClerc's ransom. Now the commander offered his congratulations to William. "It cheers me to have peace between us, Your Majesty."

"And me as well."

"I regret only that I cannot bid farewell to Lord Exeter."

William smiled. "What would you have me tell him?"

Before answering, LeClerc studied William with an unusual focus. He said finally, "Bid him remember my words about friendship. Remind him that I would rejoice to see him ever at my home." And then he smiled and added, "And tell him to claim his Nicole. He has waited long enough."

The moment Dominic entered Framlingham's walls, he was struck by a tangible sense of waiting, as though a brooding priest were hovering over this troublesome flock to see what they might do. Harrington, riding at his side, felt it too, for he grunted and said, "Good spot for an army."

Too good a spot, Dominic thought. They were in the heart of Catholic country here and it was all too easy to imagine rebels flocking to Mary in this valley. It must not come to that.

At Framlingham he and Harrington were greeted politely, but with an underlying unease that alerted all Dominic's senses. "Lord Exeter, from the king," he told a boy, who ran ahead.

Dominic said to Harrington, "Find out where Mistress Wyatt's maidservant is. Her name is Carrie. Ask her what's been happening here."

Harrington accepted the order with characteristic silence and set off for the kitchens. Dominic was met at the door to the family wing by a steward who bowed. "My lord, we are preparing rooms for you. A bath, a chance to rest after your ride—"

"Where's the family, and the Lady Mary?"

"At supper, my lord. Do you not wish to . . ." The steward gestured to Dominic's creased and worn riding clothes. Dominic and Harrington had done the 140 miles from Hastings in just four days, and they looked, at best, disreputable. That could be useful here.

"I wish to be taken to Lord Norfolk. At once."

The servants might be nervous, but not to the point of outright rudeness. "This way, my lord."

The hall was set with many tables, but Dominic focused on the one placed crosswise to the others. There was Norfolk, expression flaring into dislike before settling into neutrality; Mary, who took a minute to place him but seemed unconcerned when she did; Eleanor, gleaming like the hardest of gems. Where was Minuette?

As he crossed the long hall to the top table, he finally found her near the end, seated between two men: Robert Dudley, which gave Dominic pause, but that surprise was swallowed up by the second man. Giles Howard. Who was leaning into Minuette as though he had been whispering to her.

Her eyes were enormous and unreadable. He waited for some sign—for her to cry his name in delight or even to come to him in welcome—but she sat frozen.

"My lord of Exeter," Norfolk said at last. "What an unexpected . . . pleasure."

Dominic forced himself to attend to the duke, tearing his eyes away from Minuette and Giles. "Lord Norfolk, I apologize for my sudden arrival. I come direct from the king in France. He wished you to be amongst the first to know that the French have agreed to nearly every one of our demands. The treaty was expected to be signed this very day."

"Such an important day," Norfolk said drily. "One wonders that he did not wish you by his side."

"A mark of his deep care for you. And for his dear sister." Dominic bowed to Mary, who looked distinctly displeased. A French treaty, signed and sealed, meant war with the emperor. That thread ran through many in this room—calculation and greed and true belief and rebellion. Oh, yes, it needed but a spark to flame into war.

The spark Minuette had been meant to find.

He slid his eyes sideways and found that her eyes were still on him, still wide and . . . what? Beseeching? Warning?

"Please, join us," Norfolk was saying, and Dominic found himself at the end of the table next to Robert Dudley, one re-move from Minuette. He was about to ask to change places when she unfroze and let her face light into conversation. He knew every pitch of her voice, every tone of her laughter. It was directed entirely at Giles.

He sat appalled and silent through the remainder of the meal while Minuette shamelessly flirted—there was no other word for it—with a married man. A married man who had tried to force her just over a year ago. *I should have killed him when I had the chance,* Dominic thought, but that was only to keep the blackness away.

Robert tried to engage him, but Dominic was not in the mood for Dudley charm. He only caught a phrase or two, something about Elizabeth (naturally) and asking if the sea had been calm when Dominic crossed. He gave one-word answers when forced, and otherwise ignored Robert.

He supposed he ate something; he most certainly drank. And

all the while Minuette's teasing voice wound through his memories of a more solemn Minuette in her mother's rose garden last year: *I am trained to reflect back whatever a man expects to see.*

Clearly Giles approved of the reflection—every time Dominic looked that way, he caught the insufferable blaze of Giles's revenge. *And me?* his mind whispered. *When I touched her at Hampton Court, when she shivered at my touch . . . was that part of her training, too?*

Finally the group broke up, Mary retiring and the duke following shortly after. In the eddies of goodnights and movement, Dominic managed to get near enough to Minuette to say, "I have a message for you, from the king."

Though Giles was not standing overly close to Minuette, his stance was possessive. "How is William?" he asked with an insolence that made Dominic's fingers twitch.

"Victorious," he said shortly. "May I speak with you, Mistress Wyatt? Privately?"

"Of course." She seemed nervous, as though she didn't know how to get out of there, what to say or do.

"I will bid you farewell," Giles said smoothly, and though he did not touch her, his gaze was offensively direct. "Until later."

He left, striding out in a manner that reminded Dominic that this was the Howards' home, after all. All the more reason to get Minuette out of here.

"What did William tell you?" Minuette asked, and Dominic thought it an odd way to ask after his message.

"That Rochford had sent you here without William's knowledge or permission. I'm here to take you home."

"Is that all he told you?" She searched his face as though trying to read beneath the surface.

"He said he has missed you."

Her cheek twitched, and she shut her eyes. Then she sighed and opened them, this time with something approaching her real smile. "I will be glad when all this is over."

"When all what is over? I thought you were here to ..." Dominic trailed off as he looked around at the servants and occasional clerk passing through the hall. He chose his words more carefully, and spoke lower. "What does Giles have to do with this?"

"Do you really have to ask?" she began, then her smile faltered. "You don't trust me. You believe I am—what? Stupid? Shallow? How could you think ... I have not forgotten, and I have certainly not forgiven. I would never be so careless with Giles Howard."

"No, Minuette. I am sorry. I was just ... I have come into this blind and I let fear override my judgment. You could never be careless in your affections."

Somehow, even that was the wrong thing to say, for she was still and pale in the candlelight. "Perhaps you think too highly of me," she said. "But I promise, I have done nothing with Giles of which I am ashamed. There is a purpose, and I do not forget that."

"Well, whatever that purpose is, it's no longer yours. I have direct orders from William to get you out of here. We ride in the morning. This is not your fight."

She studied him with grave intent, and for nearly the first time in his life, Dominic was not sure what she was thinking. "The morning," she repeated. "Then I should retire, in order to prepare. There aren't many hours left."

She smiled once more, but it was her brilliant court smile, which shut him out absolutely. "I will see you in the morning, Dominic."

He stared after her as she walked away, and might have stayed there if he hadn't caught sight of Harrington. Dominic strode over to him and asked, "What did Carrie have to say?"

"That the sooner you get Mistress Wyatt away from here, the better. She says Framlingham has had a bad effect on her lady, but that was all. Said she had to get to packing now that you were here to set things right."

How can I set things right when I'm not entirely sure what's going on? Dominic wondered.

Harrington went so far as to almost offer a suggestion. "Shall I keep a watch on her tonight?"

"No," Dominic said. "I'll do that. I want you watching the gates. Don't let anyone leave tonight. Rochford sent men with Mistress Wyatt; use them if you cannot find me. Whatever's going to happen, I think it will be tonight."

And Minuette would be in the middle of it. *What are you up to,* he wondered, *that you do not want me to know?*

I will not think of Dominic, I will not think of Dominic, I will not think . . . Minuette gulped the wine Carrie had begrudgingly brought her and wondered if she could get close enough to drunk to dull her senses without tipping into insensibility.

Half an hour later—as she tripped for the third time and had to tighten her hand on Giles's arm to keep from stumbling— she thought she hadn't quite got the balance right.

Giles chuckled roughly as she swayed. "Sure you want to keep going? There are any number of quiet corners closer than the chapel."

She widened her eyes innocently. "But the whole point is to give me a private tour of the lady chapel. Isn't it?"

"Whatever you wish to call it," he murmured.

The lady chapel could be entered only from inside the larger chapel. It was a relief to finally reach the door with its pointed arch, because Giles removed his arm to use the key.

Don't let me be wrong, she prayed silently. *Please don't let all of this be for nothing.*

Giles shoved the door open, wrapped his arm around Minuette's waist this time, and pulled her against his side as they entered. Her left hand and the candle flame wavered.

"Let's get this out of the way, shall we?" He plucked the candle from her hand, lit two of the tapers that waited on the altar (Popish chapel or not, Minuette thought that sacrilegious), and set down her own flame between them.

In the time it took him, Minuette felt a whisper threading through her whole body—as if something, or someone, was calling to her. *It's here,* she thought. *I was right.*

And then Giles was on her and her only thought was how to judge the balance between eagerness and hesitation.

She made herself relax, told her muscles to remain pliable. It was nothing like William or Dominic, nothing like the melting of bones and the instinct to merge. This was calculated and an imitation—but good enough for Giles. His breath was rough and his mouth insistent, his hands grasping at her bodice, fumbling for the laces ...

She made a slight sound of protest and stiffened, just enough to penetrate Giles's awareness. This was the tricky moment. She had to make him believe she was willing, not give him a reason to force her.

"This is ... I'm ..." She made her eyelashes flutter, looked down demurely.

"What?"

She bit her lip and decided Giles was arrogant enough to believe in her capitulation. "I just think ..." She looked shyly around the lady chapel. "It's private, but not very comfortable."

Would he take the hint?

"Comfortable? Well, I can remedy that. You won't leave?"

She kissed him, even let her tongue touch his lips. He gave a soft groan and pulled back. "I knew you were wild at heart."

He strode out on a mission, leaving the door to the main chapel open. Minuette went to shut it. In these next minutes she had to look very fast, or be prepared to hit him when he returned—and for either choice she needed privacy. But as she swung the door closed, a hand grasped the edge and Dominic stepped around.

"You told me once," he said in a whisper, coming into the lady chapel and closing the door, "that I am a rotten liar. Well, so are you. I knew you weren't going to be shut in your chamber packing tonight. Although this was not what I anticipated."

His face was a blank, and she wanted to burst into tears. She settled for attack. "How dare you follow me? How dare you doubt me? Do you really think that I am here to . . ." She couldn't make herself say it, not to Dominic.

He studied her gravely. "I think you are here in search of the Penitent's Confession. I think you found Giles useful. And I think he will return rather quickly, so you'd best start looking."

"You do not think I am . . . wanton?" She wanted—needed—his absolution. But even as she asked for it, she knew what she really wanted was absolution for kissing William. And that she would rather die than tell Dominic.

His unreadable expression sharpened into something she thought she might put a name to when she was less flustered. "I think you are the most honest person I know. I think you were very clever to get in here without rousing suspicion."

He took one step, two . . . She remembered Hampton Court and the wall against her back, and the quality of his stare was like it had been that night, pinning her in place. He spoke so softly she wasn't sure he meant to be heard. The words danced along her skin as much as reached her ear. "And wanton is not always wicked. Like so much else, it depends on the context."

He stepped back suddenly. "I'll watch the door," he said. "You start looking."

Look. Right. Minuette angled her back to Dominic and breathed in and out several times to still her incipient trembling. She'd thought her only trouble tonight would be imitating passion, not quelling it.

Where to look? She regretted not having come to service more often with Mary—then she would know the interior better. The lady chapel was small, and though it was richly decorated from its gilded and painted ceiling to the intricate stained-glass window depicting Salome with the John the Baptist's head on a platter, there was very little furniture. As she could see no way in which a document could be concealed on the frescoed walls with its murals of the temple of Solomon, that left the two cushioned chairs that stayed here permanently (the others were brought in from the larger chapel as needed), the altar, and the single tapestry that hung along the back wall.

Logic said the document would be in either the least likely spot, which would be the chairs, as they might be moved, or the least accessible, which would be on the back of the ten-foot-long tapestry.

But instinct drove her to the altar—instinct and the first image that came to mind when thinking of Mary, of a woman kneeling in prayer and supplication. A woman beseeching heaven for the right course. A righteous woman who cared more for God than for kings. Deposing William would be a crusade, not a rebellion, and a crusade must begin with an altar.

She ran her hands lightly along the top, then crouched to do the same along all four sides. She tried rapping it with her knuckles, searching for some sort of hidden opening. But there weren't any handy, elaborate carvings to trigger, and the smooth wood yielded nothing.

"Anything?" Dominic called softly.

"Not yet."

She reached the back of the altar with no success and sank down completely to think. The tapestry, then? That would require Dominic's help, which meant there was no hope of finishing before Giles returned. But at least she wouldn't have to hit him—Dominic would do that eagerly. *Too eagerly,* she thought. *I will have to make certain Dominic doesn't kill him.*

She began to rise, and her eyes passed the level where the top of the altar joined the base. There, a sliver caught her attention. She picked up the candle and saw that it was indeed a line of paler wood, thin and flat, which indicated . . . She used her free hand and felt that it was slightly out of line with the rest. She set the candle down on the altar and used both hands, trying to coax movement with her fingernails. The sliver of wood didn't move at first, and she began to think they would have to take an axe to the altar, but then it groaned slightly and gave with a rush and all at once she was holding a thin, slightly hollowed wooden tray. In it rested a linen-bound object.

"Dominic!" Even as she called him, her fingers were untying the ribbon around the linen and exposing a single sheet of vellum, with faded lettering and several watermarks. But it didn't obscure the opening: *The Penitent's Confession, touching on the affair of Anne Boleyn with her brother, George, and the true paternity of the Concubine's son.* There was a name affixed to the bottom, written in the clear script of a clerk, with a woman's signature penned beneath it: *Marie Hilaire Wyatt Howard.*

She stared numbly at her mother's name, a whimper escaping her throat. "I don't understand."

Clutching the precious, dangerous affidavit to her chest, she managed to sway to her feet. Dominic took one look at her and moved. "What's wrong?"

That distraction was almost fatal, for the door swung wide and Giles came in with a heavy winter cloak draped over one arm (*So that's his idea of comfort,* Minuette thought wildly, *a fur lining on a stone floor*) and a bottle of wine in his other hand. Everything happened both too fast and too slow—too fast for Dominic to draw his sword, too slow for Minuette not to see every movement as Giles threw the cloak at Dominic, hampering his response, then raised the wine bottle and smashed it to pieces across the side of Dominic's skull. He fell with a weight that made Minuette's breath stop. It started again, fast and uneven, as Giles crouched and drew Dominic's sword, then rose and faced her.

Wake up, she silently begged Dominic, but it seemed even he was not invulnerable. This was not a good time to discover that.

She took a step around the altar, wanting to keep Giles's attention. "You're surely not going to kill the king's best friend. Even you are not that stupid."

"I'm not going to kill him. Where would be the fun in that? No." He began to walk closer, and Minuette had to make herself stand still. "I am going to tie him up. Strips of this"—he was close enough now to touch her ivory wool skirt with the point of the sword—"will accomplish two things: immobilize him, and undress you. And when he awakes, he'll have a perfect view of what comes next."

She couldn't help it; she moved back. The fact that Giles didn't stop her, that he continued to smile with that unnerving confidence, scared her. He was in control.

But not wholly. She drew her hands away from her chest, letting him see what she held in them. "You cannot hurt me before I burn this," she said.

"Is that supposed to frighten me?" he asked—entirely too calmly, Minuette thought, and her heart sank.

"It should. Everything you've been working for depends on this single sheet. If I burn it, there will be no spark left to light a rebellion."

He shrugged. "I don't know what that is, and I don't care. My intent tonight is unchanged. I might have enjoyed you willing, but I will revel in you fighting."

He lunged, and Minuette did, too. She dropped the document—her mother's terrible, traitorous document—then grabbed at the candle and threw it in Giles's face. He screamed, more in anger than pain. But it gave her time to scramble around the altar, where she hesitated. She knew she should fling open the door and scream the place down, but this was Norfolk territory and she didn't know where Robert was, and the men Rochford had sent with her were quartered too far away to hear her . . . and she couldn't leave Dominic. Not unconscious and with Giles armed.

She threw herself on the floor, feeling the crunch of glass from the broken bottle beneath her skirts, and slapped Dominic. "Wake up!" she yelled. "Dominic, wake up!"

Dominic groaned, and then Giles was upon her, sword in one hand, the other hand digging into her arm, dragging her up with a power that told her he would not stop until he'd had her. As he pulled her up, her fingers scrabbled along the floor for something—anything—to hit him with, but all she could find was a shard of broken glass the length of her palm.

He jerked her against him. "This won't take long, at least not the first time. I think we can risk his waking."

Then he was pushing her against the wall. He was going to hurt her, and his mouth was on hers and she couldn't scream or even cry. His sword arm was across her chest, so she couldn't breathe, and his other hand was freeing his laces and then at her skirt, pulling it up, and she had to do something or it would be too late, and damned if Giles Howard was going to be the first—

Her hand drove the shard of glass into the side of his neck. There was a terrible gurgle and his eyes widened as he stopped kissing her and then . . . then he was falling and there was blood on her hands, spurting wetly on her face and her dress and across the stones of the floor. *Death in the lady chapel,* she thought hazily; *will it have to be deconsecrated now?*

She slid down the wall until she sat huddled with her arms around her knees. She could not stop staring at Giles, with the glass stuck in his neck where clearly it had pierced something vital. He would never get up again.

A choking, coughing sound almost sent her screaming in terror, but it wasn't Giles. It was Dominic, on his feet almost at once and staring around as though he'd stumbled into one of Dante's circles of hell. But Dominic would never be flustered. He took charge, kicking his own sword away from Giles and then kneeling to check the man's pulse. He stayed there a moment, then turned on his knees to Minuette. He looked her over dispassionately, stopping at her right hand, which was still clenched and covered in blood. Not all of it was Giles's; she had cut herself with the force of driving the glass into him.

Dominic eased himself to sit next to her and took her hand. Gently he stroked it from the palm outward, straightening her fingers. Then he lifted it and pressed it to his cheek. They stayed like that for several minutes, until Minuette made herself look at him. He looked different through her haze of unshed tears.

But his voice was unchanged, the stable, always-right, always-loved voice of her childhood. "You did what was necessary and you did it well. I know it hurts. Trust me—the hurt will ease in time."

But she couldn't think about Giles yet. His betrayal had at least been expected. "I found it," she said numbly. "The Penitent's Confession. It's there, behind the altar. Will you bring it to me?"

Dominic brought it and, when she asked him, read it through aloud.

I, Marie Hilaire Wyatt Howard, do here confess and swear to my sins against King Henry VIII and his realm of England.

    I confess that I helped the King's Concubine, Anne Boleyn, conduct illicit sexual congress with many men not the king.

    I confess that I did many times witness her brother, George Boleyn, in her bed in a state of undress.

    I confess that Anne Boleyn did weep at her son's dark hair for, she said, "It was his father who gave it to him."

    As I pray for the salvation of my soul before God, I witness that the child known as Henry William, Prince of Wales, is no true son of Henry VIII but a bastard born of the incestuous union of Anne Boleyn and her brother, George. May God curse my own child if I lie.

Marie Hilaire Wyatt Howard

Minuette stared blankly at Giles's body and said, "Carrie told me she didn't know what my mother felt for Stephen Howard. Whatever it was, it was enough for her to lie. She must have done this for him and his family."

"I don't know," Dominic said slowly. "Do you think . . . is this her signature?"

She looked at the fading ink hopelessly. "I don't remember." Grasping at the hope, she murmured, "Could it be . . . is it a forgery?"

"It's most certainly a lie. The only real question is, who told this lie? Your mother? Or someone using her name?"

She stared at the signature as though focus alone could help her divine what had happened. Then she blinked, and when her eyes focused once more it wasn't at her mother's name, it was at the date just above it.

"The date. Dominic, look at the date."

He looked. "Seventh June of 1544."

Hope, slight and weak, sprang up. "Seventh June . . . my mother died on the eighth of June."

"And?"

"Carrie told me—my mother had childbed fever. Carrie was with her all the last days, and my stepfather. She wasn't conscious, Dominic. Not for the last week of her life. Carrie told me she didn't wake once before the end. She did not write this."

"The Howards would have known that," Dominic said thoughtfully. "So it is unlikely that they created this confession. Or at least . . . it might have been Giles. He was only a child when your mother died, he likely didn't know the details—"

"He didn't seem to care when I found it," Minuette said dully. "And why would he? If it wasn't at his family's request, then what had he to gain?"

"Revenge," Dominic answered. "A chance to hurt you. He was cruel enough to defame your mother merely to hurt you—a rebellion might have been secondary."

"All of this," she cried. "Alyce's death, my mother's reputation . . . for what? For revenge? For religion? What kind of God asks for such destruction in His name?"

"God is too often an excuse for men's ambitions. We are all of us weak, Minuette."

She wept then, for her mother's weakness in loving Stephen Howard and for Alyce's weakness for the still-unknown man who had been her death. And she wept for her own weaknesses as well: for the pleasure she'd taken in William's touch and the desire that would have seen her in his bed that very night, no better than Eleanor, and for the bright memory of Dominic's touch at Hampton Court, tarnished now forever.

At last the sobs became hiccups and there were no tears left to be wept. Dominic had held her against his shoulder as she cried, and when she straightened up he said, "What shall I do with the confession?"

The answer was to take it to William—and Rochford. This was what everything had been about. But though Minuette knew they would have to be told, she could not bear the thought of anyone else actually seeing her mother's name signed to that lie. It was illogical and unreasonable and not really her decision to make, but Dominic was looking at her as though she had the right. And he would stand behind anything she chose.

That trust meant more than kisses ever could.

"Burn it," she said.

Together they touched a flame to the Penitent's Confession and watched the spark of rebellion crumble to ashes.

CHAPTER TWENTY

D OMINIC DID NOT sleep at all that night. After watching the Penitent's Confession burn, he had carried Minuette to her chamber and handed her over to Carrie's ministrations. The maid seemed to grasp the situation at once, nodding when Dominic said warningly, "I killed Giles Howard for attacking Mistress Wyatt. Keep the Howard servants away from her until she's cleaned up."

It didn't matter if Carrie guessed what had really happened to Giles—she would protect Minuette. Dominic roused Robert Dudley and the Rochford men who had come with Minuette before sending Harrington to stand guard outside Minuette's chamber. The men took charge of the gates until Robert returned just before dawn with a company of royal soldiers. Within short order, Framlingham was firmly under royal control, with Mary and the Duke of Norfolk and his family under house arrest. Dominic himself had broken the news of Giles's death to both his father and his wife.

"How?" the duke asked, more upset at being woken than anything else.

"He intended violence. He was stopped." Never would a word more than that pass his lips.

He had not expected Eleanor to be grieved, but even he did not expect her to say, "I want to come with you to London. I must be there when William returns."

"The king does not consort with traitors," Dominic said shortly, then turned on his heel and walked out. He wanted only to be out of there at first light with Minuette.

He was worried about her, and not solely because of what had happened in the lady chapel. There was more to it than that; she had been edgy and uncomfortable since he'd arrived. He couldn't help but wonder if she knew—really knew—how he felt about her, and if she didn't want to hurt him. If she felt the same way, she would not have withdrawn so quickly from him. She would have given him some word, some sign, that the memories of Hampton Court were pleasant. A dull ache settled in his stomach and stayed with him as he spoke to Robert Dudley.

"You speak for Rochford here. What are your orders?" he asked.

"I sent a rider to bring another contingent of soldiers from Cambridge. When they arrive, Norfolk and the men of his family will be taken to the Tower. The women will be detained here—save Lady Mary. She is to be moved to Richmond at once under my personal guard. I could use you to remain at Framlingham until Rochford sends word what to do with the women."

Dominic shook his head. "I'm under orders from the king to get Mistress Wyatt to Whitehall and Elizabeth as soon as possible."

He didn't like the way Robert looked at him, or the slow smile with which he said, "Right. And I suppose after last night—whatever it is that happened in the lady chapel that you won't talk about—she'll be needing comfort."

Dominic would have retorted angrily, but he was tired and there was more to Robert's look than amusement or knowing. There was also the understanding of a man who loved where he shouldn't. So he moderated his response. "She found the affidavit, just as she was meant to do. We destroyed it. Lord Rochford cannot possibly demand more of her."

Robert shrugged and turned away. "Possibly not. Or possibly he will want to know why Mistress Wyatt was covered in blood from head to toe while you were not. It isn't possible to burn an entire gown without someone remarking upon it."

Was that a threat? Dominic dared not risk it. The last thing he would allow was Rochford interrogating Minuette. And Robert wasn't wrong about needing someone to take charge of the women. Eleanor Howard might be capable all on her own of corrupting an entire force of men at arms.

"Damn it," Dominic breathed out, then called after Robert. "If you can spare some men to ride with her, I'll send Mistress Wyatt ahead and remain at Framlingham until someone else is sent to take charge."

Tossing a grin over his shoulder, Robert said, "You're too dutiful for your own good, Dominic. We'll have to work on that."

Yes, we will, Dominic thought two hours later as he handed Minuette into the coach that would take her back to London. There were few things he'd ever wanted more than to climb in after her. "Safe journey," he made himself say.

Her eyes were bruised with lack of sleep and sorrow. "I wish you were coming with me."

She could not have said anything more piercing. He cleared his throat and said, "I will be there before William returns. I promise."

"It's just . . ." She bit her lip, and her right hand—bandaged across the palm from the glass—came up to her throat. That was when Dominic realized she was wearing the filigree star he'd given her for her birthday. As she touched it, she said, "There are things I would like to talk to you about. Things we need to talk about."

Was that pleading in her eyes? Longing? "Yes" was all Dominic could manage to answer.

Her smile was uncertain, but for the first time since he'd reached Framlingham, it was real. "Then I'll see you soon."

Dominic watched the road until long after the coach had passed from sight.

In the end, Dominic beat William to Whitehall by only a few hours. He had meant to find Minuette at once, anxious for the promised talk, but between bathing and changing—and avoiding Lord Rochford—he still hadn't seen her when he finally made it to the crowded forecourt of Whitehall Palace. As he wove his way toward the steps where Elizabeth and Rochford stood waiting, his eyes went straight to Minuette, one pace behind the princess.

The sound and vibration of hooves pounded through the voices, and Dominic turned to the gates. William was the first through, wearing the not-quite mourning balanced between a son's loss and a country's gain, a gold circlet shining on his dark hair. He was followed by Archbishop Cranmer, and then came the other lords and gentlemen of the victorious army, including the men of Dominic's command, led by Jonathan Percy carrying the Exeter standard.

Dominic turned back to look at Minuette. He heard William's voice rising above the babble as he dismounted at the foot of the steps. And then, as voices quieted and every head in the courtyard swiveled to William, Minuette alone looked elsewhere, searching amongst the crowd.

He knew the instant that she saw him, for she suddenly stilled, like a wind that drops all at once to nothing. They stared at each other until a sharp pain in his chest reminded Dominic that he needed air. As he breathed in, he was prepared to push straight through the crowd to reach her—to look in her eyes and know, for good or ill, what was written in them.

But in the next breath Minuette turned her head to greet William and the moment was lost.

Aware of the aches of fatigue and long riding, Dominic pushed through to the steps just as William was asking for him. "I'm here."

He climbed until he was level with William, who threw his arm around him and said, "Well done, Lord Exeter. We have much to speak of. Will you join me in an hour?"

"Yes, Your Majesty." Even as he answered, Dominic was thinking that an hour would give him time to see how Minuette was recovering. But from the corner of his eye, he saw her slipping away behind the others.

He could not shake the feeling that she had changed her mind about whatever she'd meant to share.

William paced the interior of his private oratory, feeling caged by the gilded space but knowing he needed absolute privacy for the conversation to follow. When a page showed Dominic in, he said, "Stand at the outer door of my bedchamber. I am not to be disturbed for anything."

Clearly perplexed, Dominic said, "What's going on, Will?"

"Please, sit. I need your opinion."

"The opinion of a man who speaks honestly when he should

not? It's yours for the asking." Dominic spoke calmly enough, but William thought there was more than a hint of hurt behind it.

"I'm sorry. I wrote a plea for your advice, and then purposely avoided you in France. But perhaps, when you know the matter, you'll understand my difficulty."

"Has it to do with Elisabeth de France?" Dominic leaned against the door, arms folded.

"In a manner of speaking." Now that the revelation was upon him, William hesitated. He had wanted to speak to Dominic for weeks—ever since Hever—but face-to-face he felt the old fear that Dominic might be disappointed in his behaviour.

After all, the last man who'd laid hands on Minuette was now dead.

Dominic prodded him. "Why was the archbishop the only one who knew you were not going to ask for Mary Stuart?"

"I told Cranmer at the last minute, so that he might not have time to question me."

"Why did you choose Elisabeth?"

There was no answer but the honest one. "Because I am in love."

"With a nine-year-old?"

William laughed at the appalled look on Dominic's face. "Of course not."

"I don't—"

"With Minuette."

The silence was so complete that William thought he had suddenly gone deaf. But then noises began to filter in from outside—the hum of voices, the creak of wooden wheels, and the impatient nickering of horses.

He focused on Dominic, trying to discern something—anything—behind that impassive face. He felt his heart sink as the silence lengthened. Clearly, Dominic did not approve. And though William was set on his decision, he wanted Dominic's approval. There would be little enough of it from any other quarter.

Sounding as though he were speaking from a distance, Dominic said, "Why Elisabeth?"

"What?"

"What has loving Minuette to do with your choice of bride?"

"Elisabeth is younger than Mary Stuart. The treaty stipulates that the marriage will not take place until she is thirteen."

Dominic's eyes cleared as he worked it out. "You don't mean to marry Elisabeth. You did it to buy time."

"Anything might happen in four years."

"Time alone won't make Minuette acceptable to the council."

William felt his temper threatening. "I will marry where I choose, council be damned."

Dominic didn't back down. "Then why bother with a betrothal at all? Why not simply marry Minuette at once?" He paused. "You do mean to marry her, don't you?"

"Yes." William bit the word off. Why was everyone so quick to believe he might intend anything else? "I cannot think only of myself, Dom. I have England's welfare to consider. I have bought four years of peace. That is not to be taken lightly."

He should have known that Dominic would not settle for the surface answer. "Four years of peace. For England, yes. But for yourself as well. Four years in which you need not be badgered on every side about when and whom you will marry. Four years in which to find a way to make Minuette an acceptable queen, so that you might not have to fight your council."

Their eyes held as Dominic added, "Are you sure you can wait four years?"

"My father waited six. I love her, Dom. I don't know how it is I never saw it before. Now that I have, I won't let her go."

Dominic nodded once. He had his hand on the door before William realized he didn't mean to say anything more.

Desperate for some word of approval, William asked, "Do you not think her worth it?"

Dominic was still for so long that he almost asked the question again. At last, without looking at him, Dominic said, "I know no woman more deserving of a crown."

He pulled the door wide and walked out.

By the time the night's banquet began, Dominic was so taut with resentment and despair that all he wanted was to fall into bed and find forgetfulness in sleep. But he feared that even closing his eyes was dangerous, for instead of blackness, he saw Minuette.

Minuette with William.

Dominic had been caught once more by his friend in the hour before the banquet and had been forced to listen to William sing Minuette's praises. Though he did not elaborate on the details of what had occurred at Hever, he said enough to make Dominic feel a rush of fury such as he hadn't felt since Giles Howard's first attack on Minuette. But try as he might, he could not persuade himself that William had forced his attentions or in some way misread her response. William was too experienced to mistake desire for anything else.

The thought of William's desire made Dominic want to strike his friend. The thought of Minuette's response made him want to get very, very drunk.

Short of feigning illness, he could not escape the celebratory banquet. And though he half considered lying about his health, the truth was that he wanted to be in the same room with Minuette, no matter how painful.

Mercifully, both etiquette and discretion prevailed at this banquet. Elizabeth and Lord Rochford were seated on either side of William at the high table, with rank and precedent determining the rest. Minuette was not even at the high table, which surprised Dominic until he realized she had been conveniently placed within easy sight of William. No doubt he preferred not to have to strain to look at her.

And he did look at her. He could hardly stop looking at her. If William thought he could hide his feelings, he was very much mistaken. Whispers would begin to grow from this night. Admittedly, Dominic was somewhat sensitive, but he didn't think many would overlook the heat of William's gaze. Elizabeth certainly didn't. Her eyes flicked more than once between her brother and her friend, and Dominic would have given much to know what was going on behind that serene face of hers. He would have given more to be able to drink himself into insensibility, but the wine had been carefully portioned and the most he could manage was a slight dulling of his headache.

He should ask William for permission to return to France. Better to be away from them both and give his own heart time to harden. Dominic couldn't stay in love with Minuette forever. Now that he had no hope, his desire would fade. There were plenty of pretty women in France. He wondered if Aimée, or someone like her, would go a long way to easing his resentment.

The feasting drew to an end, and music began in an adjoining chamber. As people drifted away from tables greasy with remnants of food and spilled wine, Dominic thought gratefully that now he could go. He would not be missed in the dancing and singing that would follow.

It seemed that he was not the only one to think as much. As Dominic rose from his seat, he saw William slip away from the crowd and exit the hall by another, more private door.

Minuette followed, her hand held firmly in William's.

Minuette did not ask where William was leading her. She did not ask why. She thought about him hardly at all, except to be annoyed that he had removed her from the party before she could speak to Dominic.

From the moment Dominic had stared at her so blankly across the courtyard this morning, Minuette had been in a fever of impatience, torn between anticipation and fear. *He knows,* her fear whispered. *He knows what happened at Hever. What must he think of me?* She wanted only a chance to explain herself, though she wasn't sure how. *"I didn't know what I was doing"? "I stopped him before it could go too far"? "I didn't mind William kissing me, but I'd much rather it had been you"?*

Minuette shivered. Dominic could not avoid her forever. She wouldn't let him.

William stopped before a door that opened into a spare, high-ceilinged chamber. The walls were unadorned plaster, but a red and gold Persian rug covered the floorboards and a fire blazed high in the small stonework fireplace.

Before she had time to wonder why William had brought her here when he had dozens of larger and more luxurious rooms for his personal use, he explained. "I apologize for the condition of the room, but I did not wish to raise more questions than necessary. And I would not insult you by taking you to my own chambers."

Minuette nearly laughed, for surely he must be joking. She had been in his chambers dozens of times. Alone with him, even. But she swallowed her laugh, for she could see that he was serious. And as he looked at her, she suddenly knew why he had brought her to this uncomfortable chamber.

As a protection—not for her sake, but for his.

Now that she was looking at him, seeing him fully for the first time today and undistracted by other concerns, she recognized the spark in his eyes. It had been there that night at Hever, and when he touched her hair before leaving Hatfield. But she knew it from before, as well.

It was the look William had often bestowed upon Eleanor in the weeks before she came to his bed.

His cheeks were hectic with colour. "I have been debating for some days how best to approach you, Minuette. And I have decided that my only hope is to speak plainly."

She sat ice-still, her heartbeat the only movement in her body. She felt almost as though she were floating above her surroundings, an observer perched in a far corner and watching with distant interest the scene playing out before her.

William swallowed. "You know that I am betrothed to Elisabeth de France. It was an important part of the treaty—perhaps the most important. England needs peace to rebuild the treasury, to strengthen the navy, to balance our own religious difficulties and protect our borders. I can't do that while fighting a war with France."

Somewhat offended, Minuette said, "Do you think I don't see that? You need not explain as if to a child."

His smile warmed the whole of his face. "No, I need not. I'm trying to ease my way into this, but I see that I only insult you by doing so." He took one long breath and spoke rapidly. "I will promise what I must to have peace. But I will marry where I love."

And then he was on his knees, catching her hands in his. "I love you, Minuette. I think I have loved you all my life. What happened at Hever was a gift—like awaking from a long dream only to find that what I wanted was in the waking world all the time. It's always been you."

Letting go her hands, he cradled her face between his palms and kissed her. It was a much different kiss from the one at Hever—a gentle exploring rather than a frantic coming together. But all the while he kissed her, her mind remained detached and separate. Though she could feel the spreading fire through her veins, there was no fear that she would forget herself tonight. She would stop him if she must.

But William had himself under control, and he broke the kiss before Minuette had to. Smoothing her hair back as he had the last time she'd seen him, he whispered, "I will have no queen but you."

In that moment she didn't see William—she saw Giles, eyes wide with shock and pain, a shard of glass driven into his neck, dying at her feet. She was afraid to look at her hands, sure that they must still be covered in blood, no matter that she had scrubbed them over and over and over . . .

I can't be queen, she wanted to say to William. *I killed a man.*

She bit her tongue and forcibly shoved the image of Giles into the depths of her memories.

They did not stay long in their borrowed chamber. A few more kisses from William, an abundance of half-whispered endearments that Minuette hardly heard in her daze, and then he was walking her back to her own chamber, where he left her with only a touch of his hand to her cheek. He looked at her for a long, tension-filled moment before striding away rapidly, as if he was afraid he would not leave at all if he didn't do it quickly.

Carrie was surprised to see her back so soon. "Isn't there dancing tonight?" she asked.

"I didn't wish to dance." But was that true? William hadn't even asked her. Not that she could imagine walking into a crowded room just now and pretending all was normal.

Minuette brushed Carrie away when she attempted to undress her. "I'll send for you when I am ready."

Carrie paused just long enough to slip a shawl around Minuette's shoulders before she left. Only then did Minuette realize she was shaking as violently as she had once before—the last time William had turned her world on end.

She had never dreamed that he would wish to marry her. She was nowhere near important enough for him to marry. Her first thought was that, for some obscure reason, he was teasing her.

Her second, more considered thought, was that he had lost his mind.

William had certainly wanted women before, had even gone to creative lengths to get what he wanted. She need only remember Eleanor's wedding to know that. But he had never let his desires override his good sense.

Until now.

But why? Minuette could scarcely believe that her charms were such that William would overthrow his ambition, his councilors, and a royal princess to have her. He was far too practical for such a course.

He is his father's son, the contrary part of her mind whispered. *What he wants, he will take.*

It had not escaped her attention that William had not asked her anything. He had taken her consent for granted. She could hardly blame him; not one woman in a thousand would decline the offer of a crown. Minuette was not immune to the temptation. And that it was William offering it to her—Will, who had ever been like a twin part of her soul—increased the temptation to snatch at what she was being offered and revel in it.

But she could not. She could not rejoice, she could not rest, she could not breathe.

She could not stop thinking of Dominic.

She closed her eyes and let everything else fade away—everything but Dominic, staring at her from across the courtyard this morning. As she pictured him—dark hair, dark gaze, dark clothes—she felt herself relax, serenity stealing its way through every part of her body and mind. She had known from the moment she'd seen him what she wanted.

Dominic was peace. Dominic was rest. Dominic was the thread of her happiness.

She stood and wrapped the heavy silk shawl tighter round her shoulders.

If Dominic wouldn't come to her, she would go to him.

Dominic was just drifting into a hazy, alcohol-tinged doze when the light knock at his door snapped his eyes open.

"All right, I'm coming," he muttered, pausing to throw on a loose linen shirt over the breeches he'd gone to bed in and rubbing his hands through his hair.

He wrenched the door open, prepared to stare down whoever had interrupted his attempt at sleep, Harrington or Rochford or even—maybe especially—William. Heaven help Will if he'd come to rhapsodize about Minuette again.

It was Minuette herself.

"May I come in?"

After a brief hesitation, he stepped back and let her enter. The brush of her velvet skirt against his leg sent shivers through his whole body. She was dressed tonight in shades of green, from the winter-rich hue of evergreens to the paler colour of spring grass. She must have been wearing at least ten yards of fabric, but he couldn't look at her without imagining the outlines of her body beneath the elaborate dress. The hollow at her throat would be echoed where the hipbones met her stomach . . .

He forced himself to speak the hardest words he had ever uttered. "May I be the first to offer my congratulations to our future queen?"

There was a long pause in which he avoided her eyes. Perhaps he was wrong. Perhaps William had pulled her away tonight merely to discuss what she was wearing, or to play a game of chess. Perhaps she would deny any knowledge of what he was talking about.

She did not deny it. "He is not serious. It is the desire of a moment, and it will pass."

Dominic shook his head slowly. "If you believe that, you know him less well than you should. He walked away from Mary Stuart for you. He will not go back."

His head was pounding with drink and his eyes ached and every muscle in his body was held tight trying to keep from pulling her against him and letting her feel all his love and hurt and desire. All Dominic could think right now was how much he hated William.

"You are in his blood now, and he will never be free of you." He could not stop the reckless words, no longer certain if he was describing William or himself.

"Dominic . . ."

"He has been half in love with you all his life. And you . . . you will be queen, Minuette. What more could you wish? William is everything you could ever want."

He turned his back on her and squeezed his eyes shut. He must get himself under control. He must look at her and wish her joy and mean it.

"He isn't you," she whispered.

He couldn't make himself move. He did not even seem to be breathing.

Carefully, as if the words were spun glass and might shatter under the pressure of too much feeling, Minuette said, "I love you, Dominic. And I thought that . . ."

He felt her come up behind him, so near that her skirts pressed against his legs. She did not touch him, but said softly into his ear, "Was I wrong? Do you not love me?"

He spun around then, unable to bear the devastating simplicity that was her most appealing quality. He put his hands gently on her shoulders and, finally, looked straight into her eyes. He had told himself that, with one look, he would know.

He did know. She loved him.

He blinked, and in that brief darkness there rose before him a dream or vision or imagining, so vivid that the back of his neck prickled. He was standing at a window, looking down at Minuette. She was walking away from him, and Dominic felt a strange mingling of despair and pride as he watched her go. And all the while, someone whispered malevolent words behind him.

Minuette moved slightly, breaking his paralysis. He wanted to move his hands from her shoulders, to feel the skin of her throat, and trace the swell of her breasts above her bodice. And not just for his own relief—more than anything Dominic wanted to make her tremble, shiver, and close her eyes as she gave herself up to him. But something in her expression held him fixed.

With those hazel eyes wide open, she leaned forward and touched her lips to one cheek and then, achingly slow, to the other. Then she drew back and examined his face, first with her eyes and then with her fingertips. She traced his eyebrows and his jaw, and drew her fingers across his lips. He opened his mouth just enough to kiss her fingertips and she did shiver then.

And that was the end of his control. Dominic slid his hands along her neck into her hair and kissed her.

He had told himself once that he would wait until she came to him willingly. But he had never dreamed of just how sweet it would be. For a piercing instant he thought of her in William's arms, but that was quickly buried beneath the taste of her mouth. He wrapped his arms around her and let the lines of her body against his erase everything that had come before.

14 November 1554
Whitehall Palace

If I were to die tonight, I would die happy.
But I hope I don't die.

"Are you certain William is coming?" Elizabeth asked, for the third time in as many minutes.

Minuette's eyes followed Dominic as he paced the king's privy chamber and gave Elizabeth the same reply he had twice before. "I'm certain."

"He's an hour late."

"Blame that on your uncle. He had something urgent to discuss with Will." For a breathtaking instant Dominic's eyes met Minuette's, and she wanted to leap to him and feel his strong, familiar arms wrap around her and kiss him as she had last night, kiss him until she was dizzy . . .

Wanton, indeed. She dropped her gaze to her hands, linked neatly in her lap, and focused on keeping her body still and her mind tranquil so that Elizabeth might not grow suspicious. Perhaps she should count in Greek, or do six-figure sums in her head, or compose silent missives to—

"Damn it!" William swung into the room, slammed the door

behind him, and dropped into the chair next to Minuette before any of them could react.

It was, naturally, Dominic who chided him. "There are ladies present, Will," he said drily.

"Sorry. But it is truly aggravating. Just when I finally get my hands on the man, he up and dies on me."

"Who?" Elizabeth perched in a window seat, facing William.

"Norfolk, late this afternoon. That's what Rochford had to report."

"How did he die?" Minuette asked, surprised. The duke had been an old man, yes, but also tough and sturdy, and she couldn't believe arrest alone would have killed him. As she blinked, Minuette remembered the spurt of blood, her crimson-soaked hand in the lady chapel at Framlingham. She shook her head. No, Norfolk's death, at least, could not be laid to her account.

William shrugged and said, "His heart stopped. I wouldn't put it past him to have died simply to spite me. Without him a case will be devilishly difficult to make."

Elizabeth narrowed her gaze. "You have others under arrest."

"But we have almost nothing in the way of hard evidence. The Spanish are denying everything, including naval involvement, and Rochford cannot seem to lay hands on the spies who brought the reports from the Continent. Perhaps Norfolk paid them to give us false information and draw us out. Frankly, it doesn't matter much at this point. The plot is finished, whatever minor points remain unresolved."

"And what," Elizabeth said intently, "will you do with Mary?"

"Mary will remain under guard at Richmond indefinitely."

Minuette nearly shook her head, as she knew exactly what Elizabeth thought but did not say: *Too soft, William. She should be in the Tower. One of these days that chivalry will cost you.*

Dominic, who had not been still for the entire last hour, finally leaned against a wall, though Minuette noticed that he kept one foot tapping. "Now what?" he asked. "You've won a war, broken a rebellion—"

"Claimed the fair maiden." William touched Minuette's cheek, then lazily drew his hand down her neck to where she wore the filigree star pendant Dominic had given her last year. Fingering the star, William said, "What we do now is celebrate. There's dancing in the hall, and I've ordered fireworks for midnight."

He sat straighter and took Minuette's hands in both of his. "Part of me wishes I never had to leave this room. Everything I want—" He looked at Elizabeth, then at Dominic, and back to her. "Everything I've ever wanted is right here."

He leaned in, and Minuette thought desperately, *Not in front of Dominic,* but William merely pressed his lips to her forehead. Even that was enough to tumble her feelings, so that happiness whirled next to guilt and confusion danced with pleasure.

It will be all right, she'd told Dominic last night. He had been all for going to William straightaway and confessing the truth. But Minuette knew William in a way no one else did—because she knew herself. *Give him time to come to his senses,* she'd urged Dominic. *I will make it easy for him. You know that I have always been able to bend Will to whatever I want.*

And I want you.

William stood and pulled Minuette up with him. "We will dance and drink and, because the French ambassador is present, we will be discreet. Dominic will keep an eye on you when I cannot. Won't you, Dom?"

Dominic had at last gone still, but there was such a sense of suppressed energy to him that it was hard to tell. William did not wait for an answer, but handed Minuette off to Dominic, then gave Elizabeth his arm. Before he opened the door, he smiled at all of them and said, "One last secret for us to keep together—the most joyous secret of all."

As Minuette slipped her hand into Dominic's arm, she shivered and looked up. Dominic's grave stare mirrored her own memory, with a sting to it she had not anticipated.

There is always another secret.

INTERLUDE

November 18, 1554

R OBERT DUDLEY PROWLED through a labyrinth of corridors beneath Whitehall Palace that few knew existed and even fewer could navigate. Beneath his carefully cultivated air of nonchalance, he was furious—enough so that he had the nerve to make it known tonight. Of course, that nerve was bolstered by a copious amount of alcohol, but as long as he got the confrontation over within the next hour he should be fine.

The door at the end of this particular malodourous corridor had been left ajar, as always. Robert thrust his way into the room, planted his feet in front of the plain table, and said, "What the hell are you playing at?"

With great deliberation, Lord Rochford eyed him through the hesitant candlelight. "How is your wife, Lord Robert? Have you gotten her with child yet?"

How he hated the man—but admired him, too, in the twisted way of wanting to exercise that sort of power. Robert gave over his temper for irritation and dropped into the chair that faced the table. "Norfolk's dead," he observed.

"Hmmm."

"The Penitent's Confession is destroyed."

"As I knew it would be—as long as you took care to plant it where Mistress Wyatt would be sure to find it." Rochford flicked a smile his way. "You did well at Framlingham."

"Norfolk and Giles Howard dead—no hard evidence—no formal charges laid," Robert mused aloud, tipping back in his chair. "How exactly is that well done?"

"You see through a glass darkly," Rochford said. "You are not required to know all."

"No, just to go where you tell me and deliver what you give me and threaten where you direct me . . . and for what? I am no nearer a divorce now than I was two years ago, and Elizabeth—"

"Remains single," Rochford said sharply.

"But for how long? You promised that you would promote our marriage."

"I promised an opportunity. That opportunity still exists, though I could destroy it in a heartbeat with a single name." In the flickering light, Rochford looked positively demonic. "The name Alyce de Clare."

"That was an accident," Robert said through gritted teeth.

"The girl was found at the bottom of a staircase with a broken neck. Pregnant with your child. How far do you think Elizabeth would trust to an accident?"

Robert shoved himself out of the chair, his head pounding with the need to get even drunker. Now.

But Rochford stopped him with an unexpected question. "What really happened to Giles Howard in the lady chapel at Framlingham?"

Robert narrowed his eyes. "I told you I wasn't there. Surely it's as Dominic reported. Giles Howard had threatened violence to Minuette before—this time Dominic didn't bother to warn him off. Why?"

With a hooded expression, Rochford said simply, "I think the young lady bears watching."

And how the hell does he know that? Robert wondered. He had not breathed a word to Rochford about Minuette's dress, soaked in blood and burnt at Framlingham.

"Has anyone ever told you that you see conspiracies where none exist?" he asked.

Rochford's smile was even more disconcerting than his frown. "Where there are kings, there are conspiracies. Trust me, Lord Robert, this is only the beginning."

ACKNOWLEDGMENTS

The Bluestocking Literary Guild: Angie Wall, Cindy Jones, Laura Boyden, Kristen Hess, Marianne Schwartz, Anna Smith, April Ramsay, Amber Burke, Anna Gilmer, Amy Chamberlain, Lori Brainard, Michelle Miller, Katie Jeppson, Ruth Hyland, Linda Crockett, Kate Boyden, and Karen Judd. You were my first readers, and you are my finest friends. Thanks for more than ten years of books, discussions, food, and laughter—and for walking with me through hell and back. I promise not to throw this book at anyone. And don't let Katie look at the cover—there might be a tiger hiding in plain sight.

The Buy the Book Writers' Group: Matt and Brooklyn Evans, Jenifer Lee, Eric James Stone, Ginger Churchill, Cindy Bechtold, Charmayne Warnock, and especially Caleb Warnock—if there are still erotic subtexts I'm missing, don't point them out now. Buckets of love!

My fellow (and favorite) writers at Cabinet of Curiosities: Ginger Churchill, Pat Esden, Becca Fitzpatrick, and Suzanne Warr. You are gifted writers, devoted friends, and outstanding women. Thanks for the generous critiques, the unvarnished honesty, and the endless patience. I couldn't ask for better women to write with.

Tamar Rydzinski: I've always said that the perfect agent was out there (mostly when so many of them were turning me down). That belief was more true than I could ever have guessed. Thanks for being my still center in the chaos of the publishing world.

Kelli Fillingim and Caitlin Alexander: I thought I would be lucky to meet one outstanding editor, and somehow I met two. Thank you for your notes, your insight, your humor, and especially your enthusiasm. The finest parts of this book belong to you.

The best parents (Walter and Dorothy Sudweeks) and the best in-laws (Dee and Frances Andersen) one woman has ever been blessed with: I'm glad you think me a good writer—but even more glad you think me a decent mother.

Which brings me to Matt, Jake, Emma, and Spencer—you are my finest creations. And like all the best creations, you are wholly your own. Thanks for letting me follow along on your life's journeys.

And always and forever for Chris. I didn't screw up. This time. Thanks for believing in me.

THE BOLEYN KING

Laura Andersen

A READER'S GUIDE

An Interview Between Anne and Minuette

30 April 1554
Hever Castle

We are here with Queen Anne in a brief pause before this summer's festivities. Even briefer than I expected it to be, since William has decided to send me to Mary's household. The queen, in a burst of sentimentality I would never have predicted, has asked me to sit with her this afternoon and speak of the past. I think she sometimes wishes to mistake me for my mother—at least, I have the sense that she has not had a friend to confide in for many years. And I am curious enough to take advantage of my likeness to my mother.

ANNE: Well, Genevieve, what shall we speak of? My opinion of the English wool trade, perhaps? The fallacies in Bishop Bonner's arguments against Protestant reforms? Last year's failure by the French to invade Tuscany?

MINUETTE: You are teasing me, Your Majesty.

A: Don't let my children know. They would not respect me so well if they thought I could tease. Very well, it is the personal you are interested in. As is every seventeen-year-old girl.

M: What personal things interested you at seventeen?

A: At seventeen I had already been years at European courts, in the Netherlands and France. You and I are not entirely dissimilar, for the companion of my girlhood was Princess Claude, later Queen of France. But my world was somewhat more expansive than yours. You've never left England, the farthest you've ever gone is . . . York?

M: As you know very well. Did you miss your family all those childhood years away?

A: Well, I was often with my sister, Mary. Also, during those years on the continent, my father was a frequent visitor on royal business. I suppose it was my mother I knew the least in those years.

M: And now? There's only—

A: Only George left. But honestly, we two were always the ones who understood each other. He is the only one who never saw me as a means to an end. For George, I have been an end in myself. That is as family should be and so rarely is. It is a pity you have no siblings.

M: It is difficult to miss what one has never had. I have my friends, and I cannot see how even siblings would be dearer to me.

A: Perhaps you are the fortunate one in that. You can choose your loyalties and not have any thrust upon you by blood. So tell me, Genevieve, what loyalties will you choose beyond your friendships with my children and Dominic Courtenay? I am given to understand that there is a young man who grows daily more enamoured. But that is only to be expected; you are a young woman poised to break men's hearts. The question is, are you as taken with him?

M: I hardly know, Your Majesty. It is . . . How does one fall in love? In an instant, or through time and experience?

A: You are young, aren't you? To fall in love is simple. To hold that love . . . Well, that's the trick. Men fall in love in a rush of desire. Women are more practical. We have to be, since we are so often at the mercy of men's desires.

M: Are you saying you've never been in love?

A: I'm saying that's a question you know better than to ask. Did I not teach you discretion?

M: You also taught me boldness. There are still stories of how your father and Wolsey forced you and Henry Percy to separate against your wishes.

A: Youth is made for hopeless romance.

M: So you're saying it was a romance.

A: I'm saying it was hopeless. It is an important distinction for a woman of the court to make. Do not trust men with your heart—or anything else.

M: How does one know whom to trust?

A: Have you learned nothing in your years at court? Trust is for saints and madmen; all else must look to themselves. A lesson I would have you learn from me, and not through hard experience.

M: Why is it that everyone thinks I am so likely to be taken advantage of? Just because I am not Elizabeth does not mean I am stupid.

A: Not stupid, no. But you have a quality very like your mother: the disposition to see the good in everyone.

M: Is that what you liked about her? I assume you liked something about my mother, since you appear to have had so few women friends in your life.

A: Friendship is a luxury for a carefree life, the kind I only had in my youth. Once caught in the snares of royal politics, I needed friends who were useful and women's usefulness will always be limited. And you needn't pity me for that. Tell me, Genevieve, excepting Elizabeth, do you have any women friends?

M: I thought I did.... Perhaps you are right. Do you think—if you had known the cost of what was to come—you would have made the same choices when the king fell in love with you?

A: That is presupposing I had a choice.

M: One always has a choice.

A: Ah, the righteousness of the young and untouched. You're right, I could have chosen my sister's path: king's mistress for a time, to be discarded when no longer wanted and married off to a man who would always know he was taking the king's leavings. That was not a choice I could live with.

M: So you have no regrets? You would not change anything if you could?

A: I won, didn't I? No one thought I would. Men lined up to watch me fall: Wolsey, Cromwell, my uncle Norfolk, the entire hierarchy of the Roman church. But here I am—the widow of one king and mother of another king. The English Church is firmly planted, no more to be uprooted by Popish interference. And for all her righteousness and piety, it is not Catherine's blood but mine that will run through the English throne for generations to come.

M: Catherine is gone, but Mary survives and many call her Henry's only true heir. If it were in your power, what would you do with Mary?

A: It is in my power, and to be ignored is a far more powerful statement than even to be punished. Mary will fade away in obscurity until history has quite forgotten her.

M: Politics, princes, popes . . . you are right, Your Majesty, I am less interested in those things than in the personal. In all that surrounded your marriage, I am mostly interested in just one thing: Did you love him?

A: What makes you think I will answer that?

M: Because no one ever asks you, and I think you like the personal, as well.

A: I loved the man who called me darling, who wrote out the great fervour of his passion, who defied his councilors to have me, who dared to claim our love as the only requisite for a proper marriage. . . . That man I have always loved. As your mother knew very well, for she asked me the same question more than once during the years Henry and I waited.

M: So I get my impertinence from my mother?

A: It is not impertinence when the motive is genuine concern. Like your mother, your heart is in everything you do. Perhaps you will be the happier for it—or perhaps it will leave you desolate.

M: Perhaps both, in which case I think I would count the happiness worth the desolation. As, I suspect, you have done.

A: And with that, I believe we are finished. Thank you for the talk, Genevieve. It has been most . . . invigorating.

Questions and Topics for Discussion

1. If "History is written by the victors," what do you think is the biggest impact of changing a story?

2. William says, "I will be the best because I've earned it. I don't need you to hand me my victories." (page 12) Do you think this is true? Is William a self-made man? Does your opinion change of him by the end of the book?

3. Why do you think their reputation within the court is so important to people like William and Elizabeth? Why are even conjecture and rumor dangerous? Do you think Minutte and Dominic feel the same way?

4. William and Elizabeth are of royal parentage. Dominic is the son of a supposed traitor. Minuette is the daughter of a trusted servant and confidante. How much do you think parentage matters to these characters? Where does it affect them most in life? How have they each overcome the generation before them?

5. The rift between Protestants and Catholics is a huge divide in *The Boleyn King*. Compare and contrast it to today's societal divisions in America, such as Republicans and Democrats, or even between the suburbs and the city.

6. In tweaking history for this story, the author opens up a world of possibilities. What historical event do you think would have the greatest impact if changed? What would that impact be?

7. In the context of this story, what qualities do you think make for an ideal servant? An ideal ruler?

8. In an age where social standing is of the utmost importance, what do you think is the most important reason for a person to be married? Why? Does your opinion change for royalty versus commoners?

9. Do you think members of royalty can have friends? What about someone like a present-day world leader? Could you be friends with your boss, or your employees, the way William and Dominic are friends?

10. Compare and contrast how each of the four main characters deal with the ideal of castle intrigue.

11. What would be the most unnerving secret message that you could receive? In what manner?

12. Compare and contrast what is deemed public in this novel versus what is deemed private. How does that compare to today's Internet culture?

13. What is said in letters in this novel versus what is said out loud? Which do you think has more impact? Which method of communication is more important to you?

If you enjoyed *The Boleyn King,* you'll be mesmerized by all of
the passion, all of the intrigue, and all of the danger in

THE BOLEYN DECEIT

by Laura Andersen

Coming Soon
from Ebury Press

PRELUDE

8 February 1547

"YOU WILL NOT tell me what I can and cannot do with my own son!"

If there was one thing to which George Boleyn was accustomed, it was his sister's temper. Anne had never been known for her retiring personality, which was just as well or she would never have caught Henry's eye.

And if she had not become the wife of one king and the mother of the next, George would still be a minor gentleman of enormous ambition and small fortune. That meant that he did not match Anne's anger. "I am not telling you, the council is. The council that Henry's will put in place."

"My son is king now."

"In name and spiritual right, yes. But he is ten years old, Anne. In practice, it is the regency council that will rule England until William is of age."

A regency council that had pointedly excluded Anne. There had been child kings before in England, and often their mothers had been central to the organization surrounding them. But Henry, for all his flaws, had always had very good political instincts and he had known that even after all this time passions ran high against his wife. Anne could not be allowed anywhere near her son except in the most limited maternal capacity.

George Boleyn was another matter. He was not just a member of the regency council—he was Lord Protector of England until his nephew turned eighteen or until the other lords could throw him out. He would not give them any opportunity to do so.

"You are mother of the king of England," he said in a softer voice, gentling Anne into listening. "William loves you and that will never change. I know that you would not jeopardize his position for misplaced pride. You would not risk the Catholics combining against him."

"They would not dare!" But her protest was half-hearted. They would dare all too well, for in their eyes Henry had left only one legitimate child—the Lady Mary who was as stubborn and righteous as her mother before her. Henry's son or not, religion made William's position as a boy king precarious.

George took his sister's hands in his. "We have won, Anne. We have broken the chains of Catholic tyranny and opened the way to a new world. William is the promise of all we hoped and dreamed. I will not let him fail."

As well as a formidable temper, Anne had a formidable mind and she knew he was right. That didn't stop her saying caustically, "And yet you will allow Norfolk a seat on the council despite his attainder. If Henry had lived just one day longer, the Duke of Norfolk would be dead."

"But Henry didn't live one day longer and to further punish the duke now would only enrage the Catholics. Don't worry about him—I prefer my enemies close enough to control. Besides, he is William's great-uncle. Pride will stay his hand for now."

Anne shook herself free of George and said fiercely, "You had better be right. And you had better be my voice on that council. William is my son, no one else's. Don't you forget it."

"I won't."

But even as George kissed his sister on the forehead, he thought *But if William is to be what we want, the world will need to think of him only as Henry's son. It is a king I am creating now, whatever the cost.*

CHAPTER ONE

Greenwich Palace
21 December 1554

I have but a few minutes before Carrie must dress me for tonight's festivities. Christmas is nearly here, but tonight's celebration is rather more pagan. There is to be an eclipse of the moon, and coming as it does on the winter solstice when darkness claims its longest reign, even the most devout are unsettled.

So why not dance and drink and throw our merriment into the dark as a challenge?

Also, there is a visitor at court. His name is John Dee and he is reputed one of the finest minds of the age. He has come to court in Northumberland's company and William has commanded him to give a private reading of our stars. Only the four of us—for it would not do to let our secrets, past or future, slip into wider circulation.

Despite the cold, every courtyard at Greenwich was filled and more. No one wanted to miss the rare and possibly apocalyptic sight of the moon vanishing into blackness before their eyes. Minuette had barely room to shiver beneath her fur-lined cloak, so closely were people packed on this terrace overlooking the Thames.

She had managed to keep away from the royal party; below her she saw moonlight glinting off Elizabeth's red-gold hair. William stood near his sister, surrounded as always by men and women. While everyone else's eyes turned to the heavens, Minuette's sought for a familiar figure in what little light the torches threw. She rather hoped she didn't find Dominic standing near William.

A whisper ran collectively through the crowd, transmitting itself more to Minuette's body than her ear. She looked up and saw the edge of the moon's circle eaten away. Despite herself, she felt her pulse quicken and wondered what terrible things this might portend.

More terrible than a star's violent fall? The voice in her head was Dominic's, an echo of his impatient skepticism.

Minuette fingered the pendant encircling her neck, tracing the shape of the filigreed star, and smiled to herself. *This night is not a portent of doom,* she assured herself, *but a sign of great wonder. And that I can believe.*

She watched the blackness bite away at the moon until it was half-covered and still moving relentlessly onward. There were murmurs around her, some nervous laughter, and the movement of all crowds that made her focus on balance as they swayed around her.

A hand came from behind, anchoring her waist. And then, after much too long, another hand until she was encircled. Minuette made herself keep her eyes open, made herself stand straight and not lean back into the comforting weight behind her. Or perhaps comforting was not the right word—for her heart was erratic and her breath skipped.

Although she could count on two hands the times Dominic had touched her since the night of her betrothal (eight), her body knew him instantly, as though it had been waiting for this part of her all her life.

Only in the dark did he dare to touch her, for only in the dark could they remain unseen. No one must know, not yet. Not a single whisper must cross the court while William threw himself at Minuette's feet, offering his hand, his throne, and his country to her. It would take time for his infatuation to die and until it did, no one must suspect either William's passion or Dominic's love.

So Minuette laughed and played and worked and flirted as though everything were normal—as though her William had not lost his mind and thought himself in love with her—as though her own heart was not fluttering madly inside a cage, wanting only to wing itself to Dominic—as though she had no secrets and everything was as it had been before. She saw Dominic every day and behaved toward him the same as always: playful and young and oh-so-slightly resentful of his lectures.

And then, like tonight, he would touch her, and she thought she might weep with wanting to turn into him and cling.

Instead, she kept her eyes open and directed at the sky as the moon's last sliver gave up its fight and slid into nothing.

Gasps went up from the crowd and in that covering moment of intense focus elsewhere, Minuette felt Dominic's mouth alight softly just below her left ear and linger. She did close her eyes then, and swayed back slightly, and for a moment his arms tightened around her waist and they both forgot where they were and who and in a moment she would turn and their lips would meet and she might die if she waited any longer—

A great cheer exploded around and below them and Minuette's eyes flew open to see the moon pulling itself away from the darkness. By the tightness of Dominic's grip on her waist, she knew his frustration. But he was—always had been—the disciplined one.

Within seconds, she was standing alone once more, only

warm cheeks and quick breathing to betray what no one had seen.

What no one must ever see.

Greenwich Palace had always been a dwelling of pleasure and luxury, of laughter and flirtation, of light and merriment. Situated on the Thames five miles east of London, close enough to the city for easy access yet far enough to be well out of the crowds and squalor and illness. The last two King Henry's had expanded the complex, Elizabeth's grandfather facing it in red brick and her father adding a banqueting hall and enormous tiltyard. Her father had been born here, as had Elizabeth herself. A beautiful palace for a beautiful night.

Even on this shortest night of the year, the palace blazed with candlelight and what heat the fires and braziers failed to provide was made up for by the great press of bodies. Men and women dressed in their finest, drinking and dancing and circling around their king as though he were the center of their world.

But what happens to that world, Elizabeth wondered, *when the center fails to hold?*

She ignored the chatter of voices directed at her and watched her younger brother, worried and angry with herself for worrying. When William had returned from France last month, he'd poured out to his sister his ardent love for Minuette along with his plans to marry her, and ever since Elizabeth had carried a thread of anxiety that made itself felt at the most inconvenient times. *It's not as though he's being open,* she told herself firmly. *He's behaving precisely as a young king of eighteen should behave.* Dressed in crimson and gold, he flirted with every female in sight (and even a man or two), he drank (but not so heavily as to lose control of his tongue), and he carried on several layers of conversation with the French ambassador at once.

And he had not been nearer to Minuette than ten feet all evening.

Elizabeth, being determinedly talked at by a persistent young cleric, swung her gaze to where her chief lady-in-waiting held court of her own, surrounded by a gaggle of men, young and old, who were clearly besotted by her honey-light hair and her graceful height and the even more appealing knowledge that she was an orphan in the care and keeping of the royal court. With the influence she held in her relationships to Elizabeth and William, Minuette would have drawn an equal crowd even if she had been pockmarked and fat. But the men would not then have been eyeing her with quite the same expression in their eyes.

A voice, very near and very familiar, broke her distraction. "How long," Robert Dudley said conversationally as he cut out the disappointed and ignored cleric, "is your brother going to continue baiting the French ambassador? William has the treaty he wanted—why make the poor man suffer?"

"Because he can," Elizabeth said tartly. "And you do the same—only with less care. Everyone knows your father continues to grumble about peace with France. How hard it is for him to swallow, a pact with the devil Catholics."

He waited a moment to answer. "My father has moved on to other concerns. He's not one to fight a losing battle."

"As fine a commentary on the Dudleys as I've ever heard."

Robert raised his eyebrows and lowered his voice that half step that made Elizabeth's blood warm. "We choose our battles with care—political, religious . . . personal."

His voice returned to its normal tones and he changed the subject deftly. "Are you looking forward to tonight's audience? I imagine Dr. Dee has found it difficult to read your stars, complex as you are."

She gave him a withering look. "I am exceedingly skeptical, seeing as this Dr. Dee comes from your father's household. No doubt you have whispered to him all the things you most want him to say of me."

"You wound my integrity," Robert said, hand on heart. But his voice was serious when he went on. "John Dee is not the sort of man to be persuaded by anything but his own intellect and the truth of what he sees in the heavens. I promise you, Elizabeth, whatever he tells you tonight will be as near as you will get to hearing God's own words. I only wish I could be there."

An hour later, as Elizabeth and Minuette slipped discreetly away from the festivities, she wished Robert were with her as well. She understood the need for privacy—anything that approached foretelling a royal's future was dangerous and though William had commanded the audience that didn't mean he wanted everyone at court to hear about it—but it was beginning to wear on her being just the four of them all the time. "The Holy Quartet" Robert called them, and not entirely in jest. And now that William took every opportunity of quartet-privacy to fawn over Minuette, Elizabeth's patience grew thinner with each day.

They wound through increasingly depopulated corridors until they came to one only partially lit by two smoking torches, its brick walls chilly and bare. There was a single guard wearing the royal badge at a discreet distance from the closed door behind which waited their guest, not near enough to overhear but only to keep the curious away.

Elizabeth opened the door to the east room herself, breath quickening with the rare feeling of unexpectedness. She was not at all certain what was going to happen in the next hour, and she found the sensation unexpectedly delightful.

The room showed signs of a hasty attempt at comfort, from the deep fireplace blazing with light and warmth to the four cushioned chairs ranged along one side of a waxed wood table. Across the table was a single high-backed wooden chair; the man in it rose to his feet and bowed. "Dr. Dee," Elizabeth said. "Welcome to court."

"Thank you, Your Highness." John Dee straightened and Elizabeth took him in. Although she'd known he was only a few years older than she, not even thirty yet, in person she was struck by his youth. Considering all Robert had said and all she had read from correspondents in England and abroad, it was something of a surprise that this young man had achieved such scientific and intellectual stature; then again, Dee had been a fellow at her father's Trinity College at the age of nineteen. More recently the King of France had tried to retain him for his court, but John Dee had declined and returned recently to England after several years on the continent lecturing on Euclid and studying with men like Mercator. He had come to the Northumberland household in the service of Robert's father, and all the court was anxious to meet this man who made things fly and read the stars and charted the heavens with surety.

Elizabeth sat down and waved Dr. Dee back to his chair. Minuette sat next to her, uncharacteristically silent. She had been less than enthusiastic about this idea, which surprised Elizabeth. Usually Minuette was the first to embrace the new and entertaining.

She eyed John Dee and was both annoyed and pleased that he met her gaze steadily. She liked those who were not cringingly cowed by her—but best not let him take too many liberties.

"Dr. Dee," she said, looking significantly at the leather portfolio that lay between them on the table, "you are aware that it is treason to tell a king's future."

A moot point. It was William who had commanded this private audience, William who had run with the idea of seeing what lay in his stars. Her brother was afraid of nothing, certainly not his future. But casting charts was legally forbidden for royalty, as it might be used as a pretext for rebellion.

Dr. Dee was no fool to fall into such an easy trap. "I do not foretell the future, Your Highness. I interpret the heavens, which is to say, I translate a very little what God himself has laid in store. And what could God have in store for our good king but glory?"

Would he lie? Elizabeth wondered. She didn't think he was an open fraud—even if Northumberland would fall for that, Robert certainly wouldn't. But it took subtlety to tell a king what he did not wish to hear without making him angry. How much would Dee avoid saying? Or was William truly charmed, a lifetime of good fortune inscribed indelibly in the heavens?

The door was shoved wide and William strode in, a little the better for good cheer, followed by Dominic dressed in all black, looking more than ever like a shadow ready to wrest the king from danger at any moment.

William ignored everyone but Minuette, bending low over her chair and kissing her hand in a proprietary fashion. Just before it would become uncomfortable for the rest of them, he released her and turned to the visitor.

"Dee!" he said. "Welcome to court. We are always glad to reward those who are useful to us."

No one could have missed the subtext, thought Elizabeth. *Tell me what I want to hear, and you'll be rewarded.*

Minuette had brightened with the men's entrance. "Isn't this thrilling, to discover what our futures hold in store." She smiled at William, who laughed, then at Dominic, who did not. "Who is to be first?" she asked.

William dropped into the chair next to hers and said, "You, sweetling, if you wish. What better way to start then with the stars of the brightest woman at court?"

Elizabeth caught the look that John Dee shot at William before dropping his eyes discreetly. *Damn,* she thought. *He may be young, but he is no fool. And that's all we need is someone leaking word of how Will behaves with Minuette in private.*

She looked at the only other person whom she knew was as concerned with secrecy as she was. Though Dominic had never spoken to her of William's romantic agenda, he radiated disapproval. Now Dominic fixed William with his eyes as though sorely tempted to tell him to behave himself.

As though that had ever worked.

Dee cleared his throat and opened the folio. On the top page Elizabeth saw a large circle divided into twelve sections, some of them blank while others contained mathematical and astrological symbols. She knew that each chart would be different based on the hour and place of their individual births. Despite her wariness, her interest flared as John Dee focused on Minuette. There was something new in his eyes, something that made Elizabeth sharpen her attention and think *This is a man who knows things.*

"Mistress Wyatt," he addressed Minuette, and even his voice had a new authority to it. "Our king is right in naming you a bright star. Your birth was a gift—to the king whose hour it shared and to those here who love you. You were born to be loved."

Elizabeth, listening hard for every meaning, felt a twist of annoyance at that. To be loved was far too passive. She herself would prefer to *do* the loving and maintain the control. But not everyone was like her—and certainly Minuette could not complain at being loved by a king.

"There has been peril in your life," Dee continued, "and doubt. Do not be too eager to escape either—peril is often the price for doing what is right, and doubt is good as it makes us search our own motives."

William interrupted. "Peril, doubt—I mislike this way of speaking to the lady. As the bright star she is, there must also be joy."

For one moment, Dee met William's gaze as an equal, assessing and perhaps understanding more than he should. Then he flickered down a notch and returned to Minuette. "Yes, mistress," he said gravely. "There will be an abundance of joy, for such is your nature. There will be marriage, passionate and deep. Though peril and doubt walk hand in hand with such joy, you will count the price well paid for what you gain."

That pleased William more, for he took Minuette's hand, raised it to his lips, then continued to clasp it as she said, a little shakily, "Thank you, Dr. Dee. You quite take my breath away."

And yet Elizabeth would have bet everything she owned that Dee was not telling all. This was vagueness, but so well finessed that he might not be accused of foretelling an unpropitious future. Peril and doubt? If Minuette were to be William's wife there would be plenty of both. And even a marriage "passionate and deep" could be a thing of disaster in the end.

"Elizabeth," William ordered Dee. "My sister must be next."

She waited for Dee to search out her page in his folio—though he had not referred to Minuette's at all, as if he had memorized their fates—but surprisingly he disagreed. "If it please Your Majesty, I had thought to speak to you next. From the youngest to the oldest—there is symmetry in such a reading."

William had been drinking just enough that Elizabeth wasn't sure if he would snarl in anger or give way graciously. After hesitating, he gave way. "Who am I to gainsay the stars?" Another subtext—*I'll let you take me in turn, but it had better be worth my while.*

Dee gave a flick of a smile as he turned over Minuette's star chart to reveal the one beneath it. "As you say. You know, naturally, that the comet that marked your birth was a portent of great power. The heavens marked you at birth, Your Majesty, and every moment of your life has been lit with the flame of that star."

"Flame can be grand or destructive," William said, not as lightly as it appeared. "Which am I?"

"A grand king in a time of destruction. The powers of Satan oppose you—"

"Wretched Catholics," William muttered.

"—and Europe grows uneasy at England's rise. There is much of darkness on your path, Your Majesty, but a burning star can blaze the way to a new world. If it so chooses."

The last words fell ominously into the silent room. Elizabeth's throat tightened. Had Dee just accused her brother of possibly choosing darkness?

William waved it away. "Of course I choose the new world. What of more . . . personal fates?"

Was it Elizabeth's imagination that Dee held the image of William and Minuette's clasped hands in his mind as he answered? "The personal and the public march together for a king. Trouble there will be, and opposition, but you will keep always your own ends in mind. You will never lose sight of what you most desire."

William gave his cat-like smile as he leaned back in his chair. "That is a future I can embrace."

But you need hardly look to the stars to know that much of William, Elizabeth thought—or any king, for that matter. Their father had never lost sight of what he desired, and had nearly riven his kingdom for it.

Feeling more nervous than she'd expected, Elizabeth met Dee's attention next. But his gaze was kind, almost . . . sorrowful?

"Your Highness," he began, and this time he did look down at the new chart he'd turned to, as though wondering where and how to begin, "your stars were the most difficult to interpret. They are changeable, one might almost say willful."

"Right stars, then," William said with good humour.

Elizabeth hardly heard him, for her eyes were riveted to Dee's. That cryptic sense she'd had earlier intensified and she felt for a moment that she was seeing the future herself. *He is important to me,* she thought, *or will be. For a long time to come.*

As though he had read her mind, Dee nodded once. "Your future is veiled even to yourself, Your Highness, for the clearest eyes cannot see straight into the sun. You love deeply and your loyalty to your single love will be everlasting."

Did he mean Robert? Everlasting loyalty . . . but that could mean anything from eventual marriage to a lifetime of unfulfilled love.

"You will command men and guide nations," Dee continued, and in that moment he crossed the line of discretion he had been walking so carefully before.

Suddenly alert (though probably he had been all along), Dominic laid a hand on William's shoulder and said, "Beware, doctor. Your king guides this nation."

"And as such, he has already given Her Highness her first command, when he named her regent earlier this year. And before another year passes," Dee returned his gaze to Elizabeth, "you will be your brother's voice in a foreign land."

That did speak of marriage—one out of England. Elizabeth

blinked, furious at herself for disappointment. It was hardly news. This wasn't prophecy; this was merely stating the obvious.

But John Dee continued to stare at her and Elizabeth had a queer double feeling that she was seeing him here, now, and also seeing him some years future, with white hair and a pointed beard. He was going to tell her how to save England, he was about to tell her what she need do for her people . . .

The moment snapped and Dee cleared his throat as he turned his full attention to Dominic. He took Dominic's measure, the only one standing, protective behind William with one hand still on his friend's shoulder. "The elder brother," Dee said thoughtfully. "The first, who would be last."

Dominic dropped his hand and said stonily, "I have no need for a star-teller. I choose my own future."

"But you do not choose that of others—and as long as your life entwines with those you love, you are not entirely free. You are the eldest, but you have the most to learn. Lessons of honour and loyalty and, yes, of choice. Not everything in this world is as it seems. You must learn to see gray, where before you have seen only black or white. There will be pain in the learning, and danger if you will not learn to bend."

William snorted. "There will only be pain because Dom thinks too much and makes everything more serious than it needs to be."

"That is your calling," Dee said to Dominic. "You are, above all, loyal and you speak always to the king's conscience. Who will tell him the truth if you will not?"

A pause, verging on uncomfortable, until William said, "Tell Dom something pleasant—how many beautiful women in his future?"

An even longer pause, then: "Only one," Dee said shortly. "There will ever only be the one."

Tension entered the room, on such misty feet that Elizabeth could not say where it centered. William broke it with a laugh as he stood up. "Well that's all right then. All we need do is identify this one beautiful woman and Dom's future is set."

And just like that, they were finished. William went so far as to clap John Dee on the shoulder. "My thanks for an interesting diversion, doctor. I hope you shall find our court accommodating to your intellect and talents."

Dee bowed. "The most glittering court in Christendom, Your Majesty."

"Ha! I'd love to see Henri's face when he finds that the English have captured what the French could not. You are most welcome at my court, Dr. Dee, if ever you should tire of Northumberland's household."

Then he spoke to the rest of them. "There is still music to be had this night. Dom, if you dance with Minuette first, then no one will find it odd when I come along and steal her from you."

"Not odd at all." Dominic's voice was toneless. "Dr. Dee, if you don't mind, I will stay until you have burned those charts."

"Of course," Dee said, and emptied the folio. There were only the four pages; Dr. Dee had written down only his calculations, not their interpretations. Those would stayed locked in his own mind. One by one he fed the pages to the flames.

"Thank you," Dominic said. He and Minuette followed William out the door.

Elizabeth hesitated, then confronted Dr. Dee who was still bowing his goodbye to the king. "Rise," she said, and when he stood and met her it was on that precarious equal ground that made her both nervous and approving.

"Your Highness?" He made it a question, but she would have wagered he knew what she was going to ask.

"What did you not say, doctor?"

"Many things, Your Highness."

"Why? What is so bad that it could not be told?"

"Why must it be bad? Even glorious futures do not come without cost. And as I believe I said before, this is not exact. God made the stars as he made men, and only He can read them perfectly."

"What did you see?" Robert's wife dead? Elizabeth married for love as William meant to do? Civil war as another Tudor king set aside wisdom for desire? Elizabeth far from England for all the rest of her life as the wife of another royal? As she thought that, Elizabeth pierced with pain and knew that would be the worst future for her of any—to leave England and never return.

Dr. Dee was silent for a long time. Then, unexpectedly, he took her right hand, letting her fingertips rest in his palm. "This is the hand of a woman, Your Highness. But it is also the hand of a ruler. The king, your father, spent much effort and pain to secure a worthy heir for England. If he had been able to see beyond your woman's body, he would have found the heart of the heir he sought."

He pinned her with his eyes, an urgency to his gaze as though there was more he could say but wouldn't. Elizabeth could almost feel words forming along her skin where he touched her hand and if she stayed here another moment she would know something she had never dreamed of . . .

She snatched her hand way. "Good night, Dr. Dee."

Coming soon by Laura Andersen:

THE BOLEYN DECEIT

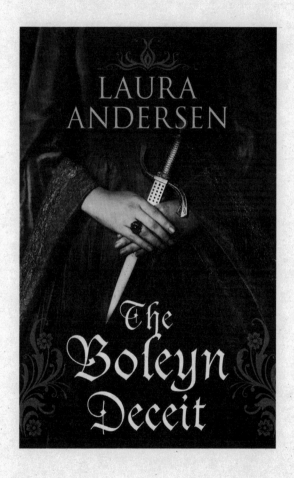

EBURY
PRESS

Coming soon by Laura Andersen:

THE BOLEYN RECKONING

EBURY
PRESS